Blood & Rain

Hidden Reaches

Blood & Rain

Descent Into Darkness

*E-Book Only
**Printed Omnibus

Blood & Rain

A novel of the *Hidden Reaches*

Doris Ross

TRINITY GATEWAYS LLC

BLOOD & RAIN

This is a work of fiction. All characters and events portrayed are fictional, and any resemblance to real people or incidents is purely coincidental.

Cover Art by Blue
Cover Design by Doris Ross

A Trinity Gateways LLC Publication
www.TrinityGateways.net

ISBN: 1941426107
ISBN-13: 978-1941426104

Dedication

For my father, David Ross, Jr.,
Who liked this one the most;
And my late grandfather, David Ross, Sr.,
Who always encouraged me when we spoke;
I would never have gotten this far without either of you.

Thank you.

August 30, 2004
Jacksonville, FL

"Ugh. You'd think people would have some consideration."
Brandy wrinkled her nose in disgust, letting the door swing shut as she moved to the next stall. Normally, she wouldn't have bothered with public restrooms. They were never clean enough, the toilet areas were all too often cramped cubicles, the dispensers were either broken or empty – the list went on. These stalls didn't even rate a comparison to closets; closets were more spacious. Yet she had no choice. She'd found herself in Wal-Mart, up a creek without a paddle with nature calling insistently. If she didn't find a decently clean stall soon she wasn't sure what she'd do. Her bladder was sending out the warning signals of impending social doom.

"Well, that's what I get for going shopping after dinner," she muttered as she inspected another hopeless possibility. "Not like I had a choice. I need some new notebooks and I know I won't be able to get up early enough to buy them before class starts... Finally."

She gave a small smile of relief at the sight of relative cleanliness. Not wanting to take any chances given the state of the rest of the stalls, she swiped a seat liner before stepping inside to take care of business. Through the ceiling, she could just barely hear the tattoo of hard rain. Thunder rolled, and she hoped it would be over by the time she left.

A crash of sound overhead had the lights flickering. Brandy prayed that they wouldn't go out. It would be like a cave in here without them. She could just imagine herself walking into things in her search for the exit. She'd experienced that before – painfully.

Footsteps echoed on the tile floor, becoming louder as they approached. Good luck, she thought. She was in the only decent stall to be had. The sound stopped in front of her stall just as she was finishing up. She noticed the toes of the boots under the door. Workman boots, she thought with a frown, then shrugged it off. There were some girls at college who wore workman boots, along with some very ratty, not-quite-matching clothing.

"I'll be out in just a minute," she called out, as she got her person in order. Flushing, she opened the door, almost running into the person waiting there. "Oh, sor – "

It was a guy.

That was her last thought.

Thunder boomed. The lights flickered. Alex Rosselle sighed as the CD player began to have audible fits. If there was going to be a blackout it would be best to shut down the computer she'd just finished setting up. She made a face at the weather outside her window as she did so. She would have to get online another time to check on her web site. The timing sucked, though. She hadn't been able to look over her site or customer orders in almost three weeks due to her move. It wasn't the kind of thing she wanted to lose track of.

At twenty-six, Alex was a modestly successful fantasy artist. While she didn't have gallery showings, she did have regular commissions for book covers, trading cards, and the occasional logo design. She did other pieces as well, selling print runs on her site. As it was the main source of her income, she was antsy to see what had sold since she'd last checked.

"Patience is a virtue, I guess," she muttered, rising from her seat at the computer desk. "Better get out the candle works."

She crossed the room to turn off the stereo system, then began the great hunt for matches. There were still so many things packed up from her move to the new apartment that she wasn't sure what was where. At least the important things were already unpacked, she mused. Her studio equipment, art supplies, her books, all her furniture, music, and electronics. Unfortunately, that didn't include matches.

After going through several boxes to no avail, she considered asking one of her new neighbors if they had any. There was a bright flash of lightning, quickly followed by an ominous roar from the sky outside. Her lamps did a strobe light effect for a moment.

Muttering to herself, she grabbed her keys off the dining room table. A tiny LED light hung from their ring, something that would be useful if the electricity failed. Running into the bedroom, she snatched a brush off the dresser. A glance in the mirror hanging on the wall made her laugh. Her shoulder-length hair was a mess. If she widened her emerald green eyes a bit, exaggerated her already fair skin, and added shadows underneath her eyes, she'd look a demented patient who had escaped from a psychiatric ward.

Making a mental note to keep that in mind for Halloween, she dragged a brush through her auburn hair before pulling it back. Then cast around the room for one last thing.

"Shoes," she murmured. The sky outside loudly proclaimed itself again. She gave the ceiling, and the unseen sky beyond it, a disgruntled look. "I get the picture already. Ease up, pal."

There were an errant pair of black pumps by the open closet, which she kicked back inside it. She hated that pair; why had she kept them? At five foot six she didn't need the height and they pinched her toes. Turning, she scanned the floor and spied one tennis shoe by the bed. As she took a step forward, something fell with a loud 'thunk' behind her. She glanced back to see her short sword had fallen over in the closet.

Exasperated, she picked it up and threw it on the bed. It landed next to an open suitcase full of clothes. She really had to organize her hunting gear. Half of it was still packed, and the rest shoved into whatever space had been handy. Right now, if she had to suddenly hare off to do battle with a paranormal bad guy, or deal with a violator of supernatural law, she'd be unprepared.

That was what she did. Aitist by day, periodically chipping in at the café she owned a percentage of, and playing paranormal lawman when the occasion called for it. She loved the role. Now if only her magic skills became more powerful, she'd be one happy hunter.

Well, this occasion had nothing to do with the preternatural. Snagging the lone shoe off the floor, she peeked under the bed to find its mate. With a satisfied grin, she pulled them on and proceeded to walk out of the apartment – only to reverse just as quickly.

It seemed that the Floridian summer had given way to a very early preview of winter. It was freezing out there. She rushed back into the bedroom to grab a sweatshirt from her suitcase. Not having a clue as to where her jacket was, it would have to do. She tugged it on before braving the chill outside.

She didn't bother with her second floor neighbor. Nate Forge, worked the late shift at a local movie theater; he wouldn't be home until after two in the morning. The thought of him made her smile. He looked just like his daddy, a man she much admired – and had actually dated once upon a time. Kent Aisley had certainly passed on his good looks to his son, and she wondered just how much of the vampirism Nate had also inherited. Her ex, a full vamp dating from the crusades, had never said. All she knew was that Nate's mother had been human.

Alex hadn't actually met Nate before the welcoming party the community had thrown for her. She had, however, seen him a few times over the years, as she did still work with his father from time to time. If Kent's son had been familiar with her name or her connection with his sire, he hadn't shown it at the party.

She paused on the first steps leading down. The rain was coming in torrents so thick that she could barely see the parking lot outside. She was grateful that she didn't have to duck in and out of the wet while going down the flights of stairs. Whoever had designed the buildings in Hidden Reaches Apartments had consideration in that regard.

Once on the ground floor, she could see that the parking lot was beginning to flood. She chewed her lip a bit nervously at the sight. The last time she'd seen rained like this had been during a tropical storm last year. It had been a hurricane the day before it had hit.

Well, the news didn't mention anything big like that. They would, if one was out there.

Mentally shrugging it off, Alex continued down the steps.

She rapped on the door with the brass characters spelling out 301A. Another crash of thunder caused the wall-mounted outdoor light to flicker. It made an ominous buzzing sound. Hugging herself against the frigid, damp wind, Alex hoped Edna wasn't in the middle of something. She really needed those matches. She sighed gratefully as the door opened.

"Why, hello, dear," Edna Bodsworth greeted her, her silver-gilt hair looking white in the twilight of the downpour. She looked like a retired grandmother, clutching the lapels of her thick, red terry cloth housecoat, and peered up with cheery faded blue eyes. "I trust you're staying dry? Would you like to come in?"

"Hi, Edna," Alex gave her an easy smile, making no move to step inside. "I'm just looking for some matches. You wouldn't happen to have some I could have, would you?"

"Hmmm." The grandmotherly woman looked thoughtful, idly tapping a finger on her chin as she considered. "I think I'm on my last book. You could always ask Michael. He almost always has little things like that."

"Michael?" The name sounded familiar. Had that been the name of one of the residents above her? She hadn't met either of them yet. "Who's Michael?"

"Michael lives on the third floor, dear. Apartment 303A. He keeps odd hours, so it's hard to tell when he'll be home," Edna explained as her cat yowled demandingly from behind her. She took a moment to shush the Siamese with an admonishment to behave herself. "Just go on up and introduce yourself, dear. Tell him that I sent you. He really is quite a nice young man. Helpful, too."

The tone, so sweet, so earnest, so innocent, set off an internal alarm. Eyeing the older woman a bit warily, Alex ventured a cautious response.

"Since there's usually a reason for such a qualifying statement, I'm going to have to ask what's wrong with him."

"Oh, it's not that, dear," Edna assured her with a sheepish laugh. "Michael can be moody sometimes. He's a sweetheart, really; it's just that there are times when it's truly hard to see that. Now," she made shooing motions with one hand, "go on upstairs, and ask about those matches."

3

Not having too much choice in the matter, Alex she went up the stairwell. It wasn't that she didn't trust Edna; it was just that she hated imposing on people she hadn't met before. She also was wary of matchmaking. If anyone bore the hallmarks of a matchmaker, it was Edna.

She paused on the top landing. The noise of the storm seemed a little quieter, more distant, on the third floor landing, though Alex couldn't figure out why it should. It was kind of weird. Trying to shrug it off, she stood in front of the apartment marked 303A. She took a deep breath to help calm her nerves, then knocked on the painted surface. A full minute passed with no apparent signs of life inside the apartment. Alex decided that Michael probably wasn't home after all. Granted, it was possible that he hadn't heard the knock, but it was only matches. She would just root through her boxes and bins until she found her own. So thinking, she turned to leave.

The door opened.

Alex turned back to face a man who could only be Michael. Somehow, Edna's description of 'sweetheart' didn't fit. Tall, lean, black-haired, and blue-eyed, the man had a face that could have been twenty-eight years old, or forty. His gaze was unreadable, yet powerful. He had the kind of countenance that said his personality was formidable, that told of hard-living while hinting at dark promises. He had a sense of presence that spoke of strength. Packaged all together, there was a definite allure. Definitely someone of interest.

A good-looking, enigmatic man like this, she concluded, was either already taken, not in the relationship market, or had a really big secret to hide that made him completely unsuitable for dating.

Okay, that's a little clichéd. Still, clichéd or not, it's generally true.

"Hi, I'm Alex Rosselle, in 302A. I was just wondering if you had some matches to spare? I asked Edna. She said that she was on her last book and that you might have some." Alex gave him her forgive-me-I'm-a-sweet-little-girl-in-need-of-some-help smile. "I'd really appreciate it."

He raised an eyebrow, the corner of his mouth quirking upwards.

"It shouldn't be a problem. One moment." His voice complimented his face perfectly. It had the four classic Ds: deep, dark, dangerous, and desirable came readily to mind at the sound of it, making her stifle a reactionary shiver.

You can't judge a man by his voice, but you could dream about it, right?

Michael didn't invite her in. Instead, he left the door open as he went to fulfill her request. Alex stayed right where she was while craning her head around to peek inside his apartment. She couldn't see much besides the small L-shaped foyer, which was awash in what could only be candlelight. No wonder Edna had recommended coming to him for matches.

The wind picked up, pouring a fresh stream of cold onto the landing. She wasn't left shivering in it for long. He came back with four boxes of kitchen matches.

"Thanks," she said, with eyebrows raised at the abundance as he handed them over. "I really don't think I need this many, though.

One would have been more than enough."

The corner of his mouth quirked again.

"Two for you, two for Edna." He glanced at the heavy rain behind her. His intense, vivid eyes went distant for a moment. "It's going to get worse," he murmured, the barest hint of an accent audible. His eyes move to meet hers. "The power grid's likely to go out. Do you have enough candles?"

"I think so…" Her answer was said to the empty air as he left the door open again. He reappeared a moment later with three cardboard boxes in his arms. Thrown slightly off balance by his abrupt generosity, she said, "You really don't have to do this."

"Two for you, one for Edna. She'll have most of hers set out already." He raised an eyebrow at her, moving the boxes out of reach when she made to take them from him. "I'll carry them. Edna first," he said. "If you would close the door."

"Um, sure." At a loss as to what else to do, she did as he'd asked before trailing after him.

Edna was pleased to have the extra supplies. She fussed over them both as Michael maneuvered into her apartment. He deposited the waxen pillars on her coffee table. Edna insisted on rewarding them for 'thinking of a little old lady like me,' after Alex handed the matron her matches. She gave each of them a Tupperware bowl of homemade chicken soup as well as a jug of spiced apple cider. As she did so, Michael made a point of mentioning the impending blackout. Edna's reply was simply, "That's what candles, matches, and gas stoves are for."

Now that was something Alex hadn't thought of. Their stoves were the old-fashioned gas stoves, an asset when it came to blackouts. She had yet to actually use hers, as it was just easier to microwave whatever frozen meals Richard, her friend and a café partner, had prepared. It shouldn't be that different from electric stoves, she reasoned. She could learn. At least now, she wouldn't have to worry about eating cold food.

After Edna had shown them out, Alex led the way back to her apartment. She opened the door, bolting inside. Ah, warmth, she thought. She waited impatiently for her neighbor to do the same so she could cut off the draft that was blowing in.

Michael navigated a winding path through the array of moving containers towards the dining room table. Thunder crashed overhead, loud enough to vibrate the walls. The apartment was doused in pitch-black darkness. Fumbling with her keys, Alex thumbed the tiny flashlight. A thin beam of light pierced the dark.

"Excuse the mess and watch your step," she quipped belatedly as she threaded over to his side. In the dining room, they unpacked the candles. Alex opened a matchbox, striking one of the sticks against the side. It flared to life with a chemical sizzle. Michael held out a thick pillar candle, touching the wick to the flame.

Together, they stationed lit candles all around the room, leaving several on the table in a haphazard centerpiece arrangement. The soft glow was a comforting buffer against the violence of the storm outside. Michael didn't seem in too much of a hurry to leave, scanning the shelves, taking in the multitude of books, the knick-knacks that had been randomly placed here and there. They picked up the light beautifully, twinkling at them.

"Unicorns, dragons, a few faeries." He seemed amused by her collection of fantasy-themed keepsakes. She shrugged in response, idly wondering if he was going to make any wisecracks about her collection as she watched him scan the room. "Every genre save horror." He swung his gaze over to where she stood. "True crime, yet no horror."

"I was never a horror fan," she replied, moving from the table to put Edna's gifts in the kitchen. She picked up another lit column of wax while she was at it.

The candle was placed on the counter to shed light on what she was doing. She fiddled with the stove, grinning to herself when she got the burner working properly the first time. She adjusted the setting, then filled a kettle with water.

"Would you like some tea? The water'll be ready in about five minutes."

"If you don't mind." He continued to look around. "You need pictures."

"Way ahead of you." Placing the kettle on the burner, she came out to lean against the dining room table. "The really big, thin box over by the computer desk has some art prints. Right now, they're waiting on the new frames I ordered."

Michael wandered over to the box. He ran a finger lightly over the cardboard top, giving her an inquiring look. More intrigued by his interest than anything else, she snagged a box cutter from the bar and tossed it to him. Catching it easily, he opened the package. Carefully, he pulled out the prints one by one to look them over in the candlelight.

None of them were her own work. Alex was of the general opinion that hanging one's art in one's own home – especially when one lived alone – was like basking in one's ego. It was begging for compliments, attention. While she enjoyed a bit of praise as much as anyone else, she liked to think that she was more subtle in soliciting them. So these were by fantasy artists that she had long admired. Fauna, both fantastic and mundane in nature, were illustrated in a variety of styles that blended instead of clashed. The binding thread, she reflected absently, was the Celtic influence evident in each.

Michael studied them intently. Finally, he slid them back into the box.

"They suit you."

"I like to think so," Alex replied, feeling a wave of bemusement at the pronouncement. They had only just met after all.

A sudden, bright flash of white through the kitchen window heralded a lightning bolt. The building shuddered again in the booming thunder that followed it. Alex sent up a brief prayer that her car remained safe from flooding while behind her the kettle had begun to whistle. She hurried into the kitchen and took it off the burner.

"What kind of tea would you like?" she called over her shoulder.

"What kind of tea do you have?" came his countering question.

With her back to him, she allowed herself to revel in the sound of his voice, like smooth ebon silk. A voice, she had to admit to herself, which sent a nice little tingle up her spine. The song *Black*

Velvet played in the back of her mind as she made herself answer

"Check in the pantry. Most of what I have is loose leaf."

She turned around to find him already following her instructions. He retrieved a candle from the counter before casually rummaging through her stash of teas and coffees. Those had been the first things she'd unpacked. She was a woman who needed her caffeine in the morning.

Alex gave her attention to pouring the hot water into mugs for them both.

"There's a canister labeled 'Richard's Specialty;' could you grab it for me?"

He handed it to her, then stepped away from pantry with another can. A glance proved that it was Licorice and Cardamom, another tea by Richard Douglas, one of her long-time friends. She dug in a kitchen drawer for two mesh balls for steeping loose-leaf teas. Handing one to him, they filled their respective spheres in companionable silence. After setting the tea balls to steep in the mugs, they regarded each other speculatively.

She raised an eyebrow, waiting.

"What is it that you do?" he asked finally. She couldn't tell if that was polite interest or just thoughtfulness in his tone.

"Oh, this and that," she said off-handedly, her smile widening into a grin. "Actually, I'm an artist. Sometimes I do special commissions, and then there are the times that I just do what I want to. I get lithographs made of my non-commissioned work. Those can be bought online through my website." She made a face. "I sound like an ad. Anyway, I do that most of the time. I also help out in the café I partially own when it's needed."

A flicker of interest came into his eyes. "Which café?"

"*Candlelight and Magic.*" A note of pride rung in her voice. Why shouldn't it, when she and her friends had worked so hard to achieve it? The ghost of a smile danced over his face. His eyes brightened with it. That little tingle she'd felt earlier spread.

"I'm familiar with it." He raised his cup to test the scent of the steam. "Most of the community is. Edna is trying to set up regular get-togethers there, although work schedules keep getting in the way."

"What kind of get-togethers? Friends, coffee or tea, board games, conversation?" She thought it over. The café could certainly play host to something like that, so long as people didn't get too loud. "Casual informality, maybe some eclectic music?"

"You should talk to Edna." Michael swirled the ball in the tea, watching the liquid go dark. Alex checked her mug. She decided to let it steep a bit longer, making a mental note to get with the elderly woman at the next opportunity.

"So," Alex began, deciding to turn the tables, "what do you do?"

He took another leisurely sip, watching her over the rim as he did so. Alex had the feeling that he was debating as to what to tell her.

Secrets, secrets, and more secrets.

"Whatever I feel like," he answered. "I'm well enough off. For the last few years I've been indulging in hobbies or helping out friends with the odd problem."

Well enough off…she supposed that meant that he didn't have or need a day job. People with that much money usually had houses, not apartments. Interesting… The way he said 'the odd problem', though, made her wonder if he sometimes dealt in the paranormal as she did. If that was the case, he might also be bound not reveal that to anyone. It was a standard rule of the Hunters' Guild, which she was a member of.

She didn't say anything for a moment, fiddling with her mug as she mulled over what to say next. She really wanted to dig a little. She didn't. She had secrets of her own to keep, so she would respect his. At least, she would until she had a reason not to.

"Must have been some inheritance," she said with just a touch of blandness, causing his eyebrow to inch upward. She pretended not to notice. "Hope it wasn't someone you were close to."

"It wasn't." He gave her a small smile and didn't correct her assumption.

Outside, the storm made its wrath known yet again. It left them both momentarily deaf and blind.

"So," Alex said after her ears stopped ringing and her vision cleared. "Do you play cards?"

The corner of his mouth quirked again.

"Yes," he replied. "I do."

The Wood

A silver moon hung in a sky studded with stars. Below it, a vast, wild expanse of trees spread through, hemmed in by mountains in the distance. Near the center of the Wood was a lake, its calm waters as clear as crystal. On the western shore, three hounds sniffed at the water's edge. Red, white, and black, they looked back at the man who knelt on the shore peering at the water's surface. He was clad in armor, not unlike the romanticized warriors of old, mantled with a heavy cloak of gray. His antlered helm was open in the front, revealing a void of darkness where His face should have been. Twin slits of silver light served as His eyes. What they saw in the lake was a picture other than His reflection. In it, a man and a woman played cards at a table lit with candles.

The two had met. Michael had taken the hint he'd been given. For the moment, He would be content with that. They would need prompting again later. The man was as stubborn as they came. He would not readily welcome the change to come. Alex was another matter. Her problem would not be accepting what would be, but in dealing with the complications that evolve from it, with it. For now, however, they sat companionably enough and played.

It wouldn't last for long.

The scene swirled into another. Yellow tape was strung across a door, an officer posted to keep civilians away. This was the beginning that would either bring them together, or force them apart. He could do little Himself. He was constrained by promises made long ago to a then newly born world. He didn't mind the vows He'd made. If His people asked it of Him, He could step into their world, their time, to make things right – though perhaps not in the way they had expected. Still, He could do it.

If they asked.

They wouldn't.

Yet that didn't stop Him from taking action altogether.

5

September 6, 2004
Jacksonville, FL

Teri Andrews couldn't understand it. It was irrational, baffling, completely unlike her.

Reason, logic. It wasn't as if she really liked the stuff, after all. There had to be a reason for it. Hormones, PMS, stress, something. Anything. A quick mental calculation led her to lay the blame on PMS and leave it at that.

Chocolate. She had to have some.

Her day had already been a long one. At twenty seven, the curly-haired brunette was the general manager for the café she owned with her three friends, and it had been her turn to open. That had meant rising before five in the morning. She was tired, she was cranky, and to top it all off, she had to drive in the rain. She hated driving in the rain. There were too many people in this city that either didn't know how, or didn't care about driving safely when the roads were wet. Music usually soothed her nerves, which is why she had one of her favorite radio stations on, with the volume turned up loud. She sang along with Springsteen as she cautiously drove down San Jose Boulevard with cars whizzing by. A truck heading the other way ran through a particularly large puddle, sending a wave of filthy water onto her windshield. Muttering curses about the driver's stupidity, she flicked the wipers to the highest setting. The station's DJ broke from music to talk about the local weather.

"As if I can't see that it's raining for myself," Teri griped as he and the weatherman described an unusually soggy day for most of the city. She rolled her violet eyes, reaching over to switch the station just as the topic turned from the local weather to the hurricane season.

Teri grimaced as she stopped for a red light. They'd had four hurricanes in less than two months, each coming close to the eastern coast of Florida. Jacksonville had only weathered the outer bands, suffering through a lot of heavy rain and wind. The southern portion of the state had not been so lucky. That was the risk of living here.

It was September. They still had until the end of November to worry about it. Shaking her head, she switched pedals as the light turned green.

"There is another storm system forming in the Atlantic as we speak. It was just promoted to a Tropical Storm, and was given the name Janice. Right now it looks like it's heading for the Caribbean..."

The weatherman was cut off as Teri fingered a button on the console, switching the station. Pantera poured from the speakers as she eased her Ford Explorer into a turn lane just as a healthy-sized gap in traffic presented itself. Smiling with satisfaction, she sent the vehicle across three lanes to enter the strip mall parking lot. Peering through the bad weather, she found that most of the lot was full – and none of the free spots were anywhere close to the front of the Wal-Mart she was headed for. With a sigh of resignation, Teri parked her SUV out in what she considered the boonies. At least the rain seemed to be dying down a bit.

She got out to dash through the drizzle, absently wondering why the weatherman kept getting it wrong. He wasn't the only one.

Just three days ago, they'd promised sunshine and cool breezes – not an altogether odd occurrence in Florida at this time of year. They had gotten wet under black skies instead. No one could seem to explain where the recent thunderstorms were coming from. Yesterday's had been the worst so far, causing blackouts everywhere.

Her speedy entrance didn't help her. She was soaked from head to toe by the time she hurried into the store. The air conditioning hit her like snowballs striking a nude target. She started to shiver as goose bumps sprouted all over her skin. Damn Florida weather. She rubbed her arms feeling the fabric of her long-sleeved shirt cling. She longingly thought of the warm jacket she'd left in the car like the half-witted idiot she felt like. Why hadn't she thought to grab it?

Well, best get it over with.

Teri darted between customers and dodged shopping carts as she headed for the aisle she wanted. Finding it full of people, she grimaced. A kitten wouldn't be able to fit in there. Maybe if she gave it five or ten minutes, it wouldn't be so crowded.

She wandered over to the jewelry counter to wait. Sparkly things were always nice to look at. She liked the dragonfly pendants. As she looked them over, water droplets hit the glass of the display. She groaned inwardly. Her sodden mass of curly chestnut hair was dripping everywhere.

"Should have gone to the bathroom first," she muttered, trudging away. She could have sopped up some of the wet with paper towels, maybe even gotten her hair semi-dry if there was a hand-dryer. It wasn't a fresh set of clothes or a big fluffy towel. Still, it was a reasonable alternative.

She zipped through the cashier lines, heading for the restrooms. She was so preoccupied with the effort to not drip on the people she passed, that she almost didn't see the yellow cone in front of the restroom. A sign had been taped to it stating that the facilities were out of order. Inside, she could hear people cleaning.

She was standing there, wondering what she was going to do now, when someone dressed in white from head to toe came out.

There were stains on the outfit – was that a haz mat suit? She wasn't sure. From the look of the blemishes on the material, she had a feeling that she didn't want to know what had made them.

"Sorry, ma'am, but this restroom's closed." He indicated the sign.

He was wearing some kind of goggles. What was that smell? Chemicals? Underneath the harsh scent was a nasty undertone. She blinked as water trickled from her hair into her eyes.

"Why?"

"It's being thoroughly cleaned." He tapped the cone. "Now if you'll excuse me…"

She let him pass, moving off aimlessly as she dripped. She couldn't help wondering what kind of mess would warrant being covered up completely. What was she going to do about being cold and wet?

"It's retail. They won't shut down unless there's no customers to buy."

"I'm sorry?" She stopped to see an elderly man sitting on a nearby bench. He wore the blue vest of an employee, his hair was silver, his face as wrinkly as a prune.

"The powder room there." He smiled. It belied the gleam of cynicism in his eyes. "We was told that this here's corporate, and corporate don't close for things like death."

"Death? Someone died in there?" She shivered again, not altogether from cold.

"Yep. Murdered."

She ogled at him. He didn't seem to notice.

"Messy one, too. They don't want us talking about it though. The manager said it would drive off the clientele." He snorted. "Fact is, custom will boom for bit after this business has aged some."

"People are sick." Her statement brought out a chuckle.

"That they are."

Teri thought for a moment, biting her lip. With a sigh, she turned a beseeching smile on the old man.

"Um, could I ask you for a favor?"

"What would that be?"

"Could you get me some paper towels?"

Fifteen minutes later, she was as near to dry as she could get given the circumstances. She thanked the man, then meandered back into the aisles. In the back of her head, the old man's words echoed. Someone had died – perhaps killed – in the bathroom.

What a way to go.

She really needed that chocolate fix now. The chill creeping up her spine had nothing to do with the cold. She quickened her step, weaving her way through the myriad rows until she reached her original destination. Thankfully, the aisle was barren of people. In a curious detachment, Teri picked up four bags of chocolate at random, then let her autopilot guide her feet to the check out. She murmured a prayer for the victim's family as she waited in line. A warm calm settled on her shoulders.

She half-smiled. Spiritual comfort. What would she ever do without it?

Go mad, probably.

She nodded hello to the cashier as her candy was rung up. Money changed hands without much notice as her thoughts turned to Alex. She'd have to share the news with her friend the next time she saw her.

Teri carried her purchases out to the SUV, crossing a parking lot that was no longer being deluged with sky-born water. Lord, it was cold. It was September, not December or January – it should have been summer temperatures still. Yet here she was, freezing in the parking lot, with murder on the brain.

She wondered why she felt compelled to tell Alex about it. It seemed, well, out of place. Mundane murder, supernatural detective – warrior – whatever. Frowning, she unlocked the door. Her inner warm calm slipped just a little. Instinctively, she began to pray silently to get it back in place.

What she got was the oddest sensation.

It felt as if strong, gentle hands had snatched her up, golden warmth pouring over her, into her, as she was lifted. She didn't feel the cool, rain-slick surface of her SUV as she braced a hand on it to keep her balance, nor did she feel the weight of the plastic bag holding the candy on her arm. Her vision clouded with white light. Her mind filled with two resonating words.

Tell Alex.

Then she was back in the parking lot, leaning against her car, still warm, as if she'd been out in the summer sun. Above her, the sky opened up to soak her again.

6

Elsewhere

It had done well.

He was pleased. His servant had done satisfactorily in its first venture into this city, bringing him a substantial amount of life energy to harvest. That was only one of its duties, one of his goals. The rest would have to be achieved soon. If this went on for too long, then he might be suspected of being involved.

He turned his plans in his mind, like a child trying to solve a Rubik's Cube. He wanted the timetable to be kept tight. Time, control, and a judicious use of his collected power would be needed to be successful. If he was good enough, careful enough, he would be blameless as well. It would be quite useful, to be found blameless, to remain sterling, unsullied in the eyes of others for at least several years yet. There was simply too much to do, too much to acquire, too much to learn. Still, it was more crucial to succeed.

He let his gaze drop to one of his recent acquisitions. The leather-bound volume was well-worn, well-used. It was not ancient, he mused. It didn't have to be, to hold clues to secrets older than time. He still had to decipher the riddles within the pages. He still had to search. While he did so, the rest of his plans would spin out as finely as a spider's web.

With the nice little benefit of increased magic...

His servant stirred in its corner, looking up with monstrous eyes set in a young woman's face. Its madness, its hunger, its need reflected in those eyes. He smiled at it from where he sat across the small room.

"There is a trinket I need you to retrieve," he told it, his voice silky smooth.

"My cursed amulet," it hissed. It had abandoned the girl's voice, he noted. "I want – need – to find the amulet."

"Of course," he soothed. "You will have every opportunity to look for it. It may very well be in the collection of things where my trinket is now."

The mad eyes stared at him silently a moment.

"What trinket?" it asked finally.

He smiled, then told it.

7

September 7, 2004
Jacksonville, FL

Candlelight and Magic. All around were used books, framed art prints, the odd bits of handmade jewelry, coffee, tea, sandwiches, candles. The air was filled with the mouth-watering aroma of gourmet lunches, freshly ground espresso, the homey scent of flame melted wax, and slightest hint of potpourri. It was such an interesting blend. The medieval, the fantastic, the Celtic, the sci-fi, the old west. Somehow, in this café, it all worked. Alex took no small amount of pride in that.

"So the news didn't say anything about who or why, just where?" She asked, sipping her coffee concoction thoughtfully. The spicy flavor of cinnamon and nutmeg rolled around her tongue. "Richard, you've outdone yourself again."

"Thanks." With hair the color of light brown sugar and a face as round as the moon, Richard Douglas grinned at her from behind the counter. He was their resident chef and her current drink his newest seasonal experiment. He was engaged to Lyselle Barinton, the petite blonde working the till who resembled a pixie more than she did café shift manager. Both were counted among her closest friends, sharing in the ownership of the café.

Richard came out into the dining room to join them at the table closest to the bar. Lys stayed at the register, leaning over the varnished wooden surface so she could hear. Her hair was done up in pigtails today, her bangs falling over her doe brown eyes in wisps. It was hard to believe that she was Alex's age; she looked about eight years younger.

Richard's voice interrupted her reverie.

"Teri, we're going to need some more vanilla-sandalwood candles and I'm almost out of Old Bay."

"Got it." Teri said as she noted down the items that they needed, then fiddled with her pen. She stared blankly at the paperwork in front of her for a long moment. Finally, she heaved a sigh, shoving the papers away. She tucked the loose curl of chestnut that flopped in her face behind her ear absently as Richard shuffled the order forms into a tidy pile. She turned back to Alex. "No, the cops have a pretty tight lid on it."

"Okay." Alex decided to get logical. Bringing out a small flip-top notebook, she borrowed Teri's pen. "So let's list what we know. A murder in a bathroom which you learned about yesterday, a divine order, and I'm supposed to do something about it. Right?" The pen scratched on the paper. "Anything else?"

"The murder probably was the one that took place last week," Lys chimed in. "There was something on the news about it but I hadn't caught where the body was found."

"I remember. It stormed that day," Richard added. "It didn't have a good feel to it."

"No, it didn't," Lys seconded, as one of their regular customers came through the door. "It gave me a migraine." She abandoned the conversation momentarily, to turn a beaming smile at the man as he placed his order.

"Hmmm." Alex thought back to that night, a little over a week ago. Her first memory was of Michael, his voice, his eyes, the way he'd slaughtered her at poker. He had known that the electricity would go out. There were a few explanations for that. It could have been a lucky guess, it could have been a supposition based on his experience of living in the building. She felt it was something more. There was an aura about him. He could be a particularly powerful mage with an affinity for Air. As such he would be sensitive to the weather, its severity. He might have been able to predict its impact on the power grid. However, that was all speculation, so she held those comments back. She made a mental note to check into it later.

"It could have been anything, realistically speaking." She sighed. "Well, I guess that I'll just have to mosey on over there, see if they've taken the tape down. If I can get a general feel for it, then I might be able to narrow things down a bit."

"I think that storm's connected, Alex." Teri looked at her with somber eyes. "Gut feeling."

Alex nodded slowly. "I just need to figure out how."

"So you'll go to Wal-Mart." That having been decided, Richard got up from the table. "Now how about some lunch before you go?"

8

Alex stood outside the Wal-Mart ladies' restroom, paper and tape in hand. Making certain that there was no one around, she stuck the "out of order" sign she held on the door, then pushed it open.

Beyond it was a gray and white tiled room, the fluorescent fixture overhead shedding dull white light everywhere. To the left stood three sinks of chipped, dull enameled metal, complimented by age-spotted mirrors streaked with soap and water. To the right stood five doors of green, one of them missing its latch.

The place was empty and almost preternaturally clean. Perhaps that wasn't so unusual when you remembered it had been a crime scene until recently. Whatever mess the crime scene investigative team had left behind would have been dealt with by the store staff before the bathrooms had been reopened.

Now it was time for a little magic.

Her mage skills were modest at best. Because of that, she didn't use them overmuch. She could imbue power in a weapon to make it more effective against a supernatural foe, but that was as far as her combative magics tended to go.

This, however, would be a bit different.

Alex paced forward slowly, murmuring a prayer to be able to sense what needed to be seen or felt. It helped her focus. She put into the words a touch of magic, the power that all mages carried with them,

There was a general feeling of – patience. Waiting. The sudden shudder caught her by surprise. The murderer had been stalking the restrooms. Butterflies started to dance in her stomach as she forced herself to reach out, to take more of it in. Disgust. That one was female, human; probably the victim.

She touched the laminate surface of the cheap structure, one stall at a time. She could sense it, like an emotional stain. Fear mixed with gleeful hunger. It was faint. The farther she went down the line of stalls, the stronger it became. Then Alex laid her fingertips on the last door.

A guy – some old guy – he shouldn't be here.

Bewilderment, indignity, outrage, the whirl of emotion gave way to shock. Pain's red haze crept through everything, covering, infusing, until it was all that was left. A flash of blood spattered on the wall. A burst of flesh being torn, rent. A sickening hunger for more. No screams – no time. So fast, so quick. The red haze became solid, dark, until finally – black.

Alex came to on the floor, sprawled like a discarded rag doll. Slowly, shakily, she sat up. She stayed there, hugging her knees, for some time.

The weather was degrading again.

The warning rumble had haunted Michael Keegan's dreams, scattering the images far beyond his power of recollection. Pent-up violence was oncoming, engulfing any lingering traces of sleep-born peace or any curious stirring of interest and desire. He remembered the sensations, wondered at them, yet their cause was lost as the darkness had spread. In the waiting depths, lightning had flashed. A foretelling, he thought. An omen of what was headed his way.

Awake, he stood on the landing of his apartment building, scanning the not-yet-threatening sky. A natural storm system had the feel of weight, the pressure of time, of water. It held a rolling pattern in place as it stirred, built, then spent itself. The weight diffused, spreading out only to be gathered again in a different place. The basic structure always remained. It might vary a bit, yet was still basically the same.

There was no such pattern here.

It had weight and pressure. They had little to do with water, only slightly more to do with time. It was wild, unbalanced, constantly shifting, ever spinning. The natural pattern was fragmented, pieces of it flashing as the weather began a slow stampede only to be lost again in the chaotic swirl. It was not the result of nature. It was the result of magic. The more it built, the more violent, the more cold the temperature became.

Even as he finished his analysis of it, he felt some of that pressure vanish. He frowned in an effort to find it. His probe told him nothing.

Even nothing was something.

Someone was siphoning power from the chaotic system. Odds were that it wasn't the person or people involved in making it in the first place. That required control, discipline. Anyone generating this kind of weather wouldn't be able to maintain it if they were also drawing from it. Michael was certain of that much.

Had the last storm been the same way? He hadn't paid much too attention to it at the time, having followed a rare urge to indulge in someone else's company. There was no way to determine it now.

With a sigh, he descended the stairs to stride out across the parking lot to the car he seldom used. He needed to find the focal point for the tempest, the origin of the uncontrolled arcane energy. Studying the phenomenon itself was getting him nowhere, so he was going to have to do it the old fashioned way. The scientific way, he supposed, using geometry.

He unlocked the Firebird with a thought, the door swinging open casually as he came up to it. He slid behind the wheel, settling himself as it closed. He focused his will on the ignition, then shifted his attention to the wheel and gear shifter beside him when the engine started.

Amused at himself, he leaned back and placed his hands behind his head as the vehicle exited the apartment complex.

10

Dammit, Alex thought when she put her fingertips to the pane of her kitchen window. It was getting cold again.

The weatherman had said that there was no chance of rain today, despite the recent freakish squalls. It had been sunny when she'd returned from her Wal-Mart excursion, as it had been all day. Not thirty minutes ago, the sky had been brilliantly blue with not a cloud to be found.

Now there were threatening clouds as far as the eye could see.

Richard's words echoed in her mind. The storm was part of it. She felt the truth of it in her gut.

The scene of the murder had been cleansed. Alex had started it, Teri and Lys had come to finish it – using prayer and spiritual ritual rather than arcane skill -- so she could go hunting. She had a scent that was psychic, magical. It was easily recognizable as what she sought, which was fortunate. She just had to find the source.

She wished it had been familiar, though. Hunts were always challenging, a reason why she enjoyed the work. Yet hunting something unknown meant it would take a while, and that could mean life or death for someone else.

Hunting for a Hag, for instance, would have been quick. They may have been relatively rare evil entities, hungry for young children and masquerading as old women, but she knew how to deal with them – had dealt with a particularly nasty one early on in her hunter's career. It had taken no more than a few days, as she recalled. No one had died after she took on the hunt.

Pulling her thoughts back to the task at hand, Alex finished the blessing of her personal arsenal. She found it comforting. Beyond that, she liked the edge it sometimes gave her over some of the things she had to fight. Still, she imagined most Christians would peg her for a Pagan as Alex had never been one to conform to some earth-bound preacher's standards. She had her faith, her beliefs, her personal tie with God. None of them had led her wrong thus far.

So long as she had faith and believed anything was possible.

Alex carefully strapped on her myriad of weaponry, making sure that they couldn't be seen by the trained eye. No bulges, no funny draping of clothing. Perfect. She wrapped a towel around her sword, stuffed a few things in her purse: blessed water in a spritz bottle, blessed rock salt and herbs in a jar, blessed olive oil in yet another bottle. There was already a crossbow with bolts, all silver tipped, stashed in her sedan, a loaded glock in her glove compartment. Locking up, she trotted down to her vehicle, stowed her sword in the trunk, then got in.

A quick glance around the parking lot revealed that the designated slot for 303A – Michael's apartment – was empty. She'd always seen his black Firebird parked there, under the oak tree in the middle of the lot. It was a classic car, one that she admired every time she was heading to or from her own sedan. That was the only reason she noticed its absence. She hadn't purposefully been looking for it. Or its owner. Or even thinking about Michael…

Which she had earlier.

The card shark. How had he managed to anticipate every single move she'd made? She wasn't the greatest card player – a fact that she was well aware of. Teri was by far better than she was, yet she had a sneaky suspicion that Michael would beat even her, hands down. He'd had the nerve to sip her tea, take her chips – they'd been playing for Doritos, not money – and give enigmatic looks all evening. The kind of look, she mused, that most women tingled over. She had tingled. By the time he'd left for the night, she'd tingled all over.

Nine days later, she could still feel the lingering effects of his company.

Damn it.

She shook her head, sighing in exasperation. Mind on business, current business, not on the sexy upstairs neighbor. With that notion firmly lodged in her mind, she sat in the front seat of her Oldsmobile Cutlass, closed her eyes, took a breath, and cleared her mind.

Like most humans, Alex had no strong elemental affinities. There was no connection with Air that she could use to track an unnatural storm. Still, there were other ways. Other methods.

Like the news station.

She turned the key in the ignition just enough to activate the radio. Tuning into a channel that played the local news and weather reports as often as music, she found it playing jazz. She waited impatiently for music to play through before the next report started.

"…looks like we'll have some thunderstorm activity on the Westside, folks, and scattered showers throughout the afternoon for the rest of Jacksonville…"

The Westside. She pursed her lips as she turned the radio off. She'd head for the Fuller Warren Bridge and see if she couldn't eyeball the origin.

The drive was…interesting. Outside, the brewing clouds darkened. The wind tossed loose trash around, tugging at the foliage growing on either side of the road. Thunder pealed, lightning streaked, yet the rain did not fall. Traffic-wise, this was a good thing. The real bonus came when she got on the bridge. She was able to see that the sky had a black patch centered over a cluster of buildings around Friendship Park – on the bank she'd just left.

She took the first exit in a bid to turn herself around only to end up on a one way street heading towards the Times Union Center. She took the next turn, following the theory that three right turns at a block apiece would get her back in the right direction. At the next light, however, she was confronted with an orange sign reading "DETOUR." Beyond the sign, she saw a crew in neon orange safety vests, doing something around a manhole.

"I *hate* downtown," she gritted between clenched teeth.

The detour steered her in the opposite direction of the way she wanted. She took the side street, not having any other choice. Her frustration was compounded when she found that she couldn't get off at the next intersection. Damn these one way streets!

With more muttered curses that alternated with gripes about the city's founders, Alex grimly drove in what she was certain were multiple circles until she found a clear street that boasted a sign proclaiming the way to the I-95. Above her, the sky thrashed. A few moments later, she was back on the Fuller Warren.

Finally.

From this direction, she got a better view of the storm. The clouds were at their blackest right above the MOSH -- the Museum of Science and History.

Wonderful. Another complication.

Establishments like this didn't allow their patrons to enter with crossbows, swords, or guns. They had security systems to protect artifacts from the exhibits. That meant cameras, maybe even security personnel, and a change in plans. She would have to leave most of her weapons behind.

Muttering about the luck of the draw, she drove past the building to park in the lot out front . She got out, then jumped three feet in the air as a white hot bolt struck the pavement next to her. The resounding crack was deafening. She stumbled back, hitting the hood of the car. Blinded by the flash, she leaned on the hood for balance until her eyes adjusted. There was a hole the size of a softball in the sidewalk.

Something's definitely off with this storm if lightning like that comes out of nowhere.

Irritated, Alex shoved off the hood and looked up. The clouds were black, striding purposefully toward the museum. She stepped through the lobby's glass doors to pause for a look around. The psychic scent rolled over her.

She stood dumbly for a few seconds as she refocused. It was strong here. Recent. As in five-minutes-ago recent. It was so thick, so powerful that she was surprised no one else seemed to notice it. She paid for her admission, listening to the desk clerk's spiel on the current big exhibit. She took a brochure and program schedule reflexively. Outside, big, fat drops of water began to fall.

Now where...?

The scent was everywhere. She wandered down the corridor to the left of the desk, idly fingering the glossy paper of the pamphlet. The windows showed the enclosed courtyard area off to the side of the building. On the wall opposite them were framed pieces hanging on the wall. There were scenes taken from historical Florida, from prehistory, and a few things from the largest attraction in residence at the moment. She frowned at a bit of framed papyrus, the colored paints drawn on its surface showing like new.

The little panel to the right of the papyrus proclaimed it a reproduction of the original in Cairo, Egypt. She glanced at the brochure, opening it to the advertisement of the Egyptian exhibit. On a hunch, she headed there.

She'd always found Egyptology more interesting than Floridian history anyway.

Up on the second floor, she found that the trail was stronger there. More intense. Alex almost choked on it. Pausing at the display just inside the room, she struggled to maintain a cool composure. It only took a moment to clear the aggravation she felt at being overwhelmed by the foreign stench from her features.

Alex turned away from a display on mummification to glance around the room. There were a few people here, poking about, despite the foreboding sky that bucked audibly overhead. They wandered among the displays that lined the walls. A few of the larger artifacts lay encased in glass atop tables or pedestals in the middle of the large room. At the opposite end of the room from where she stood was another, smaller area. Several things within glinted with gold. A glance at the brochure indicated that it was the King Tut display.

Alex approached one of the sarcophagi to pretend to study the mummified remains as she psychically extended herself with a mental prayer for protection to search. She felt the presence of – something. It was unfamiliar, undefined, elusive. Deceitful. There was another element there, one she recognized only because she had felt it just hours before.

Hunger.

It wasn't the intense, all-consuming, hunger that had left its intangible mark at the murder scene. It was an insidious whisper, faint and light. She had no clue as to where it was coming from.

Great, she thought. This was going to be fun.

11

"It will kill soon."

Michael watched Alex jolt at his quietly spoken words. He wasn't entirely certain why he'd approached her from behind. An impulse, he supposed as she spun around to face him. Her emerald eyes flashed with indignation.

"What are you doing here?" she hissed, glancing at the rest of the patrons wandering behind her.

He gave her a considering look. He was aware of what she was, the most likely reason of why she was here. What he wasn't certain of was her experience. Would she be a hindrance or a help? The creature they both tracked was close by; he might not have the time to decide if it made its move now.

"I could ask the same of you," he said quietly, looking her over. "However, I suspect that your answer would only mirror mine."

"Oh, you mean you're interested in Egyptology, too?" she asked with mock surprise. The look Michael gave her said quite plainly that he didn't appreciate her effort at levity.

"This is not a joking matter, Alex," came his cool reply.

"Tell me something I don't know," she muttered. Dimly, he

could sense her thoughts, a fleeting memory of a vile kill that wasn't truly her own.

"It's by the display of amulets." He nodded towards the middle of the room. "It's in the guise of a human female."

"What?" Then she followed his gaze and understood. Glancing back at her, he could see the hunter side of her surface. Serious eyes, a firm set jaw, the careful coiling of power around her. It intrigued him, the feel of her magic. He had thought she was a low-level mage, not someone with high-level potential.

"Can you identify what it is?" he asked.

"No. Can you?"

"No."

They watched the girl staring at the large glass case housing artifacts taken from pharoanic tombs. At first glance, she seemed ordinary enough. Her short hair was a little unkempt, as were her clothes. That wouldn't have been too unusual if she had come through the storm outside. She looked to be a young woman, late teens or early twenties.

"Who died?"

She glanced back at him, a bit startled by his question, then shrugged.

"A girl was killed in the Wal-Mart bathroom. A friend of mine kind of found out by accident. Afterwards, she got hit over the head with a divine order to tell me." She grimaced at the amusement that shone in his eyes. "She's a little religious, okay? Nothing wrong with it. Or her. What was your tip off to this?"

"The weather. There was something wrong with it. It's difficult to explain."

"It was raining hard at the time of the murder. Do you have any experience hunting – well, hunting things like this?"

"I do, yes. I am familiar with your Guild, though I am not member. Feel free to check with the Tallahassee chapter; they will know my name."

"Huh." It was her turn to scrutinize him. After a moment, she nodded decisively. "I'll do that. For now, we can coordinate, unless you have an objection?"

"I don't."

"Good." Alex moved away from the mummy, walking further into the room. She glanced over her shoulder, impatience shimmering in her voice. "Are you coming or what?"

Michael strode beside, clamping a hand on her shoulder.

"What do you propose to do? This is hardly the place for a confrontation."

"I want to see what's in the case. Something's got its attention. Just look at the way the thing is staring." She paused at the sarcophagus displayed next to it, casting a sidelong look in the direction of the creature. "How long has it been like that?"

"Since I arrived, about twenty minutes ago."

"I'm going to wander over, take a peek at whatever it's interested in." She cocked her head at him. "Back me up?"

"Be careful."

He frowned as she sauntered over to the amulets, leaning over the glass. A full minute passed. Nothing happened. Her hand, once casually laid on the corner of the case, began to clench into a fist. Her complexion began to pale.

As Alex's face took on a greenish cast, the girl's stare slowly turned towards her. The empty expression twisted into a soundless snarl.

Michael stepped forward to intercede as Alex suddenly pushed herself away from the case and swung towards him. She looked ill, her eyes unfocused and vacant. Behind her, the girl continued to glower. He wrapped an arm around her shoulders, guiding her to a timeline mounted on a nearby wall. She took deep, careful breaths. Her color improved gradually. Still holding her, he lowered his head to her ear.

"Scared?"

Her head jerked up at the insult to glare at him. "No. Why should I be?"

"Why, yes indeed." He lifted a hand to her face, idly tucking a flyaway strand of auburn hair behind her other ear. The tips of his fingers skimmed the shell of it to her earlobe, from there over the line of her jaw and down the jugular vein at her neck. Her pulse had already been beating rapidly. Now the rhythm changed. He sensed her mind whirling before; now he felt her thoughts scatter. He found some satisfaction in it.

"Touchy-feely, aren't we?" Her voice came out breathy. His blue eyes gleamed darkly, hinting at his amusement.

"You're thinking of something else now, aren't you?" He didn't wait for her to confirm or deny that. Sliding his hands onto her upper arms, he asked, "What is it looking at?"

"Some stuff that was found in the mummy wrappings, I think. Scarab cabochons, amulets, stuff like that." She frowned at him. "It's staring at us , isn't it?"

He didn't have to look behind them to confirm it. He nodded.

"You weren't exactly subtle in leaving."

"You try feeling that thing's aura, presence, whatever – it was like drowning in something foul." She shuddered. A shadow passed over her eyes, the light in them becoming muted. "The girl – the form it wears. It came from the same girl, the one murdered a few days ago. I could feel it killing her."

"Empathy." His eyes narrowed. Empaths didn't usually take a warrior's path in life.

She scowled at him.

"Yes, empathy. It's not that strong of an ability, though. There's just something about – whatever that is," she explained, referring to the creature, "that triggers it. It caught me off guard." Abruptly, she straightened, shrugged him off. "I'm okay. So, now what?"

"We'll try a different approach. We need to get it away from everyone else here."

"Got any ideas?"

"Perhaps."

Michael wandered over to the display, gesturing for Alex to follow at a distance. He saw the girl's eyes go from vaguely focused to monstrously bright at his approach. Thunder cracked outside. The building seemed to shudder as he felt energy whip up wildly, centering around the girl-who-wasn't. The fiend hissed, violently jerking away as he neared. Whirling, it stomped out of the room. The abrupt departure caught everyone's attention.

Still staring after it, he tapped the pane in front of him.

"Alex, was it studying anything in particular in this case?" If it wanted something there, it might circle back.

"I think…" She considered before pointing to a *wadjet*. Shaped like a stylized eye detailed with pharaonic makeup. "This. It's a protection charm. It still has potency, but not much. It's old, brittle. In a few years, it won't hold any magic."

"We leave it and follow."

They headed in the direction the creature had gone – the stairs. Overhead, the storm raised its voice. Arcane force surged violently as something crackled loudly. The ceiling lights flickered, then burst in a shower of sparks and glass as patrons screamed. Michael shoved Alex down, shielding her with his body from the shards that fell around them.

12

The people quieted as the emergency generator kicked on. Everything was suddenly awash in the red glare of the auxiliary lights. He stood, shrugging off the debris, then helped Alex to her feet. Behind them, the others were milling uncertainly. No one seemed to have been hurt by the incident, only scared.

"All right, people, calm down," a man's authoritative voice called out. "The power's out, so the museum's closing. If you'll come this way, the staff will direct you towards the entrance."

Michael and Alex both looked down the stairs to see a security guard ascending, flashlight in hand. He brushed past them calling out instructions for the small crowd to carefully make their way down the steps. Murmuring with relief, they obeyed.

Michael watched as the others filed past him, keeping a firm hand on Alex's arm so that they would be last. He made no pretense in his waiting. The guard gave them a cool stare as they brought up the rear, a look that he returned with equal frost. His mind could not detect the slight difference between humanity and masked monstrosity, as he had with the girl earlier, yet the scent was there. It clung to the guard's form like thick mud. There was an undercurrent of fresh blood, pain, and fear, just barely detectable.

He felt Alex tense as the last of the civilians passed. Good, he thought. She was ready as well.

"Oh!" He glanced at his temporary partner to see her patting her pockets. She smiled at the guard apologetically. "I'm sorry. I must have dropped my keys back in the exhibit. Would you mind if I went back for them?" She looked up at Michael. "You have a pen light, right? To help search for the keys?"

He nodded, understanding what she was about.

The guard said nothing. Taking silence for assent, they went back to the room. Glass was ground into the carpet by their feet as they walked. The muted sound was all they heard as they began to cast about for the imaginary keys – out of sight of everyone else.

When the attack came, they were ready.

It rushed them from behind. He pushed Alex to the side as he snapped out a whirling kick. His foot connected solidly sending the guard stumbling backwards as she hit the floor, rolled. When she came up, she had one of her little knives in hand.

Lacking a blade of his own, Michael edged towards one side. Without looking, he put his fist through the acrylic pane protecting relics of Egyptian warfare. Grabbing a curved bronze blade, he launched an offensive.

He feinted, lunged. His prey dodged, shoving a display case between them easily. The ancient stone coffin was sent to the floor amid the shattering of glass and the clarion of a burglar alarm. Somewhere behind him, Alex was making her move. Dimly, he felt magic flow, could almost hear the words she murmured as she brought that energy to bear. He caught a glimpse of something flying through the air as he evaded another attack.

Her dagger hit the target in the shoulder, the hilt flaring with dull orange-gold light. The creature hissed with pain, the human eyes giving way to something yellow, malicious. Michael sped forward, slashing with the sword. It ducked, rolled, yanking the smaller blade free.

The air in the room came alive. A sudden gust swept up from

behind them, whipping Alex's hair into her eyes. With every bit of the skill that she had shown, it threw the dagger right back at her.

Michael didn't think. He leaped over the coffin to intercept the weapon in flight, his sword missing it by the fraction of an inch as he tried to block it. The woman just barely moved in time. A part of him shuddered as the blade thudded into the wall behind her – the spot her head had been.

The lights cut off. Somewhere in the darkness, the creature snarled. Energy surged wildly, air rushing in a mad vortex. The sarcophagus suddenly heaved off the floor to fling itself at Michael. He twisted out of the way. Behind him, Alex scrabbled back as it crashed to the floor.

The distraction gave the fiend the opening it had been waiting for. It lunged. Its rampant power punched through the outer magical shields around his mind as it knocked him off balance. He fell back, rolled under, instinctively pulling the thing with him. It flipped over his head. Only after he'd done it did he realize that he'd sent it toward Alex.

He was on his feet before the fervent curse left his lips.

She met it in mid-air – foot first. The blow sent it crashing to the ground as she twisted, throwing a handful of something after it. It smashed into another display. Unearthly howls filled the room as thunder exploded outside. She began to chant in a language he didn't understand. Power stirred again, clean and pure, swirling around her like a gentle whirlwind. Specks of light sprung up on the carpet, on the guard's uniform, on the thing's face. It cried out, clawing at its visage. The tiny lights flared. It began to scream incoherently.

Outside, the storm struck again. The crack of lightning hitting the building was deafening. Sparks flew from every electrical outlet, flames spurting to life from the fried circuits. The emergency exit signs, the cameras, they all exploded with the arcane surge, sending both Michael and Alex to the floor.

In the near silence that followed they could hear shouts and running feet. Michael grimaced as he picked himself up from the floor. The room was now lit only by tiny flames from several electrical fires, yet it was still enough to see by. The creature was nowhere in sight.

"It's best not to be found here," he muttered. He yanked Alex's dagger from the wall, discarding his borrowed weapon. The hilt burned in his hand. He dug in his pocket for a cloth; he usually kept a few on him. Wrapping the blade in the fabric, he handed it to her, then took her arm roughly. She opened her mouth to say something, indignation flickering over her expression. He ignored her, closing his eyes to better concentrate.

This was the place they needed to be, *this* was the way it felt, and *his Firebird* was the beacon to guide him –

A rush of wind, blowing hot, then cold, the pounding of waves on a rocky coast, the grinding, rumbling sound of bedrock shifting, the heat, the roar of a raging fire. The sensations were all familiar to him. A dizzying kind of comfort. When they fell away, the pair stood in the harsh rain on the sidewalk. The Firebird sat beside them, parked under the trees that lined the parking lot. Overhead, the fury of the storm was reluctantly subsiding to a resentful sulk. Even so, they were both soaked in a matter of moments.

Alex clung to him, disoriented by their abrupt teleportation, shivering in the frigid downpour. Feeling her body tremble against him stirred his blood, a reaction he could hardly appreciate while on a public sidewalk getting soaking wet. He wrapped an arm around her shoulders, guiding her to her own vehicle parked a few slots down from his. Unlocking her driver side door with a touch of magic, he opened it, eased her inside. She looked up at him as he stood bent over the doorway to block the rain. He tried to ignore the fact that he could see the bra she wore quite clearly through the wet fabric of her shirt. He couldn't seem to focus his gaze on anything for very long before returning to it, something that exasperated more than irritated.

"Nice trick." She ran a hand through her wet hair. She'd apparently forgotten about what she was wearing and didn't notice his wandering eyes. He was grateful for her bemused state as he couldn't seem to stop his eyes from straying. "Got any more?"

Amusement filtered through him. Her deliberately flippant

remark was meant to dispel a bit of the tension she was feeling. He decided that he didn't want her comfortable around him — especially if *he* wasn't entirely comfortable around *her*.

"It has its uses," he replied, dismissing the urge to indulge himself by leaning closer. They had something else to talk about at the moment. "Did you see where it went?"

"No." She sounded disgusted. "Guess you didn't, either." She eyed him, taking in the drenched coat, the tousled wet hair, the rivulets of water running down his face. "You could come in out of the rain, you know."

He shook his head, almost smiling.

"Your little trick wouldn't happen to have done anything with the security cameras, would it? Both of us are on the video." Alex glanced past him, at the museum standing across the street from where they were. "It's not like we can sneak back and take tapes, discs, whatever it is that they're recording everything on nowadays."

"I doubt it will be problem. The electrical wiring was overloaded. Just about everything that was plugged in is ruined."

"If it's a digital recording, they may still be able to dig the video out of it," she pointed out. He frowned as he caught a whisper of thought from her. Something about a trashed hard drive disk that she'd had the data retrieved from. He made a note of it.

"I'll take care of it," he said, then paused as sirens sounded in the distance. It was time to leave. "We'll talk at Hidden Reaches. My place."

He didn't wait for her response. Shutting the door, he walked to his own vehicle. Above, the storm was already settling into patterns that were more normal. Some of the wild power that had formed it was still there, yet most had drained away. To where or to whom, he couldn't be certain. Behind him, Alex's sedan pulled away from the curb. On impulse, he sent a probe out in her direction. He sensed puzzlement, frustration, the sensation of being chilled. She'd turned the heater on.

He imagined that she'd take the time to change into something dry before coming up to his apartment. As he climbed into his car, he indulged in thinking about what might happen if she didn't. A warm thrill began to hum in his blood. This time he did smile, in sardonic amusement at himself.

The rain came down harder. He abruptly decided that he didn't want to fool with it. Not when it made him think of the way Alex's shirt had molded and clung. With the sirens of fire engines and police coming closer, he gathered his will once more, imagined the apartment he now called home. The car disappeared.

13

By the time Alex got home, Michael was already there. She just sat in the parking-lot-turned-shallow-lake, wearily staring at the sleek black car. She had left before he did. She knew for a fact that he hadn't passed her on the way back. What did he do – use that little trick of his to get back here with it? It seemed like such an impractical, not to mention wasteful, use of magic.

Why even bother driving at all? He obviously didn't need to.

He could have at least had the courtesy to offer her the same service.

Bastard.

Getting out, thoroughly soaking herself, her shoes, and everything she carried, she made her way to her apartment. She didn't bother running. There was no way to alleviate the degree of drenching when she had to wade through tons of water just to cross the parking lot in the first place. By the time she got to her front door, she was seriously considering stripping on the landing before going inside.

Why not? Not here, obviously, but who's to say I can't do it on the back porch? It seemed reasonable enough to her. The porch balcony faced the woods, no one was likely to be out in the this weather. A minute later, she was back in the rain, heading around the building to access the rear stairs.

On the porch, she stripped herself of the heavy clothing. She shivered as her damp skin took a direct hit from the cool air. She unlocked the sliding glass door, once again thankful for the unusual amenities of Hidden Reaches that allowed her to do so. She left her clothing on the porch. She'd collect it soon enough. The tools of her trade, though, she did bring inside; they needed cleaning. Retrieving a some fresh towels, from a bag in her room, she quickly dried herself off before doing the same for her implements.

She thought about Michael's parting mandate as she unwrapped the dagger she'd used earlier. Yes, they needed to talk. No, she wasn't going up right then. One thing that she had learned well was that no tool was left to rust, no mess from work left to stand. Michael, she reasoned, could wait.

Ten minutes later, she was clothed with her sodden outfit running through the washer. She sat at the dining room table, a bottle of oil in one hand, a cleaning cloth in the other, and set to work. As she tended to her things, she placed a call to the regional Guild House in Tallahassee. The Hunters' Guild was widespread, with a huge network of contacts who worked with, or were, supernatural. The brief conversation she had concerning Michael Keegan didn't yield many details about the man himself, so much as some of his activities.

The bottom-line was that the Guild had worked with him on several occasions prior to this, some of those instances having been decades ago. He was listed as a trust-worthy contact, his longevity due to his power as a mage.

Alex mulled it over as she cleaned.

She'd left the dagger thrown at the creature for last. Revulsion filled her as she touched it. What had that thing done to it? Frowning, she studied it minutely. Just barely within her ability to sense it, she could see an odd, yellowish pulsing. Twisted magic. Her hand tingled unpleasantly. Going with her gut, she fetched an

EMF detector from her room.

It was a little black box inlaid with a digital screen, used to measure the strength of electromagnetic fields. Electricians used the gadget to look for faulty wiring and the like. Outside that trade, it was a tool for detecting the presence of the paranormal as high EMF readings were often associated with it. Alex had found it useful in finding traces of magic, which was what she wanted to do now. Bringing the device close to the knife, she watched the little screen carefully. The numerical readout on the display indicated a measurement of 3.2.

Not magic, she thought. A reading of around 10.0 or so was standard for magic. Normal EMF levels were below 1.0, so there was something there. Given that, she moved to the next option. She said a prayer of cleansing, then determinedly brought her own power to bear on it in an effort to remove the stench of the unnatural. The magic almost seemed to slide over it, around it, a portion of it was even absorbed by the energy there.

My weapon is now a magic leech. That doesn't make me happy.

Better to conserve what she had for now, if that was the case; her capacity for arcane energy had never been more than the low-end of average. Well, Michael certainly had more magical oomph, she mused. Perhaps he could do something with it. That settled, she put everything up, enshrouding the knife in a worn piece of fabric to take with her. She didn't think to bring anything else as she headed up to his place.

When he answered the door, he did so with a lifted brow.

"You took your time," he remarked mildly.

She scowled at him. She shoved her knife into his hands as she stepped inside.

"I can't cleanse it." It bothered her that she couldn't. It bothered her more that it showed in her voice. "The black on the blade is from the oil I used. When I tried to do a prayer-spell of cleansing, it ate some of it."

He frowned at the dagger, studying. Gesturing for her to follow, he led her into the front rooms. Another wordless signal had her lingering there as he disappeared into the back. With a shrug,

Alex looked around, taking in everything much the same way he had taken in her own apartment during the last storm.

There were candles everywhere. Not a single electric source of lighting, which was odd. The walls were covered with old tapestries, a few paintings. Most of the furniture looked as if it belonged in a museum somewhere, which prompted her to wonder how long had it all been in his family. There were leather-bound books stacked here and there, some small examples of ancient-looking statuary scattered throughout. There was no TV, no stereo, no computer. The only remotely modern pieces were the cordless phone on a narrow table against one wall, the brass-studded leather couch, and the matching armchair in his living room.

Wow. A person could only inherit so much. The man must have been rolling in it to have all of this. Once again, she couldn't help wondering why he'd chosen an apartment for a home.

"I have little use for a larger space at the moment."

She turned to see him standing at the mouth of the back hall, blade in hand. She lifted an eyebrow. She raised her chin in silent challenge, a move that he seemed to recognize for what it was.

"Sorry," he murmured, more amused than embarrassed. "The blade's been contaminated. I don't think it will ever be cleansed. It would be best to get rid of it and find a replacement."

She glanced at her weapon. Whatever he had done to it had turned it completely black. It looked charred, as if it had been engulfed in flame.

"Alright." She huffed out a breath. She hated going through the trouble of replacing a tool. "You wanted to talk."

"Yes."

He didn't give the knife back. Turning away from her, he headed for the kitchen. The dagger had disappeared by the time he'd come back with two steaming mugs of what smelled like heaven. He offered her one, then carelessly waved for her to sit as he took his own seat on the couch. She perched in the armchair, pleasantly surprised to find the leather warm instead of cool to the touch.

"You should know that I did some checking on you."

"With the Hunters' Guild." He nodded, unfazed. "Were you satisfied?"

"I guess. Intrigued is the better word," she admitted with a slight smile. "You've lived a long time, Michael."

"Yes. I do have a question." Michael sipped his tea, watching her over the rim of the mug with eyes that were darkly intent.

"Yeah?" she quipped. "Are we moving on to more pressing matters then?"

"Partly. What language were you chanting in? Just before we left."

"Language?" she asked, giving him a startled look. She could feel the mild embarrassment creep up her face as she remembered. "Oh, that. It's a prayer thing. I find it easier to use magic if it's in the form of prayer." She shrugged a little sheepishly.

He contemplated her for a moment, then let it go. She couldn't tell what he thought of it. When he didn't say anything else immediately, she spoke.

"My turn: why is a powerful mage like you – and someone who 'poofs' a car across the city is powerful – here in Jacksonville?"

The corner of his mouth quirked as he sipped from his mug.

"Why are you here?" he returned.

"It's home."

He nodded.

"I landed here sometime ago, doing a favor for a friend. When it was done, I saw no reason to leave. As for being powerful, I'm not. At least, not in the way you perceive me to be. I'm just... different."

She frowned as she let that statement sink in. He leaned back, continuing to talk as if the question had never been asked.

"It won't be back to the museum," he said, thinking aloud. "Have you seen the news?"

She shook her head.

"One of the security guards was killed. The same one," he went on with great significance, "that we fought."

Alex wasn't surprised. She had caught the underlying stench of death about the thing.

"It works fast." She leaned back in the chair, resisting the urge to draw in her legs and curl up. There was more than enough room to do just that. "It's not natural," she murmured, brows knitting as she thought about it. "At least, it's nothing like any of the shapeshifters I'm familiar with."

"Doppelgangers are known to sometimes kill those they wish to emulate."

"That's true. However, there are other things that don't fit."

"Such as?"

"It's speed, for one. Have you ever fought a doppelganger?"

He shook his head in answer.

"They're not that fast. They don't think quickly on their feet, typically. They also don't have a predominant personality. They stick with the personality of whoever they're mimicking until something forces them to step out of the role." She drank again. Then frowned, bemusedly at her mug. It didn't look as if she'd been drinking the wonderfully spiced tea at all.

A smile ghosted over Michael's face, quick as thought, and just as swiftly gone. Alex noticed it just the same. She gave him a suspicious glance as he picked up her thread of reasoning.

"Another factor would be that Doppelgangers don't have as much substance as this thing does." A brooding look slipped over him as he stared off into space. She could almost hear the gears working, the pages flipping, as he rifled through his memory. "Like you, there's nothing in my experience that resembles this."

"For me, that means research," she said with a sigh. "I'm not looking forward to it."

He lifted an eyebrow. "How will you go about it? Wade through books, myths, cultures? The internet?" He sounded almost disdainful, especially of that last option.

She smirked at him, unable to resist the urge.

"The internet? Mostly incomplete and unreliable. Books? Takes too long. I've got something better, to start anyway." She took another sip, then did a double take. It wasn't the same tea she'd been drinking. She didn't bother hiding or toning down the accusing glare she sent his way.

14

"**D**on't like it?" he answered with a query of his own. His voice was threaded with humor.

Alex gave him a stern look. Thing was, she did. She couldn't tell what it was she was drinking. It was warm, spicy, tasting wonderfully of apples and pears. A few minutes ago it had been caramel with a hint of cinnamon. Though she wasn't certain which she liked better, she still didn't appreciate her drink being switched without her consent.

This time he did smile, the expression doing interesting things to her stomach.

"Answer the question," she ground out, trying to ignore her reaction for the moment. Pursing her lips, she pointed at the cup.

"My dishes are…unique. I'm sure you've heard of the mythical Cauldron of Plenty." He paused as she nodded. "It conjured feasts upon demand, thus the ogre – or witch, depending on the story – it belonged to never went hungry. These are smaller, more modern variations of that."

"You have magic dishes." There was a flat note of skepticism in her voice. She studied his serious face, then her mug. "Dishes of

Plenty."

"It's convenient."

"Where did they come from?"

"There was a time, long ago, when I wasn't actively involved in situations like the one we encountered earlier," he began. "I had the time, the power, and a desire not to learn things such as cooking or cleaning. So…the dishes."

"How long did it take you? How the hell did you do it?" One things kept going 'round and 'round in her mind. The sheer amount of magic that it would have required…much more than needed to teleport, right? Had to be, to create something that could sustain its own magic in some way. Why was he *here*, in an apartment of a city like Jacksonville?

"Years, decades. To be honest, I didn't mark the time it took. The collection is a small one, created one piece at a time." He shrugged. "The process was complicated, arduous, and extremely drawn out."

She shook her head slowly in disbelief.

"What are you thinking now?"

"That I want my EMF detector to test this mug. I'll do it later." She gave a little laugh. "You say you're not powerful yet you make Dishes of Plenty."

"Yes."

"If you can do that, then why not do more with that monster at the museum?"

"A valid question." He cupped the mug with both hands, looking at her with sober eyes. "One has to be careful when walking the Dark. I am not familiar with the creature. There are shadings to it that I don't understand, characteristics I cannot define the shape or purpose of. Until I'm sure that it won't take a magical attack, or take that energy for its own, I'll refrain from using magic." He sipped, locking gazes with her. "Too many people can get hurt trying to fight something they don't understand. I'm not going to be one of them. There were also civilians to consider."

"Okay, I can accept that." Mostly because she agreed with it one hundred percent. The bystanders had been a concern of hers during the event. "So now what?"

"Research." He gave a speculative look. "You were saying that you had something other than books and the internet."

"Yeah, a database."

He regarded her with interest. "How large a database?"

"It's sizeable, bigger than will fit on my computer hard drive, anyway," she answered. "Doesn't have everything in it, of course. Still, things are being added to it all the time."

"How did you come by it? The Guild?"

"It's been in the works for about eight or nine years now," she replied. "So I'll search the database. You will do – what?"

"Wade through books," he stated dryly.

"It's a bit late for a trip to the library. You have your own here?"

"Yes."

"We can probably save a bit of time by going over the database first. It'll narrow the field, at least." Outside, fresh peals of thunder rolled through the sky. Before she could say another word, a loud boom reverberated the building. Fast on its heels came a blinding flash of light through the windows.

"Electricity's out," he murmured with a sigh. Of course, his place was still well lit as he used nothing other than candles. Alex cursed fervently, then closed her eyes in resignation. She needed the computer and a working internet connection to use the PASAC – Paranormal and Supernatural Analytical Catalogue – that the Guild had developed. There was the UPS battery as a backup power supply. She had one that would last a few hours at least. However, it didn't guarantee the internet.

Michael abruptly stood up, crossing over to the phone. He checked for a dial tone.

"Dead. Will this affect your database?"

"Yeah. My connection's DSL." She grumbled a bit under her breath. He went to her, his mug in one hand, extending the other for her take.

"Time to leave already?" she asked ironically, then sighed dramatically. "So nice to be wanted."

He chuckled, the first time she'd ever heard him do so. She felt a warm flutter in her stomach. "You're not leaving. You can bring your tea with you."

She rose, ignoring his outstretched hand. Nonetheless, she found her hand in his as soon as she was on her feet. She allowed him to lead her to the back hall, glancing curiously to the right as they turned left. There was a door there, left half-open. Beyond it was what looked like a bedroom, with a very large bed at the far end of it. She got only a glimpse of it, leaving the impression of warmth, dark wood, and rich, heavy fabrics.

The room to the left was much larger, almost as large as the living room. The walls were covered from floor to ceiling with wooden bookcases. More jutted out from the wall every four feet or so. In the center of the room was a small table with two comfortable looking chairs. Candle stands of wrought iron and glass were everywhere, most of them coming up to her elbow or shoulders. A few were actually taller than she was. The moment they entered the room, the simple ivory candles flickered to life. If not for the slightest whispers of arcane force or the light, she might not have noticed them.

Alex saw something move out of the corner of her eye. Magic rose in an intangible breeze, flowing around the room as she turned to look. A book glided off the shelf, sailing towards the table as they approached. It opened itself, flipping its own pages as it went. It wasn't the only one. They came from every direction, at varying speeds, converging on the room's central point. Michael ignored the flurry of volumes that zoomed around his head as he sat down. Alex stayed where she was, certain that if she moved that she'd be hit with the heaviest tome there. He glanced over at her as the books settled themselves in a high pile on top of the table. When the last pages stilled, he crooked his finger at her.

"These are the books that hold something similar to what we are looking for," he explained as she gingerly sat down in the chair opposite him. "Just think about the creature, its characteristics. The book will flip to any section that may be relevant."

With that, he buried himself in the first tome that came to hand.

Alex stared at him. Abruptly irritated with him, both for the surprise of the flying library and the commanding attitude he'd assumed, she scowled at his bowed head. Snatching a leather-clad volume at random, she muttered about great magicians – making the very word a slur to anyone affiliated with magic – being great showoffs. She was so preoccupied with her own search that she missed Michael's amused smile as he read.

Elsewhere

A lamp crashed against the bedroom wall, shattering into a thousand pieces, the cord flailing wildly at the impact. The wanton destruction was only nominally satisfying. It was an outlet, though not what he wanted. That was to break the duo that had delayed his plans.

His servant was healing. It would be at least a wee-k before it could venture out again, unless he found a way to aid it. He was loathe to waste any of the power he'd harvested on bringing his slave back up to readiness. It would heal through other means.

Whatever that woman had done to it had left it scarred. There were pits on its face, its limbs, and until the healing was done those bloody, scabbed sores would identify it immediately to the enemy. Whoever the enemy was.

There had been two of them. Both had reeked of magic. Yet it had been the man that the creature spoke of. It claimed that it was the man that could see past the form it wore, the man that was the more powerful. It was the man that made him – *him* – look like a novice.

The servant now bore bruises to go with the pockmarks.

The woman was the one that intrigued him. Her description was as familiar to him as the man's was not. Yes, familiar, and expected. His minion had not been able to give him names. Still, he was sure of who it must be.

The trinket, though lost, had served its purpose. It was a silver lining to the cloud of wrathful disappointment he felt. With the seed planted, it would now be nurtured. He would bide his time, make a few contacts, put out his lures. With the servant out of commission for the moment, he had little else to do.

As he thought about the staging ahead, his temper leveled out. Perhaps the servant's injuries were not so bad a thing after all. It wasn't necessary for all preparations. Some of the bait could be set without it. The woman…yes, he needed to watch her a bit more, bring himself up to date on her capabilities.

It was the man that nagged at him. There was something about him, the description, that lodged in the deepest recesses of his mind. He had to learn more. Learning required more brains than brawn. The slave, he felt, lacked the kind of intelligence and comprehension needed.

His plans would soon be back on track. This hitch was already smoothing out. With one minor prize sacrificed for the greater good of his ambitions, it left two more waiting in the wings. All he had to do, was find them. All he had to know was who to kill.

16

Jacksonville, FL

Alex was still muttering two hours later when her stomach started to rumble. Loudly. Then her complaints turned to obnoxious people that starved their partners even if they had plate-ware that could fill with food at the owner's slightest inclination. Dishes of Plenty, she called them. Vastly amused, Michael let her ramble on for a bit. It wasn't all grievances and he found her choice of words entertaining; they certainly made the dull task before them less of a burden, at least for him.

He would have to feed her soon, though. It was more of a matter of what, and he was still trying to make up his mind. What did one offer a human hunter like this one?

As he continued to mull that over in the back of his mind, she broke off from the subject of food. Instead, she gave a sarcastic and somewhat skewed commentary on what she was reading break through the griping.

"Getting naked just to wear some animal skin – what is this? A fetish?" She snickered. There was a bizarre image of wolf-skin lingerie. It was followed by another of a loaded hamburger and French fries, complete with a pickle spear.

Always one to prefer solitary study, Michael thought it something of a small miracle that he'd found her company entertaining as opposed to irritating. He wondered if she did the same thing when she was alone in her work. A picture came unbidden of grilled cheese sandwiches and tomato soup, both herbed. Not his usual fare; the thought hadn't been his to begin with. In her mind, they smelled delicious. When she thought of someone called Richard with longing he felt the amusement drop away. An unpleasant rush of heat began to thrum in his blood as he remembered the canister of "Richard's Specialty" in her pantry.

"Who is he?"

"What?" came the absent response. Alex look up at him from across the table. "Who?"

"Who is Richard?" His voice was cool, even to his own ears.

"Richard?" She frowned at him, confused. "Richard Douglas? Where did this come from?"

"The tea blend in your pantry." It hadn't seemed important enough to ask that night. He felt more than just a little irritated with himself that he was asking now.

"Richard's an old friend. Teri Andrews is another, and so is Lys Barinton. Richard is engaged to Lys."

"How long have you known him?" His eyes narrowed at the page he was skimming, not really reading it. He hadn't meant to ask that.

"Not as long as Teri and Lys." She paused. He could feel her thoughts flash through her mind as she tried to see where this was going. "I met Teri first; we've been friends since grade-school. We met Lys in college, then Richard a year later when he came down to see Lys. They'd gone to high school together. I think they started dating when she was getting her AA. They got engaged the day we opened the café."

His mood lightened, though he gave no response.

"Now why are you asking?" Her suspicious question stopped him before he could begin to sort out the reason for his mood swing.

"Grilled cheese and soup," he muttered, not wanting to discuss it further. He made an abrupt gesture. A plate of the meal she'd been daydreaming about appeared on top of the book in front of her, with a thick tapestry place mat underneath it to protect the pages. It smelled better than she'd imagined. In fact, he found his own mouth watering. He conjured a portion for himself.

As he began to eat, he wondered about his own behavior. He was so deep in thought over it that he missed her reaction to the presentation of dinner. Her sigh drew his attention back. Full of longing for the food, it had him unwillingly thinking of something else.

"Smells heavenly." Alex bit into a sandwich wedge, almost moaning in pleasure. "Hate to say it but it's better than Richard's."

"Richard's." His eyes flickered toward her. He saw several of the candle-flames nearest them dancing uneasily. He needed to get a handle on whatever it was that he was feeling.

"Yeah." She happily dunked her wedge into the bowl of soup that had come with the plate. "He's our gourmet chef. Kept us all fed through college. Stocked my fridge and freezer when I moved here. I keep telling Lys that she better not lose him. We might very well starve."

The flames stopped dancing.

"So why the sudden need-to-know on Richard?"

"Why not?" He couldn't tell her if he wasn't sure himself so he changed the subject. "What's the closest thing you've come across to our quarry thus far?"

"Nothing really. Lots of human-animal shape-shifters. So far, there's nothing that has to kill in order to change form."

She sighed, spooning up some soup. He let the conversation give way to quiet as she ate. He made sure that he paid no outward attention to her as he did the same, continuing to skim the same page he'd been looking at for the last ten minutes. When they were finished with the meal, the used dishes whisked themselves away.

"Where did they go?"

He looked up to see her emerald green eyes alive with curiosity as she asked, "Never-Never Land? The Land of Lost Socks?"

"The sink in the kitchen." He frowned at her. "The Land of

Lost Socks?"

"Don't tell me you've never lost a sock in the wash." She grinned up at him, humor apparently restored by food. Laughter echoed in his mind. "I've lost thousands. One of the reasons why the socks I wear are all white and of the same style."

He shook his head, momentarily baffled.

"Do you even do laundry?"

That question had the corner of his mouth quirking. That was one chore of many that he'd never had to endure. "No."

She stared at him, those intriguing green eyes going from bewildered to puppy-like. "Please, please, please, oh, please tell me the secret. I absolutely *hate* doing laundry."

He didn't know where to begin. Magic was so much a part of what he was that he'd never had to think about it. He gave a slight shake of his head as he settled for a simpler answer.

"I have an…arrangement that takes care of it."

"Oh." She pouted for a moment, then shrugged it off philosophically. "Oh, well. Guess I'm doomed to doing laundry for the rest of my life. Have you had any luck with your end over there?"

"No more than you." He eyed the remaining pile of books on the table, thinking of the long hours required to go through all of them. "How reliable is your method of doing this?"

"Hmmm. Hard to say. Needs electricity, though." She leaned back, her face thoughtful.

He debated with himself. In theory, he could power her computer. He had done so before with other, smaller electronics. It was not an option without risks, however, as there was a chance to blow the contraption's circuitry – or whatever it was that passed for a computer's innards.

"Can I ask you something off-topic?"

He glanced up at her, frowning. "What is it?"

"Did you know that you're God-touched? Some people don't, even when they are." She smiled cheekily. "You don't strike me as the kind of person who wouldn't."

He sat back, studying her.

"You've got the aura thing going," She began to flip through another book idly.

"Aura thing. You see auras?"

"Not normally. Just when someone has a real powerful presence to them. Yours is a dark purple, for instance, with gold flecks in it. It's the gold that tells me you're God-touched."

"Are you?"

She laughed. The sound was rich and bright.

"I have no idea. I can't see my own aura, Haven't had any encounters with God, either, so I'm not sure I have a reason to think I am. Have you? Had an encounter with a deity, I mean."

In his mind, he felt a familiar, slightly impatient nudge, one that had his jaw clenching. He sent a jab back. He got a response of sensation rather than words. Reassurance, amusement, slightly-mocking laughter, more impatience. There was a definite feeling that He approved of Alex. Muttering an oath, he heard Gwynn's rumbling chuckle in the back of his mind as His presence left. Alex raised her eyebrows.

"It was a long time ago." He didn't elaborate, feeling vaguely resentful of Gwynn's 'encouragement.' He was grown, with over a hundred human lifetimes behind him. One would think he could be trusted to decisions for himself by now.

"Sore point?" For the first time, she hesitated, uncertain. "I'm sorry."

"No," he sighed heavily, then sipped his tea. "Only occasionally irritating." He studied her again, this time looking with more than just his physical eyes. Mixed in with the fiery red of her own aura were traces of sparkling amber. He didn't mention it. "There are times He annoys and times He irritates. Our relationship isn't an easy one."

"Would you have it any other way?" she asked.

"No." The answer was prompt.

"Why?"

"Because He has always been there."

17

When Alex and Michael left his apartment, the downpour had died down to a drizzle. Neither of them had noticed how late it was. She judged it to be after ten or so. Not for the first time, she was grateful that she could command her own hours. She didn't have to get up early the next day.

The landing lights were on – a sign that made her happy. Not only would she not have to fumble with her keys at the door, they wouldn't be stumbling around her place in the dark. A few minutes later, she stood in the foyer, feeling around for the light switch. When her fingers found it, light flashed on. After the relative gloom of Michael's library, it was blinding.

"Let me bring up the database and we'll be ready to rock'n'roll." She hurried over to the desk in the far corner to boot the computer up.

The candle on top of the hutch lit up as Michael came to stand behind her.

"Most of the candles are scented," she commented.

"I noticed. Tell me about this database."

"It's been a Guild project for well over a decade now. As

hunters, we need to know what we're up against. The more info we have, the better off – and more successful – we are. This database helps narrow the field when it comes to looking for stuff. It cross-references hard copy files, books, etc. – pretty much everything we need a search engine to do."

"Search engine?"

"Yeah." She looked up at him, saw the blank face. "You've never heard of a search engine?"

"No." The corner of his mouth quirked upwards. "I'm afraid that technology isn't my strong suit."

"Think of it as an electronic index."

She manipulated the mouse, clicking items on the screen until she got to the file she needed. A prompt for her password popped up. Her fingers flew over the keyboard as she logged into the secured site. The database loaded. She typed in her query and let it run. Michael laid a hand absently on the back of her chair. She tried to ignore the fact that he was there.

"Does it bother you?"

"Hmm?" Distracted, she glanced over her shoulder at him. He was watching the screen as the little hourglass graphic kept siphoning its pixels from top to bottom, then flipping over to do it again.

"How close I am."

"Not really. This shouldn't take long."

It was a lie, she admitted to herself. Well, a smidgeon of one. He was an interesting, mysterious guy. Good-looking, nice to have at your back in a fight – what wasn't there to like? She couldn't help that warm and fuzzy feeling that growing inside, could she?

You're not in high school, anymore, Alex. Get a grip. Stay on track...think of something else...

"I don't suppose it would be possible for you to go back up and fetch one of your mugs?" She really could use a drink right now. He didn't reply. With a sigh, she let herself slump back in the chair to wait.

Behind her, Michael shifted a little. He handed down one of his fabulous mugs, filled with steaming tea. With a surprised sound of delight, she took it. Looking up to thank him, she found him watching her with those dark blue eyes. There was something in his gaze that was a little disconcerting. She told herself not to be silly as she smiled, then gave him a proper 'thank you.'

The screen changed. Alex sat up straight to scan the results of the initial query.

"Not bad," she mused.

"Only three hundred or so possibilities," came his dry reply. Obviously, he'd been hoping for a narrower scope.

"Three hundred and fifty-eight. That was just step one." She typed in a different query this time, searching within the results only. Keyword searches were such useful things. The ones that allowed for multiple criteria were even better.

Within five minutes, the choices had been narrowed down to ten. All of them had matched the descriptions she'd typed in: shape -shifting, killing humans, possessing a connection with the weather. Alex scanned the list, chewing her lip thoughtfully as she clicked on the link that brought up another window containing yet another list, this one of various references. Looking at each one, her heart sank. She didn't have most of them.

"Recognize any of the titles?" she asked wearily, rubbing her eyes. What time was it? It had to be late.

"Two in the morning," he murmured. She cast a startled glance at the computer clock. She'd been way off in her initial estimate of how late it was. "A few. I went through them earlier tonight." He straightened. "I might be able to get access to some of the others but it will take a few days."

"Ditto." Alex sipped her tea, suddenly bone tired. "So, now what?"

"We rest." She could hear the trace of weariness in his voice. "We got farther than I had expected to."

"Hmm." She swiveled her chair around. She continued to drink as she considered him. "Before we call it for the night, I have to ask something."

"Yes?"

"This partnership thing. Are we making it official? I know it's kind of late in the game to be asking about it."

"Define 'official.'" There was the slightest hint of wariness in his voice. She couldn't read his expression.

"Do we share the hunt as well as information? Do we let each other in on whatever it is that we discover on our own? Can we follow leads on our own? Do we back each other up when Hunting? That sort of thing."

He stood quiet as he thought it through. She had the feeling that he didn't care for checking in with someone else. Well, neither did she. She also got the impression that he didn't like the thought of her going out on her own, either. At least, not for now.

"I just wanted it laid out, that's all." A yawn caught her off guard. "Sorry. Feel free to go the lone road if you want."

"No." He raked a hand through his hair, then rubbed the back of his neck as if to ease the tension there. "Partners. Officially. Two are better than one when faced with a unknown adversary."

"Okay." She gave him a tired smile, leaning her head to one side. "Crick in your neck?"

"Yes."

"Probably from staring at the monitor from over my shoulder. Hold still a minute." She got up, came around behind him. She began to rub his shoulders and neck methodically. Alex wasn't the best masseuse in the world nor did she think she was the worst. Slowly, the muscles underneath her hands relaxed as the tension was worked out.

He was certainly built under the clothing he wore, if what her hands were telling her could be believed. She'd always been partial to well-toned muscles. Thinking of that, she suppressed a smile. It probably wasn't appropriate to fantasize about her new partner. With the last of the kinks worked out, she stepped back, letting her hands slip off his shoulders.

"Better?"

"Yes." He turned to face her, eyes fathomless. They gave her the eerie feeling that he wasn't unaware of what she might be thinking. "Thank you."

"No problem." The room descended into an awkward silence as

Alex tried to think of what was next on the partner agenda. She hadn't been a part of one in a very long time. "So, um, what's the plan for tomorrow?"

"We try for some of those books. I don't think the creature will attack again anytime soon."

"Nope." It didn't take much effort at all for the grin to spread over her face. "Those wounds should be slow to heal."

He gave her a querying look. She shrugged.

"It ticked me off. It also wasn't natural – we'd agreed on that, remember? Blessed rock salt tends to leave unnatural things in a world of pain."

"Ah." He seemed amused at her nonchalance. "Let's meet again tomorrow. Until then, we can work on our own."

"Sure," she replied with a smile. "Say around noon? At the *Candlelight and Magic*?"

"Alright."

With that set, Michael took his leave. Alex locked the door behind him, then leaned against it. She could still recall the sensation of his shoulders under her palms. No, she affirmed, fantasizing about one's partner was not at all appropriate. It would be embarrassing if he could pick up on it. Thinking back over things that had been said or done throughout the evening, she really had to wonder if he could.

Shaking her head, she pushed away from the door. She would sleep in. Not by much, though; just enough to get about six or seven hours of sleep, and put in a call to her parents. She'd have them fax over some of the research material she needed, maybe gather some supplies for sketching at the café. It had been a long time since she'd drawn there. The patrons usually liked to see an artist at work.

Plans set, she headed for the bedroom. Not bothering to undress, she laid in bed to let herself slip into dreams.

The Wood

They were working together now.

It pleased Gwynn. Alex slept amid dreams of fantasy while Michael lay awake thinking furiously about feelings he didn't readily understand.

It was hard for him. He was so used to walking his path alone. He had developed the habit of maintaining distance between himself and the rest of the two worlds he moved through. It was a protective measure. One did not live for centuries without acquiring a few.

There was a war in the preternatural underworld, that aspect of reality that most people didn't see. It had raged on since before the time of Eden, pitting followers of Light and Dark against each other. So long as there were those who chose evil or placed their own desires above all else, there would always be Darkness in the universe. Perhaps the war would never end. Perhaps it would never be won. Yet what mattered were the lives that people led, the choices they made on their own. Their beliefs, their faith.

Every victory over the Dark allowed the positive to bloom.

Every victory required soldiers to fight, to believe in what they fought for. Michael was one, Alex another.

A gauntlet covered hand moved to absently rub the ears of the huge white hound beside him. Hard times would be ahead for both. Especially Alex. The daughter of His heart had little inkling of what lay in her way. It was His hope that the son of His heart would choose to stand by her when the time came. It would happen soon enough.

She would draw tomorrow. He would meet her, see her work, be introduced to her friends. What would he think, He mused, to find her sketching something near to him? It would be humorous to find out. Michael needed prodding, though he wouldn't admit it. A little joke such as this would do that.

The wind shifted, bringing the smell of fresh air, clean water, and a woodland valley. Two of His hounds skittered into the clearing, each pulling at the end of a stick in a game of tug-of-war. He watched them play, a father observing His children, then decided to join them.

19

September 8, 2004
Atlantic Beach, FL

Alex was not a morning person. It didn't matter what time in the morning she woke; it was the same. Every day began with the ordeal of getting out of bed, stumbling to the kitchen in a zombie-like state, and brewing that first pot of coffee. It normally took two or three cups to make her human again. Her routine usually allowed for enough time to have a fourth, maybe even a fifth cup of coffee before leaving the house for anything.

Today, she drank the third cup while seated in a tea shop out at the beaches. Though not directly on the beach, *Timeless Teas* was close enough to benefit from the off-shore breezes and beach-goers. Its well-dressed proprietor sat across from her, fussing over the table setting.

"I appreciate you meeting me so early this morning, Ms. Stanton."

Nora Stanton was a middle-aged brunette with a passion for English traditions. Tea time was a particular favorite of hers, one that she had based her business on. She hosted tea parties for all ages groups, also selling anything having to do with making tea. There was a stack of her business cards for interested customers at the café.

That wasn't what brought her to *Timeless*, however. Besides being a business peer, Nora was a medium. While she may have left off giving séances and readings years ago, she had never cut off contact with the spirit world.

"Not a problem at all, dear. Are you sure you don't want any tea?" She shook her head, holding up a hand. "Silly me, of course, you are. Would you care for a scone to go with your coffee? I've got blueberry."

"I'm fine, thank you."

"Good." She brushed her hands over her navy slacks. "I suppose we'd best get it over with. I've a new hire due in about half an hour."

"I'll try to be brief. Mind if I record? It's easier than jotting it down." At the other woman's nod, Alex pulled the digital recorder from her pocket, putting it on the table between them. She recited date, location, subject matter, and the names of those present. "Has the weather of late felt odd in any way to you? Have you heard anything regarding them?"

"No, I'm afraid I haven't felt anything in particular." She tapped her chin with a ringed finger as she mulled it over. "David, now – he's sensed something."

"Who is David?"

"My nephew. He's more sensitive than I am, though in a different way. He lives on the Northside. Let's see…what did he tell me…" Her brow furrowed. "Something about the storms giving him migraines, and his housemate giving him fits on top of it. He was talking about leaving town for a while, take a road trip somewhere in the west until things settled down again. His housemate was being rather insistent on it, actually."

"Is his housemate sensitive as well?" Alex sipped her coffee.

"Oh, no, dear. His housemate is quite dead. A ghost." She smiled. "I can't remember his name. I've never seen or heard him. David says that he is as much a recluse as he is, so they fit well together. I'm not sure where he found him," she went on as Alex tried to recall what haunted dwellings were on the Northside. "I think he's attached to an antique trunk that David picked up while he was in college."

"Would David be willing to speak to me?"

"I can certainly ask him to call you. I doubt he'll venture into a public place. As I said, he's a recluse of sorts. What is it that you're after?"

"We not sure. It's killed twice." She described the creature and the events surrounding it. "So far, it's kept to Mandarin and downtown. You haven't heard anything on the grapevine about it?"

Nora pursed her lips.

"No. The only thing that I've heard of significance is that Drake Howell is back."

Alex blinked, sat back. That was a name she hadn't heard of in a long time. It was one she would have been quite happy to never hear again. She sighed, rubbing her temple.

"Why? What's here for him?"

"I couldn't say." Her tone took on a prim, disapproving edge. "He isn't being greeted like a prodigal son. No one who's familiar your family, and quite a few who don't, have no reason to love him, Alex. Frankly, I'm surprised the Guild kept him on as a hunter."

"His father was senior on the Florida Council," she muttered, answering the unspoken query. "Okay, so he's back. Anything else I should know about?"

"He's asked about you." Nora's gaze held hers. "Not in a flattering way, either. If anything, his superior attitude has gotten worse. He hasn't asked me, mind. My friends and customers – those who are part of our grapevine, as you put it – have told him little. From the way he was talking, however, it looks as if he plans on staying for at least a couple of weeks."

"Great." She sighed. "The last time he was in the area, he made a point of looking me up. He'll do it again. Thanks for the warning, Ms. Stanton."

"You're welcome." They rose together, Alex scooping up the recorder as she did. "Have you ever wondered why he singles you out?"

She gave the older woman a humorless smile.

"No. He does it because he's a sore loser. He does it because he has the maturity level of a tadpole. Lastly, he does it because he can." Her smile brightened as she remembered the most recent change in her life. "Drake's going to be in for a bit of surprise this time around, I think. Will you get back with me about David?"

"Yes, as soon as I can get a hold of him. Be careful, Alex."

"I will."

She left the shop, deactivating the recorder as she walked to her car. The wind picked up. Shivering in the sudden chill, she pulled her lightweight jacket closed. Checking her watch, she saw it was after ten. She calculated the amount of time to get back to her place, then the café. With weekday traffic...no side trips. There wouldn't be enough time to do more than set up a meet with another contact or two before she had to be at *Candlelight and Magic*.

Getting into the sedan, she headed back.

20

Jacksonville, FL

Alex was humming with the music when he came in, sketching away on a large pad of paper. She hadn't changed in the years that had passed since they'd dated, Drake noted. Still drawing, still dreaming.

Glancing around, he took in the atmosphere. It wasn't the type of place he normally frequented. A man like him, who made certain that his gilt hair was well-kept, the line of his suit was smooth, and that his career was on the fast track towards his private ambitions, preferred other, more sophisticated establishments. Still, he supposed she had done well for herself. The little café was doing brisk business and she owned a percentage of it. No doubt it supplemented her income.

He didn't bother approaching the counter to order anything. The little blonde girl manning the register had already spotted him, her brown eyes narrowed in dislike. She looked vaguely familiar. It took him perhaps two minutes to recall who it was. When he did, his lips thinned in a disapproving line. He'd met her only once, when he had encountered Alex during college.

Drake had never liked any of Alex's friends. They were all

strange – not that a Guild hunter or any of a hunter's contacts could be considered ordinary. Alex had a knack for attracting wild cards – mystics, eccentrics, the exception to every rule ever dreamed of by the Guild. Perhaps what was so irritating was that, unlike him, she could somehow get away with it.

It was just one of many reasons of why they were at odds.

Well, on to my real purpose here...

He walked to the table Alex had taken for herself, pulling up a chair. The sound of the legs scraping against the hardwood floor had her looking up from her work. Whatever had been in her eyes before she'd seen him was replaced with chilled abhorrence.

"What are you doing here?" she demanded flatly, flipping her drawing pad closed. She slammed it on the table.

He hadn't expected her to be civil. It was always nice to be proven right.

"Straight to the point, as always. I'm here on business." He gave her a cool smile that didn't reach his eyes. "Still doodling? I'd have thought you might have picked another, more...sensible profession by now."

Though temper was in her eyes, her face remained calm. He reluctantly had to give her points for that; she hadn't been as successful at controlling her expression in college. She gripped her sketching pencil like a weapon. With repugnance, she spoke in a voice hard and brittle.

"What do you want, Drake?"

"I'm glad you asked. I need to borrow something, for research," he explained in a tone that purposely conveyed his opinion of what was a superior occupation, "on a relic I found last month on the Aegean Coast. If I remember correctly, you have a few volumes in your library that aren't to be found anywhere else. In particular, *The Crete Index* – which I'm told is your family's own work."

Her library, her devotion to it, had been one of her very few redeeming qualities.

"This relic would be – what?" Her eyes narrowed suspiciously.

"Ah, that's the thing, now." His smile turned patronizing. "I can't tell you. It's Guild business, after all, for the Grecian branch. The only reason I'm involved is that I was the one who found it in the first place. Alas," he spread out his hands in insincere apology, "they took over the bulk of the hunt as soon as they found out. Their territory. You understand."

"Of course, I understand." Her reply was cool. "I understand a truck load of manure when it seats itself at my table."

"Now, really." Drake let the smile slip from his face. "Surely, you won't let this childish grudge of yours interfere with Guild business. I need that book to proceed with my hunt."

"Then procure it through the Guild Libraries. The one in Tallahassee has a copy."

He frowned.

"You're really going to make me drive all the way out there for a volume you have on hand?"

"Drake, what makes you think I'll let you borrow anything of mine after you stole a book from my parents' Library when we were in high school?"

"Youthful high jinx." He dismissed the past with a wave of his hand. "I was over zealous in my efforts to resolve my hunt and pass my trials. You know how important it is for any trainee to be pronounced a full-fledged hunter. Besides, the book was returned unharmed.

She gave a look that would have intimidated weaker men.

"No."

"Alex," he began with every sign of outward impatience. He was not at all surprised by her reaction. In fact, he was inwardly smug about it. "Be reasonable. We are playing on the same team, after all."

"Bull." She curved her lips. "We were never on the same team. Now, be a good boy, and get out of my friend's chair."

Feeling a dim rush of annoyance, he glanced over his shoulder to see that friend she'd spoken of. Dramatic enough, he concluded derisively, dressed all in black with a leather duster that just barely skimmed over the floor. The expression on his face was unreadable, his eyes unfathomable.

There was something about him that nagged at his mind. A predator, as most hunters were, yet more – primal. There was understated power there, an arrogance. Deception, too, he thought as he eyed him appraisingly. There was definitely something deceptive about him, though he couldn't tell what it was. Intrigued despite himself, he stood with the air of one much put-upon.

"Aren't you going to introduce us, Alex?" he asked. "Or are you bent on being unreasonably rude?"

"The latter, I'm afraid," she replied coolly, without apology. "Now get lost."

Drake gave her a disapproving look, then turned to the newcomer. "I'm afraid that you'll find that she isn't gracious in the least. Not even to dear acquaintances."

"You were never 'dear,'" Alex retorted with an indelicate snort. "Are you going to leave or do I have to have you removed? I'll be sure to make it the most humiliating scene you've ever had the misfortune to witness, let alone be involved in."

"Really, Alex," he began, a thread of warning running through the reason in his voice. "You can't just – "

"She can." The quiet words were steely. It seemed the silent mystery man had finally decided to add his two cents worth to the conversation. "She will. I believe you know where the door is."

Drake swung his gaze to lock with the other man's, noting with interest the flecks of color in his blue eyes. Magic whispered in the air, the presence of it as subtly menacing as the man's expression. Deeming it time to back down, he stiffly nodded to both of them as he began to make his leave.

"Oh, and Drake," she called after him pleasantly. He paused at the entrance, a little wary at the tone. "Chairs here are reserved for paying customers. Unless you intend to actually patronize our excellent café, I wouldn't come back."

"As if we'd serve him if he did," the cashier put in tartly as she rung up another customer.

His jaw tightened visibly, the only sign of a reaction that he would give them. He stepped outside, letting the glass door slam shut behind him as he walked to his rented Sonata. With ironclad determination, he shoved his temper to one side and found himself smiling sardonically.

Alex had taken a partner. Imagine that. It had taken her some time to replace him, he mused as he thumbed his key chain, unlocking the car. Quite some time. That didn't bother him so much as amuse him.

Well, this trip was just full of surprises.

Perhaps he would have more of an opportunity to show her how many before he left.

21

"Who," the word was spoken in a deliberate, neutral tone, "was that?"

The answer Alex gave Michael was in a cheerful enough voice, despite her churning stomach, yet she could hear the undercurrent of dislike in it. As for what she said, it didn't bear repeating. She didn't seem to have shocked him with her choice of language; that actually made her feel a little better. He didn't even raise that eyebrow of his. His apparent distaste for their uninvited visitor almost made her smile as she finished her diatribe.

Before he could give a response to it, Lys hurried over.

"What did that bastard want?" she hissed. Then she took notice of Michael watching them. She gave him a dazzling smile. "Sorry, old business." She turned back to Alex. "Well?"

Lys had never liked Drake. Though they'd met only the one time several years ago, Drake's high-handed manner would have made any woman with sense turn up her nose at him. That the man had sneered at Alex's single status, implying that she hadn't gotten over him in the least, had made Lys as angry as Alex herself had been.

"He wanted to borrow a book. As if I'd let him." Alex deliberately reopened her pad, giving her immediate attention over to the large sketch she propped up in front of her. She needed to do something that she enjoyed, something fulfilling, to proverbially wash the vile taste that Drake's impromptu visit had left in her mouth. Picking up a pencil, she began to add detailed striations to the horns. Should she do jeweled caps on the tips or ornate cuffs around the bases?

"I hope you told him to go Hell," Lys said vehemently, raising Alex's spirits a tad higher. Her friend was nothing if not loyal. "With explicit directions. He probably wouldn't be able to find it on his own."

"Come on, Lys," she replied as she experimented with light strokes of graphite. "Hell wouldn't take him. They'd be disgusted with his conniving and bitching in less than a day, then just kick him back out again."

"I really hope he returns," her friend muttered. "I'll get Richard to slip some hemlock in his salad. Just for him."

"Much as the thought warms my heart, it would violate everything you believe in, sweetie." Alex gave her a grateful smile. "Appreciate it, though."

"Yeah." Lys sighed. She turned to give Michael another bright, perky smile. "Oh, don't mind us. Would you like something to drink?"

"Tea," he replied with a glance at Alex. "Dealer's choice."

"Coming right up." She hurried back toward the bar, stopping momentarily to speak with a curious old couple along the way. The reply she gave to their questions had them all chuckling.

"Does the bastard have a name?" he asked after she'd left.

"Drake Howell." Thieving ass, she added mentally. Manipulative son of a bitch.

"Howell." He frowned. She swore she really could hear the files flipping in his mind. "He's a collector, in Richmond, I think." She gave him a startled look.

"You know him?"

"Of him."

"We're not fond him of here." Shrugging, she gave him a humorless smile. "As you can see."

He nodded.

"He's made it his business in the last several years to locate and acquire many things, most of them with some degree of power. I've had offers from him – through others, of course."

"Really?" Interesting. She refrained from asking what Drake had wanted. "Somehow I don't see you selling anything."

"No." His blue eyes darkened. Purple and gold glints surfaced in them briefly. "I don't sell. Did you have any luck?"

"I talked to one of the local sensitives, put out some feelers. I received some docs via fax but there wasn't much there that matched everything." She considered the decorated horns she'd just finished. Yes, that was right. She gave a satisfied smile. The sinuous neck was next, she thought as she retraced the lines more firmly. The chest would follow with -- a breast-plate or a collar? "It did occur to me that since it's not a natural creature we might not find anything on it in the records."

"It isn't a construct," he stated, referring to a mage-created entity similar to a golem. "It's old as well. There was a feeling of age to it when I got close. How old it is, is anyone's guess. However, if it has been around people, there's a good chance of some kind of record or tale."

Lys arrived with his tea. She set it on the table with a smile before leaving again to intercept the next customer. He picked it up, sipped, then nodded slightly with approval before continuing.

"I should have some information coming my way within the next few days." Reaching over, he began to toy with one of her pencils that lay on the table between them. "I've also begun looking for police reports."

"Homicides." Alex stopped drawing to look over at Michael.

He nodded. It didn't surprise her that he would have the necessary contacts for it, let alone think of it.

"Well, it probably has killed before." She frowned. "Where are you looking?"

"Nationwide. I put out a general inquiry. It may be weeks

before I get any feedback on that end."

She sighed. "I hate the waiting game."

"I'm not fond of it."

"Do we have any hunches to play with?" she asked, returning to her picture. A breast plate would be too much, so it would be a collar, thin at the back, broad at the front. A jewel at the center? With Celtic knot work along the band, she decided with an imperceptible nod.

"Not at the moment."

"I guess we just keep on plugging, then. I've a shift to work here this afternoon, so I won't be able to do much until afterwards."

"That's fine. I'll see if the museum has reopened, check with a few people I know."

"I should have more text to go through by the time I get off, if you want meet to up after I get off work." Her lips curved. "Having Guild Librarians for parents is a big help."

"Yes, I imagine it would be."

Richard popped in out of nowhere, food in hand, before he could say more. He placed the dishes on the table, the aroma making her mouth water. She set the pad on the extra chair beside her as she took in the meal in front of them. No soup or sandwiches today, she noted. Some kind of chicken salad on a bed of greens, a fresh herb roll, the scoop cheese spread, and a ramekin of the house vinaigrette.

"Richard, you're a God-send." She grinned at him. "Michael, this is Richard Douglas, gourmet extraordinaire. Richard, my neighbor, and new partner, Michael Keegan." They shook hands as she prepared to dig in.

"Don't mind Alex," Richard said drolly. "She has no manners despite all we've tried to teach her. We've been trying for years."

"Indeed," Michael replied, amused. "It's a wonder you let her out in public places."

"Ha, ha," Alex managed to say around a bite of her salad.

Richard gave him a quick, appreciative grin, then left them to enjoy their meal. Neither of them spoke for several minutes, which suited Alex as she was thinking about what to tackle next with the

new drawing. It was a good piece, she thought. A very good piece.
It would probably sell very well, especially if she decorated the
matting to match. Something a little Celtic, a little medieval. An
illuminated border, maybe? Vines interwoven with trees worked
into the pattern would be good. The cornerstones of the could
depict miniature scenes from the dragon's imaginary life…

"Do you often draw dragons?"

The question scattered the image of the finished picture in her
mind as she looked up to find him studying the work-in-progress.

"When the spirit moves me," she replied, her curiosity pricked.
"Dragons have always been one of things that fascinate me."

"How long will it take you to finish this one?" he asked,
nodding toward the pad.

"Depends on how much time I'll be able to devote to it. Could
be a week, could be a year." She shook her head. "I'm hoping no
more than a month."

"Will you sell it?"

"Full of questions today, aren't we?" She smiled as he
shrugged minutely and speared some of his chicken. "I'll have
lithographs made for sale. I don't know if I'll sell the original yet.
Sometimes I do, sometimes I don't. It's too early to tell which way
I'll go."

"If you do, I would be interested in purchasing it."

"Alright."

A moment passed without a reply. Deeming the subject done,
she gave her attention back to her food.

"You did the faerie on the wall by the bar."

She smiled, pleased that he'd noticed. "Sure did."

"Does it belong to the café or is that for sale, too?"

"It's for sale." She glanced at the fragile figure with the
gossamer wings and wildflowers around her. "There's a price tag
tucked into the bottom right corner of the frame."

"Do you sell most of your work here?"

He really was full of questions today. It made her wonder if he
was just making conversation or if he was truly interested in her
work. The idle tone didn't help her make a distinction one way or

the other. She cheerfully chose to believe that it was the latter. If she happened to be wrong, well, she wanted to remain blissfully ignorant of it. She saw the corner of his mouth twitch as she answered.

"Some of it. I've got a website that features everything currently for sale. The more expensive ones are rarely hung here."

He gave her a questioning glance, and her smile softened.

"In the café, we get ordinary people with ordinary budgets. If I'm going to dangle a pretty picture in front of them, I'd like it to be something that they might actually be able to afford. We get dreamers here, Michael. We want them to be able to take a little magic home with them."

22

" **S**o that's why no one's allowed up on the second floor, sir. Do you want to pay nine bucks for just the first floor exhibits?"

Michael watched as the young clerk glanced over his shoulder. There was the entrance to the aforementioned exhibit, a gaping thing shaped like human giant's maw. Dental hygiene was the theme. They even had a table set up in front with free samples of dental floss, cheap toothbrushes, brochures, and lollipops with white teeth depicted on them.

"I mean, I know the planetarium – which is still open – is pretty cool but the next showing is in two hours."

"No, that's alright." Resigned, he flicked his disinterested gaze at the gargantuan mouth. He tried not to grimace. "I'll come back another time. When do you think the exhibit will be open again?"

"Haven't a clue, sorry. My boss said it could be a few days to a few weeks, depending on stuff. He said that we were lucky to be open today, actually." The boy handed him a sheet of paper with the museum's schedule and exhibit listing for the month. "You can check back with us, though. Our number's on the flyer."

He took the brightly colored sheet with a nod, then exited the building. Stepping out into the afternoon sun, he tucked it away in his coat pocket before heading for the parking lot across the street.

So much for going back to square one.

He'd come alone, as Alex had been busy tending to one of her jobs, to find out what he could. While the trip hadn't helped with their hunt, he had garnered some information. The surveillance cameras in the building had been replaced with something better than the ones they'd had previously. The placement of them seemed to be the same, on the first floor at least. If the second floor followed suit, it meant that sneaking back into the MOSH after hours to take another look at the place wouldn't be feasible. Not for him, anyway.

Another bit of information was that there had been two separate sections of the museum blocked off: the second floor exhibit area, and part of the back offices. The security guard had been killed in the latter section. Still, it didn't help him if he couldn't get to the scene to examine things for himself.

He dug out his keys as he approached his vehicle only to stop and peer at the car parked a few slots down. The white Mustang gleamed in a familiar way. He moved toward it for a closer look. His eyes had trouble focusing on the license plate. Concentrating, he 'looked' with his mind's eye to see the esoteric symbol that overlay the stamped metal characters.

The disappointment he'd felt lifted. He knew what, if not who, the Mustang belonged to. If he or she had worked this part of town a few days ago, they might have more information about the creature. Glancing around, being sure to see with more than the normal optical senses, Michael found no one around.

Recalling that there was a hospital just down the street from where he stood, he began to walk that way. Cars drove past him, on the road beside him and on the overpass above him, as he hiked down Prudential Drive. Pausing for traffic at an intersection, he smiled. Coming from the other direction was a shadow that few others could see. The dark figure played idly with the most famous tool of his trade as he waited for the light to change in his favor.

When it did, Michael stood where he was expectantly.

"Oh, hi, Michael. Nice day, isn't it?"

"So it is, Tom."

Thomas A. Gordon was a young man in an old profession. Dressed in the uniform of a hooded monk, he was reminiscent of figures from old horror movies or, worse, bad horror parodies. It occurred to him that perhaps the uniform should be upgraded to something more befitting modern standards. Then again, people in Tom's profession weren't usually seen.

There was a saying that people saw only what they wanted to see. Michael supposed that a Reaper was not one of them. Even those fascinated by the concept of Death feared meeting their own end. Yet he could see the Reapers at their work if he chose to do so. He had given up trying to understand how or why.

"I thought you worked the night shift, Tom."

"I do, normally. Things got re-arranged since one of the guy's is on vacation right now. Can't wait until he gets back, though. I like nights."

Michael nearly chuckled at the cheerful tone. Tom was evidently one of those rare people who enjoyed this particular line of work.

"How is the job treating you?"

"Pretty good," he replied. "The Boss is great, and there hasn't been anything especially ugly on my schedule for months. Mostly, it's been naturals with a few accidentals thrown in."

"So you weren't working this circuit a few days ago."

"The museum murder." Tom's good spirits seemed to deflate. "No, none of us worked that one. The Boss did. He said it was bad juju or something. He, uh, also said we weren't to talk about it. Company policy."

"I won't press you. I might ask you to relay a question or two to your Boss later on if I find myself at a loss, though."

"Can't promise you answers."

"I'm aware of that."

The Boss, as he was called by his employees, was the most aloof and silent of those who tended to the needs of the universe.

Michael didn't expect to gain much from Him, yet was unwilling to discount the possibility entirely. Death was an entity that was knowledgeable about a great deal.

Michael gave the black-robed man a slight, reassuring smile.

"It's fine. What else had been going on?"

"There's a rumor that The Boss is moving to Jacksonville for a while. No one knows why. I mean, the company's doing well and there are no problems up the ladder that I can see. Oh, yeah." He snapped his gloved fingers as he remembered. "We're hiring. Two of us are retiring soon. If you can recommend anyone, we'd appreciate it."

"I'll think on it."

"Thanks." Good humor restored, Tom brought out his keys, thumbing the remote attached to them. The trunk popped open as he collapsed the scythe he carried. "Well, I've got to get to the next appointment. It's been good talking to you."

"I'll see you some other time, Tom. Take care." The two shook hands, then parted ways.

On the drive back to his apartment, Michael wondered if Alex might get home before the café closed. A glance at the clock in the dash revealed that it was barely six. If she got off at nine, or nine-thirty, it was unlikely that she'd be able to leave this early.

Thinking of his partner reminded him of other things as well. There had been vague dreams during the night, fleeting glimpses of chasing something through a forest, catching it only to fall on the ground, a lithe form beneath him. Alex's voice had whispered to him in the dark. More than that, he didn't recall. He'd woken with a tension inside him, need warming his blood, and a mind foggy with sleepy impressions.

It made him question whether he could keep their partnership a business one. He wasn't certain that he wanted it to go in any other direction. She felt the same; skimming her thoughts the night before last had revealed that, in addition to her own attraction. Besides, he liked his life as it was, simple, relatively uncomplicated.

EVEN THE LONE WOLF TAKES A MATE.

He scowled at the steering wheel. Not all lone wolves took mates. Especially not the ones who were occasionally nagged by trumped up deities. Deities that spread their influence further than they should, he thought grimly. He had a very solid idea as to where the notion for Alex's drawing of the dragon, as well as its dressage, had come from.

There was heavy sigh in the recesses of his consciousness. A twinge of guilt stabbed through him. Gwynn didn't deserve his attitude. He was the father figure of Michael's long life. With it came the privilege to meddle and worry.

It had been a recent concern of His that Michael so seldom took up with anyone. For his part, he had lost track of when he'd last taken a lover. The interest was there, certainly. It was just that he hadn't come across anyone whose lifestyle could mesh his own for more than a single night. Such brief liaisons were not what he wanted.

Gwynn's presence touched his awareness briefly, much like a father might run his palm over his child's head. There was understanding in the contact, and something else that he couldn't quite decipher. The presence withdrew before he could it explore it further.

The introspection had carried him through the journey home. He pulled into his customary place in the lot, then sat for a long moment with the engine shut off. Alex…partners…

He would consider it, he decided.

However, there was one thing that he hadn't considered. He had never thought to ask if anyone else had a claim on her. It was important, wasn't it, for partners to know these things?

He had until evening before he could talk to her. It wouldn't hurt for him to stop by Edna's. If anyone possessed even a hint of anything about the residents of Hidden Reaches, it would be her. With that in mind, he got out of the car to pay her a visit, pausing by an azalea bush along the way to snap off a bloom.

All he had to do now was figure out a way to avoid her

matchmaking tendencies.

"Michael, this is a pleasant surprise."

Edna accepted the flower he handed her. She made a fine show of sniffing the fragrance of the pink petals as she studied him. Her eyes were still sharp despite her age. The hints of brooding she saw in his face made her all the more curious as to the reason for his visit.

"Oh, do come in, dear." She moved away from the door, ushering him in. "I was just listening to the weather report. They say there's another depression out there that could give us some rain in a few weeks. There always is during hurricane season." Leading the way into the living room, she waved at the settee. "Sit down and I'll make us some tea. I have chocolate chip cookies – just baked today."

She patted herself on the back for giving into the baking impulse as she bustled into the kitchen. Freshly baked goods generally were enough to prime the information pump, she thought with a chuckle. She fetched a small bud vase for her flower, then went about the business of playing hostess. Water was heated for the tea, the cookies were arranged on a platter. Prepared with the tools of her friendly interrogation, she brought it all out on a tray.

"Tea will be just moment. Is Earl Gray all right?" she asked, shifting the trinkets on the coffee table to make room for the tray. Her cat, a fire-point Siamese named Mystery, appeared at her feet as if by magic. She yowled a plaintive query. "No, dear, you can't have any cookies. The chocolate's not good for you. I'll get you a catnip biscuit in just a minute."

"Earl Gray is fine, Edna." Michael watched as she fussed over her things, then crossed the room with Mystery prancing behind her. She opened a tin, laughing as the Siamese went crazy. The cat spun, jumped, made little cries like an eager child, trying to snag the biscuit with her claws. Edna let her have it, still chuckling.

"She's such a sweetheart," she said fondly as she joined Michael on the settee. She smoothed her long skirt as she gave her guest a bright, deliberately vapid smile. The man was still watching her cat's ecstatic throes over the treat. "Now, what prompted you to come visit?"

"Do I need a prompt to visit?"

"No, dear, you certainly don't." She eyed him thoughtfully as she foisted a cookie on him. Food had a way of relaxing people. Relaxed people had relaxed tongues. "Now, don't let these things go to waste! What you don't eat will have to go with you when you leave. I couldn't possibly eat them all."

He gave her an amused look as he took the proffered cookie. "If you didn't want them, Edna, then why did you make them?"

"Oh, it's not a matter of wanting them," she explained, fluttering her hands in a way that made her look flighty. "I just like baking. It's so soothing. Since I can't eat everything that I bake, I give it all away." Her faded sky colored eyes twinkled. "No one's complained so far."

"They'd be crazed if they did," he murmured as he bit into the sweet. He fell silent as he ate, his eyes of blue going dark and distant.

The poor man was preoccupied with something. Something worrisome, she decided with an imperceptible nod. Maybe even personal. Well, she'd get to the bottom of it before he left or her name wasn't Edna Bodsworth.

She fetched their tea, launching into a full blown description of Mr. Willis' recent misadventure. The man was in charge of maintaining the landscaping of the complex, possessing an arcane green thumb. In an effort to help with mosquito control, he had been experimenting with predatory plants, like the venus fly trap. One of them had somehow gotten one of his secret-home-made-formula nutrient spikes in its proverbial teeth. The thing had gotten quite lively, snapping up small animals much to gardener's dismay. It had taken two days – and her beloved Mystery – to put it down.

"She looked so smug," Edna told him with a laugh, "Sitting there on top of the twitching thing and swatting at it. Mr. Willis has sworn off using plants like that around here from now on. He said that they just can't be handled when they're 'magnified' as he calls it."

The cat, having heard her name, mewled. She licked up the last of the treat's crumbs before climbing into her owner's lap, purring the entire time. The corners of Michael's eyes crinkled as he sipped his tea.

"What have you been up to?" She asked, curious. She really didn't expect much of an answer. Michael was ever discreet about most of his activities. "Meet any nice young girls lately?"

He merely gave her a look.

"I'm only teasing, Michael." She smiled complacently as he fingered the handle of the teacup. "What did you think of Alex?"

"Intelligent, open-minded, capable. She's a great deal like Vincent Johnson."

"Oh?" Intrigued, she leaned forward. "Do tell."

Vincent Johnson had been the landlord at the Hidden Reaches before the current one. He, like Alex, had been a hunter with the Guild. The residents who had been there prior to his retirement in 1989 remembered that. It had been on one of his hunts that he had found his successor at the Reaches, Morgana Lake.

As she listened to the explanation, the comparison, something dawned on her. She had never heard Michael speak so much about a single person. Alex had apparently caught his interest.

"Morgana was asking about her the other day," she said. "She doesn't know much about her, or what she does – aside from what she put down on the application form, that is."

"I'll stop by the office in a little while to bring her up-to-date. Did she seem especially concerned about it?"

"Not really, no. She trusts the Reaches."

As with all residents who came to live at the Hidden Reaches Apartments, Alex had passed an undefined test before she could put in her application. She had seen the entrance, had been able to travel through it easily. Whoever, whatever, had founded the complex had given it sentiency and the ability to protect itself. The reason for that had been lost somewhere along the way. It was just one of several mysteries about the place that had fascinated residents and landlords alike during the last few decades.

Thinking of the Reaches' protective nature reminded her of something else.

"Oh, she also said that it would be wise to keep behind locked doors when it rains. She couldn't be very specific as to why, though."

"Yes; I'm the one who told her." Michael's expression took on a grim cast.

" I don't think anyone's told Alex." She sipped her tea, picking up another cookie.

"Alex knows as much as I do." He looked faintly disgusted for the briefest of moments. "Which isn't much."

"Are you working together?" she asked, surprised. "I didn't think you liked working with anyone."

"I don't." Two words, flatly stated. "However, this one isn't the usual type of enemy. It's an unidentified quantity with a link to the local weather. We were both tracking it independently before we decided to become partners – for this hunt only."

Now, wasn't that interesting?

"I'm going to be unforgivably nosy, Michael," she warned as she put her cup down on the table. "Do you like Alex?"

"Liking has nothing to do with it." He got up, began to pace the room restlessly. She hid a smile.

"So you don't like her?"

"Edna." His voice was mild. "Don't."

"I'm just trying to understand how things are between you, dear," she assured him soothingly. He muttered something about one matchmaker in his life being enough. He didn't need two. She wondered who he was talking about. "Is Alex trying to set you up with a friend of hers?"

"No."

"Oh. Well, then." She beamed at him, deciding that she was going to meddle after all. "Since you're not interested, I've got a grandson that might suit her. He's so sweet, and about her age. I could have the two of them over for dinner, introduce them."

"No."

Her eyes widened a little at the force that backed the single vehement word. The electrical lights dimmed momentarily. Mystery suddenly launched herself off of Edna's lap, fur bristling. She streaked into the back of the apartment – undoubtedly to hide under the bed, Poor thing, she thought to herself as she calmly retrieved her tea. She'd get over her little fright soon. As for Michael... She gave him a dreamy look, ignoring the snap of power in the air. It seemed he was interested in Alex after all.

"Why not? They'd make a lovely couple." She had never noticed those specks of purple and gold in his blue irises before. Fascinating. The lights began to flicker around the room. She pretended not to see it.

"Forget it, Edna." The tone was flat.

She gave an exasperated sigh. "Then take her out yourself, Michael. There's no sense in brooding about it or snapping at me." She gave him a sharp look, frowning as fiercely as she could, before continuing tartly, "I'd appreciate it if you fixed my lights before they give me a headache."

He closed his eyes, turned away. Gradually the flickering stopped. Shaking her head, she poured herself a fresh cup of tea. He really needed some help in this area.

"I don't need your help with this, Edna."

The tight voice raised her eyebrows almost as much as what he said did. "Read minds do you?"

"You aren't exactly keeping it to yourself."

Another interesting tidbit. She filed it away with a mental note to keep it herself. While she prided herself in having nothing to hide, there were plenty other residents who would be bothered by his little ability.

"So what are you going to do?" she asked after a moment's consideration. "Slay the big bad wolf together and walk away?"

"Edna…"

"You're smarter than that, though," she went on, cheerily certain. "Only a stupid man would walk away from that girl. You're not a stupid man. Only a fool wouldn't give her a bit of romance. You're not a fool, either. All women like romance." She paused as she thought back lovingly to how her late husband had wooed her. She sighed to herself before she went on.

"Anyone who doesn't has something wrong with them. Now, you listen to old Edna. March back upstairs, knock on that door of hers, and ask her to dinner."

"Edna – "

"Don't dawdle."

"She isn't home." Resigned, he slipped his hands into his jean pockets.

"Even better." An idea taking root, she beamed at him. "That gives you more time. Get her some flowers. No roses – she doesn't seem like a rose kind of girl. I'm sure you can find something that'll suit her. Have you been inside her apartment?"

"Yes." He sounded resigned. She had to suppress a chuckle.

"So have I. She likes knick-knacks, especially those little glass figurines. Get her one. Does she go out on her porch at all?" She waited just long enough for him to shrug. "Ah, well. Just box it up all nice and pretty. Wrapping counts, my boy. Leave it on her doorstep for her to find. Don't leave a card with it, dear," she instructed with a wink. "Let her wonder. Then show up after she's had about an hour or so to daydream. That's when you ask her out. Now, you'd better get going if you're to have it all set before she gets home."

He sighed heavily.

"Don't forget your cookies, dear. Let me get you a container for them."

It seemed Michael had the answer he'd been looking for. Alex was not currently seeing anyone. To complicate matters, Edna was pushing the notion of wooing.

He had never courted anyone prior to this. His trysts had just... evolved, he concluded. They'd grown out of association, mutual respect, and pure physical need. There had not been the shadings of long-term commitment or deep emotional attachment. He thought back to Gwynn's remark about a lone wolf taking a mate. That implied a long-term relationship, didn't it? Wolves mated for life.

He needed time to think it through. There was more than just the two of them to think of – there was the hunt, their partnership, their individual obligations. There was even the fact that they didn't hail from the same race. That point would be a difficult one to navigate around.

As he mulled it over, he made his way up the stairs, heading back to his apartment. He paused when he reached the second level landing, glancing behind him at the parking lot. Alex's car was nowhere in sight. Idly, he looked back at the stoop, wondering if he should leave her a note. He wasn't sure...

There was a box sitting in front of her door.

It was wrapped in gold paper, with an ivory ribbon tied around it. A card peeked out from underneath the bow. It looked very much like the type of thing Edna had described as a suitably wrapped courting gift. He felt a very strong urge to invade her privacy – something he had been trying very hard not to do – to find out what the card said. More to the point, who it was from.

Yet they were partners. Partners didn't go through each others' things. He forced himself to walk away, thinking of other possibilities. It could have been from a friend, a relative, maybe as a 'thank you' from one of the other residents for a favor she had done. That line of thought gained him several steps up the second flight of stairs. It didn't have to be from someone significant, he reasoned. Even if it was, it wasn't his business. His hand gripped the rail until the knuckles went white.

The hell it wasn't.

He whirled around, hurrying back to her door before he could talk himself out of it. Snatching up the gift, he examined the card. The envelope flap was merely tucked in. He opened it and read.

To the woman with the eyes of Old Eire, from Your Secret Admirer.

A suitor. A courting gift. The landing light began to flicker wildly. He forced himself to put the package down, to turn away from it. Struggling for calm, he sought to analyze the emotions rising within him. It was confusing. He could pick out anger, something that might have been jealousy, another that was disappointment. She apparently mattered to him more than he'd realized.

He didn't have the right to destroy the gift as he wanted to. It would be left alone. It was not, however, the end of this. He would find out who it was, determine what needed to be done to make sure that the would-be-suitor didn't stay in the picture very long.

Edna had not believed her to be involved with anyone. She had been unaware of anyone taking an interest. Yet she wasn't the only one who might have some insight regarding this. He stalked up to his floor to make a few phone calls.

"I appreciate the help, Alex."

"Hey, it's my café, too," she replied with an affectionate smile for her friend. "Besides, the lovebirds need the time together."

"Have you had time to finish unpacking yet?" Teri asked, remerchandising the candy on the counter.

"Not by a long shot. I've got the kitchen set to rights, though, so I haven't been completely slacking."

"Richard will be proud." Teri laughed. "Took you long enough."

"Yeah." She grinned. "It did. Now the only thing left is the stuff I hid in the bedroom closet and what's in the living room."

"Oh, Alex." she sighed with good-humored exasperation.

They had a lull at the moment. It was Thursday, the slowest day of the week for them. There were only two customers in the café, one snoozing quietly in an overstuffed armchair while the other sat sipping a latte, a newspaper in his lap. Without a need to tend to customers, the girls had decided to get a head start on the closing duties. Condiments would be restocked, the floor swept, the trash taken out.

Behind them, the phone rang. Teri hurried over to it as Alex continued to wipe down the empty tables at the café. Once a week, she worked a ten to twelve hour shift so that Richard and Lys could have a day off together. It was a change of pace, talking to the customers about food, drinks, décor – anything, really.

She also helped out with the events they hosted. There was an auction scheduled a few weeks away; they had just posted the notices for it. Flyers detailing what would be for sale sat in a neat pile by the door, held aloft by one of those cute little wooden French maids lifting a wooden tray toward anyone who walked in the door. That was a new addition, one of Lys' contributions. It worked perfectly for things like that.

She could hear Teri talking to the caller behind the bar as she turned from the tables to the small dresser and hutch that held their condiments. She replenished the various sweeteners, non-dairy creamer, straws, etc., taking mental notes of what needed to be brought out from the storage room in the back. The only things they were in dire need of were napkins.

She finished up, then headed to the storage room for those napkins. She strolled past the bar, glancing over to see her friend still on the phone. It must have been some conversation she was having. Her face was alive with excitement, her eyes sparkling with laughter as she listened to the receiver. Shaking her head in bemusement, Alex left her to it. When she came back to the front, laden with boxes of paper napkins, Teri was no longer on the phone.

"Who was that?" Alex asked her friend, preparing to tease. "New boyfriend?"

"You tell me," she replied, coming around the counter to help out. "Tell me about Michael Keegan."

"Michael?" She began unpacking napkins, handing them over to her business partner as she did so. "Not much to tell. We're working together on that little project you handed me."

"Uh-huh." Teri neatly placed the napkins in the dresser drawers. "And?"

"And what?"

"And so the lovebirds told me you had lunch with him."

"We had a business meeting." Alex waved her off. "We met here to fill each other in. I wanted to eat good food while I was at it."

"Yeah, so?" Teri wasn't going to let it go. She sighed.

"So it's business. The hunt. You know – tracking down the big, bad things lurking in the shadows of the big, bad city?"

"Okay, it's business." The prompt agreement made Alex suspicious. "So he just interrogated me about your love life just to make sure that it wouldn't interfere with the hunt."

"He what?" Alex set done the napkins in her hands, staring at her friend. Her stomach started doing somersaults. "That was him?"

"Sure was." Teri couldn't be more pleased. Or smug. "He was asking about who might leave you a little something on your doorstep. Sounded kind of intense about it, too. Who's been leaving you gifts?"

"What? Wait." Bewildered, Alex grabbed Teri's arm. "What are you talking about?"

With eyes that shimmered with glee at her friend's surprise, she told her.

Elsewhere

It was all coming together.

No plan was without its pitfalls, however. He glanced at the corner where the servant slept restlessly. It had returned to its original form during the night. It was ugly, naked, grotesque. Not dirty, as that was one thing he would never tolerate. It whimpered in its sleep as he turned away from it to contemplate his reflection in the mirror.

As always, what he saw pleased him. Well groomed with the few physical imperfections only enhancing his image, he was a man that made a statement, one of cool triumph, of suave finesse. He was a tad vain, perhaps more than a little prideful. They were weaknesses, he could admit, ones that he did his best to compensate for. Yet he wasn't so partial to them that they couldn't be sacrificed for success, especially if the deal was sweetened with vengeance.

The prize was part of that. It wouldn't – couldn't – be all of it.

He was closer to that last goal. He had the geographic location to seek out now, something he had verified earlier that day with a private courier service. Soon he would be able to pinpoint the entrance, to see what was perhaps the greatest mystery of his career.

Anticipation filled him, a dark thrill that made him chuckle. Yes, he would have to wait. The waiting was part of the game, after all. It didn't have to be without its tiny pleasures, however. Smiling, his mind turned towards the hunter, running an idle finger along the lapel of his blazer.

Surprise, he thought. Surprise.

Jacksonville, FL

Alex stopped at home, not intending to stay there for very long. She needed to talk to Michael. Nerves skittered through her as she climbed the stairs. He wasn't going to bite her head off for asking about the phone call he'd made to *Candlelight and Magic*. She just wasn't sure how to brooch the subject. Something would come to her, or so she hoped. It was probably nothing much anyway so why was she worrying about it?

Her stoop was dark; the light must have gone out. She fumbled with her keys as she approached the door. She had a small penlight on the keychain...

Her toe hit something. She stopped, found the tiny flashlight, switched it on. The gold package glinted at her feet. So this was what had prompted Michael's call in the first place. Kneeling, she opened the card, reading it as she nibbled her lip thoughtfully. A Secret Admirer. Somehow, she wasn't impressed.

It seemed so clichéd. So typical. So, well, ordinary. Leave a mysterious gift with a mysterious note to make her swoon. She'll be yours before you know it.

Yeah, right.

Alex wasn't going to deny that she was curious. She was. Yet the one guy she might have wanted to receive gifts from wouldn't use this tactic. Even if he was interested in the first place, which she wasn't certain he was. Probably not. She sighed. Well, she'd deal with it. She always did.

She picked the box up, unlocked the door, and went inside. She wondered what she was going to do with it. It didn't matter what it was, she wasn't going to keep it. Dumping it on the table, she decided to clean up before going any further. It would freshen her up, make her ready for the long night of research ahead.

One quick shower later, she was pulling on her usual attire of blue jeans and a V-neck shirt. The green shirt matched her eyes, something she hadn't realized until she'd looked at herself in the mirror. She had to laugh at herself; it seemed like something high school girls did to catch the attention of some boy they liked.

She'd almost forgotten about the package until she came out into the front rooms. Scowling at it, she began to unwrap it.

"Secret Admirer," she muttered. Right. High school stuff, first crush stuff. Probably some moony teenager. She crumpled the paper into a wad along with the ribbon, then lifted the pristinely white lid of the box. Tissue paper sprinkled with gold glitter obscured whatever it was inside. Impatient now, she shoved it to one side.

It was a wooden box, stained a dark mahogany with the pewter outline of a heart affixed to the lid. It was simple, lovely. It was also not her taste. She would have preferred Celtic knot work to the heart, the pattern either engraved or stained onto the wood rather than formed with metal. It was a jewelry box. She didn't have any need for a jewelry box. What few pieces of jewelry she possessed were hung on a little stand her father had given her for her sweet sixteen. She had no intention of ever using anything else.

Of course, whoever had sent it wouldn't be aware of that. With a sigh, she lifted the lid. There was another layer of glittery tissue on top. She moved it out of the way, her fingers brushing against something odd. Her hands stilled as she saw it. Nausea surged into her.

All went black.

Where was she?

Michael scowled at the time on the phone's digital display. Alex was supposed to have been at his apartment at ten o'clock. It was now almost eleven.

Concern drove him to abandon his apartment to stand at her door. Something wasn't right. Her car sat in the lot outside – he could see it from the landing – the gift he'd spied earlier was gone, she was home, yet she wouldn't answer when he knocked.

Several things ran through his mind. She could have recognized the sender of the gift. She could be on the phone with him, or had walked to his place if he lived nearby. She could have been in the rear of her apartment, far away enough not have heard him. She could be in the shower. Yet if she was running behind, wouldn't she have called him? She had his phone number.

In his mind, the image of the gold box flashed.

Perhaps it was jealousy causing him to circle back to that gift as being part of the reason for her detainment. He knocked again, louder this time, backing it with enough power to be felt within the confines of her home. He prowled the landing as he waited.

Concern, irritation, and impatience began to bleed through his consciousness. The porch light began to flicker as the minutes dragged by.

The tell-tale sign made Michael force himself to cool down. She had a right to privacy, a right to change her mind, alter her plans. The least she could have done was tell him. He rubbed the faint ache in his temples. She would have. She would have come up, maybe spent ten or fifteen minutes explaining why she wanted to postpone things, and maybe even given him the green light to go through the papers and books on his own. That was the way she was, or so he believed.

He thought about calling the café again to ask Teri if Alex had told her about anything, only to remember that the café had closed for the night. Another thought occurred to him. She'd been on her feet all day, serving meals, fixing drinks. She was bound to be tired. Could she have taken a nap? Maybe have sat down with the intention of resting for only a few moments then falling into a sound sleep?

He sighed, suddenly feeling a bit embarrassed over his behavior. He had worked himself up over – what? A mysterious package and woman who was probably napping on the couch. He didn't much care for the feeling.

Still, he wanted to be sure.

Laying a hand on the doorknob, he touched the lock with magic, heard it click. It was a bit uncomfortable for him invade her in this way. If he was wrong for doing it, well, he'd pay the price later. Once inside he paused in the foyer, shutting the door behind him as he noted that the lights were on. He frowned, then shook his head. He'd jumped to enough conclusions for one day. He stepped into the apartment proper.

Alex lay sprawled on the carpet like a discarded rag doll. Hurrying to her, he checked her pulse and breathing. Both were strong. Moving with exaggerated care, he felt the back of her head, working his fingers into the damp hair. There was a small lump just behind the left ear. Had someone hit her or had she cracked her head on the way down?

Satisfied that there were no other injuries, Michael lifted her off the floor. He took her to the bedroom, then laid her on the bed gently, unable to resist trailing a fingertip over her cheek. Sitting beside her on the bed, he tried to envision what might have happened.

She had come home to find the box. She brought it in, showered, put on clean clothes. After that, she had returned to the front living area...

Getting up, he went back into the dining room. He hadn't noticed much beyond her when he'd first come in. Now he saw the open package on the table.

He didn't bother to hide the snarl that moved across his face at the sight of the gold paper and glittering tissue. Moving closer, he saw that the present had contained a box – a jewelry box from the look of it. The lid was still open, a flap of tissue curled over the contents.

He didn't touch it. Instead, he gathered in power, gesturing abruptly. A translucent shell of purple light appeared around the gift, shrinking until it fit like a second skin along the myriad planes. It faded into the box, triggering nothing as it did so. There was no spell, no trap. Nothing even remotely magical. Leaning over the table, he carefully lifted the tissue flap away to look inside.

The scent – both psychic and physical – hit him a bare millisecond before the image caught up. Death, old death, old pain, dried blood. The sick, twisted hunger that had characterized the creature they'd fought two days ago. It clung to the intact human eyeball that peered up at him.

The organ was secured to the cushioned lining of the box with a hatpin tipped with a twinkling rhinestone. Just below it was a gold charm that was pinned in place the same way. Two words, wrought with exquisite curves and loops, were accented with a single red stone that sparkled in the light. The original sentiment of the charm had been endearing, meant to be given to someone much beloved. Paired with the eye, it took on a new meaning.

I see only you.

29

Alex woke with a groan. Her head was pounding. Even as she wondered where the hell the headache had come from, she felt her hair fall across her face, tickling her nose. She lifted a hand to brush it away. Someone else beat her to it.

Her eyes blinked open to see Michael sitting on the edge of her bed. He looked...grim. Almost angry. Had she fallen asleep, missed their meeting? She shifted sluggishly in the bed to prop herself on the mound of pillows. If he'd come looking for her, how did he get in? Had she given him a key?

He watched her without a word, waiting. The tension in him seemed contagious; she could feel it creeping out to envelope her. What had happened? Whatever it was, now he was upset with her.

She'd left work, arrived here. She remembered that much. They had a study session scheduled...going through stuff for the hunt...there was something else she'd wanted to talk to him about, as well.

"I – Did we talk already?" Her speech was slurred with sleep. Lord, she didn't even sound coherent.

"No."

His voice was very – controlled. Even. Neutral. She winced. Yeah, she was in trouble.

"Um, Michael – "

"Hush." His eyes raked over her, almost as if he could see right through her. A mug appeared in his hand with a whisper of magic. He pressed it into hers, wrapping her fingers around the ceramic with a gentleness that confused her. When he spoke, some of that control slipped, his voice coming out harsh and clipped. "Drink. Don't say anything yet."

He sounded furious, so she did as she was told. The hot tea was bitter. It reminded her of Theraflu, almost making her gag as she swallowed. Was this some kind of punishment? If so, then what had she done? The harder she tried to think back to when she'd come home, the more the headache intensified. Finally, she gave up. She continued sipping the tea, absently noting that it didn't replenish what she took from it. Just as well, really. She wasn't enjoying it.

When she finished the drink, she stared down at the empty mug in her hands. The headache was easing, the pain seeming to fade away from every section of her skull except just behind her ear. She rubbed at the spot without thinking. Pain lanced from there to just behind her left eye. She dropped her hand, wincing.

"What did I do? Fall down the stairs?"

"No." His intense eyes flickered. "You blacked out in the dining room. You hit your head on the table on the way down."

"Blacked out?" That didn't make any sense. "I fainted?"

"I wasn't here when it happened."

"Oh." Wonderful. He couldn't tell her why she'd fainted. She closed her eyes, feeling inadequate. "I don't remember."

"Do you recall the package?" The chill in his voice made her feel as if she was failing some test. Resolutely, she pushed the feeling away.

The package. She thought back to the moment she'd gotten out of the car. She locked it, come up the steps to the second floor. She'd been thinking of the talk they had to have. Package, package. Yes, there had been a package. Her foot had kicked it when she'd opened the door. It was why he'd called, wasn't it? It was why they needed to talk. She'd looked down –

She couldn't see it. Everything else was crystal clear in her mind, yet she couldn't see the box that had been left on her stoop.

"It was made up like a lover's gift," came the terse prompt.

Definite frost there.

A lover's gift. *Secret Admirer.* Yes, she could see it now. Wrapped in gold, tied with ribbon. She'd taken it inside, she remembered. Put it on the table. She'd showered, gotten ready to meet with Michael. Then she'd opened it.

"A box," she murmured. "Wood, right?" The picture in her mind was fuzzy. "I remember thinking that it was all very unoriginal."

Michael said nothing. He sat watching her like a hawk waiting for a rabbit to bolt from its hole. Alex strained her brain, trying to recall if she'd opened the wooden box. The elusive image refused to come. She shook her head. The room began to tilt.

She found herself laying back on the pillows, with him bending over her, a hand on her cheek. It took a moment for her eyes to focus. His face had that stony look, a cold fury burning in his eyes. It slowly dawned on her that he might not have been angry with her.

"No." His voice was quiet as he brushed his thumb along her cheekbone. "Not with you." He eased back into his former position on the bed. "You opened the box. I believe that's when you went under."

"What was in it?" The image wouldn't come. Uneasiness crept over her, through her. "I don't remember seeing what was in it."

"A warning." Something violent glimmered in his eyes for a moment.

Closing her eyes, she was thankful that she was already reclining. She could see it now, the box, the tissue. The way the light sparkled on the glitter. She'd moved the paper aside. Underneath –

Pain, fear, blood, hunger. Something new – anger. Anger at them. Fear. That was there, too. It had nothing to do with the pain.

Need. It needed something. It had to go back. New shape. Uniform. He would do. Quick, messy. Spray of blood on glass, gurgle as sound pushed through liquid. More violence. More bloodshed. It needed more from this one. More pain. More –

The blow came far out of nowhere. The overwhelming flow of foreign memories cut off. She didn't realize she was shaking until her body was dragged up against Michael's. He held her as tears tracked down her cheeks to soak into his shirt. She buried her face in his shoulder and let herself go.

It was a long time before the sobbing ceased.

The empathic flashback had caught them both unawares. Michael hadn't realized how strongly they came on, how vivid they could be, until this one. It was little wonder she'd fainted. He rocked her gently, stroking her hair, listening to her breathing.

What he felt was hard to describe, harder to understand. There was a protectiveness that he hadn't anticipated, a pleasant warmth in feeling her body against his. Perhaps what confused him the most was the possessiveness, the jealous rage that seethed beneath the rest. It was underscored by a fierce desire to kill the bastard who'd sent the message.

He quelled the urge as best he could. It wouldn't help anyone at the moment.

Instead, he forced his mind to consider the so-called gift. The package had to have gotten to the landing somehow. Someone may have seen it delivered. Their land lady would have had to let a delivery service in, if it was sent that way. Later, when Alex no longer needed him, he would contact Morgana.

The so-called gift left another question begging for an answer, however. The thing they'd fought was twisted, unnatural, the magic it possessed was contaminated. It had lacked the sophistication of thought in their first encounter with it, relying more on brute force than tactics.

It hadn't placed the eye in the box, or wrapped it up. The only thing that bore that peculiar taint was the piece of dead flesh. That meant it had a partner, or master. It had been that individual that had put it all together.

She shifted a little in his arms, drawing his attention. He reluctantly loosened his hold. She eased away, wiping at her face before looking up at him. He felt his heart do a slow tumble in his chest. It was the oddest sensation. Was this what it felt like, he wondered, to look at someone and see only her?

"Sorry. I don't normally cry all over people." Alex offered a half-smile. "Honest."

He studied the cheek he'd struck to bring her out of the flashback, saw with relief that the red mark had already faded from her skin. Lifting a hand, he tucked a few stray strands of hair behind her ear, careful not to touch the bump. His eyes drifted over her face, catching the look of puzzlement in her eyes. Leaving his reservations on the wayside with a sigh, he let himself sink into what he felt. He leaned forward to touched his lips to hers.

The kiss started gentle, one arm coming around her waist to bring her against him again. She didn't pull away, hesitating only a moment before yielding to him. She gave a soft moan, the sound spurring him on. Need began to take over.

His mouth slanted over hers. Her fingertips skimmed over his torso, had him growling deep in his throat. He ached, the throbbing of desire intensifying at the little sounds of arousal she made. His blood roared in his ears, rushing south as his body rubbed against hers. His hand found her shirt hem, sliding beneath it, along her skin. She arched under the contact as his mouth left hers to trail down her throat. He caressed her back, slipping his fingers up along her spine towards her bra clasp as she tugged his shirt loose from his jeans.

Michael.

His name echoed in his mind, piercing through the hot haze. He struggled to a halt, burying his face in her neck as he tried to calm his body. Her labored breathing mirrored his own. It was then that he realized that he had all but taken advantage of her.

Part of him was mortified. Part of him cursed Gwynn for interrupting something they both wanted.

He pulled himself away, searched her face for some sign of outrage or hurt. He found stunned passion. She blinked her eyes back into focus.

"Wow."

The simple statement had him chuckling.

"Yes, I'd have to agree."

"That was...wow." She took a deep breath, leaning back on her hands to study the ceiling as she gathered her wits about her. "Just wow. You're really good at that. Really good."

"Thanks."

"You're welcome." She dropped her gaze to meet his. "So, um, why'd...?"

"Bad timing," he murmured. "It wasn't what you'd call appropriate given the circumstances."

"Not – oh." She sighed. It sounded disappointed. "I guess not."

"I will kiss you again."

"Yeah?" She smiled, then let it fade. "What about being partners on the hunt?"

"We'll work it out." He wasn't going to sacrifice one for the other. Not if they were to be long-term lovers hunting the same thing. "Do you have a problem with this?"

"I don't know." She bit her lip. "I got involved with the partner I had. It didn't end too well. That was back in high school – God, about ten years ago."

"Drake." He had suspected that there had been something deeper there. She nodded.

"He was an immature ass, though. You're not. It makes a

world of difference."

He touched her cheek with his fingertips, let them drift down to her jaw.

"I can't promise that this won't affect our partnership. What I can promise, is that I won't intentionally hurt you. Will that suffice for now?"

"Yeah. For now."

He got up, holding out a hand for her. She took it and he pulled her to her feet. He led her out of the bedroom, pausing only when she stopped in the hall.

"Where are we going?" she asked.

"Out." He gave her hand a little tug. "You need to eat."

"Let's take those papers I got yesterday. We can get at least some of the research done tonight."

31

September 9, 2004
Jacksonville, FL

Teri hummed to herself as she pulled up in the back of *Candlelight and Magic*. Today was a good day, she decided as she got out of the SUV in the twilight gloom. All was right with the world. She had a business she adored, a vehicle that worked, a steady paycheck, friends she loved. Her favorite song had played on the radio as she'd driven in, she'd finally found the back cover for her remote, and three movies she'd been wanting were coming out on DVD.

Yep, life was great.

Unlocking the back door, she slipped into the café. Flipping on the lights, she began the rewarding process of preparing to open. Ovens were heated, pre-filled trays of pastries were inserted to bake. The menu was updated, coffee and tea were brewed, the cash drawer was counted. There were a few last minute details that had to be seen to in the dining area. The condiment stand needed to be double-checked, the floor needed to be swept again just in case, the newspapers needed to be received then put out. She found the whole routine very satisfying.

When they'd opened last year, it had been the most terrifying moment of her life. What if they failed? What if they couldn't compete? What if their eclectic atmosphere didn't take?

So many what-ifs. Richard had been frantic in the kitchen. Lys had been nearly sick with nerves. Teri had been beside herself. Alex had just rolled her eyes.

It'll be fine. It'll be fun, and, for God's sake, Teri, if you don't stop nattering I'll have to hit you.

She laughed at the memory. Only Alex.

Now the café was one of the five best things in her life. She loved it.

She put on some music, wondering what had been left in the CD changer the night before. That piece of musical gadgetry had been the first thing they'd bought with the profits of the café. With eight trays holding twenty-five slots each for CDs, it never needed fiddling with in the middle of the day – or the week, for that matter. Through the speakers came Bon Jovi. Nice choice.

Teri busied herself with chores until the grandfather clock announced that it was six in the morning. It was time to open for business. With a smile, she turned on the lights outside before hurrying to the front.

There was the stack of newspapers, just outside the door. They must have been delivered only a few minutes ago. She undid the deadbolt, singing along with Aerosmith. She glanced around the lot out of habit as she opened the door to gather the stack. The parking lot was empty. That would change in the next half-hour or so. Still humming, she bent down – that's when she noticed it.

Silver foil, white ribbon. It was small enough to fit into her palm. It reminded her of what might be purchased at a jewelry store. A tiny card was affixed to the wrapping, half-hidden by the simple bow. She nudged the white loop aside for a better look. There was no name, only a single line written in elegant cursive. Wasn't that interesting?

She frowned thoughtfully as she contemplated the handwritten note. *Destiny awaits, flying on a bird's wings.* Who was it for?

Plopping it on top of the newspapers, she carried it all inside. She finished the final tasks of set up for the day, then wandered back to where she'd left the present sitting on the bar. Teri studied the foil wrapped box, seeing that the lid was wrapped separately. It wasn't taped down. The ribbon was loose enough that she could slip it off and on again easily. It wouldn't hurt to peek, she decided.

She pulled the ribbon away, a ball of tension settling in her stomach. Anticipation? Maybe. Or maybe it was the fact that didn't know who it belonged to.

"Well, if they didn't want just anyone opening it, they'd have addressed it to someone," she reasoned.

The lid was lifted away. White tissue dusted with opalescent glitter twinkled at her. Pretty, she thought. A nice touch. More Lys' style than hers, though. It certainly wasn't Alex's. She hated glitter. It got everywhere.

Taking it to a trash can, she did her best to knock off most of the stuff into it. That done, she peeled back the flaps of paper to stare at the gift nestled inside.

It didn't look like much at first glance. While it was certainly jewelry, it wasn't anything she recognized. Beaten silver shone white in the shape of – was it a hammer or an anchor? She wasn't sure. Lines of gold twining in a vaguely Celtic design were inlayed over it, with a silver chain running through the hole punched at the top.

Turning it over, she saw nothing on the back. No jeweler's stamp, no little notation proclaiming the purity of the metal. No sign of where it had come from, or who had sent it. It seemed ordinary enough, she supposed as she held it up. Even if she couldn't tell what it was.

"Hmmm." Maybe it was intended for Alex. Hadn't Michael said yesterday that she had gotten something, a kind of mystery gift? She grinned. He'd been ticked about it, too.

"Time to call Alex," she said to herself, then looked at the clock. She sighed. "Later."

Alex was rarely up before eight. Calling before seven was a death wish.

3

A lex awoke, not really wanting to get up. Instead of opening her eyes, she hugged the pillow and rolled over. Her legs didn't want to move with the rest of her body. Frowning, gave a little kick only to find that material was wrapped tight around her lower half. She reached down to pull the sheet away. Her fingers encountered twisted blue jean.

Oh.

Well, that explained it. She'd fallen asleep in her clothes often enough that it didn't surprise her that she'd done it again. With another sigh, she opened her eyes, promising herself that she was just going to strip out of her clothes, then crawl back into bed. When she did, she saw rich reds, heavy brocade. A canopy overhead. Were those curtains all round her?

Now wide awake, she sat up to get a better look.

Definitely not her bed. It made hers look like a child's bed it was so big. The comforter covering her legs was a kind of fancy quilt. She identified brocade, chenille, satin, and velvet sewn in rectangles of various sizes. Beautiful. She ran an appreciative hand over the fabric, yearning for one just like it on her own bed. Nice.

"Sleep well?"

She looked up to see Michael leaning against the doorjamb. His doorjamb, she realized.

"Um, yeah." She dredged up a smile. "What did I do? Fall asleep on you?"

Well, duh, Alex, of course, *you fell asleep.* God, she sounded inane. He smiled, amused.

"While reading."

That was right. They'd come up to his place after grabbing a bite to eat at IHOP. No other place served breakfast at one in the morning.

"How much work did we get done? Did you find anything?"

"We went through most of the material last night. I finished the last of it this morning. Nothing matched."

She rubbed her eyes, muttering a half-hearted curse. He paced forward as she swung her legs off the bed. He caught her hand in his, skimming his thumb over the back before hauling her to her feet.

"So what's on the agenda today?" She stifled a yawn.

"Breakfast. After that, we split up. I need to check with some contacts in the area, see if anyone else has gotten wind of the creature. I assume you have people to tap as well."

"I do. I, ah, don't suppose I'd be allowed to go home and change before we eat?" she asked, rising. She wanted a shower, clothes that weren't all wrinkled, her brush. Her hair probably looked like a thousand-year-old rat's nest.

"You would be," he replied with a smile, humor gleaming in the blue depths. "And it doesn't."

That was wonderful to hear, even though she didn't believe it.

He released her hand with a low chuckle. They left the bedroom, Alex giving that sumptuous bed one last lingering glance. Where had he gotten that mattress? It had felt like she'd been lying on a cloud.

"What time is it?"

"Nine-thirty."

Not too early to feel human, then. She looked around as it

dawned on her that she'd spent the entire night in his bed and he hadn't. It left her feeling vaguely disappointed. "Where did you sleep?"

"On the couch." He glanced at her from over his shoulder. His eyes held amusement along with heat. "It wouldn't have been wise for me to share the bed with you."

That statement did some very interesting things to her insides. Since he was being a gentleman, however, she tried not to think about it. She failed.

Feeling a little awkward, she took her leave. Halfway down the stairs, it finally registered that she'd left her shoes behind. In his bedroom, probably. With a sigh, she dug into her pocket to find her keys. She would consider it a small miracle if there wasn't a bruise from sleeping on them.

Unlocking the door, she ducked inside, grateful that no one had seen her. She heard the beeping of the answering machine, muttered a reassurance to it that she would be back in a bit to hear what it had to say, and hurried to her private quarters. Once in the bedroom, she took her time cleaning herself up.

As she did so, she wondered what would happen at the morning meal. He'd said he would be kissing her again. Those words sent a thrill up her spine. They also had her bursting out with laughter. She sounded like a love-sick girl on the verge of womanhood and tarnished innocence. It was ridiculous. Funny, yet still ridiculous.

She stepped out of the shower to dry off. She dressed quickly, grinning like a fool when she reached for her shoes then remembered where they were. Running a comb through her wet hair, she debated whether or not she should blow dry it. As thick as her mane was it would take at least twenty minutes. Her rumbling stomach wasn't willing to wait that long.

Before heading out, Alex crossed through the dining room to check the answering machine as promised. A glint of gold caught her eye. She stopped. There was no wooden box, no glittery tissue. The wad of paper was gone, the only sign of its prior existence being a small scrape of the foil lying on the table.

She licked her lips, a little anxious. What had he dzone with it?

Not that she wanted to keep the thing. She shattered the image that had begun to emerge in her mind before she could recognize it for what it was. Two episodes were enough, she thought. She didn't need a third one.

Still, Michael had to have done something with the 'gift.' She checked the trash. There wasn't even a speck of glitter to be found. She couldn't think of any other place it might be. With a deliberate shrug, she dismissed it. She could always ask him.

Now for the answering machine. She hit the blinking button, listening as it relayed her messages for her. The first was from her mother. They had a line on something and had just wanted to update her on it. They would have more information for her in a day or so. The second was from her best friend.

"Hi, Alex, this is Teri. Just calling to see how you spent your night. I've got something that might be yours at the café. Give me a call when you get a chance. Bye."

The voice was cheerful, untroubled. She'd call her back in an hour or two. Food came first. She took off her clean socks as she didn't have her shoes, then exited the apartment.

33

Alex found Michael standing in his doorway talking with one of the neighbors. Her neighbor, to be exact. Nate Forge, manager of the movie theater a little ways down the street, had come calling.

Is it me or does he look more like his father every time I see him?

"Is this a guys-only conversation or can a girl join in?" She smiled as Nate started, then smoothly stepped to one side to look at her. The corner of Michael's mouth quirked.

Nate glanced at Michael. The uncertainty in his posture pricked Alex's curiosity.

"What?"

"We were talking about the incident last night." Her partner's response came out flat.

She pursed her lips. She wasn't sure that she appreciated having her fainting spell, however justifiable it had been, spread around the community. The worst-case scenario was that Nate would tell his father, Kent would call, and she would end with a bodyguard tailing after her. Well, maybe not, she conceded with a sigh. Nate was probably still ignorant of her relationship with his father.

"Mind telling me what, precisely, about the incident you were discussing?"

Michael remained silent. Her neighbor gave a discreet cough.

"Well, sugar," he began with a southern drawl. "He told me that you'd gotten a bad package. He was asking me if I'd seen anything before I went to work yesterday, or if I'd heard anything else-wise." He turned to the other man. "Hadn't and haven't. I'll get with Morgana, see what she has to say on it."

"I spoke with her and a few of the others earlier." Michael cocked his head to one side. There was a faint barking somewhere below. "I believe Ivan is calling you."

"Yeah, I hear him, I'll leave it in your hands, then. Call me if you need help with anything." He flashed Alex a smile as he headed down the stairs to take care of his dog. "Nice seeing you, sugar."

She nodded, still gazing steadily at her partner. She waited until she heard Nate's door close downstairs before speaking.

"You had a meeting about me."

"Yes."

"You don't think I should have been there, been apprised of it, anything like that?" She should have been. That was how a partnership worked, dammit.

"You were going to be told." His tone was cool.

"Fine." She reined in the irritation, bottling it. "Tell me about it now."

He opened the door, gesturing her inside. She went, stopping in his living room to face him with arms crossed.

"I asked that packages from unknown senders be re-directed to me."

Her jaw dropped.

"Excuse me?"

"I will not walk into a room to find you on the floor again." The words were intense, the voice low. His eyes flashed with the anger she'd glimpsed last night. "Next time it might not be an eye,

Alex."

"I'm aware of that. Don't think for a moment that I'm taking it lightly. But – God, Michael, you can't just make an arbitrary decision like that without me. It doesn't matter what the motivation is, it comes down to it being my life, our partnership, and you not respecting either of them."

His face darkened.

"What would you have me do? I am a warrior. I act. I do what I feel is needed." He moved closer. She resisted the urge to step back. "I value your life. I won't stand for another harming it."

"Neither will I. You have to trust me enough to hold up my end of things. If I take a tumble, make a mistake, fail in some way, you can step in. That's part of what being partners is about." She took a deep breath. "Tell me this: if our roles had been reversed, if you had been the one to get the package, with the same results, would you have told me about it? Would you have let me help with it?"

He went very still, hesitating. When he said nothing, she figured she had her answer. It was one that hurt.

"That's a no. Maybe we should rethink this partnership thing."

She started to brush past, intending to go home. He grabbed her wrist, yanked her back. The candles in the room flared to life.

"Don't."

"Don't?" Anger and bafflement mixed with the hurt. "That's all you have to say, Michael?"

"Understand that this is frustrating for me. I've never had a partner before this." He lifted a hand to her face, traced the shape of her cheek. "I have never had someone else to rely on, not as you describe a partner should be. You're the first."

She had suspected as much. His admission alleviated some of what she felt.

"Okay. I'll accept that. Still, you have to promise to talk with me. Clue me in. Don't let me find things out by hearing it from someone else."

"I'll try."

"Good." She gave a wan smile. "We're straight now."

He kissed her. It started out gentle, then began to heat up. His hand fisted in her damp hair, his tongue coaxing hers out to play. He tugged her up against him, letting his free hand rove over her back. She gripped his shirt, striving for balance as he shifted them to one side. He pulled on her top as they moved. Excitement sparked in her blood. She lowered her hands to his waist, her fingers fumbling with his belt.

Her t-shirt came free of her jeans. A dark thrill ran through her as he slipped his hand underneath to seek out her bra clasp. His belt loosened. Her fingers brushed hot skin as they worked to undo his buttons. Her bra went slack as he lowered her onto the couch.

He broke the kiss long enough to yank her top over her head, taking her bra with it. She reached for him, shoving his now open shirt away to caress him. His mouth nibbled on her throat, his hands cupping her breasts. She gasped, moaning as his thumbs brushed over her nipples.

"Michael." The name came out in a harsh whisper of need. Closing her eyes, her nails dug into his shoulders as he nipped her neck.

The phone rang.

She heard it dimly, not recognizing it at first. Her world had devolved to pleasure, anticipation, the man that brought both. Energy stirred in the air around them, raising the hair on her arms. It moved along their straining bodies in a magical caress. Even as it registered, Michael drew her attention back, this time by turning his clever tongue to her breasts. Her body arched against his, a hand moving to run fingers through his hair. He gave a low growl in response.

The phone rang again. The power coiling around them lashed out with an audible snap. The phone went flying into the far wall.

The sound of the crash had her turning her head. Not quite focusing, she saw the damage through a haze of passion. Michael didn't seem notice, continuing to tease her with fingers and mouth.

"Michael – " She whimpered in her throat, she tried to tell him what he'd done. "There's – a hole – in the wall – "

The last word devolved into a moan as his slipped south to stroke her through her jeans. Her center wound tighter, the ache becoming almost painful. The phone rang again.

He snarled, pressing his face to her breast. His hands clenched into fists against the couch cushions as a low, feral growl clawed up his throat. The sound was vicious, bestial.

Instinctively, she ran her hands along his shoulders and back to soothe. As his breath came in jagged gasps, the stirring of air that tantalized them both faded away.

Michael pulled away to sit on the cushion beside her, his hands covering his face. Still achy with desire, she lay in a daze as she tried to sort herself out. Had the phone completely ruined the mood for him? She eased herself up to look at him. Apparently, it had. She, hesitated, then reached to floor for her top and bra. Her hand shook a little as she gathered them up, put them on.

The phone rang a fourth time. She put her shirt on, leaving the other for the moment. As he sat mute beside her, she fingered the simple white material in her lap. A tear spilled out of the corner of her eye. Damn it. She closed her eyes, willing herself not to shed the tears that inexplicably welled up. *Damn it.*

She'd wanted that. She'd wanted him. Now she needed him to tell her why he'd stopped.

She hugged herself for comfort, looking over at him. He was staring at the wall now, at the gaping hole he'd put in it. His expression was one of fury edged with frustration. Something dangerous flitted over his face as the dratted phone rang for the fifth time. Shoving off with enough force to move the couch, he stalked across the room. He snatched the handset out of the hole, looked at the caller ID on the tiny screen. With a murderous glint in his eyes, answered it.

"What."

The eminent death conveyed in that single word sent a shudder through Alex, her pulse quickening. He listened, eyes flashing with ire, before crossing back to the couch. Without a word, he handed her the phone before disappearing into the back rooms. She looked down at it, bewildered by the string of zeroes on the tiny screen. She almost hung up, followed Michael.

"Alex."

The caller said her name loud enough to be heard across the room. Wary, confused, she brought the receiver to her ear.

"Yes?"

"It's too soon for this part of your journey." The voice on the other end was gentle, almost fatherly. It had an underlying note of steel. "You both need a little more time."

"More time for what?" she demanded, uneasy. "Who is this?"

"You can call me Gwynn." He paused as the name rang a bell in her mind. "There is much about him you need to know before either of you take that leap."

"What – "

"Let him calm down. That will take some time, perhaps an hour or so. Then the two of you need to get back to work. Finish redressing, Alex."

Before she could say anything, the line went dead.

34

Michael resisted, barely, the urge to destroy something. He stood in the middle of his bedroom, letting his raging libido work its way into embarrassment and anger. The ache of thwarted need that filled him served to only deepened the rage.

You are not a stag in rut.

The reprimand spoken over the phone echoed in his mind. With it came shadings of shame, of guilt. It made him angrier. As his emotions intensified, his control of his magic faltered.

The heavy bed frame trembled, his chest of drawers shook. Candlewicks burst into hot flame. The ancient tapestries that covered his walls moved as if rippled by a strong wind. Seeing it, he fought to choke his feelings back, to rein in his magic. All he accomplished was moving the bed towards him by a few inches.

He couldn't stay. If he couldn't pull himself together here, he couldn't stay. He had to leave, to go, and come back only when he'd mastered himself again. Alex –

What would he tell Alex?

Would she understand? He didn't know. He raked a shaky hand through his hair. Distance might be best for both of them. It would certainly be best for him.

There was one place he suddenly wanted to be, the one place that had always given him peace. He fixed the image in his mind, gathered his will as best he could manage. It answered him, the power bucking against his control as he reached out with his mind. Magic swirled around him. He felt searing heat, frigid cold. The gust of wind, the feel of stone. A splash of water, a wave of sunlight. When the whirlwind settled, he was gone.

The Wood

Gwynn felt the shift in the fabric of reality that heralded a visitor. He had anticipated this. His only disappointment was that Michael had not spoken to Alex before he had departed.

The air stirred with an arcane breeze. It twisted up from the ground in a vortex, mixing sensation and light. It flashed once, then dissipated to reveal the son of His heart. Michael scowled at the trees before swinging his gaze towards Him.

He stepped forward to meet him. There was resentment, anger, keen frustration in his stormy blue eyes. He'd expected that, perhaps deserved it to a degree. It had been His intention to pair the two of them off, after all.

Neither spoke as they faced each other. Gwynn took the time to study the man. His ebon hair was tousled, his shirt still open. His clothing was black. Michael had ever been fond of black. It amused Him that His son would cling to some of the subtlest elements of his true form while employing the one he wore now. Some found the man in black imposing, intimidating.

He didn't look intimidating now, He thought. He looked absolutely furious.

"Michael," He said finally, inclining His helmed head in greeting.

"Why?" Arcane force whipped out, breaking twigs from nearby branches as it raced erratically around them. He closed his eyes with a curse, once again trying to rein it in.

Gwynn remained as He was until Michael had achieved some control. Once he had, He motioned him to follow. They walked past the aged trees, sunlight filtering through the leaves above to speckle the ground with gold.

"What do you feel for Alex?"

"Gwynn – " Frustration strangled His name.

"If it were not important, I would not ask," Gwynn replied calmly. "If it were not important, I would not have called."

Behind Him, Michael muttered in a language that very few would recognize. Small wonder, He mused. It hadn't been spoken on Earth for nearly six thousand years or so. His son fell silent, brooding. They continued to walk as he searched his mind, his heart. The white hound bounded in, greeting Michael with a wagging tail, yips, and a lolling tongue. He paused , turning back to see that His son was distracting himself with the dog. The hind leg thumped madly on the ground as he scratched its belly.

"I want her. I care about her, for her. I don't want her hurt." He continued to pet the hound as he spoke. Gwynn nodded, saying nothing. "I'm not sure what else there is."

"What of the enemy's gift?" He asked.

"What about it?" The tone was flat. He stood up, glaring at Him. Resigned to the loss of attention, the hound flipped over to gain its feet. It trotted off. Neither paid it notice.

"You weren't pleased to see it on her doorstep." Even as He said it, He could feel the echoes of jealousy and protectiveness reverberating through Michael. His son still hadn't come to terms with it. "I believe that you were thinking along the lines of removing the sender from this life."

"So?" The belligerent response put Him in mind of a rebellious human teenager.

"So what does that mean? Why would you feel that, if caring is all there is, if all you want is to bed her?"

Michael looked away. *Still stubborn.*

"Until you have the answers, until you can tell me, you can't have her, Michael." That brought those blue eyes back to meet His gaze, the flecks of purple and gold glittering. "Do you know how much you could hurt her – or yourself? You are the son of My heart, Michael. There is little I would deny you, littler still that you have asked of Me. Harsh I may have been, yet have I ever failed you?"

"No." He sounded subdued, unsettled. A good sign. He was thinking now, not reacting.

"Trust Me in this." Gwynn came forward to place a comforting hand on his shoulder. "What will you do now?"

He sighed.

"Go back. Deal with it." He kicked at a rotting log, still frustrated though no longer as angry as he had been when he'd first arrived. "I did promise her breakfast."

"Is that all?" Gwynn had not meant pledges.

Michael looked up. Azure storms still roiled within his eyes.

"No."

"What else?"

The answer was a long time in coming. When they came, the words were a whisper.

"She worries me."

36

Alex walked into the café late that afternoon, having had a long, annoying, and unproductive day. Her local contacts hadn't given her any leads. All had mentioned Drake, which further spoiled her mood. Yet what plagued her the most, was Michael.

She didn't talk to anyone as she entered the back. Snagging a chair in the kitchen, she waited for one of her friends to come see what was wrong. She buried her face in her arms on the small break table, feeling the numbness around her heart.

What a load of BS.

It was all she could think about. Not the hunt, not the murders, not the thing that was laired up somewhere just waiting to heal again before it killed someone else. All she could think of was that leap that she'd thought she would never make, and the fall that inevitably came after it.

Richard bustled in with an empty tray. He didn't say anything, just set it on the counter before fetching her a strong cup of hot tea. He put it beside her before departing out to the front.

Lifting her head, she began to toy with the mug as Teri and Lys hurried in. They sat, taking in her pale face, her turbulent eyes.

"What did he do?" Teri was the first to ask. Alex loved that about friends so close that they were more siblings than anything else. She didn't even have to tell them who it was.

"Nothing. He didn't do anything." That was part of the problem.

"Is that it?" Lys persisted. "That he didn't do something?"

"It shouldn't matter. It really shouldn't." Alex got up to pace, feeling all at once edgy. "I've known him for all of – what? A week? How can I feel miserable over some idiot man after only a week?"

Lys gave a silent 'oh.' Teri pursed her lips, eyes narrowing.

"Did he kiss you?"

"Kiss me?" Alex suddenly felt like throwing something. Snatching up the first thing that came to hand, she did so. The oven mitten went flying into the wall with an unsatisfactory 'whump.' "Kiss me? He damn near had me. Would have if the phone hadn't rung. Then he left. Just *left*."

She cast around for something else to throw. Getting up, Lys began gathering anything that could be used as a projectile. Alex thought of that blasted phone call. It had been so weird, so disconcerting, even for her, that she couldn't tell them. Instead, she concentrated on heaping all the blame on Michael, conveniently forgetting what would have happened if the phone hadn't rung.

"The bastard. He comes back and it's like nothing happened. He served me breakfast. We talked about shape-shifters, about the hunt. Then he showed me the door. I feel like a fool."

"He never said why?" Teri asked as Lys laid an understanding hand on her shoulder.

"No." That was the main reason for her current state. "He pretty much patted me on the head and sent me on my way." Alex slumped into a chair, putting her face in her hands. "I wanted him. I thought he wanted me – I was so sure at the time he did. Now he's all brotherly towards me. I don't know what to think."

"Jerk." Lys was, as always, absolutely loyal. It made her feel better to have her support. The blonde girl scooted the tea across the table to give her a hug. "Let's make him suffer."

"They're supposed to be partners on this whole murder thing," Teri reminded her, brushing a few brown curls away from her face. "How's that going, anyway?"

"Slow." Everything else had gone too fast. "We split up for the day. I've come up with zilch so far."

"What was that present?" Lys asked, deciding to change subjects. "Anything good?"

"No, that – " She broke off as she remembered Teri's message from that morning. Forgetting her misery, she grabbed her friend's wrist. "You said you had something that might be for me."

"Well, yeah." Teri shifted a little uneasily at the urgency in Alex's eyes. "This little silver box. I opened it since it wasn't addressed to anyone – "

"What was it?"

"A necklace," she said thoroughly puzzled now. "I put it in the safe if you want me to go get it."

"Necklace?" Now Alex felt confused. "Nothing gory or gross?"

"No. Give me a minute and I'll show you." She got up, heading for the small office where they kept the safe.

"The present on your doorstep?" Lys asked hesitantly. "Was it gory and gross?"

Feeling slightly faint, Alex nodded.

I see only you. Michael had told her about the statement, the ruined eye, the blood that had stained the lining. Discussing it after breakfast had been surreal; he hadn't seemed very upset over it. He'd been almost nonchalant. That didn't add up with his behavior just a few hours before.

"Here." Teri placed the box in front of Alex, breaking through the reverie. "It was tied with a white ribbon; I'm not sure what I've done with it. The card that came with it is inside."

Her hands were a bit unsteady as she lifted the lid. Underneath the card, tissue paper sparkled with specks of glitter. Her mouth went dry. Opening the small card, she read words written inside.

Destiny awaits, flying on a bird's wings.

Wrapped in the tissue was the necklace. A silver chain running through the hole punched in the top of the strange looking pendant. It looked naggingly familiar. Where had she seen it before? She chewed her lip thoughtfully, cudgeling her brain to no avail.

"So what was in the first package?" Teri asked.

"An eyeball." She tried to sound flippant. It fell flat. "I – it was a warning."

"Do you think that whoever it is knows you're after him?" Lys' voice was worried.

"Of course, he does. He sent the package, didn't he?" Teri responded with agitation. Then all the color drained from her face. "Oh, God. He has your address."

"You can't stay there." Pale herself, Lys was adamant. "You'll stay with one of us. You can't be alone with that thing out there looking for you."

Alex wasn't paying attention. She turned the pendant over in her hands, tangled the chain around her fingers. "I have to tell Michael."

"What?" Teri pushed away from the table, scowling. "Oh, right. The partnership thing. Tell him you're staying with me. I'll be sure to give him hell when he comes calling."

Alex gave a weak laugh at the fierceness in Teri's voice. What would she do without her friends, her sisters? Still, there was something else she had to tell them before she lost the gumption to. Setting the necklace back in the box, she replaced the lid.

"I – I think I might be in love with him."

Silence filled the kitchen.

"Wait, you've only worked with him a week," Teri protested anxiously. "It's just an infatuation. Right?" She looked to Lys for support.

"I'm not sure." Lys looked from Alex to Teri and back again. "It didn't take me long to fall for Richard."

"How was it for you?" Alex asked, not having met either of them before college. "How long did it take?"

"It – it depends." Lys sat down at the table, twisting her fingers. "For me, it was only a week or two. Richard was fun to be with. He made me feel special. He'd come around and I'd be on Cloud Nine."

All at once uncomfortable, Alex fidgeted with the gift. She hadn't reached Cloud Nine. Maybe she wasn't in love after all. There was chemistry, she supposed gloomily. She enjoyed his company, the way he made her feel, the dark mystery of him. She enjoyed the feel of him against her, yearned for it. None of that equaled love. If it had, she could justify feeling miserable, could justify making him suffer for it.

"Forget I said anything." Thoroughly depressed, she stared at the silver foil of the box. She didn't notice the look that her friends exchanged, or the tear that leaked from the corner of her eye.

"Alright," Lys said softly.

37

Elsewhere

The stage was set. He was looking forward to watching things play out. A cold smile touched his lips. His servant was ready. The pawns were in place. It was time to raise the curtains and begin.

His original timetable was in shambles now – not that he minded too much. There was simply too much opportunity not to take advantage of the delays. He would work things out to his satisfaction. He would gain his prizes and much more before he walked away.

Still, he had to be cautious. The servant especially. He had spent a great deal of time instilling that need into the creature. It would venture out into the city soon, to take something more, something dear. His enemies would quake before it was done. The price, his price, would be exacted.

In the end, he would have it all.

Content with his plans, he opened the journal once again to read.

38

Jacksonville, FL

M ichael hadn't heard from her all day.
      Perhaps it was just as well. He'd ushered her out the door
after breakfast, concentrated on finding more clues for the hunt.
His efforts had yielded him nothing. It didn't help that the memory
of that morning haunted him. He could see the questions lingering
in her eyes, the ones that he had evaded because he didn't have an
adequate response to them.

      His return home from his last meeting had been uneventful.
Her car had been missing from the lot so he hadn't stopped by her
apartment to check in. Instead, he'd fixed the hole in the wall, then
reinstated the phone. A few calls to various courier services had
netted some information about the package Alex had received. He
found the delivery company, even spoke with the young man who
had taken the order. However, he couldn't relay much about the
sender. The box, as well as a second, smaller package, had been
picked up from the front desk of the Sea Turtle Inn in Atlantic
Beach, along with a cash payment; the concierge had been the one
to arrange it. As the other delivery had gone to different address,
the clerk wasn't willing to divulge any details concerning it.

Michael called the hotel only to be told that it was against their policy to give out any particulars about their guests.

That the packages had come from an inn brought another possibility to mind: Drake Howell. Could he possibly be connected to this?

As he was a member of the Hunters' Guild, it was unlikely. Still, he wanted to explore that avenue, see where it led them. Doing so required his partner. Alex was far more familiar with the man than he was.

He checked the clock to see that it was after eight. Going to his kitchen window, he found that she had not yet come home. There had to be a way to find her. They needed to share what they'd discovered, or didn't, needed to discuss this new angle related to the so-called gift. He would also have to do what he should have done earlier: explain why he was stepping back from her.

He dreaded it. He didn't have the words as Gwynn seemed to think he did.

Coward.

Though said with affection, it stung. It was also accurate, he realized with a wince. He wasn't acting like the warrior he claimed to be. Picking up the phone once again, he dialed the number for the café. Odds were, if she wasn't home, wasn't pursuing some lead, she would be there.

"*Candlelight and Magic*. This is Teri. How can I help you?"

Teri had been happy enough to answer his questions last time. Somehow he doubted that she'd want to do the same now. Feeling a bit grim, he replied.

"This is Michael. I need to talk to Alex. Do you know where she is?"

"Why?" The perkiness left her voice, leaving it cold.

Closing his eyes, he took a deep breath. "I need to talk to her."

"You've already said that. I'll have to ask again," she retorted. "Why? She doesn't particularly want to talk to you."

He winced, muttering a quiet, pithy oath. How much damage had he done?

"If you're going to cuss at me, we'll end this conversation right now."

"I'm sorry. This is between Alex and myself," he told her, his temples beginning to throb. "Is she there?"

"You'll have to do better than that," Teri replied mildly.

"Is she coming home soon?" He ran a hand through his hair distractedly.

"Why?"

He was beginning to hate that word. "I don't want her staying there alone. I need her safe, Teri."

"She isn't going home. She's staying with me."

His head was starting feel like a mineshaft being worked over by Scandinavian dwarves with pickaxes.

"Is she there?"

There was a long pause. For a moment, he thought that she'd hung up on him.

"Yeah, she's here." The answer was given reluctantly. He could hear the scowl in her voice. "We close at ten tonight."

The dial tone sounded in his ear. Placing the handset in its cradle, he figured that he would need every minute before the café closed to make his case to Alex. He vetoed using the car; it wasted time. Focusing his magic, he envisioned the café, willed himself there. He vanished from his living room, reappearing in a remote corner of the café's parking lot.

Taking a minute, he let his eyes adjust to the twilight that followed sunset. A survey of the area revealed himself to be alone; no one had witnessed his sudden appearance. He walked through the lot, past the empty tables outside, to the entrance. Business seemed to be at a lull. It would pick up again with an hour or so, when the after-movie crowd came in.

He wound his way to the bar. At the register, Teri looked up with startled lavender eyes. They'd never met before this, yet it didn't seem to matter. They recognized each other, both based on Alex's descriptions.

"That was extremely fast," she said, then remembered that she wasn't happy with him. She scowled at him. If he hadn't been so intent on getting past the guard at the gates, he might have found the switch amusing.

"Where is she?" He kept his voice low. Locking gazes with her, he saw the ferocious loyalty in her eyes. He doubted that Alex had a better friend or honorary sister.

"You wait right there, buddy," she commanded, leaning forward so that her voice didn't carry beyond them. She pointed to a table in the far corner of the seating area. "I'll see if she wants to talk to you. If she says no, you're out that door. Understood?"

His jaw clenched, but he nodded. She stalked into the back, head high, spine stiff. He took a seat at the table she'd indicated and waited. As the minutes ticked, his gut knotted into a ball of tension. He rarely experienced nervousness nowadays. That he did now seemed just.

Alex stepped out, pausing at the door leading to the back to scan the room.

She looked tired, he noted. Dulled. The vivacity that normally shone through was gone. Had he done that? He must have. No wonder Teri had been so protective of her.

She spotted him. With a mug in hand, she joined him at the table. Her eyes, now unreadable, gazed directly into his. They made guilt slither through him again.

"You wanted to talk," she prompted in a quiet tone.

"Yes." By Gwynn, this was hard. How did he begin? "Alex, this morning – "

"This morning was a mistake." The statement was like a slap to the face. Even as the numbness began to spread through his chest, he saw that her hands were clutching the mug a little too tightly. "A fluke. It won't happen again."

The emotionless certainty in her voice jabbed at his temper. He let it lead his rejoinder.

"No, it won't happen again. Not like that." An indefinable glimmer came and went in her eyes. "I lacked control, discipline. I didn't handle it well."

"No, you didn't." The agreement came quick. "It wasn't appreciated."

She had good aim. Her words struck true, bruising to the bone. He took a careful breath, absorbing the pain.

"I'm sorry. I broke the promise I made to you, and I'm sorry for it."

He went against his natural instinct to drop his gaze, look away. He couldn't be dominant here. He wasn't sure if he should even be equal, not in this matter.

"Apology accepted." Her quiet reply was cool, distant. Her eyes, however, reflected inner turmoil. "We don't have to work this as partners, Michael. We can work separately. Maybe we should."

"No." Letting her walk away from any aspect of their relationship was unacceptable to him. "We work as partners. That's business, Alex. We'll get to that. First, we need to deal with the personal."

"It's supposed to be the other way around," she reminded him.

"Not tonight. I need to explain. I should have, before you left," he admitted, regret flickering over his face.

"Before you pushed me out the door." Her reserve finally snapped, green eyes flashing with anger and resentment. It relieved him to see it. "Pat the poor girl on the head, send her off before she gets into something she shouldn't." The glare she aimed at him was lethal. "As if I couldn't handle trouble on my own, couldn't possibly take care of myself. Here's a news flash for you, buddy, I *can* take care of myself. As for that – " she paused in her tirade as she looked for the right word, her eyes narrowing " – fiasco this morning, it's over. There is no personal, Michael. Just business."

He let the words slide over him, tried not to take them to heart. On one hand she was right. On the other, she wasn't. Taking that leap he dreaded, he tried to explain.

"I needed the distance. I don't expect you to understand that." Michael met her gaze steadily, feeling echoes of the too-well-remembered rush of need. "Without it, I would have taken you. Without control, without a thought for the consequences. There would have been consequences."

"Like what?"

"Like Gwynn's wrath." She almost flinched at the name. He leaned towards her, catching her hands before they could be yanked away. "Gwynn is like a father to me. While that didn't stop me from cursing His name to hell and back again after He called, it does make me want to do my best to obey. Especially when He's right."

"Right about what? Us needing time?" Ire sparked in her eyes.

"That, as well as other things,"

"And that justifies – " He cut her off.

"Nothing. It justifies nothing. It is a reason." His thumbs started massaging the underside of her wrists. He wasn't even aware of it. "I have to agree with Him. There are many things about me you don't know. When you do, you might not be as inclined to be with me."

She said nothing, pulling her hands free to cross her arms. Her posture dared him to continue. He found his mouth dry as he did.

"I am not human."

She stared at him a good long while, leaning back in her chair. She took her time studying him. Finally, she spoke.

"That's all?"

He almost laughed as some of the tension in him eased. With a shake of his head, he reached for her mug. He played with it as he considered what to say next.

"It's more the what, then the what-not," he murmured. "I've never told anyone. I've never wanted to, never needed to. Perhaps I should have when we became partners. I didn't foresee us going this far, or this deep, though. Didn't think it necessary."

"Obviously it is now." The frown on her face was more searching than angry. "So tell me. What are you? It's not an illusion."

"No, it's not." Michael sighed. "I've never felt free enough to tell anyone what I am. My kind is seldom welcomed. We are frequently misunderstood, or subverted. Most believe that I am a powerful human mage, a misconception that I am content to let them have. A few – a very few – are aware that I am a shape-shifter."

"Wait." She searched his face intently. "I didn't think that there were any true shape-shifters left. Just the weres."

He nodded slowly, carefully watching her. "I'm not one by blood."

"Then what are you?" she asked again. Her expression held concern, puzzlement, consternation, yet no fear. He wondered if that would soon change.

"I am a dragon."

A dragon.

Michael sat across from Alex, sober, serious, and tense. He believed what he was saying. More, she saw that he was anxious as to what her reaction may be.

Alex had been afflicted with an avid interest in dragons since early childhood. It had amused her parents, how she had gone through every book in the Library, in the bookstores, on the internet, compiling every scrap of information she found into a thick file kept in her dresser drawer. By the time she had reached high school, that file had been the most comprehensive document on dragon kind to be found outside the Guild. Her father had it printed and bound as a book for her seventeenth birthday; he'd even added a copy to the Library.

She still had the original file on a CD. The book, titled *Draconia: An Overview*, sat on a shelf in her own library. She didn't need to reference either. Most of what was in the text had been lodged in her mind for years.

"A dragon." She sounded a little faint to her own ears. "What kind?"

His eyes darkened, becoming more inscrutable than usual.

"I'm not entirely sure as to what you mean."

"Eastern, Western, or Sea?" she asked, with a trace of impatience. Her voice sounded anything but faint now. "Those are the three types of dragon, as classified by the Guild. Sea live in the ocean, if they still exist. Eastern are more serpentine. They were revered as semi-deities at one point, having withdrawn since then, Western – well, I haven't heard much good coming from Western dragons."

Something flickered in his eyes. She sensed, more than saw, his tension increase.

"I – it's hard to say."

"Really." Why did trying to get anything out of the man feel like pulling teeth? She pinched the bridge of her nose, trying not to give into the urge to just walk away.

"Don't." He gripped the edge of the table, staring at the wooden surface as he tried to find the words that would explain it. "I wasn't born here. I don't know the draconic types as you do, nor have I seen the need to research them."

"What do you mean, you weren't born here? In the States?"

"The mortal world." His voice was all at once tired. "I was born in a place called the Haven. The Kindred – that's what we call our race – took refuge there some six thousand years ago. Some stayed. Most went. Others left the Haven after a time to see what had transpired here. I was one of them."

"Wait. Back up." Alex looked him over, trying to discern how much of what he was telling her was truth. Michael returned her searching gaze warily, as if he expected a blow, physical or verbal, to come at any moment. "I think you need to start at the beginning."

As he told it, his birthplace was a peaceful paradise. It was full of the one thing that every dragon needed to survive: ambient magic. Earth was being depleted of it, by war, religion, and disbelief. The Kindred had appealed to their deity for a solution. That solution had been the Haven.

Not all dragons were content there, however. Some left,

yearning for adventure. Others left intending to see what the legends they'd been told since hatching were about. Most died of one thing or another. The few that returned did so within a year's time, possessing a new appreciation of the home their race had been gifted with.

"The dragons that you're likely familiar with are the exiles," he went on, now sounding like a history teacher lecturing a class. It hadn't taken him long to regain some of his confidence. "Chronic troublemakers are banished to the mortal world. Here, their lifespan is greatly shortened. They can live up to perhaps five years before perishing – if they're not killed first, which they usually are."

"So, St. George's dragon was a troublemaker for more than just the one city?" Alex asked dryly, intrigued in spite of herself. The medieval tale of the knight who saved a city from the dragon's predations had been her favorite bedtime tale as a toddler. He nodded.

"That particular dragon was what I would call borderline."

"Borderline, how?" She absently lifted her mug to her lips. Finding the tea cold, she set it down again without drinking.

"When a dragon has been in the mortal world for a year or more, he becomes tempted by the Dark, no matter what his natural inclination may be. Most are approached in one fashion or another by the end of the second or third year, when they're usually desperate enough to accept a lifeline, no matter the cost." Idly, he reached across the table, plucking her mug out of her hands. He cupped the ceramic vessel as she felt the slightest whispers of power. "In most cases it leads to enslavement or indentured servitude to a Dark Lord. As I understand it, that one had had already declined any assistance from the Dark once. It was being courted a second time, with only slightly more success, when George killed it."

"Why did it attack the city?"

"It attacked the livestock in the lands around the city. When the people tried to protect their property, it turned on them." He gave her a look that told her that he'd gone through a similar phase at one time. "As a dragon, you starve here. You don't realize that part of your diet, for lack of a better term, incorporates arcane energy. All you feel is the hunger, yet nothing satisfies it."

It made sense. She just wished there was a way to verify it.

He gave her the mug back. She accepted it, not surprised to find it warm again. Sipping it, she found the tea had been replaced with something that tasted of chocolate covered cherries. She raised an eyebrow at him.

"I thought you needed one of your magic mugs for that."

"It makes it easier, but it isn't necessary." He studied her a moment, hesitating so briefly she almost missed. "Do you mind?"

"No." She sighed. "It's fine. Michael, how come you're not out there, serving a Dark Lord?"

"Gwynn got to me first."

"Gwynn." She frowned, her eyes narrowing. "Oh, yes, Tell me about the guy that started this whole mess with that bloody phone call of his. He knew you had me half-naked, by the way."

"Yes." He looked away, as if the reminder bothered him.

"What is he – another dragon?" Her voice held a thin veneer of casualness. She felt her temper begin to rise again, dangerously. "Is he always that nosy?"

"No, He isn't." Michael took a deep breath, returning his gaze to hers. "When I first came to Earth, I observed people. I was fascinated by the various cultures of humanity, how they had all sprung from a single race and yet were so vastly different. I was young, small. I could hide easily." A kind of wistfulness came into his eyes. "I didn't stay that way. The more I grew, the more frequently I was found out by the people I had come to watch. Each time, I fled to a different place, a different culture. Eventually, I found myself in a small valley in a region now called Wales."

"Wales." Alex chewed her lip thoughtfully, then stopped as it hit her. "Gwynn. The Valley of Neath."

"Yes, Neath was spelled differently at the time," he added.

"N-u-d-d. Good Lord, don't tell me that was Gwynn ap Nudd on the blasted phone," she said incredulously, color seeping into her cheeks.

"Sorry." The corner of his mouth quirked. "It was."

"God." She stared at him a little helplessly. First, he was a dragon. She was coming to terms with that. Now he was a dragon that followed an ancient Welsh deity. "Michael, is He just as powerful now as He was back in the day?"

"Yes." He watched her with dark eyes.

"He – oh, Lord." She slumped onto the table, trying to think it through. Had Gwynn been eavesdropping on more than just the physical happenings? Had He delved into her mind, too? More importantly, had He shared any of what He'd seen with Michael?

"No. He hasn't told me anything, Alex." She raised her head to look at him suspiciously. He sighed heavily, massaging his temples as if trying to ease a headache. "All He's told me in regard to you is that I can't have you just yet."

"Have me?" She closed her eyes. This was getting to be a little too much revelation for one night. "Okay, we're circling back to that for a minute. Why would a dragon want a human girl?"

"I don't know."

It could have been the obvious frustration in his voice. It could have been the tension in both of them. It could have been the expression she'd glimpsed on Teri's face from where she stood at the bar watching them both, full of bafflement, suspicion, and concern. Whatever the reason, it had her grinning like a fool. She laughed as he glowered at her.

40

"It isn't funny, Alex," he snapped, temper fraying.

"Oh, yes, it is!" Conquering her mirth was a battle, one that she eventually won. The grin, however, didn't leave her face. "God, Michael. Think about it just a minute. Here we are, a dragon-man and a human girl, sitting in a café, drinking tea or whatever this is. We're talking about history, about deities, about us as a possible item. If anyone else had told me this was how I would be spending my evening, I would have driven them to the shrink's office myself."

"Why?" he asked, his voice taut with irritation. "Because the dragons you've heard of fight with the Dark while you fight against it."

The grin faded from her face. She'd hurt him, she realized. Without meaning to. She reached out to touch. Her fingers closed around his before he could draw away.

"I didn't laugh because I'm not taking it seriously – taking you seriously. I just found it ironic. Improbable. The issue of good and evil aside, just how many people can claim to knowingly have a conversation with a dragon?"

He lost some of his rigidity. "Very few, if any."

"It's going to take some getting used to." She gave him a wan smile. "I really needed that laugh. First, this morning, then this – well, it's huge. I felt like I got hit with a two-by-four both times."

"I meant what I said about this morning," he said, his gaze locking with hers. She saw frustrated desire flicker in them, to be replaced with rock hard. "I want you. Badly. You wouldn't be the first I've bedded, Alex, yet you are the first I've told about myself, what I am. You're definitely the first to haunt my dreams."

"You dream about me?" Pleasure filled her at the thought. Her smile deepened.

"Yes."

"When?" She rested her chin in one hand, watching him.

"In the early hours before dawn," he replied with some of his usual quiet amusement. "After I've tossed and turned for half the night."

Alex sipped her drink. It was nice to hear that she'd gotten under his skin the same way he'd gotten under hers.

"What about you?" He tightened his fingers around her hand as she set down the mug. His thumb ran over her skin in a somehow intimate way. Between the feather-light touch and the gleam in his eye, her pulse began to quicken.

"What about me?"

"Do you dream about me?"

"Yes." The mood had changed between them. She now found herself flirting with the man – the dragon – she'd been depressed about all day. It felt good.

"When?"

"When I sleep." She left it vague on purpose. He leaned forward.

"When you wake."

She blushed. Satisfied to have gotten the upper hand, he released her hand.

"So now what?" she asked finally.

"We finish it." He sobered. "I want to continue our partnership. I want to maintain our relationship. Perhaps, as you've said, we should do neither. I hope otherwise. It takes two to makes this decision, Alex, so…" He spread his hands. "I leave it up to you."

"One thing at a time," she murmured. "I like you. I like being with you, working with you. I haven't felt an attraction this strong in…" She couldn't think of when the last time was. "…ever. I want to explore that, but I don't want to be hurt by it. This morning hurt."

"My fault. It didn't have to hurt." Guilt darkened his expression.

"No, it didn't." She sighed. "I'm a sucker for second and third chances, Michael. We'll see where it goes."

He grasped her hand, brought it to his lips in a courtly gesture she hadn't anticipated.

"Thank you."

"Don't make me regret it, okay?" She took a deep breath, got her thoughts in order. She caught a glimpse of Teri at the bar, saw her mimed query. She sent her a reassuring smile. Teri gave her a disgruntled look in return.

"She's less than happy with me." Michael stated, noting the exchange without seeing it. "She cares for you very much."

"We've been friends a very long time." Her face softened as she thought back. "Teri's always been there when I needed her. She's the sister of my heart, and I love her dearly." She dragged her mind back to the matter at hand. The personal issues had been settled. For now at any rate.

"I guess we're back to business. I've got something."

"As do I." His grim tone had her eyebrows rising.

"You first, then."

"I managed to track yesterday's package to a hotel in Atlantic Beach." As he relayed what he'd learned, she pursed her lips thoughtfully. He ended his dissertation with a question. "Do you believe Drake to be the type of person to send a 'gift' like that?"

"The style of it fits," she admitted. "Not the content, just the style. It was flashy, clichéd. Almost classy. That's him to a T. I just don't think he has the balls to have someone killed and the eyeball plucked out. He's not the type to work with anyone, either. Not unless they play servant to his lord."

"It was an idea." He sighed, a bit disappointed. She smiled.

"Yeah, one I wouldn't mind pinning on him. Maybe we'll run him down wherever he's hiding, ask him about it."

"I would like to be the one asking." The glint in his eye indicated his level of dislike for her ex. "You mentioned that you had something."

"When I went home to change clothes this morning, Teri had left a message on my machine saying that she'd found a present that she thought might have been meant for me."

"A present." His voice went flat. "Did she open it?"

"She did. It wasn't addressed to anyone, and, no, it wasn't like the first 'gift,' either." She leaned back in her chair, waving her friend over. "It's in the safe. Teri," she addressed her as she came within hearing range, "could you get that necklace from the back, please?"

"Did he make it up to you yet?" Teri demanded in answer, scowling at Michael.

"Yes, he – " Michael cut her off.

"No." He met the glaring Teri with quiet dignity. "I've apologized. I've explained. I do intend to make it up to her; it will take more than a single night to do so."

"Hmmph." She wasn't impressed, yet Alex could tell that she was giving him brownie points for honesty. She would relent – eventually. "You'd better."

With that, she headed for the office as requested. Michael turned his attention back to his partner.

"What necklace?"

"A silver chain and pendant." She gave him the brief description. "I think I've seen something like it before. Can't think of where, though."

Teri came back, calling out a greeting to the customer waiting at the register. She tossed the item to Alex, then hurried back to work. The throw went wide; Michael got up before she could, catching it before it hit the floor. Frowning, he turned it over in hands as he reclaimed his seat.

"It feels old, yet looks brand new," he said, frowning. "That could be the design of it. It is familiar, yet, like you, I'm not sure where I've seen it."

"We'll think of it eventually." She sighed. "Teri wants me to stay with her until this is over."

He nodded. "She had mentioned it when I called earlier."

"You called? When?"

"Just before I came here." His eyes lifted to her face. "Are you going to?"

"I'm thinking it might be a good idea." She glanced toward the front of the store. She hadn't realized how late it was. "I don't want to lead the enemy to her, though. Do you think the necklace could be the second package sent out from that hotel?"

"Odds are, yet what its purpose is…" He shrugged, handing it back to her. "It presents another problem, however. Your connection to the café isn't a secret. Any of your friends could be a target, Alex."

"I don't want them hurt," she replied vehemently. "I don't want them to be victims in this." She paused, closing her eyes. "How likely do you think they'll be targeted?"

"I couldn't say."

"Do you think I should stay with Teri?"

"Do you think you should stay at your apartment?" he countered, his voice becoming intense. "Wherever you go, wherever you stay, I don't want you alone. I certainly don't want you having empathic flashbacks without someone there. Once was more than enough."

"And I can't stay with you." Even as she said it, it surprised her how much she wanted to.

"No." His hand covered hers. "Not yet."

She turned her hand over to grasp his on the table. She would spend the night with Teri. Then later, maybe, they could be together.

41

N *ot that one.*

Michael knelt beside an open suitcase, one of Alex's shirts lifted in his hands for inspection. An overnight bag to his right. The shirt joined the first in a discard pile on his left. So did the next top he pulled out.

The woman had more T-shirts than any other single article of clothing, except perhaps underwear. He wasn't sure of that was because he had yet to find them. Didn't she have something that wasn't white, stained, too suggestive, or dirty? Looking at a blouse that was designed to show the curves of a woman's body, he decided that she didn't.

Just when he was on the verge of giving up, he found one that was suitable. It was a tunic, the style of it reminding him of what the emerging middle-class of medieval Europe had worn. Where had she gotten something like this? Frowning, he examined the collar, found a tag. It was hand-stitched. Perhaps she'd had it made.

Deciding it wasn't important to matter, he folded the tunic neatly, then stashed it in the bag. The Great hunt for her undergarments commenced.

When Alex had made the request for him to make up an overnight bag for her she had said sheepishly that none of her clean clothes had been unpacked. They were all still in suitcases or boxes she'd used for the move. They were hard to miss as her closet was full of them. Having already gone through everything on one side, he began on the other.

An hour later, he still hadn't found them. He was about to call her at Teri's house when one of the plastic bags he'd ignored fell off the top shelf. Silky, lacy items tumbled out onto the floor in a vibrant array of color. He ran a hand through his black hair in exasperation before delving into the mess.

It was hard not to imagine the woman he wanted in the garments. Mere scraps of cloth, he thought. That's all they were, yet Michael found the thought of them alluring. So long as they belonged to her. It baffled him. Dragons had never bothered with such things; only human females did. A chuckle sounded in the recesses of his mind. He heaved a long-suffering sigh, choosing several items at random. If he'd missed something crucial, she would have to live with it. He wasn't coming back to go through them again.

Having packed her clothing, he moved on to the spare bedroom she used as her art studio.

She'd mentioned her art every once in a while. He hadn't seen any of it save the faerie piece on sale at the cafe and the dragon picture she was still working on. He couldn't help wondering if it was as disorganized as her bedroom at been.

It wasn't.

Of all the rooms in the apartment, this space was the cleanest. Several framed pieces hung on the walls between dozens of wall shelves. Studying them, he could feel the joy they gave her. Her work was part of her happiness, holding threads of her wishes and dreams. Did she feel that wonderment, impart those wistful things with each of her pictures?

One painting in particular drew his attention. An antlered helm, an armored masculine body, a gray cloak with blue highlights from the ball of light held aloft by an outstretched hand. A cauldron steamed behind the figure, the wisps depicting a forest in the dead of winter. There were no hounds, no horse, no stag, none of the other recognizable trappings that went with the myth. No wonder Gwynn was fond of her. He studied it, noting that she'd shown more skill in drawing the dragon. Going by the date notated in the corner, it had probably been one of her first pieces.

Had she conjured His image on her own, or had He shown her in some way?

As fascinating as her workspace was, meandering through it wasn't what he'd come here for. He selected two pads from a rack, nabbed her bag of various pencils from a shelf, and chose a T-square at random. With one last lingering glance at the watercolor of Gwynn ap Nudd, he left for Teri's apartment.

Michael drove there. Not having been to her place before, he couldn't just teleport there as he was want to do. So he followed the directions Teri had given him before he'd left the café, a bit surprised to find that she lived so far away from Alex. It was, by his estimation, a twenty minute drive from their business, with another fifteen minutes added to that from the Hidden Reaches. As close as the two women seemed to be, he would have thought they lived closer together.

He was halfway there when the first roll of thunder rumbled above him. Looking around, he spied a grocery store parking lot ahead, and turned in. Stopping the car, he left the engine running as he extended his awareness up toward the dark clouds gathering overhead.

He felt the rush of air, the churning of vapor, the sizzling heat of charged ions clashing. Magic flickered amid it all in a manner similar to natural lightning. Even as he tried to pinpoint its origin, a chill began to take hold in the air. Though he sat warm in the car, he could sense the temperature plummeting. He felt the punch of raw electricity discharging, heard the roll of thunder that followed on its heels. Letting his consciousness fall back from the storm, he gripped the steering wheel.

It seemed that the creature had made a full recovery.

The system was moving. He could see the clouds churning in the direction he was headed. His first thought was of Alex. Was it following her? How would it have known where she was?

Putting the car back in gear, he peeled out of the lot. He wished, fervently, that he'd delved into his partner's mind for his destination. He could have teleported if he had. He wouldn't be racing through the streets of Jacksonville, missing turns laid out in the directions, or cursing slow drivers.

Then Michael saw the entrance for the community Teri lived in. The houses so small that they looked like dollhouses rather than homes for people. The yards were tiny. Searching, he glanced up at the street sign as he came into a cul-de-sac. Stafford Road. Teri lived on Stafford, in a little green two-story. The house sat right in the middle of those ringing the court.

A blinding flash of light had him hitting the brakes out of reflex. The crack of thunder that followed it nearly deafened him. Gazing out his window, he could see that the clouds had stopped their trek across the sky. They crouched above the subdivision as if waiting impatiently.

He pulled up into the driveway. He shut off the engine, sitting with his awareness extended to the storm again. Sensations trickled in. The sizzle of wild electricity. The rising of wind. It carried with it something foul, cloying. Straining, he probed as far as he could manage with just his mind. The element he sought slipped away. Instead, he found something else. Caution, hunger. Recognition. Wariness warring with new anger, new fear. A fierce need that tainted everything else.

It had seen him.

Alex and Teri probably didn't have a clue.

With feigned casualness, he snagged the overnight bag from the passenger seat as he got out. He paused, letting the car door slam shut behind him. Seeing no one around, he locked the Firebird, then hurried up the walk to ring the doorbell. A long moment passed before Teri answered it.

"The enemy is in the neighborhood, Teri." He stepped through the entrance, holding out the parcel he'd put together for her friend.

She took it, yanking the door shut quickly. Michael looked around the foyer. "Where is she?"

"Upstairs. How do you – " She broke off as he headed up the steps, taking them two at a time. Muttering something uncomplimentary, she raced after him. "She's in the shower, Michael. How do you know the thing's in the neighborhood?"

Her voice, sharp with anxiety, stopped him in the hallway.

"The storm out there is wholly not natural. It has the creature's influence all through it." He glanced at the bathroom, where he could hear the shower running.

Teri opened her mouth to say something else, then changed her mind. Shaking her head, she moved past him to knock on the bathroom door.

"Clothes! Hurry up!" Setting the bag against the jamb, she turned back to him. A mixture of anxiety and anger began to smolder in her expression. "Alex has told me some of what's been going on. How did it find out where I live?"

"I'm not sure." He shook his head. "If it had access to the records concerning business licenses, it wouldn't be too hard to find out. Or it could have tailed you from work."

"From – Oh, God. Lys – Richard – " Before he could say anything, she dashed back downstairs. He might have followed, just to double-check the house while she called her friends. The bathroom door opened before he could.

Alex stood in the doorway, still toweling her hair dry. With skin still damp and wearing the tunic that clung to it, Michael found himself staring. She looked at him, then herself.

"What?"

He muttered an oath under his breath, dragging a hand through his hair. He had to keep his mind on track.

"Teri's downstairs. The creature's here."

"Where?" She tossed the towel in the hamper behind her, her face grim. "What did it do – follow us?"

"I don't know. As to where, its someplace in the neighborhood." He led the way to the first floor as he spoke. "I can't pinpoint it beyond that. Teri's calling Lys and Richard to warn them."

"You don't think they're at risk, do you?" she asked anxiously, grabbing hold of his arm.

He wished he had an answer for her.

"Alex, we'll handle it. I'll set up something for each of them. I promise. Right now, I want to see if we can track the thing down while it's here."

"Alright." She let him go. "Okay. I don't have much in the way of an arsenal with me, but Teri has some things I can borrow."

"I'll see what I can do to make this place safer for her to stay in." She sent a look of gratitude his way as they entered the kitchen. He wondered how Teri was going to react to what he wanted to do.

Outside the little house, the wind picked up. It whipped through the foliage that lined the streets. The lamps that ran along the road glowed, illuminating the neighborhood. From an unseen backyard, a dog barked while a tabby cat slinked from under one parked vehicle to the next. A single raindrop fell on the pavement, a dark splotch on the dark gray asphalt. The fiend took no notice as it stared at the green house down the road.

He was there. The master had warned it of the girl, yet the man was who concerned it the most. She was different. Skilled. It remembered well the pain she had given it. The man, though – the man was more.

The master was a fool. It never voiced this. He was weak, not a warrior. Soon, soon it would be free of him. That promise, that hope was what kept it going. How close was it to that goal now? Did it matter? It would keep trying, keep searching, until it found the amulet, the key to its prison. Once freed…

Magic stirred, drawing its attention. Eddies of arcane force flowed smoothly to surround the house. It couldn't see the energies, couldn't touch them, but it felt them like a vital warmth.

Crouched in hiding, it could almost taste the magic, a distinct flavor unique to its user. It recognized the signature.

The man was using his power on the house. Was he aware of its presence or was he merely being cautious?

It padded to a nearby hedge, creeping underneath the foliage to crouch, watch, and wait. The flow of energy eased then ceased. Still, it observed in silence. It was a warrior; it had patience. Need may have driven it here, a whim may have led the master to release it for this one night to try to find what it sought. It would not allow its need to dictate its actions here. The man was not to be underestimated.

The front door opened and two people stepped out. It bristled at the sight of the woman who had hurt it. The man was with her. It watched as the pair left the small yard to walk along the road. The man grasped the woman's hand as they strolled. Both of them surveyed the landscape as they passed. They were looking for it, it realized. Yet they were ignorant of the form it wore. It looked down at its paws. For the search, it had been ideal. For the next step in its plan, it needed something else.

The two disappeared around the bend, as it crept out of hiding. What it wanted was in the green house. Another woman lived there. At the moment, while the others were off seeking, she was alone. It sensed the protections around the home. In this instance, they would be of little consequence.

It knew just how to get in.

43

Teri replaced the cap on the bottle of blessed oil she'd just about emptied. Anointing the house had seemed only logical to her. First, it had given her something to do as her best friend went off hunting a murderous maniac with her partner. Second, it gave her peace of mind.

Magic had never been something that she'd been all that comfortable with. Alex used it occasionally. As Teri saw it, her heart-sister used magic as an extension of prayer. Michael, however, was a different matter.

The man had insisted that he do something to keep that – thing – out of the house. Between his dire warnings and Alex's concern for her safety, she hadn't been left much choice. So she'd given in to appease them. Letting him do whatever to her home was almost like giving it away. She hated that feeling. Going back, blessed oil in hand, to each point in the house where he had stood, doing something, made the place seem like hers again.

Still, she did feel safer knowing that it was there. His only word of warning about it was that it could still be circumvented if she invited the enemy in.

With a sigh, Teri put the bottle away. Outside, thunder boomed again. After the sound had faded, she heard another coming from her stomach. It was time to think of tonight's evening snack.

She always ate something after closing for the night. Usually, it was a bowl of cereal. Tonight, though, she wasn't alone. A meal? Sandwiches? Soup? Mentally, she went through her inventory of food items. Richard had left some things in the freezer, hadn't he? She crossed the kitchen to open it, digging through everything to find cartons of ice cream, packages of raw chicken, some bacon, a huge bar of chocolate that she had forgotten about, and boxes of frozen veggies. In the door were four bags of miniature candy bars.

For someone who didn't particularly like chocolate, she certainly had a lot of it. Maybe she could persuade Alex to eat most of it. Michael could certainly take some with him when he left. Until then, it could just stay in the freezer.

Not finding anything remotely like a prepared meal, she shut the freezer. It would have to be pizza. There was a late-night pizzeria that delivered not too far away. Lots of meat, she decided, extra cheese, and mushrooms. She had already picked up the phone to call in the order when she remembered what Alex had told her about the creature. A shape-shifter that could take on the form of whatever it killed. She'd be courting disaster, wouldn't she, ordering pizza now? With a sigh, she put the phone down. Maybe she could bribe Alex into cooking dinner.

The doorbell rang.

Frowning, she hesitated. Would a killer ring her doorbell? Who would be coming by after – she glanced at the stove clock – eleven o'clock at night? When it rang again, she tried to quell the butterflies pirouetting in her stomach as she hurried to the door. She peered through the peephole. No one there. The bell rang a third time. Whoever it was had to be short. Cautiously, she cracked open the door to see Chris, the eleven-year-old boy from next-door.

He stood in the scruffy jeans he used to play outside in. His shirt and ball cap were grass-stained; he must have been wrestling with friends earlier in the day. He grinned up at her guilelessly, eyes twinkling mischievously. She answered it with a smile of her own, caution dropping away. Instead, relief mingled with worry. Chris could hardly be a cold-blooded killer, but he could very well be a victim of one. What was he doing here?

"Hi, Miss Teri," he greeted cheerfully. "Mom sent me over. She wants to borrow some brown sugar for chocolate chip cookies. Can she?"

"Cookies?" Teri asked, puzzled. "She's baking cookies this late at night?"

Chris nodded with a sheepish smile. "I forgot to tell Mom about the party I've got at school. I'm supposed to bring cookies."

"Hmmm." That sounded like Chris, alright. Always waiting until the very last possible minute to remember that something was needed the next day. Like a book report. She cocked her head to one side as if debating. "Okay, but she's gotta pay the toll. If she can give me some of those cookies, then I'll let her have a whole box of brown sugar."

"Okay." The response came quickly, with humor. "I get mine first, though."

"Come on in," she invited, stepping back so he could. "Let me see if I can find it. I know I've got two or three boxes of the stuff somewhere." She led the way back to the kitchen. "You've got a game coming up, don't you?"

Chris played little league. The sport was his obsession. He wandered around the room, taking in everything.

"Uh-huh. Saturday, at two. Are you gonna come?"

"Don't think I can this time, kiddo," she replied apologetically, rummaging through her cabinets. "I got work."

"Oh. That's okay." He meandered over to the breakfast table, playing with the salt and pepper shakers she kept there. "Maybe next time."

"Here we go." Teri plucked the box from a cabinet shelf. She turned around just in time to see Chris home in on the silver box Alex had set there earlier. "Don't touch that."

"What is it?" He didn't take his eyes off it.

"Just a necklace," she replied casually, a little uneasy at the intensity of his stare. "It's my friend's. She'll be back in a little bit for it."

"Can I see?"

The butterflies were back. Apprehension began to build, bit by bit, as she clutched the package of sugar in her hand. "No, I don't think so. Here's your sugar, Chris. You better get it home before the rain hits."

She forced the sugar into his grasp, then took the box to tuck it out of his sight. He looked up and her mouth went dry. Eyes of yellow glared, monstrous eyes that held no hint of humanity. He snarled, the child's face contorting grotesquely. She stepped backwards as he launched himself at her.

Teri let go of the necklace, grabbed the nearest chair. She swung it wildly. The chair struck the thing in mid lunge. It went down with a grunt, rolling to regain its feet. Muttering a prayer, she took another swing at it. It dodged to the side. Grasping her arm with the strength of a grown man, it flung her into the counter. Pain exploded. Her vision hazed. Stunned, she slumped against the cabinets by the sink.

Her side was on fire. Was this what broken ribs felt like? It hurt so bad –

A crash snapped her back to reality. The creature had overturned the table to get to the silver box on the floor. Using the counter, she hauled herself onto her feet, hobbled along the length of the faux granite away from it. Its hands had just closed over the box when the front door banged open. It let out a sound that was part laugh, part howl. The noise galvanized her.

Teri made a mad dash for the door. Her legs were like jelly, the agony in her ribs increasing. She couldn't move fast enough. She wouldn't get away before –

Behind her, she heard an inhuman shriek. It had realized that she wasn't down for the count.

Just go, just leave. The thought was desperate, losing coherency as shock set in. *You have what you came for – leave –*

Power surged throughout the house as Teri stumbled towards the front. Her feet fumbled over a wrinkle in the rug. She felt herself begin to go down. Strong hands caught her, Masculine hands, she thought dazedly. Michael? She didn't notice Alex run past as the world spun. Sound and sensations rushed over her as her consciousness slipped away.

Alex met the enemy just outside the kitchen.

Dagger ready, a fist full of blessed rock salt in one hand, she rushed it. Recognition flickered over its face as she flung the salt at it. It stumbled back, covering its eyes. She slashed in with the blade, unsheathing another as gashes opened up on its arms. It shrieked, striking out. The small fists hit like heavy stones. With a scream, it lunged at her. Its mouth clamped on her shoulder. She stabbed its middle, shoving it aside as it released her.

Lights began to flicker wildly. Magic rose and fell in erratic waves, making the hairs on the back of her neck stand on end. The storm outside burst into full-fledged fury. Another boom of thunder sent the house into darkness.

Oh, hell...

She didn't have back-up. Michael was taking Teri to safety. Now she couldn't see. The little monster made a cackling sound, harsh and evil. A tremor of fear ran up her spine.

Work with it, Alex. You can do this. All you have to do is survive until he gets back.

She backed up against a wall, feeling the edge that meant the entrance to the kitchen. There was a little ambient light in there; the sliding glass door had no curtains. She darted in as it hissed at her. Energy slammed into her, knocking her off her feet. She skidded across the tiled floor to hit the table. She scrambled up, was hit again.

Then it shrieked, almost wailing. The din was piercing. She clamped her hands over her ears, trying to see into the pitch blackness beyond her.

Colors flared in quick bursts. Sickly yellow warred with purple, punctuated by crashes and incoherent shouting from the creature. Another inhuman cry rang out, answered by an equally inhuman roar. She crawled into a crouch, felt her way to the wall. As she listened to the sounds of fighting, it dawned on her that the fiend was facing off with her partner.

It strained against the other's magic, wildly spinning out whirlwinds that tore around the hall. As her eyes adjusted, she could see its silhouette in the dark. It darted back and forth, attempting to break out of its position. It couldn't go backwards, she realized. There was – she struggled to visualize the layout – a wall there. It couldn't go forwards because of Michael. That left –

It slipped under an attack, running for the kitchen. Alex moved to intercept. It flew into her, knocking her sideways. She lashed out with a knife, felt the resistance as the blade bit into flesh. There was another shriek of pain. She was hit again. Her head struck wood, stars rupturing her vision. Glass shattered. Another frustrated roar followed.

Her head throbbing from yet another knot on her skull, Alex groped for the counter lip. She tried to haul herself to her feet, fingers slipping when she was half-way there. She hit the floor with a groan.

"Stay there."

The terse command took a moment to register. When it did, she was more than happy to obey. Leaning back, she closed her eyes. She heard the crunch of broken glass, then silence. Minutes ticked by. The pounding in her skull wasn't going away. Teri usually kept her meds in the kitchen drawer, didn't she? There should be over-the-counter pain-killers. Of course, that meant moving, something she wasn't sure she wanted to do.

The sound of footsteps on the glass caught her attention. She opened her eyes to see a pinpoint of light form above her head. It grew until a floating sphere the size of a golf ball shone in the air. She squinted, thinking that it was much too bright. It toned down in intensity. Michael knelt beside her, gingerly probing her skull. He swore softly when he felt the second lump.

"It's gone?" she asked, turning her head towards him.

"Hold still," he ordered, his voice harsh. She could feel a rage boil within him. Reaching out to touch his face, she tried to soothe. He ignored the effort, continuing a ruthless inspection of her injuries. "It's gone. It was after the necklace."

"Mmm." She winced as his fingers found one of the deeper bruises on her shoulder. "That's gone, too, then."

"No. I've got it. We're not staying here." With that pronouncement, he gathered her up in his arms, lifting her from the floor. The abrupt movement brought on motion-sickness. "You're the only person I know who's managed to get two concussions within twenty-four hours," he snapped, biting the words off. "Don't make a habit of it."

"I won't."

Alex closed her eyes as the light faded. She pressed her face into his shoulder, feeling the tension in him as he began the teleportation process. Her sigh was lost somewhere in the transition between places. Much as she might like to, she couldn't stay snuggled in his arms like this for long. When she opened her eyes again, they were back at Michael's. He set her gently on the couch, then fetched one of his mugs. He gave it to her with orders that she drink all of it and left the apartment.

It was the same bitter stuff that she'd been forced to drink last time.

Wrinkling her nose at the taste, she continued to sip as she idly looked around the room. It hadn't changed much. She frowned. Wait...he'd put a hole in the wall. It had been right across the room, opposite the couch, plain as day and as large as a basketball.

Guess he fixed it. She wondered if he had done it with magic or the old-fashioned way.

She finished her drink, setting the mug down on the coffee table just as Michael walked back in. He still looked ready to kill someone. His expression reminded her of what he'd looked like that morning when they'd both been tearing at each other's clothes. The memory had heat rushing to her cheeks. Determined to ignore it for the moment, she asked the first thing that came to mind.

"Where's Teri?"

"Hannah's," came the terse reply, referring to his neighbor. He moved restlessly into the kitchen. Alex raised an eyebrow in mute query. "She's a Healer and Teri's got two cracked ribs. She's fine," he added before she could ask. "She'll spend the night there."

"Alright." There really wasn't much she could say or do about her best friend at the moment. While she hadn't met Hannah, she did trust Michael. If he thought that Hannah could take care of Teri then she could. Resolutely setting that matter to one side, she asked another question. "What about your car?"

"What about it?" She could hear him turn on the faucet and move dishes around the sink.

"You had it at Teri's, didn't you? Or did you just..." Alex let her voice trail off as something clattered loudly.

"It's here. In the parking lot. So is hers." He turned the spigot off. The clanking noises didn't stop, and water splashed sporadically. He was doing dishes, she realized, by hand.

"It's either this or strangle something," he said from where he stood in the kitchen with his back to the rest of the apartment. "Or take up where this morning left off."

Oh. Well. That certainly brought all kinds of tingles to bear.

"Do you mind if I call Lys and Richard, check in with them?"

"You know where the phone is."

The mug disappeared from the table. From the splash she heard coming from the kitchen, it had landed in the sink. Bemused, she called her friends, made sure that they were okay. Both promised to come by in the morning.

She sat for a while, amused at his industrious method of venting frustration, as he meticulously cleaned the kitchen. He came out into the living room to begin cleaning up the wax drippings from his candles. She suppressed a grin. When he started looking for something else to do, still restless, she impishly decided to give him more options.

"If it's cleaning you're wanting to do," she said, using an exaggerated sage-like tone, "there's a dwelling just below you that could use your immense skills. The kitchen, the living room, the dining area – it's deplorable. A man of your talents could easily set it to rights within a day or two." She grinned at him, marveling that she was in good humor despite her throbbing head. She added cheekily, "That is, if it's cleaning you're really wanting to do."

The long look he gave her was, for once, very easy to read. Feeling all at once lightheaded, she concluded that both of them needed something else to think about. Especially if he was going to be obedient to Gwynn, as he seemed so bent on being...

The hot, predatory desire in his gaze vanished, sardonic amusement taking its place. He held out his hand to her, which she took with only the slightest hesitation. He pulled her carefully to her feet.

"Let's go clean your apartment."

45

September 10, 2004
Elsewhere

It had failed, as he had anticipated it would.

The servant was not taking its failure very well. Its rage kept it moving, heedless of its wounds. He found it fascinating that these injuries, unlike the ones inflicted at the museum, were healing rapidly. What was the difference? Alex had done the first set; these had come from her and her mysterious partner.

The partner. Michael Keegan. He had unearthed the name through some delicate inquiry. The people he had spoken with either didn't know him, or didn't want to talk about him. One had given up the name – and a few other things – at a steep price.

A crash drew his attention back to the creature. The lamp lay in a broken heap by the bed as it lashed out with crooked fingers at the comforter. The fabric ripped. It growled at the sound, its body expanding a bit more, losing the shape it held. It was losing control of its form. It had a harder time keeping it when injured.

"They shall pay."

The hissed words had him nodding in agreement.

"Yes, they will." He smiled coldly. "Tell me of the man."

"Hurts." It clamped a hand over its abdomen. The fingers were clawed now, no longer child-like.

"Yes. It's healing." He paused, considering tactics. "They both hurt you, the man, the woman. The woman I know. It is the man that I need to learn more of to help you, as I promised I would."

"No man. Beast." It bared its teeth in a grotesque grin. "Like me, like her, only not."

A shape-shifter? Weren't all true shape-shifters extinct? Intrigued, he made a mental note to check his sources on that. The rest of the phrase caught up with him just as he was about to speak.

"Like her?" His eyes narrowed. "What do you mean?"

It cackled. He suppressed the surge of irritation at its amusement.

"I was a man once." All mirth fled its face. "She is a woman. I changed. So will she."

Cursed? Blessed? Either could result in such a change, yet there were other things that also could. Blood, for example. The spilling of it, the giving of it, or the inheritance of it. Perhaps he needed to do some genealogy work, discover more about her blood heritage.

"What else can you tell me?"

"He has magic, old magic. Cautious. Caution makes him weak. He protects, and that makes him strong." The servant sat on the bed, began to rock in place. "Strong. So strong…"

"Stronger than you?" He made certain to keep his tone sympathetic. He didn't flinch when it snarled at him.

"Need the amulet. I will be the strongest, the greatest, with the amulet."

"Of course. We will find it again. In fact, that is all you have left to do here. I have what I need." He reached over to the table beside his chair, stroked the leather cover of the journal he'd been studying. Then he paused, as if struck by a sudden thought. "The girl. The one you said had the amulet. I almost forgot. I apologize."

Bringing out a small notebook from inside his blazer, he began to flip through it. Finding the page he was looking for, he read aloud.

"Teri Andrews. She works at the *Candlelight and Magic Café*. She will know where it is."

"Yes…" It's monstrous eyes began to glow with an eerie light. "Yes…where is it?"

"About a forty-five minute drive from here. I'll take you when you've finished healing. Perhaps a bath would speed up the process?"

It took a bit of persuasion to coax it into taking a shower. As it ambled off to the bathroom of the suite they shared, he contemplated his next move.

Alexandria Rosselle was fairly predictable when it came to her friends. She wouldn't let Teri returned to her house alone, wouldn't let the woman stay there overnight until things were resolved to her satisfaction. Teri would be staying with her at her new apartment.

The Hidden Reaches. Putting the notebook away, he picked up the journal to scan its pages once again. The book spoke a great deal about the place. There were many mysteries there, a treasury of secrets that called to him as a flame did moths. Yet beneath all the enigma was something else – something hinted at in the carvings of an Incan ruin in the Andes.

The Key to the Pit.

He felt the rush of lustful power, the eagerness to obtain it. He allowed himself to revel in the sensation, not questioning where it came from. Nor did he hear the laughter that echoed in the back of his mind.

Jacksonville, FL

"Now. When did you finally pull this place together?"

"Shhh. He's sleeping on the couch. We didn't turn in until around four so let's keep it down."

"Sorry."

It was too late, Michael thought. He had woken when Alex had stepped out the front door to check on her friend. Still, he kept his eyes closed as they passed him on their way to the back bedroom. He was dimly aware of the dull aching in her sides. It sat in her thoughts like an unwanted child, lurking in the shadow cast by the curiosity he sensed. She was wondering what had transpired the night before.

When he heard the bedroom door close softly behind them, he sighed, reluctantly opening his bleary eyes to stare at the ceiling. Like Teri, he was feeling the effects of the evening's events. The fatigue came from using magic; the teleportation in particular was draining. The bruising scattered over his torso came from battling the monster. The cobwebs in his mind came from the lack of sleep.

As it didn't look as if he would be getting that sleep, he dragged himself into a sitting position. He looked around with the air of a man who had no idea what he was looking for until he saw the clock Alex had installed on the wall in the dining room. According to it, it was barely seven o'clock in the morning.

Had she slept at all?

No. She has other things to do, as do you.

Scowling at the voice that echoed in his head, Michael shoved himself off the couch. His body protested as he walked into the kitchen, splashed water on his face at the sink. The muscles would loosen up in short order. It was those cobwebs and the fatigue that would hamper him throughout the day.

Skipping meals yesterday does not help matters any.

"Will you stop?" He muttered it to the sink basin. A headache was beginning to form right between his eyes. "I wasn't hungry anyway."

Gwynn's response came in sensation: amusement, affection, and a kind of parental push to get going. With a grunt of acknowledgement, he turned to the refrigerator. The mention of food had piqued the interest of his stomach. Opening the contraption, he didn't find much. There were eggs, some bread – why did she keep that in the fridge? – orange juice, lots of coffee creamer. Other things in containers graced the shelves. None of it resembled ready-to-eat food.

There was a knock at the door. He closed the fridge with a frown. Who...oh. He remembered. Lys and Richard both were expected to come by this morning. He went to answer the door.

Both of them looked well rested, he noted, a thread of envy weaving through him. Lys, perkily dressed in a sky blue outfit, stared at him. Richard, not-so-perkily dressed, just glared.

"You look exhausted." There was concerned sympathy in Lys' voice. It might have irritated him, if Richard hadn't scowled at her from behind. "Did we wake you?"

"No. I was awake. The girls are in the bedroom." He stepped back from the door to let them in.

"You stayed the night?" Richard's disapproval was plain. Lys frowned at him.

"Yes." Michael did not feel up to a confrontation. Instead, he ignored the attitude, something he wouldn't normally have done. "I slept on the couch."

"Should have slept in your own apartment, considering the way you'd treated Alex."

"Would you have left her alone for the night?"

"Teri – "

"Teri spent the night upstairs at Hannah's, as she's a healer. She didn't come down until about twenty minutes ago."

"Stop it." The two words, said quietly, were enough to draw both men's attention to Lys. "Just stop it. Neither of you are going to have an argument in Alex's home." Silence followed her words for a moment.

"I'll make some breakfast for everyone." With that abrupt announcement, Richard disappeared into the kitchen. Sighing heavily, Michael looked to Lys.

"I'm sorry."

"It's okay. He's just protective of us girls. Sometimes a little too protective, but that's Richard." She offered a smile. "Why don't you go get Alex and Teri. We can eat, then figure out what it is that we're going to do next."

47

" So."
Alex looked around the table. Teri was doing okay. Hannah had worked a miracle on her ribs. The bones had been mended, though the massive bruising on her torso remained. It would be a while before that faded away, along with the still present pain. Lys caught her eye, rolled her own in her fiancé's direction. Richard was miffed about something. Given the way he ignored Michael, it was probably him. As for his part, Michael just seemed resigned to it. He looked tired. So was she. Yet while she had caught a third – or was it fourth? – wind, it was obvious that he hadn't.

"That thing, monster, killer, whatever you want to call it." She paused to drink more coffee and thank God for the almighty bean. "Which did it follow to Teri's home? Teri or the amulet?"

"I couldn't say. She wasn't what it was after." Michael dug into his jeans pocket to bring out the jewelry in question. He laid it in the center of the table. "I mentioned last night at the café that it felt older than it looks. I think it might be a replica of another piece. As for the creature, it's main focus was the necklace. That's not to say that it would not have killed anyone once it had it, but it did not kill Teri when it could have."

"That doesn't answer the question." Richard's stiff tone spiked the tension level in the room. Alex moved to counter it.

"Actually, it kind of does. It knew the necklace was there. Everything else was secondary." The caffeine was kicking in now, shifting her mind into full gear. "Now we have to trace the replica. Who made it? Why? Was it done locally?"

"Jewelers." Teri said it with a sigh. "There are a lot of jewelers out there. Couldn't say as to whether or not anything they sell runs to that sort of thing."

"You can call them up to ask. Save some time and gas that way." Lys got up to begin collecting everyone's plates now that the meal was over. "We can help with that."

"We'd have to work around the café."

"Good point." Richard's face lightened a bit at Alex's agreement. "Who opened it today?"

"Sherry was on the schedule to open. Lys and I have the mid-shift. Teri was supposed to have the evening." He sighed, looking at Teri. "I guess with your being hurt, we'll have to cover that."

"I can still come in," Teri protested stubbornly. "I can do paperwork, supervise, count the tills, that sort of thing. Hannah just said no heavy lifting. If I follow that, I'll be fine."

"While she's there tonight, she can shift the schedule around so that she won't be stuck opening or closing. She can take the majority of the mid-shifts. There's less heavy lifting involved." Lys gave her fiancé an encouraging smile. "We won't have to do double-shifts."

"I've got a concern about that, though," Alex broke in. "It knows Teri's face. It may have connected her with the necklace."

"It may have tracked the necklace to the café first, or discovered that it went there." Everyone turned to Michael as he spoke. He looked thoughtful as he considered the dilemma. "A solution might be to have a bodyguard."

"Like you?" Richard's tone was derisive.

He sighed as Alex gave Richard a warning glance, then responded without rancor.

"I was thinking of Nate Forge. It's his day off and he has experience with the supernatural."

"I'm familiar with some of his work," Alex put in. "He'd be a good choice. He's Kent's." She exchanged a smile with Teri.

"That's good enough for me, if he's willing to do it, that is."

"I'll ask him." Michael got up to leave. "I'll take the time to shower afterwards."

"Alright." Alex stretched, also getting up. "Just send him over. Meanwhile, I'll start compiling a list of jewelers to interrogate."

After her partner left, she turned to Richard.

"So what gives?"

"I just don't like him." He shrugged, retreating to the kitchen to start on the dishes. "He hurt you."

"Yes, he did. We've worked that out." She studied his back from the kitchen doorway, trying to figure out what had turned him off Michael. "I like him. A lot. He's my partner, which complicates things a bit, so he was right to put the brakes on it when he did. Could he have done it another way? Yes. He admits that."

"You could do better than him."

Did they all feel that way? She looked back at her friends. Lys shook her head; Teri just shrugged.

"I appreciate how you feel, Richard. I don't agree with you, but I do appreciate it." She smiled. "I'd like to give this a chance, see where it goes. Can you at least be nice to his face? For me?"

"Alright." He sighed. "I'll try. For you."

"Thank you."

She leaned against the wall, turning her head to see Teri pensively tugging at the hem of her top. It reminded her of another issue in need of addressing.

"Why don't you move in with me until this is over? Just to be safe. In fact, does everyone just want to meet here after closing? Okay, with you?" She directed her question at Richard.

"Sure." He continued to wash dishes as he answered. "We can bring over some leftovers from the café for a late dinner."

"Since everyone's working at the café except for Alex, why

don't you two leave your car here and take my SUV? We can car pool." Teri hesitated, then asked, "Um, Alex? Do you mind taking me back to my place and dropping me off after? I need a fresh set of clothes." She gave a wry smile, gestured at the jeans and oversized t-shirt she wore. "I'd like to be able to give back the clothes I borrowed from Hannah. I just don't feel up to going by myself."

"Sure, we can do that."

"She can drop me off after we run by my place." Teri patted her pockets absently, then remembered she wasn't wearing the pants from the previous day. "I need my keys. Be right back."

"What about Michael?" Lys asked. "Won't you wait for him?"

"Yeah." The trio heard their friend bellow the word from the back bedroom. Alex pushed off the wall.

"On that note, I'm getting started on that list."

Teri looked out the window of the car, trying to decide on what she needed to get without imagining what her house might look like. Alex had mentioned that the kitchen had been trashed. The thing, whatever it was, had done quite a number on her cooking area despite the diminutive stature of the form it had chosen.

Chris. She closed her eyes as grief weighed down. The boy was dead, wasn't he?

"It's more than likely that he is." Alex's quiet voice drew her gaze. Her hand left the steering wheel to grip Teri's. "I'm sorry."

"Maybe – maybe there's a chance. Maybe it just hurt him – just a little – and he's not dead."

"Maybe."

She could tell her friend didn't think so. Still, Teri clung to that hope, burying the rest under denial. Slumping back in the seat, she stared hard at the dash until the urge to weep passed.

"Talk to me, will you? I need a distraction."

"Richard doesn't like Michael," Alex commented. "Do you?"

She thought a moment. She could see that it bothered her so she wanted to give an honest, thorough answer.

"It's complicated. I mean, I don't know much about him. He's your partner and I can see you're all starry eyed for him. He hurt you." She gave her a sideways look. "I could have given him hell for that. But, well, he seems to care about you. A lot. An idiot can see that you're important to him."

"That doesn't answer my question."

"I'm getting there. On one hand, I want you to be happy with him. I want to accept him as part of our rag-tag family. Big brothers are cool." She smiled thinly. "When they're not a pain in the rear. On the other hand, I think he's hiding a few secrets. That makes me think twice about having him around."

"He does have secrets. He's told me a few of them." Alex stopped at a light. "I can't break confidence, Teri."

"I wouldn't want you to." She turned in her seat to face her. "Just tell me this: is he human? I get this distinct feeling that he isn't."

"He isn't."

"Fey?"

"Nice try." She gave her an apologetic smile. "It's one of those secrets. What I can tell you is that he doesn't follow the Dark. He's oath-bound to a Welsh god to fight those who do."

Teri's expression became pained.

"Alex, I love you dearly. Still, I've told you before that there are no Pagan gods in my world."

"Sorry." She chuckled. "Let's call him an aspect of God, then."

"That's better."

They continued to chat until they came to Teri's neighborhood. The conversation died off as they turned into it. The car slowed to a crawl as they caught sight of the police cars parked along the curb close to the cul-de-sac. Yellow tape was strung around Teri's home, a CSI unit was parked in the drive. It wasn't the only house cordoned off. Her neighbor's was as well. There were more vehicles in front of it. One looked similar to the vans used to take the bodies away in TV shows.

No – God, no –

Alex stopped the sedan in the street as Teri fumbled with her seatbelt, then flung the door open. She took a few steps toward the blocked off area, stopping when a cop called out to her. She stared numbly, not needing to fake the shock and confusion on her face.

"I live here." She said faintly. She felt Alex place a comforting hand on her shoulder. "I live here, this is my home. What happened? Nancy – Chris – " She covered her mouth as she saw people come out of the house, a black bag was strapped to the gurney between them. "Oh, God."

Her eyes swam with tears. She heard Alex murmuring to her, yet couldn't make out the words. She watched as they loaded the bag into the back of a parked van. An ominous buzzing fill her ears. Alex stepped in front her, shook her shoulders.

"Teri." She refocused on her friend, the tears streaking down her cheeks. There was sorrow and understanding in her eyes. "Let's go sit down now. The cops are going to want to talk to us both."

The questioning took a long time. A brief interview at the scene was followed up by a more formal one downtown. There they were separated, their answers recorded. Alex was done before Teri.

She sat on a bench in the hall, wondering if her friend had been in the frame of mind to pick up on any of the cues she'd tried to give her. She hated it when the police crossed over into hunter territory like this. Things usually got very tricky.

She couldn't tell them the truth. Who would believe that a shape-shifting monster had killed the neighbors, then used the boy's shape to gain entrance into Teri's home?

The door to the interview room opened. Teri stepped out, pale and red-eyed. She rose to hurry over to her.

"Hey, you okay?"

"I guess." She sounded tired, weary. It made her heart ache for her.

"Before you go, Ms. Andrews, we need to get contact information for you." The detective came out of the room to motion them to follow. "I'm afraid that we can't allow you back into your home just yet."

"That's – I – okay." Teri scrubbed her eyes with her hands.

"She's staying with me." Alex put an arm around her friend's shoulders. They reached his desk in the bullpen, sitting down as he shuffled papers aside to take notes. She gave him her address, her phone number, the café's info.

"Neither of us have cell phones," she went on. "I've got an answering machine, though, and so does the café. Did you need anything else?"

"Not at this time. Thank you for your cooperation, Ms. Andrews, Ms. Rosselle. The department appreciates it."

They shook hands, then left him to confer with his partner on the investigation. Once outside, Alex breathed in deep. As they walked to the car, she studied her friend, debated whether or not to take her to the café as planned. She looked so worn out.

"I'll be fine. Really." She managed some semblance of a smile as she opened the door to get in. "Don't worry about me."

"Hard not to. Are you sure you want to go to work?"

"I need something to do. I need work." She looked down at herself as Alex cranked the engine, sighed. "I need clothes."

"We can swing by Wal-Mart on the way back."

"Not Wal-Mart. Target. Let's go to Target. Ah, what about Michael?"

They'd left him at Hidden Reaches, making those calls to jewelers around town.

"I called him when we got here, told him what was up. I can call him again from Target, let him know that you're still going to work." She hesitated. "What did you tell the cops?"

"That we'd left there around ten-thirty to crash at your place. I figured the truth was best there." Her mouth tilted in what might have been a smile. "The time's an estimate. I told them I wasn't clear on it. I said that I'd come back for some more clothing as we'd decided to extend the unpacking project."

"Oh, good." The relief was audible in her voice. "I said more or less the same thing."

"You missed your turn." Alex muttered a mild curse. It got a tired chuckle from her passenger. "Thanks for being there."

"Hey, that's what friends are for."

It took another missed turn, what seemed like a dozen different roads, and half an hour to get onto I-95. Their detour to the store added another forty-five minutes to their commute. By the time they got to the cafe, it was close to four o'clock. A visibly exhausted Teri walked in with her new clothes in a bag, making her way to the restrooms in the back to change.

"She doesn't look well at all." Alex looked over at the register, saw Lys staring after their friend. The blonde turned to her. "What happened?"

"The cops were there when we got to her house." She kept her voice low so that it wouldn't carry to the customers. "Her neighbors are dead. We had to go downtown for questioning."

"Oh." Her expression became distressed. "Did she see...?"

"She saw a body bag. That was enough. She hasn't eaten, probably isn't hungry, but she needs to have something."

"Okay. I'll tell Richard." She darted through the door leading into the kitchen.

"Who's the lead investigator?"

She glanced over, saw Nate sitting at the bar with a mug of coffee. His golden eyes, so like his father's, were serious. She leaned against the counter, edging a tad closer.

"Detective Nelson. He has a partner, Detective Grady. Haven't a clue as to what they're impressions were."

"I'll dig up a few contacts in that area. Let me check on it."

"Thanks."

Teri came out. She said nothing as she made her way into the 'employees only' area. She ducked into the kitchen.

"I don't know what to do for her," Alex murmured.

"Find the fiend. Bring it down." Nate sipped his coffee, eyes going to the front as someone else came in. "Let her work, as it'll keep her mind off it. Trust me to watch her while she does that. Hello, Michael."

"Nate." Michael touched her arm, studied her face. "How is she?"

"She's taking it hard."

He nodded, letting his gaze wander to the back. They unfocused for a moment.

"Lys and Richard have her for now. How are you?"

"Okay." She took a breath, closed her eyes. "I'd met the boy only once, so it's different for me. I won't break, if that's what you're asking. I can do this. I will do this."

He nodded.

"Go say your goodbyes. I've got a lead we can follow. The sooner we find the creature, the better off she will be."

50

They had dinner first. Neither of them had eaten, so it seemed that it was the thing to do. Michael chose a steakhouse, which suited Alex's need for protein. It didn't take long to be seated, or to give their orders. Once the waitress had left them, he studied her over the rim of his water glass.

"Will you tell me?"

"Hmm?" She seemed to come back from that place her mind had wandered to. "Sorry, I'm not paying attention."

"Tell me what's on your mind."

"A dozen things." She sighed, slumping back in the booth. "There's something out there that has no qualms about killing children. Teri's torn up about it, which I can't help worrying over. I haven't checked on pending orders for art prints in a couple of days, haven't checked with my agent to see if any commissions have come through. The cops – I'm not sure if Teri's on the suspect list or if they have any leads in their investigation. I can't look into the future and say whether or not that particular incident will double back to us. We both lied in interview today."

"The police are unlikely to believe tales of shape-shifting

murderers."

"True enough." She began to toy with a sugar packet. "Richard doesn't like you."

"I've noticed." He could see it bothered her. "I am aware that he doesn't approve of what I did, how I did it – how it hurt you. It will be a long time before I'm forgiven for that."

"I usually have more support from him. Teri likes you." She flicked the packet at him, got another. "She's not entirely convinced that you're good for me, yet she's willing to give you a chance. Lys likes you." Now she gave a little laugh. "She thinks that bumps in the road are natural, which they are, I guess. She just seems to have more blind faith in happy endings than Teri."

"She strikes me as a wistful faerie," he murmured, thinking of the petite blonde. "She's bright. Teri shines. She is like a unicorn. Pure of heart, strong of mind, and utterly loyal."

"Yeah? What about me?"

"I'm not sure yet."

Hot bread arrived. Flicking her second packet at him, she broke the loaf, slathered on butter. He slid the pack of sugar to the side with the first.

"So what did you do today?"

"Talk." He took the piece she offered. "I've learned that I don't particularly like phone work. I've called and spoken to more jewelers than I thought existed in this city. Most didn't know what I was talking about, a few didn't have time for an inquiry."

"What was your approach?"

"I described the necklace, asked where it could have been acquired." He saw her expression and sighed. "How would you have done it?"

"Like you did, but I would have asked if it sounded like something that had to be custom-made. I'd have spun a story about having borrowed a friend's necklace, that I liked it so much that I wanted one of my own. As it was a gift, she wouldn't have a clue as to where it had come from." She shrugged. "Did you get anywhere? You mentioned a lead earlier."

"There's a place on the Northside of town that does custom

work. I was directed there. One of the people I talked to mentioned novelty shops."

"Novelty jewelry. Hmm. It's an angle."

"I didn't call any of those shops. I did, however, contact the Northside one. The proprietor mentioned that it sounded similar to some pieces he had on display. He closes in two hours."

Her grin lit the room.

"That is fantastic. Let's make this meal a quick one," she said. "I want to get over there tonight."

51

"How are you doing, sugar?"

Teri looked up from her paperwork to see Nate seating himself across from her table. They sat at the back of the dining area, in a spot tucked in behind a few small bookcases displaying tea and coffee blends for sale. Everyone could see them, yet no one could sit around them. It was her favorite table at the café for that reason. She didn't appreciate someone else using it while she was there.

Nate studied her face a moment, then sighed heavily.

"Sugar, you had your sad face on, so I came over to check on you. Now, you've got your pissed face on. Is it me you're objecting to, or that I came over to see if you were okay?"

"I just want to be left alone for a bit. I've got work." Pointedly ignoring him, she went back to the stock form she was filling out. She had done foodstuffs earlier in the week. This one was for the locally crafted items they sold.

They needed more of the hand-dipped candles. Halloween was next month, after all. Orange, purple, lime green, white, and black. She jotted the colors down, made a note to inquire about seasonal votives. Two of the smaller art prints had sold this week, too. She shuffled papers, found the one she wanted. One had been Alex's. The other had belonged to a college student. A check would have to be cut and sent, another piece requested –

"Are you going to go away?" she snapped, glaring at him.

"I figured that I'd give you a target to hit, sugar. I think you need one."

Gripping her pencil in both hands, she scowled at him. Who was he to say that? She never hit anyone, even when she wanted to. All she needed was to be left alone, dammit. Why couldn't he get that? Why couldn't they all get that? She didn't need or want any of the hovering, plaguing her with the same damn question every damn time she turned around –

There was a sharp snap of wood. She looked down at the broken pencil in her hands, then promptly burst into tears. Even as she sobbed, shock flooded through her. She never cried. Ever. At least, not in front of other people.

Nate got up without a word, fetched napkins from the condiment stand. He laid them down on the table as Teri attempted to get herself under control. Grabbing a fistful of the napkins, she buried her face in them and just breathed. She didn't see Lys' concerned visage as she stood at the register, or the nearest patrons peering over to see what was wrong. She hadn't a clue that Nate had waved them off.

It took her a few minutes to pull herself together. As she mopped the tears away, she felt embarrassment color her cheeks.

"I'm sorry. I don't usually fall apart like that."

"You were due for a break down, sugar." Nate edged a seat to one side, blocking her from the rest of the café as best he could. "You want a drink?"

"No – " She stopped, closed her eyes. "Yeah, thanks. Water."

He went to the bar, spoke to Lys. When he came back, he set to a cold bottle in front of her.

"Some things happen," he began in quiet voice. "You can't stop them, can't change them, and they hurt. They leave wounds on the heart, sugar, ones that got to be cleaned before they can heal. If you just cover they up, they only fester. It can make you sick."

She studied his face as she opened her water. He had a point.

"You sound like you've been there, done that," she murmured. He smiled at her. It didn't reach his eyes.

"Sugar, I'm over two hundred years old. You don't live that long without getting a little wounded. You feel better?"

"A little." Her chest didn't feel so tight. Funny how she hadn't really noticed it until it was gone. "It's just – he was like a nephew to me. I was friends with his mom, but we weren't as close as Chris and I were."

"You like kids." His golden eyes seemed to stare through her a moment, then went thoughtful. "You'd probably make a great mom yourself."

"Well, there's something missing from that particular equation." She held up her left hand, wiggled her bare ring finger. Then she slumped forward on the table, began turning the water bottle in idle circles. "I'll miss him. I miss him now."

"You'll remember him long after most others have forgotten him. Sugar, don't you think that it means something? You'll have his memory, and a piece of him, with you for the rest of your life."

"Yeah."

"Ah. Here comes the rest of the gang."

She looked up to see Richard and Lys heading toward them, with one of their part-timers now manning the counter. Richard, she noted, kept giving Nate the gaze of eternal death. Great. Now she had to play referee, too.

"Teri, are you all right?"

"I'm fine," she answered Lys' query. "I just broke the pencil and had a crying jag, is all." She turned to Nate. "Sorry, I was bitchy."

"Sugar, you weren't bitchy."

He was sincere, she realized. It made her feel that much better.

"Are you sure that you're okay?"

"Yes, Richard, I'm fine." What was with him? "Nate's just offered himself as my punching bag should I need one. Um, could I wheedle a small chicken sandwich from you? I think I may have an appetite now."

"That's good." His lips curved at the news. "I'll get right on that." They watched him go.

"While he's doing that, I think I'll buy me a water of my own." Nate got up. "You're doing good, sugar."

As he walked away, Lys took his place at the table.

"Since it's just us girls, what really happened?"

"I was bitchy. I guess I was bottling things up too much. Nate came to check on me, I snapped at him. Then I broke the pencil and started crying." She ran her fingers under her eyes. She could still feel the tear tracks. "It was mortifying. He didn't make me feel like an idiot, though. No pampering, no crowding, no panicking. He just..." She groped for a suitable word. "Understood."

"Good." She smiled. "I like him. He's sweet."

"His father's a vampire."

"So?"

Teri laughed. Lys had never been the type to care about race.

"Yeah, he's sweet." She picked up a fresh napkin, blew her nose. "He calls me 'sugar.'"

"I'd noticed. He calls me 'ms. Barinton.'" She rolled her eyes. "I think that's because of Richard. He's been touchy lately."

"Yeah. What's up with that?"

"The situation maybe." She chewed her lip, considering. "He's worried about us. I mean, the paranormal stuff that Alex gets into doesn't normally touch us. Now it has. He's trying to deal with it in his own way."

"Maybe." She remembered the conversation between Alex and Richard that morning. "Maybe."

Alex and Michael arrived at their destination half an hour before it closed. *Custom Jewelry by Ormond.* Finding it had been an education for Alex. She hadn't realized how ignorant she was of the Northside part of town.

Her Hunts tended to lead to her to the seedier areas, the ones where the shop owners had bars on the windows. They were where the buildings show their age, the people keep to themselves, and no one would admit to anything. Whether they were nice or mean, it didn't matter. Retaliation tended to be the biggest fear.

Pecan Park Road was different. Out by the airport, it had a clean store front, clear windows, with bright lights all around it. Security cameras were perched on the eves of the shop. She counted four as they climbed out of her car. Below the center two were the bright gold letters spelling the business' name on the wide glass.

"It's a nice little place," she commented as they approached the entrance. Michael's only reply was to step ahead and open the door for her.

The interior was nice as well, if not flashy. Finished pieces were displayed in glass cases, with a section devoted to ready-to-engrave items. Binders sat on a shelf by the front, holding designs or customization ideas for customers to peruse. A smaller showcase behind the counter displayed loose gemstones, some cut, some raw.

Also behind the counter somewhere was a radio.

"...The National Weather Service has just raised the alert for Monroe, Broward, and Miami-Dade counties. A Hurricane Warning is now in effect with a Hurricane Watch issued for Palm Beach and Martin counties. Watch out for increased traffic volumes along the major highways as folks will be fleeing Hurricane Janice..."

Alex suppressed an inward wince as she listened the rest of the report. As things stood now, Jacksonville was at the farthest edge of a Tropical Storm Watch. That, as the announcer went on to say, was likely to change at the rate Janice was going.

When had she become a hurricane? She hadn't known that there'd even been a named system out in the Atlantic.

"Oh, sorry, about that." A bespectacled little man came out of the back, the overhead lights glinting off of his bald head. "I heard the jingle but had my hands full. What can I do for you today?"

"Paul Ormond?" At the man's nod, Michael continued. "I'm Michael Keegan. We spoke over the phone earlier."

"Oh, yes! You were wanting me to look at a necklace, correct?" He fished a cloth from a counter drawer to spread on top of the case in front of him. Michael laid the pendant and chain on it. "Well, I can tell you now that it's good work. Not the normal style for these things.." He examined the anchor-like piece closely. "No jeweler's stamp. I'd have to test it to tell you how pure the metal is. I'm afraid that the absence of a stamp indicates that it's not likely to be pure silver. It could be solid nickel, or some other cheap base metal with silver plating."

"It's really the style of the pendant we're interested in, Mr. Ormond. You recognize the shape?" Alex smiled at him. "It's been driving me crazy, trying to figure out what it is. I've seen it before, yet can't place it."

"Well, they are fairly common. It's Thor's Hammer." He turned it over in his hands. Alex resisted the urge to smack her forehead. "I've made a few of them over the years, though not recently. Most have more bulk than this one. See how it's thin and flat? The ones I'm familiar with are thicker, heavier, a fully three dimensional shape. Still, it's a pretty piece."

"How easy would it be to acquire a Thor's Hammer pendant like this one?" Michael tapped the tail of the chain still on the cloth.

"Very. They're all over the internet. Novelty shops sometimes carry them. I'd wager that all renaissance fairs sell them." He put it back down on the cloth. "Were you looking to have it appraised?"

"No." Michael glanced into the case to his right. "I would like to see that piece, however."

"Of course. I can engrave the back of it for you…"

As he and shopkeeper talked, he handed the necklace to Alex. A tilt of his head toward the door had her rolling her eyes. What was he buying that she couldn't see it? Squelching her curiosity, she marched out to the car. Having finally identified the jewelry, she was in the mood to accommodate him anyway.

Thor's Hammer. Grinning, she did a little jig in the parking lot. PASAC would have listings for that. Norse mythology and folklore would be the key, or so she hoped.

Please don't let this be a red herring.

By the time Michael joined her, she was seated in the Oldsmobile, listing all the books she had with Nordic themes. It gave her something to do. Glancing over at him, she didn't see a package or little box.

"Did you buy something?"

"I did."

"What was it?" She flashed him a smile when he cocked an eyebrow at her. "I'm nosy."

He seemed amused.

"It's for later. You'll find out then. For the moment, it's back to your apartment, and your database."

As Alex started up the car, she tossed the necklace in his lap.

"I have a good feeling about this one."
"So do I."

53

Vengeance.

It was sweet like the honeyed mead of home, intoxicating and as satisfying as...as...

It couldn't remember.

True satisfaction had become a foreign concept, something it had not felt in a long, long time. Centuries. Had it experienced it before its hideous transformation? The memories were vague ghosts in its mind. It barely recalled the period of its existence when it had once been human.

Satisfaction, pleasure, happiness – perhaps it would feel it all again when the amulet was in its hands. Maybe it would taste them when the turbulent power it was amassing poured into the talisman and melted it to nothing. Possibly. Hopefully.

It didn't know what hope was.

The door opened as the rain pelted down around it, on it. It ignored the drenching. Soaked to the skin, it watched as three people came out of the building. It had been watching since before the storm had broken overhead.

First, it had hidden in the shrubs, amid the cars of the parking lot, observing from those vantage points until the last of the customers had driven away. It had seen the girl from the previous night working at a table, the counter. She'd been pale for most of the day. Grief-stricken. Fearful. It could almost smell those emotions when she had broken down earlier, like a lingering perfume in the air.

The scent had it salivating.

The café was now closed up, the four having exited the back to climb into the only mechanical beast there, a thing called a 'sports utility vehicle.' Four. It's eyes narrowed suspiciously, shoving the hungry craving clawing at its stomach aside for the moment. What was he, the stranger? The master had shown it pictures of those who worked at the cafe. This one was not one of them, yet there he was, helping to close up shop, leaving with them. He was not like them, yet was not like the other man – the man that was not a man. The Unknown. Caution. It had to be cautious.

The girl was who it wanted. It might have chanced taking her with the other two there. The third – no. It could not risk itself, not with the goal – its goal – so near completion.

The girl had the amulet.

It had killed again, before coming here. The form it wore now was that of a young woman, plain-faced and anonymous, It would not be recognized. Still, it waited until they were all inside the moving contraption before creeping up behind it. The engine started up. Moving much faster than anyone could believe, it threw itself at the rear bumper. Grabbing hold, it hooked itself up and under the SUV. Its hand and foot holds were tenuous at best. It was be strong, though. It would keep its grip.

The mechanical contraption backed out of the parking slot, moved onto the road. With heat from the exhaust burning into the flesh, the pavement passing quickly beneath it, it shoved the slim frame of its form against the undercarriage. It grinned.

Teri made the turn that took them off Baymeadows Road. Richard and Lys sat in the back seat of her Ford Explorer, holding hands in silence. Nate Forge sat in the front passenger seat, scowling at the sky whenever thunder rumbled overhead. No one spoke.

Teri tried to concentrate on driving. It hadn't begun to rain in this part of town yet, but it would soon. She refused to think of what might be happening when it did. She was having a hard enough time as it was trying to figure out what they were going to do, about the café, about the creature. Not to mention her house…

How long would the police keep it as a crime scene? They had only said that they would contact her when it was released. Even then, she wasn't sure that she could stand living there anymore. She kept seeing Chris in her mind's eye, then the monster that had stolen his image and his life.

God.

"Easy, sugar." Nate murmured the words beside her. "We're almost there."

"Yes." Almost to Alex's. She shoved the memories away, took

a steadying breath.

She braked at a stop sign, waiting for a car to pass through the intersection. Nate leaned forward, bracing himself against the dash as he stared at the storm overhead.

"I swear that it's following us," he said suspiciously. "Those clouds look they're moving with the vehicle. That's not natural."

"None of the storms of late have been," Richard pointed out from the rear. "They've been connected to that – thing."

Nate unbuckled his belt to twist around in the seat. He peered through the windows as Teri sent the Explorer on its way again. She had a bad feeling. All she wanted to do now was get to their safe haven for the night.

Finally, they came to the tiny sign that indicated the entrance of the apartment complex. Teri slowed, turned, going over the first large speed bump in the narrow road carefully. She heard something hit the underside of the SUV towards the rear. Gritting her teeth, she slowed down even more, glancing in the rear view mirror.

Then stopped the vehicle abruptly, pitching everyone forward, as shock flooded her.

There was large patch of red on the speed bump.

"Teri, what are you doing?" Lys squeaked out as she tugged on her seat belt. The thing had gone taut, cutting into her neck.

Teri just stared into the mirror. Nate turned the rear view a bit so that he could see. He hissed, a vaguely cat-like sound. It broke through her stunned stupor. Shaking, Teri put the Ford in park and fumbled with the door latch. Had she run over an animal? Someone's pet? Oh, God, she hoped not.

"Stay in the car." He barked out the order, causing her to freeze. "Keep driving."

"But – " she protested. "If – "

"Teri, don't. It could be anything, it could be nothing. Do you want to risk your life because you think it's a dog when it's really that fiend?" His golden eyes seemed to glow orange with intensity. "Drive. We'll be safe enough when we get into Hidden Reaches."

Her shoulders slumped. He was right. She shifted gears,

touched the gas, yet wouldn't go any faster than a crawl. Another speed bump loomed just ahead; she wanted to be sure that they didn't hit it going over. She turned the wheel slightly just before the bump passed under the front bumper, taking it at an angle.

Again something under the rear of the Explorer hit.

Lightning flashed over to the side of the SUV, followed by a deafening crack. Startled, she let out a small shriek. Nate ignored both her and the storm, staring out the back window with narrowed eyes.

"Keep going," he ordered. "We'll be within the threshold of the Reaches after the third bump. We can check the undercarriage then. For God's sake, Teri, speed up. Please."

Swallowing at the bite in his voice, she continued down the lane at a faster clip than before. When they came upon the third speed bump, she again took it an angle, slowing only slightly for better control. As before, something hit. Unlike before, there was an explosion of sound.

She slammed on the brakes. The squeal of the tires was lost in the cacophony. Shoving the shifter in park, she turned around to stare at the kaleidoscope of colored light sparking outside the rear the Ford.

Now she heard the screaming.

It was high, impossibly shrill, utterly inhuman. It hurt to hear it. She covered her ears with her hands and saw that everyone else was doing likewise. Nate was wincing in pain, pressing the side of his body into the back of his seat.

"Move the car!" Richard yelled from the rear. "Get us out of here!"

Teri immediately reached for the shifter and the steering wheel. She regretted it. Pain pierced her eardrums like stilettos, driving into her brain, lancing down her spine. She struggled against it, fumbling for the vehicle's controls. Seconds of agony ticked by like an eternity before she put it in gear and gunned the engine. The SUV shot down the road recklessly.

Fat drops of water splattered on the windshield, thrown by the wind that came up out of nowhere to shove at the automotive. A violent gust nearly sent it off the road. Wrenching the wheel hard, Teri avoided hitting a palm tree only to come within a hair of driving into the fence on the other side of the road. The wind then seemed to vanished. More rain came down, thick, fast, and heavy. Visibility was cut drastically.

Teri couldn't bring herself to take a hand off the wheel to flip the switch for the wipers. Nate, bracing himself against the dash, leaned over to do it for her.

The screaming, thankfully, didn't follow them. She slowed down as they rounded a curve, then stopped the Explorer. They could still hear it in the distance. Fortunately, it didn't hurt anymore.

"What was that?" she asked, her voice raw.

"It – it l-l-looked like a-a girl. A young woman," Lys stammered, almost sobbing. "Oh, God."

"The monster," Teri murmured, feeling so utterly helpless and vulnerable. "Why did it scream?"

"Hidden Reaches," Nate's grim voice was harsh. "That was the threshold. It can't get past it. Nothing bad can."

"How – how did it get here?" Lys asked. Richard answered before anyone else could.

"All I can think of is that it rode under the car." As prompt as his reply was, his voice shook. "I – We need to get to Alex's."

"Yeah." Heart hammering, Teri numbly shifted gears again to resume driving.

55

The Master watched as the servant writhed on the ground. It convulsed like a fish on the asphalt, clawing its way to the side of the road, dragging itself out of the entrance of the Hidden Reaches. It really was a pathetic sight to behold.

Amazing, he thought, just how bloody the creature had gotten from a few collisions with the huge speed bumps. The jeans and blouse were torn, the wild mousy hair was matted. Its eyes had that fever-bright look of an animal pushed over the edge by pain. Even from where he stood across the way, standing in the shadows of a few trees, he could see the skin beginning to mottle in grotesque colors. He supposed that someone could mistake it for bruising. It was actually the prelude to the servant's shift back into its neutral shape.

"Let's see..." He paused as he gauged the time on the watch. "It's had that form for only eight and a half hours. The protections on the place must be formidable indeed to have it changing back before the third day."

Soon, that wouldn't be an issue for the thing he had used all this time. It could feel the presence of its coveted amulet anywhere in the city – or could when he allowed it. Once it attained its goal, it would no longer be restricted in its forms, its power.

Would it return here to test its regained strength against the Reaches? He considered as he took out the prepaid cell phone he brought with him with a gloved hand. No. It would seek to destroy the one thing that was its greatest threat first. He would have to do some research, perhaps some recruiting or acquisitioning, before attempting to breech the Reaches himself.

He punched three numbers, waited for the other end to pick up.

"911 Dispatch, what is your emergency?"

"There's a woman injured on the side of Bayberry Road, about halfway between Baymeadows Road and Phillips Highway. I don't know how badly hurt she is." He smiled thinly as his former slave continued to screech as it writhed. "I can't get close enough to see. She's charged me a few times."

"She charged you?"

"Like a raving mad bull. She's covered in blood. You can see it from across the street." He watched as the creature curled into a fetal position. Its screams had devolved into harsh sobbing now.

"I've got officers and paramedics on the way. Can I get your name, sir?"

He hung up, tossed the phone into the bushes, then walked away.

Time slid by in a haze of pain. A thought crawled through the fog in its mind that it needed to move, to get up. It needed to heal. It could do it quickly now. The master had taught it how.

It heard the rumble of an engine. Other sounds joined it. Voices. It cracked one lid open, saw a blurred version of a box like machine on wheels. It closed the eye, opened it again. A spark of recognition flared in the fading memories of the woman whose life it had taken and assumed.

An ambulance. That was significant. People rode in them. Anticipation stirred, coiling like a serpent. Yes, it could use that.

It let itself go lax as several men approached. It was touched, its wounds inspected. The sky rumbled, the wind picked up. It sensed the movement and sound more than felt it. That, too, could be used.

It listened as it was loaded onto a stretcher for transport. They wanted to take it to a hospital for treatment. It felt itself being lifted and shoved into the back of the vehicle, heard the paramedics climb in after it. There were two here. A third would be driving it. The sirens came on, the ambulance began to move. It opened its eyes as the men continued to check its vitals.

"Ma'am, you just hang in there," one assured it. "We're gonna get you to a hospital."

They would never get there.

57

"I should have recognized it. Why didn't I?"

Michael sighed as Alex, once again, berated herself. He understood by this point that the question was rhetorical so it didn't require an answer. What he didn't understand was why she kept asking it.

"Alex, please."

"Sorry."

They were in her apartment, with an angry sky outside making itself known now that sunset had passed into night. Alex sat at the computer, running the PASAC database through its paces. He sipped tea while he browsed through the books in the living room to kill time as they waited for the search results.

"Well, the third round is in."

"How unmanageable is it?"

The problem they were encountering was that, as the jeweler had said, Thor's Hammer was a very common item. Nordic myths, legends, folk lore, archeological treatises – all of them featured Thor's Hammer in some way. Thor, it seemed, had been a very popular god. That made his hammer, Molnjir, just as prevalent.

"Not too. Okay, so this bunch has been refined to entries on the hammer itself and its use as a warding agent," Alex began. "What took so long is that the Molnjir icon didn't just take the shape of an actual hammer or amulet shaped as one. It's also featured in carvings, metal works, and leather."

"What about the shape-shifting killer we're after?" He studied the list over her shoulder. It was still longer than he liked.

"That's a problem." She angled her chair away from the screen towards him. "I can't enter it into the criteria because that term isn't used. I want to say that there were several terms used for different types of shape-shifters for this culture. Don't quote me on that, though. We're going to have to look that up separately – which is what this window is doing." She pointed to a smaller window on the monitor. It displayed the words "Searching...Please Wait."

He stared at the words, sipped his tea, dug into his memories. He had, at some point in the distant past, spent time among the Germanic tribes of Europe. Most of them, particularly in the north, were associated with the Nordic beliefs and traditions.

"What was Sigfreid called?" He rubbed the side of his nose as he concentrated. "A berserker? They took on bestial attributes in battle."

"What we're after hasn't taken animal form that we know of, though." She frowned as she considered. "I could do a search for it if you want."

"Give me a minute."

They'd worn skins into battle. Some of them had worn nothing else. Frothing at the mouth, flailing their weapons with surprising precision, they would charge the enemy. It had been intimidating, startling. Yet she was right; they didn't fit. Berserkers didn't hold the kind of cunning and deceit that their quarry used.

That wasn't the only thing that could come close, however. A vague recollection from the early Viking age began to surface. Then the front door burst open.

"Alex!"

She rose just as Teri rushed to her, skin white, body shaking.

Richard and Lys followed suit, all three babbling at their friend in a confusion of sound. Michael motioned Nate to follow him as he went into the kitchen.

"What happened?"

Nate wasn't as pale as the others, he noted. He was steady. When he spoke, he dropped the southern drawl he was so fond of using.

"It had taken another form, a woman's. It must have been at the café, waiting for us to leave, but instead of attacking us there, it latched onto the underside of Teri's Explorer." He grimaced. "No one noticed. Don't have a clue as to how it got past me, Michael. I was the last one in."

"It doesn't matter. Go on."

"It matters to me," he muttered. "It rode in through the entrance with us. Then all hell broke loose."

He described the scene that had taken place, how Teri had kept herself together until they'd gotten to the parking lot. That had been where she'd broken. As Nate related the tale, Michael kept a mental ear tuned toward Alex and the group. She gave them assurances, was getting their version of the story.

"So that's it."

It wasn't. It was another problem.

"How likely do you think it might be that someone will see or has seen the creature on the side of the road?"

The half-vampire hissed to himself.

"Point. One I didn't think of." He cursed. "I should have."

"Don't start," he said wearily. "I've heard a lot of that today. We'll deal with it now." He led the way back into the living room and caught Alex's eye. "We're going to see if it's still there. Did you want to stay with them?"

She hesitated. He could see the war in her eyes. Yet she nodded as she glanced at her friends.

"Odds are it won't be there anymore," she stated. "It'll have run off to heal somewhere."

"Probably. We'll check anyway."

They left as she turned back to the others.

It was pouring outside.

Nate slanted his eyes upwards as they trudged through the rain towards the front entrance. The clouds had a strange look to them. Even with the water falling into his eyes, despite the dark, he could make out the hint of color in the sky. It was a bad omen.

"If one touches down, it won't be here."

Nate gave Michael a pointed look.

"And you know this how?"

"A tornado has never entered the premises of Hidden Reaches. One bounced off the boundary some years ago." He peered through the sheets of droplets to the illuminated sign marking the edge of the property. "It's not here."

"Yeah, I see that." He could also see that they weren't the only ones to have come out to poke around the entrance. Under the streetlights, Morgana Lake, was walking towards them from the road, an umbrella shielding her from the worst of the weather. Their English-born land lady was a practical woman, despite the elegant pant suit and fashionable heels she was wearing out in the wet. Nate shook his head as they met, Morgana falling in beside them as they walked back. She was going to ruin those shoes.

"Cops came to the office," she started without preamble. Her voice was crisply British, a sign of her agitation. "An injured woman had been found at the front. Michael, what's going on?"

"Nate."

He took the ball tossed to him, explaining everything a second time.

"They came and went pretty quick, didn't they?" he asked, his summary finished. "Kind of surprised, really. I'd think it would have taken longer."

"Yes, well, it didn't." She muttered an oath as she stepped into a puddle. "These shoes are ruined. Is this thing connected to that package that was left on Alex's doorstep?"

"I believe so," Michael answered. "It's working with someone; we don't have much information on who that someone is."

"What are they after?"

"That's the thing, isn't it?" Nate hopped over a deep puddle, held a hand out for Morgana so she could do the same. "The fiend wants a necklace. The other?" He shrugged.

"Did they take it or was it gone when they left?"

"They took her – it." Her gaze was sober as she looked at Michael. "They were taking it to a hospital."

"They won't get there." He said it softly. Nate felt a wrench of guilt inside. If he had stayed behind to deal with it... Michael flicked his eyes, brilliantly blue, to lock with his.

"Stop. Someone would have died. If not them, you. If not you, someone else. That much is fact." He paused as they reached the walkway leading up to the leasing office. "You have a radio, can you access to the police and emergency channels?"

She nodded.

"Listen for anything that might pertain to this and let me know."

"Alright." She started up the path, then paused, turned back. "How much longer until this is done?"

"I can't say. We're hoping to finish it soon."

"Keep me advised, okay?"

They watched her trot into the office, then trekked through the downpour, heading back to Alex's.

"You can't regret seeing to the protection of others, Nate."

"Hard not to think that if I'd stayed, sent them on ahead of me, that I could have ended it right there." He flicked wet hair out of his face. "They were only doing their job." His voice was bitter. "They were only trying to help a woman in need. Now they're dead."

"I could be wrong."

Nate retorted with something crude. "You don't believe that."

"No, I don't." He placed a hand on Nate's shoulder, one comrade speaking to another. "'What might have been' distracts from 'what is', and the 'what is' is what can kill us all. Remember that, if nothing else."

"Yeah." Yet remembering that didn't vanquish the guilt.

59

The ambulance sat in an empty parking lot, behind a business that had closed earlier in the evening. Wearing the guise of a man in a paramedic's uniform, the creature shut the back doors of the vehicle. Seeing a bit of blood spatter on the back of one hand, it paused to lick it clean. Sated, not wanting to stay out in the open for very long, it went around to the cab, yanked the driver side door open, and climbed in.

It had never driven before. That didn't present a problem. It had three sets of memories to draw upon.

Those memories flowed more easily now. Was the amulet weakening? Maybe. Maybe. It licked its lips, felt its heart leap in its chest. A feeling of elation, of yearning moved through its body in a building surge. Was that hope? Perhaps it was, perhaps it wasn't. Whatever it turned out to be, it reveled in the sensation.

It could be free.

It wasn't free yet. There was the master, the amulet. It had to be rid of both of them to be free. Which to pursue first? The one whose location it already knew.

It turned the ignition, grinning as the engine roared to life.

Gripping the steering wheel, it allowed itself a broad, feral grin. Then it began to drive.

60

September 11, 2004

Alex opened the door, then crept out onto the outside landing as quiet as a mouse before closing it behind her. The chill of the early morning caught her off guard. She hadn't dressed for it. Shivering in her t-shirt and jeans, she rubbed her arms as she traversed the stairs to Michael's apartment.

She knocked on his door, waiting a bit impatiently for him to answer. He did just as she was about to knock again.

"It's not even seven," she muttered without preamble, brushing past him into the warmth of his home. "I haven't even had my first cup of coffee this morning."

Dressed in his customary black, he watched her pace his living room as she groused.

"I have people sleeping in my apartment who kept me up until well past midnight. You – " She pointed an accusing finger at him. " – bailed. Nate wasn't any better, using his monster of a dog as a handy excuse. They kept asking me what they were going to do, as if I had all the answers in the world. I couldn't tell them. They've got a business to run, Nate's got to work his shift this afternoon, we've got a killer to catch, and my agent called last night with a commission for me."

He held up a finger, going into the kitchen. She didn't stop.

"Everyone wants a damn answer. Now I've got to figure all of that out before I go back downstairs." She resisted, barely, the urged to kick at the sofa. Instead, she stared hard at the tapestry hanging above it. "Then you made me get up at a God-awful hour of the morning to discuss the next move."

"Alex."

She turned to see the large mug he offered. The aroma rising from it was heavenly. Her eyes met his.

"Please tell me that's coffee."

He smiled.

"It's coffee."

Taking it, she stepped forward to plant a kiss on his mouth.

"Thanks." She sipped, relishing the caffeine-rich flavor of a good roast. "I'll need about three gallons of this before I'm set."

"The obligations of living often complicate things." The words came out softly. "I'm sorry they are a burden to you."

"I'm just bitchy this morning." She sighed, then drank deeply. "We'll work it out."

"Your friends need to work, yet Nate cannot be there as he was yesterday." He mulled it over as she finished the mug.

"More, please." She tipped it toward him to show that it was empty. He righted it in her hand, a whisper of power moving through the ceramic. When it had faded, it was full again. "Nice trick. I think I may have a solution for the bodyguard gig. I have a contact that I can tap. I can probably set it up this morning. It'll go smoother if I take Nate with me."

He raised an eyebrow in inquiry. She offered him a smile.

"My contact's his father."

"Kent Aisley." He gave her a thoughtful look. "I know him. Not well, though we've worked together a few times in the past."

"Teri and I have known him for years. Since I'm bypassing the normal procedure for a meeting, I'll need Nate with me. Also, since he keeps tabs on the medical community, he might be able to give us a lead on that ambulance."

"Which leaves your friends to me, as they have to be at the cafe." He sounded resigned. She winced.

"Sorry."

He waved off the apology.

"Someone needs to be there until other arrangements can be made."

"I can give you print outs of that list we generated last night. Going through them would give you something to do in addition to the guard duty. I'll call the café if Kent provides that lead."

"I would appreciate it." He reached out to brush his fingertips along her cheek. "When do you leave?"

"As soon as I've got things set with everyone – after I finish my coffee, that is."

"Be careful." He kissed her, slow and easy. "Humor me."

"I can do that."

Elsewhere

He'd fled.

Like the rabbit before the hungry wolf, he had run. Despite the frustration that plagued it, it couldn't stop the toothy smile that creased its face. Still grinning, it sniffed the air delicately. What was that? Fear, anger? Could emotions leave a scent in the air? It had never smelled anything like it before.

It was wonderful.

Intoxicated by the fragrance, what its ability to detect that scent might mean, it cast its gaze around the room. It was clean, neat, tidy. Some of the furnishings had been replaced while others were absent. It marked each change, finding both satisfaction and wrath flowing from the newfound knowledge.

There was so much to do, so much to make clear. The master would pay, as would the people that hurt it. The women, the man. Especially the man.

Thinking of the ebon clad stranger brought on a shiver, the chill of fear. Its fear. What was he? Was he cursed, as it was cursed? Bracing its hands on the dresser it stared into the face of a stranger in the mirror. Memories slid in front of its mind's eye. The coastal village, the rugged terrain, the boats at sea. Conquests, battle, the rape, the pillaging – it hadn't been enough.

Its desires had been answered with a curse, the price, it had been told, for glory. Had the man received the same? It couldn't be sure. The only certainty was that freedom was close at hand.

Soon, very soon, it would be all, have all. Hadn't it been promised that, all those long centuries ago? When it had first become – this?

It turned away from its reflection to move towards the window. With a violent shove, it parted the vertical blinds, scowling at the overcast sky. It could feel the churning, the power that surged through clouds. The flow was weakening. Too soon, the clouds would lighten in color and drift away. The sun would shine through the hours of the day before it was overtaken by night.

To change that, it would have to kill again.

With a darkening mood, it left the room. There was no point in staying. The master was gone, the bill was likely paid. The room would be rented to someone else. Another haven would have to be found. In the meantime, it would scour the city. Its amulet was out there.

Somewhere.

62

Jacksonville, FL

"I can't believe you talked me into this, sugar." Nate's voice was grim as they got out of her car. "We're gonna be lucky if all they do is throw us out."

"They won't." Alex was more confident about this than he was, obviously. She returned the baleful look he shot her with a cheerful one of her own. "Trust me, Nate. It'll be fine."

"As fine as two brand new caskets," he muttered.

"Oh, come on. I wouldn't have asked you if I thought you'd get hurt." She gave him her best please-dear-just-for-me smile. "They're not going to kill us."

"How many vamps have you dealt with?" he demanded.

"Oh, a few." Her nonchalant answer didn't assure him. They weren't in any real danger, something that Nate also knew. His protests were more for form than anything else. They could still get kicked out, maybe even banned, she mused. It wasn't likely, though.

There was a bit of risk involved when dropping in on a vampire conclave unannounced, however. Vampiric guards tended to attack first, then dispose of the corpse when caught unawares. That was especially true of the youngest in the ranks.

They'd parked the car in a grassy lot behind their destination. The gray cinderblock building looked ordinary enough. It was two stories, lacked windows, and could use a new coat of paint, squatting on the corner of East Church and Parker. The business housed here was a legitimate one. Kent had started his printing company, Aisley Printing, in 1959, operating it out of the same location he had started it in. It was also the central meeting place of his conclave.

There was only one glass door at the front. She could see a single female behind a desk, with two males – guards, presumably – loitering nearby. They entered the lobby, pausing just inside the entrance for the receptionist and company to give them a visual once over. Nate approached the desk to speak quietly with them. Alex remained where she was, giving a nod when any of the group looked her way. One of the men gestured to the receptionist who picked up the phone to speak to yet another person as they continued to wait.

Protocol. It was tedious as it was necessary.

From the depths of the inner offices came the vampire lord himself. He wore a charcoal suit today, she noted, without a tie. Long black hair, amber eyes, perfect skin marred only by an old scar on his chin acquired before his Turning. For a vampire who had spent many lifetimes traversing the world and fighting in it, he looked no older than his son.

A cool smile curved his lips, but there was warmth in his eyes when he spotted her. He inclined his head, then turned a mild, questioning gaze toward Nate. She could only imagine what kind of speculation was running through the vampire lord's mind.

"Alexandria. Nate." A faint English accent was evident in his voice. *Like father, like son.* Both seemed to be fond of affecting accents.

"Lord Aisley," she said in greeting. "Thank you for taking the time to see us."

He gestured for them to follow, leading the way through a maze of corridors, stairs, and offices to his own on the second floor.

Walls painted a soft white, wooden furniture, floral arrangements on the bookcases, a neat stack of magazines his company had printed up on the antique mahogany desk, deep green carpet on the floor. The prints on the walls were lithographs of artists. She smiled to see the piece she'd given him years ago among them. It was one of the very few non-fantasy pieces she'd ever done, depicting a rugged mountain landscape.

"You know, as nice as this office is, Kent, it would drive me crazy if I had to work in it."

"So you always say." Kent Aisley chuckled as he seated himself behind the desk. He waved them toward the chairs in front of it. "I trust you've been well, Alex?"

"Very." She gave him an impudent grin. "Though I'm afraid poor Nate's likely to clobber me. I didn't tell him we'd met before."

"Ah." Kent's eyes narrowed thoughtfully, darting between the two of them. "I don't suppose the two of you are here to tell me something of – personal significance, are you?"

"No, sire," Nate answered before she could, dropping his usual country accent. The look he shot her way told her exactly what he wanted to do to her. 'Clobbering' was a mild description. She winked, grinning impishly before she turned back to Kent.

"I asked Nate to intercede for me since it would be easier than dancing around for two days," Alex said briskly. "I'm here on two counts, one personal, one professional – and not my art."

"Of course. Business first." Kent relaxed back into his seat. "Not any trouble from my conclave, I trust."

"No, it's coming from a different quadrant altogether." She pursed her lips. Where to begin? "Much as I hate to say it, we haven't been able to find out much about it, let alone what it is. Other than a murdering nuisance, of course."

That sent an elegant eyebrow winging up. "An ignorant hunter? With all the Chronicles the Guild keeps?"

She made a face at him. "Don't make it worse than it already is. You've got connections throughout the medical community."

He nodded cautiously, eyes now slightly wary.

"Do those connections extend to ambulatory services?"

"Why?"

"Because the creature that we're pursuing was badly injured last night. Someone called for an ambulance. I need to know what happened to that ambulance." She met his eyes squarely, saw something flicker in them. "Odds are good that the paramedics are dead. It's probably running around looking like one of them right now."

"Tell me everything, from the beginning."

He listened as she related the sequence of events, raising an eyebrow when her partner's name was mentioned. He restrained from speaking until she was finished.

"I've worked with him before. He doesn't run with partners as a general rule."

"There's a first time for everything." She shrugged. "Anyway, now it's targeting people close to me."

"Teri?" Kent's eyes went hard, tense. "Your family?"

"Teri, not my family. They're fine, Kent, for the moment, at least." She rubbed her right temple wearily. "This is where the personal thing comes in. Michael and I can't pursue this thing and guard them at the same time. Nate's helped where he can…"

"Yet cannot be there all the time. The protection you are entitled to." Kent caught the inquisitive look on his son's face. "I've told you some of this. Teri is who the others call the Prayer Lady."

"Really?" He looked intrigued. "I'd thought she was a nun or something. How did this come about?"

"It began when Alex was in high school. There was a car accident – "

"Oh, Lord, you're not going to tell him the whole thing, are you?" Alex groaned.

The vampire shrugged.

"She had just broken up with her boyfriend at the time – "

"He wasn't a boyfriend," she muttered.

"If he wasn't a boyfriend, then what was he?" Nate asked.

The description she gave him left his ears burning and Kent

chuckling.

"After the break up, she wasn't paying too much attention to her driving – " he continued, only to be interrupted a second time.

"*I* wasn't paying attention? If you're going to tell the story you had better tell it right. *You* weren't looking where you were going."

"I was minding my own business," he told Nate, as if Alex hadn't said a word, "I was crossing the street when she came around the corner. She hit me."

"You hit him?" Nate gave Alex an incredulous look.

"Direct hit. I had an impression of his too-pretty face on the hood of my car." She grinned at him. "I was freaking out because I thought I'd killed someone, then realized what he was. I told him off for not watching for traffic."

"After that, she insisted on taking me home." Kent chuckled as Nate shook his head. "I'm afraid I had completely misunderstood when she offered the ride."

Alex snickered. "I took him home alright – *my* home. Frank, my mentor in the Hunters' Guild, patched him up. Teri just happened to be there, too, and decided to exorcise him."

Nate burst out laughing.

"It was – an unusual experience," Kent said dryly. He smiled. "Definitely not pleasant, but not what it could have been, either. It was the result that interested me. The blood craving is no longer anywhere near what it once was. Life, such as it is, has been much easier for me since. Teri has been able to reduce the craving in others among the conclave, as well – any willing to undergo the exorcism, that is."

"Ah. Hence the entitlement." Nate nodded.

"Just so." He leaned back in his chair, looking at Alex. "I can have the arrangements made in a few hours. Where are your friends now?"

"The café." She hesitated a moment. "You have a network of informants on the streets."

"I do, yes."

"Would it be possible for you to pass on anything that may be pertinent to our hunt? Things like, oh, storm locations, unusually violent or highly suspicious murders, theft of magical artifacts. Eye witness accounts. That sort of thing."

"That shouldn't be a problem." He flicked a glance at his son. "Give us a minute."

"I'll be in the lobby."

Kent studied Alex intensely as he left.

"Michael is more than a partner," he stated, his voice soft.

"Yes, he is." Alex felt just the tiniest trickle of guilt. Kent was a good ally, a good friend. They'd dated briefly and she was aware that his feelings had run more deeply than hers. "I'm sorry, Kent."

"There is nothing to be sorry for. The heart is a willful thing, Alex." He smiled wanly. "Take it from someone who has lived centuries and learned the hard way. So he is the one." Kent sighed, closing his eyes in a kind of serene resignation. "You will not cast aside friends or allies for him."

"Not now, not ever. Nor will I ask the same of him."

He nodded. When he opened his eyes, they were clear, warm, and just a bit sad.

"You will always be welcome here. You will also tell me if he hurts you."

"Thanks." She gave his hand a squeeze, then decided to change the mood. In a teasing tone, she said, "You never told Nate about me."

He flashed her a smile, with only a hint of his fangs.

"Well, now, there are just some things a father doesn't need to tell his grown son, until a certain point has been reached."

63

Michael sat at a table towards the back of the café, two stacks of papers in front of him. He took another page from the smaller stack, studied it. Frowning, he made notations in the notebook to his right before placing the page on top of the larger stack. He had repeated this process since the beginning of the café's mid-shift.

He looked up every time a customer came through the door, yet didn't notice when Lys placed a coffee at his elbow as he pored over the print outs. Without referencing a clock or watch, he broke from the routine every forty-five minutes to patrol the café. He ignored Richard's speculative looks, kept his exchanges with Lys to a minimum, and only occasionally spoke to Teri. When he noticed the coffee – one of several that been given to him unasked for – he slipped the money for it to Richard before taking his 'walk' around the perimeter.

It was almost time to take that walk again. He finished going over the entries on one more page, intending to do his duty afterwards. Something on the paper caught his attention.

The cursed hamrammur: a shape-shifter of the Icelandic berserker tradition that was cursed for his ambition and greed by the Nordic gods.

There was a reference to a little known folktale. The brief summary lacked too much detail to go on. Still, Michael's blood had begun to hum, the way it did when he scented prey. This was it. He circled the entry, jotted down a reminder to have Alex contact the Guild Library in that region. No sooner than he had finished the note than Alex herself walked in.

She was in good spirits, so he could safely assume that she had been successful in securing bodyguards for her friends. Nate came in behind, looking more relaxed than he had when they'd left. It was Kent, following his son, that surprised him. He hadn't anticipated the vampire lord venturing out at this time of day.

Alex waved to her friends, stopped at the register to speak to Lys. Nate and Kent nodded their way, as they joined him at the table.

"It's been an interesting morning," Nate drawled. "How's yours been?"

"Productive. I may have found the reference we need to catch the creature." He flicked his gaze to Kent. "I would have thought a lackey or two would be here, not you."

"Nice to see you, as well, Michael." The dry reply had his mouth quirking up. "The only lackeys I've available at the moment are old school, not willing to venture out during an overcast day with only clouds and sunscreen for protection against the sun. That will change in about three hours."

"I've called out from work. Family emergency," Nate put in. "I'd thought about doing it earlier, but, well…" He shrugged. "I'll probably get written up for the trouble. It'll wash, though, when I go to HR."

"I don't see why you bother working there." His father's frowning statement had the half-vamp grinning.

"I love that silver screen."

"Since you're off, you can be in charge of Teri's protection." Michael laid the single page on the notebook, then combined the rest of the print outs into a single stack to be disposed of later. "She's the one the thing's gone after twice."

"You're certain it's Teri."

"Yes." He glanced up as Alex took a seat beside him. "It's looking for a necklace, an amulet. It believes that Teri has it."

"She did, the first time it went for her." Alex scooted his notes around so she could read them. "Iceland…that's Nordic. Settled by the Vikings. I think the regional Guild Library is in the capitol there." She smiled at him. "Very cool."

Warmth spread through him under her approval. He squeezed her hand once before releasing it. Reaching into his pocket, he brought out the silver jewelry piece, laying it on the table for everyone to see.

"We know this is significant. How, in what way, why – those are things we'll find in that Guild reference."

"It'll take time to get it. The request has to be put in, it has to be found, then sent over. I'll see about having it faxed or e-mailed as that's quickest." Alex nibbled on her bottom lip thoughtfully. Michael found it mildly distracting. "It seemed to be able to track this amulet, though. Can we lure it out somewhere? Trap it?"

"This isn't the original; it's a replica. Once it gets a good long look at it, it may not even try for it."

"Hmm." Kent picked it up, turning the pendant over in his hands. "There's not a great deal of power to it. It feels older than it is, has a certain 'flavor', we'll say, but that won't hold for any longer than it would take for the creature pick it up."

"It's held it before," Alex murmured, thinking back to the attack at Teri's house. "We were fighting it, so it didn't have time to take notice of anything wrong with it."

"A trap would be a one-shot deal." Nate stretched his arms over his head as he thought aloud. "Not sure if we could set that up safely with what we have. So, here's another idea: it can track the amulet. Can we use the amulet to track it?"

Kent looked at the necklace, then at Michael.

"It might be possible," he said finally. "I have no idea how accurate it would be."

"Right now, the tracking method we have is the weather. It's not all that accurate, either," Alex pointed out.

"I'm not certain that it's feasible. It's a clone." Michael nodded towards the necklace. "The copy isn't associated with the creature, only the original. We'd be better off looking for that. Once we have the real amulet, we should be able to trace it."

"The rules of associative magic." The hunter gave a wry smile. "I'm afraid that this isn't really my arena, folks. I'm not that much of a mage."

"I can work with this." Kent re-wrapped the necklace in its silk cloth, pocketed it. "I'll call you when I've got something that may work."

"I guess we'll try hunting the old-fashioned way. There's nothing like driving around the city and looking for clues." Alex's amiable tone belied the futility of the endeavor-to-be.

They might get lucky, Michael thought. If there was a storm. Still...

"I have a starting point for us." He turned to Nate. "The café's all yours."

Nate gave a mock salute. Then he dug into his pocket to bring out a key. Handing it to Alex, he made a request of his own.

"If you happen to stop by Hidden Reaches, do me a favor and check on Ivan, would you?"

"Sure. Give me a few minutes to contact the Guild and get the ball rolling on this bit before we take off." She took the key, then the sheet of paper. "What's our starting point?"

"The Sea Turtle Inn. The ambulance was found in its parking lot. It was on the news."

Teri looked up from the paperwork she was filling out at the bar in time enough to see Alex wave on her way out. Kent came to her side with his son trailing behind him. He placed a comforting hand on her shoulder.

"Teri, you are well?"

"As well as I can be." She sighed. "I just want this whole deal over with. Are you helping Alex now?"

"Yes. Nate will continue his bodyguard duties for now. I will have others here shortly to aid in that." He hesitated a moment. "I don't suppose that you would consider closing the café for the interim?"

To her embarrassment, the suggestion had her eyes stinging with tears. It was her café. Right then, it was the calm center in her emotional turmoil. The vampire lord said nothing as she fought them back.

"I don't want to." The words came out in an intense, low tone.

"We may have to, Teri." Lys came up to the counter, a black coffee in hand. She handed the mug to Nate. "Have you seen the weather reports recently?"

She shook her head.

"Hurricane Janice – you did hear about it?" Her expectant look was met with a blank one from Teri. "There's a hurricane. Right now, it's stalled off shore around West Palm Beach. They expect it to continue up the coast sometime tonight. If it moves at the same speed it had before it stalled, they say it'll be parallel to us in about two days."

Teri sat silent, her mind jumbled. Then she tilted her head up to study the ceiling. She had to decide, didn't she? She wasn't the only one who owned the business but she was the store manager. Their employees would be relying on her to give them time to be with their families, to flee the city if necessary.

It wasn't just about her or the damn amulet.

"We'll try for one more day, depending on the storm. I'll check on it in the morning, make the calls from Alex's if we're closing. We'll need to board up the front."

"Richard's already calling places about plywood." Lys offered a sheepish smile which faded as she remembered. "Oh. We'd need to pick it up, bring it back…"

"You'll have an escort when you do," Kent reassured her.

"God, sorry. I forgot my manners." Teri rubbed her forehead. A slight headache was beginning to brew. "Kent, this is Lys Barinton. Lys, this is Kent Aisley, head of the local vamp conclave."

"Hi." Lys gave him a smile tinged with curiosity. "Would you like some coffee or tea? Or is that something that you can't have? I'm afraid I don't know much about vampires."

"Thank you, no, though I do drink tea. I leave the coffee to Nate and Alexandria." He swung his gaze back to Teri. "I do need to get going, however. Call me if you need anything, or have Nate do it."

"Thanks, Kent. I appreciate it."

They watched him leave.

"He's cute."

Nate choked on his coffee. Teri blinked, then turned to stare at Lys as he coughed.

"What? Did I just hear that?"

Lys giggled at them both.

"Just because I'm engaged to Richard doesn't mean that I don't notice. He is cute." Her expression became thoughtful. "I wonder if I can get Richard to grow his hair out like that."

"Lys," Teri began firmly. "Do us all a favor. Don't tell Richard and get Nate another coffee." She glanced over at him. "I'll get him some napkins to clean up with."

"Sure." She paused. "Um, I do have a question…"

"Sunscreen."

"Ah."

65

Atlantic Beach, FL

"There's a spot."

Michael pulled into the slot Alex pointed out and cut the engine. He peered around the parking lot as they got out, frowning.

"They've already taken the ambulance away."

"Yeah, I thought they would have since it made the news. It's a conveniently mobile crime scene." She contemplated the hotel as she asked, "Can you detect the creature's scent?"

He said nothing, no doubt casting around with all senses on alert while she waited. Meanwhile, she studied the multi-storied building in front of her. The Sea Turtle Inn was a posh place. She had never been inside the resort hotel. They hosted events, like weddings, and had some sort of spa deal. A room here wasn't cheap.

Hadn't Lys and Richard taken a weekend here once? A kind of mini vacation? It hadn't been too long after they'd gotten engaged. Her friend had gushed over the fancy design of the place –

"It's there. Extremely faint, yet there. It's not definitive enough for me to determine where it leads."

"That figures." She turned away from the building to face her partner. "Tell me something: why would something that, presumably, has no job or income come here?"

"We had speculated that it was working with someone."

"Right..." She chewed her lip as she thought. They had some clues about the killer yet none where its cohort was concerned. Had they based themselves here since day one or had they hopped from one set of lodgings to another?

"The package came from here."

Her train of thought veered off the tracks.

"This place? Huh." Her eyes narrowed. "You had asked if Drake could have sent it."

"Yes."

"Looking at him hadn't been a priority before this. Looks like I'll have to bump it up. This hotel is classy, just his style. A nice, luxurious statement of self-importance," she murmured, mostly to herself. "Showing off. Proving he's better, or trying to."

"My impression of him was of a petty man with a superiority complex."

"It's an apt one."

"You don't want to think he's involved in this." The quiet tone caught her attention. His gaze was unreadable. "Underneath all the negative emotions you harbor for him, you will not believe that it could be him."

She didn't answer right away. She had a feeling that he was talking about the naive girl she had been, the one that had been infatuated with a young Drake Howell. That wasn't the case.

"I don't want it to be him because he is a hunter. Unlike me, he is more of a – a curator, I suppose. He collects arcane artifacts for the Guild when they surface. Still, it doesn't make him any less of a hunter. I would like to think that no hunter would break his vows like this. As for the rest..." She took a deep breath. "Well, I'm biased. I like thinking that he's the scum of the earth, too caught up in himself to be truly worthwhile or capable of anything significant."

"And now?"

"Now I have to consider him as part of it, don't I?" She

grimaced. "We'll need proof, though."

"If he is part of it, we'll find it."

They began to walk towards the building. He reached for her hand as they moved, gave it a gentle squeeze. She smiled at him, then turned her attention to finding someone to talk to.

A few minutes later, they stepped into the lobby. Alex took in the sand-colored furniture, the coordinated carpet, the modern aquatic design. It made her feel as she was in some kind of weird, serene aquarium.

The front desk was busy with people. The sitting areas were filled with men and women dressed in fancy attire, probably from a wedding. The ambulance was the story buzzing on everyone's lips. Mingling with the crowd, it didn't take much effort to draw the tale from several people.

The ambulance had been discovered that morning. There had been bodies in the back of it. No one could say how it had gotten there or when. Those details were the only ones that all accounts had agreed on. The number of dead varied, the visage of the vehicle had multiple descriptions. Reactions went from gruesome fascination to utter fear, which explained why the desk had its hands full of check-outs.

They didn't bother with the hotel personnel or trying to snoop around. The psychic scent of their quarry was so faint that it couldn't have been here for long. That it had brought such attention to the place indicated that it wouldn't be returning for a while, if at all.

Alex checked the time as they climbed back into Michael's car. They'd spent over two hours at the Inn. The sky looked untroubled. Searching now wouldn't get them anywhere.

"Let's head back to my place. Maybe the Icelandic Guild Branch came through with that reference."

"Then we'll eat something. You need to."

"Yeah, that sounds good, too."

It could sense it.

The pull of it was like fine mead, the kind one expected to be served in Vahalla – the kind used to mask poison. It knew it was close. It had to be close for the tug on its awareness to be strong enough to taste.

Taste…

The thought distracted it as it trudged down the sidewalk. The sun was lower in the sky, with only an hour or so before sunset. Street traffic passed by. Pedestrians walked on without so much as a glance at it. It didn't see them, didn't hear them. It couldn't even say where it was, only that there were shops, the scent of the sea in the air, and a few restaurants. It was trying to remember what taste had been like. It despaired when it couldn't.

Once, long ago, it had experienced taste. Honey, spice, vegetables – flavors that weren't raw muscle or fresh blood. It hadn't been aware of this sacrifice when the deal had been struck back then.

Had it asked?

No, it hadn't. It hadn't thought of the cost, only of the prize.

A woman passed him, tugging a small boy behind her as she traveled from one place to another. The child looked at it with wide eyes. The innocent look had it snarling at him. The mother glanced back, saw the expression on its face, and pulled her son closer.

"Come on, Jeffrey. We'll just go and get that ice cream cone for you like I promised."

It turned away from them, mindful of the wariness in the woman's backward glare as they picked up their pace. It hated people. They never held it in awe, even the ones from its own era. It hadn't commanded the respect of a great warrior…

That was why it had this curse now. The Master had been correct in that, at least. People were why it was as it was. He had known so much, yet had learned so little.

It was beginning to think that he was the worst of them.

It stopped that train of thought before it got started. The amulet. That was what was important.

The woman at the café had an amulet. It could hear its distant call across this sprawling city yet it didn't have quite the same pull as what it felt now. Had it been a copy? A fake? Had it broken in two pieces? Was that why it was being tugged in different directions, with one source far closer than the other?

It would have to find both to see.

It paused in front of a bus stop, breathed deep. Closing its eyes, it concentrated on the insidious sensation drawing it in. It was somewhere ahead. Stationary.

Ignoring the curious looks of those waiting for the bus, it took off at a trot. It passed a plaza, rounded a corner onto a side street, slowed. Stopped. It was…getting closer?

A large brown vehicle drove past it. So did the pull.

With a growl it gave chase, eyes fixed on the yellow lettering of the shipping service logo.

Jacksonville, FL

"Feel like a little walk, sugar?"

Teri paused at the steps leading up to Alex's apartment. The sun was setting now, the sky clouding up again. The latest weather report they'd gotten at the café reported that Hurricane Janice was moving again. Three employees had already asked about taking off to make sure their families and homes were safe. She had given in, deciding to close shop for the next few days.

They'd closed early so Lys, Richard, and the two bodyguards that Kent had lent them could fetch the plywood that Richard had purchased over the phone. They would board the place up. It was a job that Teri couldn't help with. Her ribs still twinged with pain if she bent the wrong way. All of it, added to the urge to cry whenever she thought of her house or Chris, made her feel like a failure.

It meant that she wasn't in the mood for things like a walk. What she wanted to do was sulk over a bowl of cookie dough ice cream. It must have shown on her face because Nate gave her an understanding smile.

"I just got to take Ivan out, sugar, that's all."

"Oh." She'd forgotten about the dog. "Alright, fine."

They continued up the stairs. A box and a couple of large brown envelopes sat on Alex's doorstep. Nate placed a restraining hand on Teri's shoulder, then stepped forward to inspect them.

"They're all addressed to Michael."

She frowned, puzzled.

"Then why are they sitting in front of Alex's door?"

"Beats me." He picked them up to hand them to her. "Why don't you take them inside while I get the big, bad dog?"

She did so without much enthusiasm. She put the packages on the dining room table, next to a note from her friend. Apparently she and Michael had gone out for a bite to eat. Wandering into the kitchen, she idly checked the freezer to find it devoid of ice cream. Neither the fridge or the pantry held anything of interest. She felt the disappointed pout form on her face.

It was childish. She was a grown woman with a successful career, a close circle of friends, and good sense. It was not the end of the world that there was no damn ice cream in the damn freezer.

Nate came in, fighting Ivan's insistent yanking on the leash as he did so. He couldn't get further than the foyer.

"Teri?"

She went to him, then stopped to stare at the dog. She had heard of Ivan. He'd been described as a big, friendly dog. She had heard him barking from next door a few times, the baritone sound indicating that it belonged to a large canine. The reality was somehow…more.

Ivan was huge. As big as a St. Bernard with a coat that looked more like a Husky's, he wagged his tail, surging forward to greet her. Nate snagged his collar before he could leap up to give her doggie kisses.

"That is a small horse," she stated, her depression momentarily forgotten. "A pony in dog's clothing."

"Nah, he's just a great big mutt who thinks he's a puppy." He wrestled his dog onto the landing. Teri joined him, eyes still on Ivan.

"What's wrong, sugar?"

She blinked.

"Wrong?"

"You looked bummed when I came in." He released the collar to scratch his roommate's ears. She felt her cheeks warm a little.

"No ice cream," she muttered. Ivan gave a pitiful whine. "We'd better take him down." She began to lead the way to the ground level.

"I've got pecan praline at my place."

She halted, turning narrowed eyes on him.

"Don't toy with me."

"It's almost a full half gallon. Ivan!" The admonishment came after the animal jerked forward on the leash, straining for the bushes by the walkway. "Okay, okay! I get it."

They visited every island of greenery around the complex, letting the overgrown dog enjoy the outdoors a bit. Teri didn't talk much. Instead, she let Nate regale her with anecdotes about his pet. He'd found him at the pound, fell in love, and now suffered being wrapped around Ivan's paw. Some of the stories made her smile a little.

It was dark by the time they came back to the building that her friend called home. She hesitated at the bottom of the stairwell. She had the mail key with her; she might as well check it since she was down there anyway. So saying to Nate, she ducked around the stairs to where the mailboxes were.

An older woman stood shuffling through the bundle of magazines she'd just taken out of the her box. She hummed a jaunty tune as she juggled the mass of glossy paper. It slipped.

"Oh, drat."

The disheveled pile scattered on the ground. The flustered matron glared at them as if they had done it on purpose. Smiling, Teri stepped forward to help her pick them up.

"Why, thank you, dear." She beamed at her. "My back isn't what it used to be, and apparently my grip isn't either."

"You're welcome. I'm Teri Andrews – a close friend of Alex's." She stacked what she'd gathered in a neat pile, then handed it over.

"Oh! Well, nice to meet you, Teri. My name is Edna, Edna Bodsworth. I'm the nosy gossip who lives on the first floor and tries to keep tabs on everyone else." She laughed at her own description, coaxing a chuckle from Teri as she jammed Alex's mail key in the lock. "I'm just fascinated by people."

"Yeah, people can be a weird bunch." Teri took out the mail, absently noting several bills and a letter with no return address. She frowned at the envelope.

"Now, Teri, would you mind terribly if this old woman imposed on you for a small favor?" Edna asked, eyes twinkling. "Just a little one."

"Um, kind of depends on what it is," she replied with a smile. "I try not to make promises I can't keep."

"That's a very good habit, dear." Edna nodded approvingly. "Now, it's really two favors. The second one shouldn't trouble you at all, I don't think. I'll get to that one in a moment. I just wanted to know if Alex really spent the night with Michael earlier this week. I haven't had a chance to corner either of them yet."

"Ah – " Caught off guard by the request, Teri wondered if Alex would want it spread around who she was sleeping with, if she was sleeping with anyone.

"It's a fact that Michael's interested in that girl," Edna went on, fussing with her magazines idly. "Told him to take her out, give her a little gift. Dinner. Flowers. That sort of thing. I'm also certain that he didn't." She sniffed disapprovingly, light blue eyes gleaming. "That man. Do you know what we call him?"

Teri shook her head, bemused.

"The Mystery Man of Hidden Reaches," the older woman announced with a beaming smile. "No one knows much about him on a personal level, you see. He also never works with anyone else yet is always in the thick of things. I haven't heard of him dating anyone. Still, I'm convinced that he's a very sweet man inside." She nodded in smug emphasis. "More to him than what's on the surface. Yes, indeed."

"Well, Mrs. Bodsworth – "

"Oh, just Edna, dear. I haven't been Mrs. Bodsworth around

here for ages."

"Edna. I really think you need to talk to Alex about her relationship with Michael," Teri told her with a small smile.

"Oh, well. Can't blame a nosy old gal for trying."

"No, I suppose not." Teri edged a little closer to the steps. "What was the other thing?"

"Oh, yes." Edna beamed at her. "I was baking this morning. It relaxes me. I can't eat even half of the cookies I made, though. Why don't you take some up to your friends? Nate's fond of my cookies. I understand that he's been spending time with all of you. That's all to the good, I say. The boy needs to get out more. Just wait right there – I'll be back in a wink."

Without waiting for a reply, the matron dashed into her apartment with a spry agility that left Teri blinking dumbly after her.

You'd think she was a kid, the way she moves.

"I see you've met dear old Edna."

She looked up the side of the staircase. Nate leaned over the railing, several DVDs in hand. He traipsed down the steps and held up three cases for her approval.

"I figured we could watch a movie. See anything you like?"

"I don't see any ice cream."

"It's waiting for you in Alex's freezer."

"Thanks. Umm, this one." Teri tapped a finger on *Die Another Day*. She'd seen it before, like any good James Bond fan. It was one of her favorites. "Is Edna always gossipy?"

"Why, sugar," Nate smiled blandly at her, "we're all a little gossipy. What was she asking about? Alex and Michael?"

"Yeah – "

"Here we are. Hello, Nate. I've some cookies for you and your friends, dear." Edna came out with a huge platter of various cookies, topped with something that looked vaguely like a brick wrapped in aluminum foil. "That's banana nut bread on the top."

"That's mighty sweet, thank you." His southern drawl had thickened much to the matron's amusement. Nate handed Teri the DVDs so he could take the platter with both hands. "Edna, sugar, what was your question about Alex and her man?"

"Her man?" She hooted. "Michael will just love that one. I'll have to share it with him when I see him next. All I wanted to know was if they really had spent the night together."

"Oh, they did." He ignored Teri's mutter of protest as he answered. It was her friend's privacy, damn it, not some celebrity couple in the society column. "Can't say how serious they are right this moment."

"Still, that's good to hear. I think they make a lovely couple." Edna gave a nod of satisfaction. "That girl's got enough spunk to get under his skin. Now you two run along. Nate," she sent him a stern look, "don't forget to share those cookies with the rest of your friends."

The tart reminder delivered, she went back inside her apartment. Nate was still chuckling to himself, Teri scowling at his back, as they climbed the steps.

"We got a movie to watch." He gave her a cheerful grin. "You'll have to open the door, sugar. My hands're full."

T he credits were rolling when Alex and Michael returned.
The first thing Alex saw was Teri sprawled on the floor asleep, one arm slung around a snoring Ivan. A throw blanket had been draped over her. Nate sat next to her with his back against the couch. He glanced at the slumbering figure beside him, his golden eyes softening a little, then turned to give the couple a quiet greeting.

"How did it go?"

"Pretty much like a stone in water." She gave him a tired smile. It had been a long day – several long days, really. She wanted some down time and could tell that Michael felt the same.

"We found no sign of the thing, and no other information in either her library or mine." Michael sighed.

"Were there any messages or anything? I'm expecting a few calls, maybe a fax."

"We let the answering machine pick up the calls; there were two. I heard something like a fax machine in the back. I didn't poke into the room." A particularly loud snoring sound from the dog had Nate glancing back with an affectionate smile. "They're cute, aren't they?"

"Yeah, they are." Alex allowed herself a minute to wonder how much of his evident affection was for his pet.

"Some stuff came for Michael. It's on the table." He gestured towards it. Michael went off to go through it as he continued. "Did you want me to hang for the night or take off?"

"You might as well stay. You come with the dog and I think parting her from him will wake her. I'd rather let her sleep. She didn't get much last night."

"I don't think any of us did. We closed the café today."

"Oh." The news had her stomach sinking. Teri would not have taken that well.

"The main reason is the hurricane. The others are boarding up the store front tonight; they'll be dropped off in a bit. I got a check-in call a while ago."

"The escort?"

"They'll be back in the morning. Everyone's safe enough at the Reaches."

"I was expecting this." The statement brought them both to stand on either side of Michael as he flipped through photocopies of news articles.

"What is it?" Alex asked, coming up alongside him.

"It's from a few of my contacts, people who have an interest in events that hint at the supernatural. If you'll recall, I had asked for them to look into artifact theft associated with some kind of shape-shifter," Michael answered, now studying what looked to be a report. "There were two murders in Seattle last year. They made the local headlines. A small time collector of Indian artifacts and a teacher. No overt connection between them, other than the way they died."

"They were killed the same way," she murmured. "Pretty much torn apart – mauled, as the news described it here in Jax. Does it say whether or not anything was missing from the collector's cache?"

"It's not noted in the summary. I'd have to read the whole report." Michael glanced at Nate, a considering look in his eyes.

"You and the others can go through it, see what you can find. I'm expecting more packages like this. It may not help us find the thing itself, but it could help locate its partner. We'll need a timeline," Michael continued, skimming his gaze over the newspaper clippings before them. "Details. Victims, occupation, what was stolen, where things happened, and weather reports for the dates of the murders."

Alex angled her head.

"You want to see how rapidly it built power, why it's peaking now."

"I also want to find out when, where, or how the creature might have hooked up with its partner."

"We can see if Drake was in the area for any of the incidents. If it was business in any way, the Guild would be able to verify." She still felt a twinge at putting his name forward as a suspect like that. Hunters weren't supposed to go bad.

"So while we're doing all this," Nate drawled, resting a hip against the table, "you two will be hunting for the thing here."

"Speaking of which, I'd better go check that fax." She headed for her studio, leaving the two men discussing what to look for in the mailed content.

On a printer stand just inside the door was the fax machine. She tore off the print out, scanned the cover page. It was from the Library in Iceland. Appended to it was the reference they'd been looking for.

69

It had followed the truck from the beaches to the city.

It didn't know what part of Jacksonville it was in now. That didn't matter. All that it cared about was that the big brown box on wheels had stopped again.

It watched from the sidewalk as the driver climbed out of the front seat with a package in hand. The man trotted across the residential street, towards one house in a row of many. It walked to the vehicle, keeping one eye on the driver. Its blood was pumping hot as it climbed into the cab. Ducking through the doorway into the back, it swept its gaze over the racks of boxes and envelopes. In one of them was the amulet it had sought for, yearned for, in all the years since it had ceased being a man.

A man.

Human.

It keened as rage and despair ripped through it. It remembered. It could see in its mind what it once had been. Human, respected, a warrior to be reckoned with. It had grown powerful, more powerful as it had been promised, only to be reduced to this...

No. It took a deep breath, sought for control. It could

overcome this. It *would* overcome it. The amulet – that most hated link to the past – was here.

A frantic need to tear through everything in its search rose in a great wave. The air stirred around it as it snatched the first one that came to hand off the racks.

"…Nah, I won't be in the area then."

It jerked its head up, freezing in place as it heard the man climb into his seat. The air went still.

"Well, Sal, if you want to meet me for dinner, I'll probably be…" There was the sound of papers being flipped. "…in the Regency area. Steak'n'Shake's quick and easy…Okay, I'll see you there."

It crouched low in the back, easing behind a large box. It saw him reach over to deposit his cell phone on the dash. Ah. It relaxed minutely. It was just the driver. He would be easy enough to deal with when the time came.

The engine started up, the truck began to move. The man began to sing. It bared its teeth in a predatory smile. Overhead, the sky rumbled.

70

"It used to be human."

Alex's statement jarred the two men out of their discussion. They looked up as she joined them at the dining room table, fax in one hand, a book in the other.

"What used to be human?" Then realization dawned in Nate's amber eyes. "Oh."

"According to this story I received from the Guild Library in Iceland, the creature used to be a Viking berserker," she continued. As she spoke, Michael plucked the pages from her fingers to read them himself. She didn't need them to tell the story anymore.

"It seems this guy was so full of pride and ambition that he decided to become the strongest, most fearsome warrior in the history of the Norse. To that end, he appealed to the gods to find out how that might be done."

"Well, that's never turned out right." Nate interjected. "Most legends and tales I've heard where that's been done almost always ended badly for the mortal, or came with some really big strings that made the bargain not worth it."

"Well, yeah. Not all of those types are true, according to Guild

Lore. They were used as object lessons for young people. Anyway, this warrior made his appeal. It was answered by Loki."

"Who is never someone to be trusted." This came from Michael as he skimmed the next page of the fax.

"No, he isn't." Alex idly drew shapes on the table as she went on. "So Loki basically says, 'okay, I'll do it.' He promises that the world will tremble at this guy's approach, blah, blah. The Viking asks what Loki will get out the deal. He just replies that seeing his affect on the world will be satisfaction enough for him. So the offer is accepted. The warrior will become stronger each time he berserks, taking the essence of his defeated enemies into himself."

"He takes their forms as well." Michael looked up from the fax, setting it in the middle of the table. "He was so eager to test the offer that he picked a fight with a wolf."

"Mind if I make some coffee, Alex?" Nate rose from seat as Alex waved her hand in assent. Heading for kitchen, he glanced back over his shoulder to ask, "They have wolves in Iceland?"

She shrugged.

"I guess. Anyway, he kills the wolf and takes its shape. Then things start to get weird." She paused as the faucet was run for the coffee pot. When it was shut off, Michael took up the story.

"He couldn't handle everything that came with the form – the instincts, the memories. The longer he was a wolf, the more crazed he became, yet he didn't know how to become human again. He started attacking livestock. Eventually, he began killing the people of his own village."

"Which is where the amulet comes in." Alex opened the book she'd brought with her. She flipped through the pages until she found the set of photographs she wanted. "The village had a seeress; in most Nordic traditions, magic is used primarily by women, with some exceptions. The seeress appealed to the gods to show her a way to get rid of the monster in their midst. Her plea was answered by Thor who gave her the amulet. The story described it as being similar to one of these." She tapped a photo of a gold pendant. The shape was a match for the necklace that had been left at the café, though the ornamental design was more crude.

"This is a charm in the shape of Thor's Hammer, Mjolnir, which was used to ward off evil. In this case, it was made of enchanted silver by the dwarves and was intended to bind the magic of the shape-shifting creature they called a *hamrammu*r."

"So it limits the thing's power. Huh." Nate came back to the table as the coffee maker percolated. "No wonder it wants it back."

"The story ends with the thing being trapped in a cave." Michael added. "There's no mention of what happened to the amulet."

"So what's the next move now?"

Alex shrugged at her neighbor's question. "I guess we look into old Nordic magic while we try to find the real amulet. The *hamrammur's* still in town; I would think that it would be here, too."

"My father's working on that angle, so that would leave you two free to do more research."

"My not-so-favorite word." She sighed.

"I have a contact who might tell us more now that we've reached this point."

Alex looked up at Michael with a hopeful expression.

"Yeah? Who?"

"Gwynn." The corner of his mouth curved upwards. "It's time you met Him, anyway."

71

Michael took Alex up to his apartment first. It had already been a long day for both of them. He wanted to make sure that there was some time of relative peace, and an opportunity to eat, before they went to the Wood. It would also give him a moment to settle. He was feeling a strange mix of anticipation and dread regarding the visit.

"So when I meet Gwynn face-to-face can I slap him for the phone call he made a few days ago?"

Her cheery tone had him wincing.

"Please don't." He ducked into the kitchen to pull dishes out of the cupboards, trying to keep busy. He had to think of a meal for them both. He prayed that Gwynn and Alex would like each other. "I – He's a deity, Alex."

"I was just joking. I know you see him as a father figure." She'd followed him. He could sense her now, leaning against the wall of the entryway, watching him. When she spoke next, he heard amusement and surprise. "You're nervous."

He fell back on the first meal they'd shared together. Words were muttered in another language – completely unnecessary yet somehow appropriate – and the grilled cheese sandwiches took shape on the plates he'd placed on the counter.

"Hey." She came up behind him to lay a hand on his shoulder. "What's wrong?"

He handed her a plate.

"I've never taken anyone to meet Him before."

"Oh." She picked up a sandwich wedge as she mulled it over. "It's like taking your first date ever home to meet the parents, right? You hope they'll like each other, that Mom and Dad will approve, and no embarrassing anecdotes or pictures crop up during conversation."

"Dragons don't have this tradition," he said, cautious as well as puzzled. "I will have to do this with your parents?"

"Eventually." She gave an encouraging smile. "We're taking it slow – per Gwynn's orders – so you don't have to worry about it any time soon."

"Good." He paused, then asked, "Pictures?"

"Usually naked baby photos." She shrugged as he tried to see what was so embarrassing about them. Why would anyone take those images to begin with? Dragons had no use for them. It was another thing about humanity that he had never understood. "Anyway, I'll be on best behavior, okay?"

He nodded. They finished eating, leaving the dishes in the sink for later.

"So where is the Wood?"

"Everywhere. Nowhere." His lips quirked at her scowl. "It is the domain of Gwynn ap Nudd, Alex. I barely fathom it myself; how can I explain it?"

He took her hand, pulled her close.

"I want time with you when this is done."

"The hunt? Alright, but – "

He could feel her thoughts derail as his lips took hers. As he deepened the kiss, he mentally reached out for the one place he called Home. Wind stirred, whipping around them. The earth shifted and shuddered. The apartment faded away in patterns of darkness while the two of them disappeared in a flash of warm light.

They broke the kiss as the world settled around them. Alex looked around at the forest, then back at him.

"I hate it when you do that."

He knew. It gave him a kind of perverse pleasure, which is why he did it. Still not giving a reply, he took her hand, swinging it gently between them as he led her through the Wood. Feeling the way her hand fit in his, it didn't seem as if they had only known each other for almost two weeks.

TIME IS A RELATIVE THING.

He ignored the voice in his mind, though hearing it was always a kind of comfort. They walked in silence, pausing once in a while so that he could point out a wildlife resident of the valley. He spied a wood violet in full bloom and thought of something Edna had mentioned to him. He dropped Alex's hand to pick the flower, then stood twirling the stem until she came to stand next to him. He offered it, watching as the unexpected pleasure suffused her face.

THAT WAS WELL DONE, the voice said softly.

"Welcome to the Wood," Gwynn spoke aloud from behind them. They turned and He gave a nod of greeting to Alex. "It is quite rare that we have new visitors."

"We?" she asked. Distant thunder rolled. She looked up reflexively. Michael could sense the automatic thought that the storm heralded the *hamrammur*.

"There is no hunting here unless I permit it," Gwynn assured her, knowing, her mind. "The rain will not yet break. As for the 'we' I spoke of..."

A big red dog came crashing through the bushes next to her. Tail wagging, tongue lolling, he sniffed her legs, then leaped up to plant his paws on her chest. She laughed, rubbed his ears, and shoved him away.

The deity gestured for them to follow Him. The closer they got to the center of the Wood, the more spots of lovely solitude, places that glowed with the nuances of faerie lore they saw. Alex seemed particularly fond of a beautiful glen with a bubbling brook, wild flowers, and rich green moss. Oak trees and rounded boulders accented the raised banks. Sunlight twinkled like gold on the rippling surface of the water. She studied it intently, memorizing every detail. Gwynn and Michael both stopped to let her look.

"Michael used to sit here, thinking for hours, when I first brought him to the Wood."

He remembered. He'd been contemplating life, death, and two possible futures. Choices. Pixies had played on the water or danced on the rock. The subtle music of the brook had lulled him to sleep in the endless afternoons. The moon, always full, had guided him back to camp when he woke. The memory was a cherished one, one of many beloved moments he'd lived in the Wood.

"Oh?" Alex glanced up at Gwynn.

He had to admire how she had the knack of conveying a thousand questions in that single syllable.

"He was always thinking," Gwynn went on in a dryer tone. His gaze seemed to grow heavy with indulgent exasperation as He shifted it to Michael, making him smile. "You'll find that he thinks too much. Some things should be taken as they are given, enjoyed, loved, and honored as they should be."

"Such as you, O Glorious Father?" Michael jibbed in a slightly mocking tone. He'd missed the teasing, the needling. He hadn't realized how little of it there'd been recently until now.

"Of course," Gwynn answered with dignified aplomb.

Alex watched the exchange with a smile, then looked back at the beautiful spot by the creek. Michael could all but feel the pencil in her hand, the pad propped on her knees. She was already composing the sketch in her mind: the glen, dancing faeries, a slumbering dragon curled up on the bank. He stepped closer, brushing her hair away from her ear and leaned down to whisper, "One piece at a time. You still have to finish my dragon."

"Your dragon?" She looked up at him with narrowed eyes twinkling. "Who said it was yours?"

"I did." He gave her a confident smile, then a quick kiss.

"We'll just see about that," she muttered.

He kissed her again, because her tart reply seemed to warrant it. Gwynn cleared his throat. He glanced over to see Him shaking His head in mock admonishment. Beside him, Alex blushed.

"Yes?" Michael queried.

"You'll have time enough to romance her later, Michael," Gwynn told him with a trace of amusement that dropped from His voice as He continued. "There are things you wanted to discuss. We'll do so at the camp."

"Yeah, that's the main reason why we're here." Alex sighed.

He put his arm around her waist as they travelled along an old game trail. It was, to Alex's delight, still used. She identified several different kinds of tracks, and laughed a bit over the ones left by a raccoon. They looked almost like faerie hand-prints, she said.

Her simple, almost child-like enthusiasm warmed him. He loved the Wood. It mattered to him, perhaps too much, to see her here, reacting to it as she did.

IT ISN'T TOO MUCH WHEN IT IS RIGHT.

The whispered words echoed in his mind; he shoved them away. He wasn't sure if he was ready to go there. He wanted her, enjoyed her, yet...

There were always complications. He was beginning to think of them more these days. Now was not the time for that, however, so he firmly locked those thoughts deep inside himself.

The trees gave way to a clearing, a roughly circular break furnished with a fur-covered tent, logs for sitting around the campfire, a bare spit set up over the flame. The red hound raced forward to join his fellows lying at the tent flap. The other two canines, one black, the other white, raised their heads then scrambled to their feet to race toward them. Michael stepped in front of his partner as they came at them.

They jumped, barked, and wagged their tails at him, each getting a scratch behind the ears before trotting more sedately to Alex. She held out a hand to each in turn.

"What are their names?"

"I..." Michael stopped, brow furrowing. "I don't know that they have any." He looked quizzically at Gwynn.

"They have many names, though I seldom use them here. My son," he indicated Michael with a tilt of his head, "has always called them by their colors."

Before Alex could reply, Red launched himself at her, knocking her flat on her back. The dog proceeded to bathe her face with his tongue. Black and White joined in, sniffing, licking, and barking. She laughed as she shoved at the dogs. Michael just stood grinning like a fool.

At an unspoken command, the hounds suddenly abandoned Alex to race toward Gwynn. The deity was seated on one of the logs lain around the campfire, calming His companions with absent strokes. Alex, still laughing, struggled to sit up as she wiped at her face.

Michael pulled his partner to her feet, then conjured up a warm, damp cloth to hand her. Magic was so much easier to use here, he mused as she cleaned up the dog slobber. She gave the cloth back to him as he escorted her to the campfire.

Gwynn waited, His helmeted head cocked to one side. It was for His son to start.

"I know that there are lines you can't cross."

"Laws are Laws for a reason, My son," was His quiet reply. "Without them free-will would not exist."

"We have found something that explains the origins of our prey. It involves another deity, Loki. Can you tell me if this is true?"

The glowing white eyes seem to burn brighter for a moment.

"You are concerned about retaliation. There is no need for it at this time, though the story you've unearthed is true enough." Red leaned against Gwynn's knee for attention. "This situation is unique – fragile. It is not one that I can touch directly."

Michael frowned.

"So Loki still retains some power." Alex's thoughtful conclusion brought to mind grim visions of war. Gods battling mortals rarely ended favorably for the latter.

"Yes, and no." His glowing white eyes looked down at His hound as He found a good spot to scratch. The dog's leg began to thump with pleasure. "Loki's fate is well recorded in the Annals of Man. At present, his position is tenuous at best. He cannot yet act should you slay his tool."

"It rains – or seems to – whenever it kills. How much does it really affect the weather?"

Her question triggered something in Michael's brain. Rain and blood...Blood magic required the spilling of blood. The more blood, the more agony, the more death, the more arcane energy to be gained...

"That I cannot answer, save only to confirm that there is a link."

"It can't contain the magic it generates, can it?" His blue eyes met Gwynn's. "It can't control it – that's why the weather is affected."

"It's the least stable natural pattern of magic." Alex nodded with a humorless smile. "Too little ambient power, the pattern falls apart. Too much, the pattern expands, linking systems and pulling them in towards the epicenter."

"It is affecting a hurricane out in the Atlantic Ocean."

"It generated it," corrected the deity. "This *hamrammur* continues to tug it closer to your city with every kill it makes."

"I didn't even think about that. Not really – certainly not as part of all this. God." She rubbed her temple. "Well, how can you stop something like a hurricane? You can't. You don't. So we concentrate on finding the monster, and pray that we stop it before the storm hits."

"The amulet." Gwynn inclined his head as Michael continued. "Do we need it to destroy the creature?"

"So long as it is bound by another god's power, it cannot be terminated by any of Mine." He gestured to His adopted son.

"This includes you, as your magic is derived from Me."

"It's a Law thing, isn't it?" Alex sounded aggrieved. The Laws governing deities could never be broken, unlike the secular laws of mortals. A human criminal could be executed for his violation but a Law-breaking god could send the world into chaos.

"The amulet was forged by the dwarves at Thor's bidding," Michael recalled. "What if the amulet was destroyed?"

"It would regain all its former power. Isn't that something we don't want?"

"It would then be vulnerable to me." He turned to Gwynn. "Can I affect the amulet or is it also covered by the same Law?"

He seemed pleased with the question.

"It protects, yet is not itself protected."

"Even the Laws of the gods have legal loopholes." His partner gave a little laugh. "Why am I not surprised?"

"We will think on this. Kent may have some input as well." He stood, holding out a hand for Alex. "If we can find it before the *hamrammur*, we can trap it."

"What about its partner?"

"We'll continue the hunt for him but unless he sends you another gift I'd rather deal with the more immediate threat first."

Gwynn watched them depart in a flare of light. He had been right to pair them together. His son may worry about the centuries down the road, and she may refuse to think that far ahead for either of them. In the end, they would learn that those concerns were needless.

He stared into the fire, Red's gaze following His. In the flames He saw the possibilities for the future. There was death, destruction, salvation, and a man known to His hunters trapped in a nightmare of another's making.

74

September 12, 2004
Jacksonville, FL

The UPS delivery man hadn't kept his dinner date. He lay sprawled on the floor in the back of his truck, ribcage torn open, skull punched through. Crude sigils had been inscribed in the flesh not covered by the tatters of his uniform. The lines of them were ragged. They still glowed when looked at with an arcane eye.

With the sound of a heavy downpour hitting the metal roof above, the creature called the *hamrammur* studied its handiwork, its skin still tingling in the aftermath. It wasn't perfect. The master would have sneered at the way it had made do with whatever implements were handy. He would have preferred a knife to morphic claws, for one. A lip curled at the thought, a low growl building in its throat. It didn't care what the master thought of its attempt. It would find him, repay him for those years of using it for his own avaricious ends soon enough. For now, what was important was the success of its first major blood rite.

It had taken all night. The experience had been exhilarating. The mix of fear, power, and blood – even the memory of them had its blood pumping hot. It would have enjoyed it more had it allowed the man to scream.

"Not wise…not wise to be heard…"

The hoarse voice had an almost sing-song quality. It grinned to itself, continuing to murmur.

"Rain, thunder – it wouldn't cover it…tear your throat out… wonderfully warm…wet… delicious…" It reached into a crimson stained pocket to withdraw its prize. The tarnished silver of the pendant glinted dully in the light cast by the overhead lamp. It hung from a stiff leather thong, dangling from its clawed-tipped fingers as it stared at it. "Your time comes soon…so soon… Let's try – now."

The rite had granted it more magic. It could see that arcane force as a sullen red light that traced its own body, crawling over it like tiny snakes. Concentrating hard, it forced one of the serpentine lines to slither toward the amulet in its hand.

The thread of magic moved like a convulsing snake now. Reaching the hand, it slipped onto the thong. Progress slowed tremendously as the power neared the pendant. A final mental shove had the tendril of arcane force touching the metal. Yellow sparks began to fly as the ancient enchantment strove against the blood magic.

Sweat began to bead on the *hamrammur's* brow as a second arcane tendril joined the first. Then a third. Its head began to pound in a vicious rhythm. As the *creature* brought more of its stolen energy to bear on the artifact, faint yellow bands appeared on its body. They twisted, tightening. Its legs weakened. Its chest constricted. Breathing became torture.

With a loud snarling noise, it fell to its knees next to the corpse. It wouldn't fail – not now – not when it had the thing in its grasp and was so close –

Blindly, it stuck its free hand out to brace itself. The talons tore into cooling flesh as it clutched at the arm it had landed on. Its breath a thin wheezing. Spots began to appear in its vision. Grayness swam around the edges of awareness.

It wouldn't give up.

It was a warrior. It had been the best of its era. It would be the best in this one. It couldn't – concede – to –

The world began to fade. As darkness claimed it, it heard something snap. It didn't feel the electric shock that shot through the vehicle like lightning. It didn't smell the fire as the packages began to burn.

In its hand the metal of Thor's Hammer flashed white hot.

Alex woke to find herself in Michael's bed, still fully dressed. The man – well, man-shaped dragon – was nowhere in sight. She sighed, rolling over to hug the pillow.

She didn't want to get up. The bedding smelled of him, which made her want to snuggle into it to daydream like a lovesick school girl. That would have been mildly embarrassing if she had been more awake than she was. She didn't want to call the Guild office in Tallahassee to ask certain questions about Drake Howell. In her current mindset, Drake did not belong in the same thought track as Michael, even if it was hunt-related. She also didn't want to go downstairs and explain to her friends why she hadn't come home last night. Well, to be fair, she didn't want to deal with Richard's unspoken disapproval over where she'd slept.

He really needed to get over it. She really needed to get up. With a groan of heartfelt protest, she forced herself to rise. She refused to shine before coffee.

The door opened.

She lifted her head, caught the glorious scent of rich, brewed caffeine. Michael crossed to her, put the cup in her hands, then brushed her lips with his. If this was going to be how mornings with him went, she could get use to it. She took a long sip of the coffee, waited for the first hit to kick in.

"Where did you sleep?"

"The couch." He sat beside her. "I've spoken with Kent. We're due at his office around noon. He hasn't had much sleep since we gave him the replica to work with."

She grimaced in sympathy.

"He gets crabby with no coffin time." Not that she believed he slept in a coffin. "Did he say if he has anything for us?"

"He has two -- prot – " He paused trying to recall the word. "Poto –"

"Prototypes?"

He smiled.

"Yes. He also said that we would have had them sooner if either of us had a cell phone."

"I refuse to have one. They're a bloody nuisance. If my agent knew I had one I'd hear from him all that time and wouldn't get anything done." She stared into the mug that was almost empty. "I don't want to make the call."

"I have contacts in the Guild that I could tap, Alexandria. You don't have to do it."

"Yeah, I do." She leaned against him, letting her head lay on his shoulder. "I have to be able to. So I'll finish my coffee, go downstairs, check on the others, eat something because – hey, got to eat. Then I'll call. What will you do?"

"Check the news at your place. If our quarry has been active there may be a report of some kind."

She drank the last of the coffee, handing him the cup. Getting up, she glanced down at her rumpled clothes.

"I think I'll shower when I get down there." She smoothed her wrinkled shirt as best she could. " Okay, let's get started."

76

Lys had woken first. Teri was in the bedroom. Nate had gone back to his place after Lys and Richard had arrived last night. She and Richard had taken Alex's studio to sleep in; she left her fiancé slumbering there to creep out into the front rooms.

There was still no sign of their hostess.

She frowned thoughtfully, hoping that nothing had happened to Alex while she was out hunting. Maybe she'd spent the night at Michael's. Cheered by the thought, she bustled into the kitchen to make coffee, then into the living room to turn the TV on. She tuned it to the news channel, listening to the latest report on Janice as she poured her first cup and debated over breakfast. The storm was on the move again. The beaches were already evacuating in preparation for the worst.

It was just as well they had closed the café.

She rummaged in the fridge and pantry, finding the ingredients for French toast. She was dipping the bread slices in egg batter when she heard the door open. She peered over the pass-through bar to see Alex and Michael walk into the apartment proper.

"Morning," she said in a loud whisper. "Everyone else is still asleep. I'm making breakfast if you want any."

Alex came in to give her a hug in greeting, sniffing the scent of the toast on the griddle.

"Yes, please. I'm going to take a quick shower, first. Mind if Michael surfs for news?"

"No, he can go ahead."

"Where's Nate?" This came from Michael who had come to stand in the kitchen entrance.

"Next door. He said we're safe enough here." The last came out as more a question than a statement. Michael nodded. She smiled in relief. "He should be back when he wakes up."

Alex stepped around Michael to go to the back of the apartment. He glanced after her before asking, "Is anyone going anywhere today?"

She began to shake her head, then remembered.

"We didn't get everything shuttered at the café. We have to go back to finish that up this morning. Richard didn't want to leave anything in the safe, either, just in case." They had all heard stories about the looting that had gone on in the wake of Hurricane Andrew in South Florida. "It shouldn't take long."

"Is Kent's escort going with you or is Nate?"

"The escort." She flipped the bread, adding another two battered slices to cook. "They were very good about helping us out last night." A frown crept onto her expression. "Richard wasn't too keen on them, though. I don't know what his problem is lately."

Michael didn't reply to that. Instead, he wandered over to the TV to watch the news, leaving her to finish breakfast while she scowled over her fiancé's behavior.

Alex didn't take long in the shower, coming out with a towel wrapped around her head as Lys turned off the griddle. She offered her friend two laden plates.

"For you and Michael," she said. "Can you get the butter and syrup out? I'll bring the rest out in a minute."

"Sure. God, this smells good…"

When Richard and Teri stumbled out, the three of them were

seated at the table, already halfway through their portions. Richard grunted a 'good morning', but didn't say much else. He wouldn't with Michael there. His fiancée was beginning to find it more than a little irritating. This wasn't the place, however, for a pre-marital spat, so she kept her peace.

The meal passed in relative silence. When she was finished, Alex excused herself to make a phone call. Michael took both his empty plate and hers to the kitchen to take care of them. That was nice, Lys thought. They were acting more like a couple all the time. It was wonderful to see.

When they were finished, she collected everyone else's plates. Michael took them from her when she came into the kitchen. He'd already washed the dishes from before. Murmuring a thank you, she left him to it, then decided to check on Alex. She found her in the studio, wrapping up her call.

"Yes, just let me know if he still wants it whenever you talk to him. I appreciate it. Thanks." She clicked off, putting the phone back in its cradle. "Well, that went better than I'd expected."

"What's up?"

Alex yanked the towel off her head to shake out her damp hair.

"Drake. The Guild office was unaware that he was in the country, let alone the area. They thought he was still in Greece." Her brow furrowed. "If he collected the – whatever he was supposed to get – he should have reported it. The Grecian Branch hasn't heard from him since he first arrived. What the hell is he up to?"

"Sounds shady, if you ask me." Lys could easily envision Drake doing something unlawful. "So where does that leave you?"

"It leaves me wondering what he's really doing – if he's connected to our hunt here. Michael has a packet of stuff from a contact – reports, news clippings, etc. – things that could be attributed to the creature we're after. As soon as I find a way to convince the Guild office to send me a list of Drake's activities for the past few years, we can cross-reference them." She tossed her hair over her shoulder and laid the towel over the back of her chair. "I'm not buying coincidence. Not from a snake like him."

"It still doesn't help the hunt now, does it?" She cocked her to one side.

"No, it doesn't." She sighed. "Come on. We'll get everyone up-to-date on what's going on, then my partner and I have to leave for Kent's. If we're lucky, we'll have this thing done before Janice hits."

Elsewhere

It just couldn't do anything on its own, could it? It had to be herded, helped, guided.

The Master paced across the filthy store. He looked out of place in the abandoned hole-in-the-wall shop, dressed in a sleek gray suit and tie. The trash littering the boards beneath his feet skittered out of his way as he walked. Even the dust wafted away from him. He didn't notice it. Nor would he take note of the clear path he'd left in his wake. Other things occupied his mind, demanding his attention.

He stopped to stare down at his pawn, sprawled on the floor like a rag doll and oblivious to the world. It no longer looked human. The grotesque shape it wore now held only the vaguest resemblance to the Viking it had once been. One clawed hand was fisted tight. It held the amulet in a steely grip, unwilling to let go even though the metal had burned into the flesh of it. The burns were healing quickly. The blistering was decreasing even as he watched.

The *hamrammur's* hand was the worst of its injuries. The clothing had been singed by the fire, yet the flames had not touched its body. Had it been left in the UPS truck any longer, that would not have been the case. The fire had gutted the vehicle before the firefighters had arrived to snuff it out.

While it had been foolish in its choice of venue, what it had accomplished there could not be discounted. A cold grin slid across his face as he crouched down beside his former servant.

"You learned well, even if you fumbled through it," he murmured to it. "No need to thank me. You'll be paying the price of my aid soon enough."

It would be ravenous when it woke. Healing wounds used up so much energy, he thought. Still, he had provided for it. He was still its Master, after all, and it wasn't finished with the task he had left it to perform.

Glancing behind him, his eyes glinted with an eerie yellow light as he spied the homeless man sleeping in the corner of the room. Old newspapers lay scattered underneath him, a worn trench coat served as his blanket. He had given him a meal, supplied him with water. The drug he'd suffused the drink with would keep him asleep through most of the pain to come. A small mercy, he thought. Well, he could afford to be merciful now.

It was too bad that many of the city's inhabitants were readying to leave. Their flight before the threat of Janice meant fewer victims for his former pet. Well, it would just have to get creative, wouldn't it?

Standing up, he slipped his hands into the pockets of his slacks. Things would be back on track soon. When his creature finally freed itself, Janice would hit the city. The storm would be fierce enough to crack the defenses of the prize he'd come for.

With the wonderful side benefit of killing Alexandria Rosselle.

The man would still be an issue. He frowned at the thought. There was something about him… He had tried to spy on him, tried to get others to do so. He had failed. Even scrying for him seemed to be impossible. He had scried for Alex. There had been difficulty in it but it had been possible.

Was the man protected somehow?

The notion made him uneasy. Deep in his mind darkness stirred. The uneasiness faded.

He would deal with him in good time. When the Reaches fell, the way would be open. No god could protect Michael Keegan then.

Jacksonville, FL

"If either of you had a cell phone, you would have had these yesterday."

Michael and Alex both scowled at Kent. They had just come into his office to find him grousing at his desk, the surface of it covered with gadgetry, tomes, and papers. The vampire lord didn't look as if he'd slept at all in the past few days. He was pale. Dark shadows ringed his eyes. Michael caught the tinge of crimson in them as they join him.

"You need to feed, Aisley."

"I don't need a bloody nursemaid, Keegan," he retorted. "I need allies who have the means to be contacted."

"Kent." The quiet way Alex said his name had him deflating. "We didn't expect you to work on this night and day, without any rest."

"Do you have any idea what having a thing like that in the city does for my conclave?" She shook her head. He dragged his hands through his dark mane of hair. "We become suspect. I've been queried by no less than five other lords in the state. If this doesn't end soon, they'll arrive to audit us. They'll look for anything that could possibly be construed as being of the Dark. That's the first step in a non-hostile takeover."

"I'm sorry, Kent." She reached across the desk to lay a hand on his arm. Michael had to suppress an unexpected flash of jealousy. "We'll do our best to finish it before that happens."

Getting up, he left his partner to console the vampire as he fetched a glass from the wet bar in the corner of the office. Closing his eyes to better concentrate, he gathered his magic in, focusing on the blood running through his veins. A surreal feeling built along the edges of his awareness as his blood level decreased by a pint. When he opened his eyes again, the missing pint was in the glass. He took a moment for the lightheadedness to pass before walking back to the others. He gave the glass to Kent, who frowned at it.

"That isn't cattle blood. That's what's in the mini-fridge over there; this isn't that."

"No."

"Drink it." Alex pushed it towards him. "You'll feel better."

His expression faintly suspicious, he took a small sip first. He sputtered a little as he swallowed.

"Gah, what is that? Poison?" he managed between coughs. "God, Michael."

"No, it's not poison. Drink all of it."

"What did you give him?" Alex asked as the vampire grimaced, then tossed the rest of the blood back like a shot of whiskey. He slammed the glass down on the desk as he shuddered in reaction.

"Something he's probably never had, and may never have again." He gave her a slight smile. "He'll be better for it. I wouldn't hurt him, Alex."

"Could have fooled me." Kent's voice was hoarse as he spoke. "That was stronger than any spirits I've partaken of, before or since I Turned. I need some water." Alex waved him back into his seat as he rose to get it. As she went to fetch it for him, he asked, "What was it?"

"Dragon's blood."

Michael felt a spark of perverse pleasure in seeing the shock on his ally's face. The vampire lost enough of his composure to gape at him.

"Dragon's blood? Where in bloody hell did you get dragon's blood?"

"I have a pet hatchling I keep in a dungeon hidden in the Alps. I bleed it every once in a while to sell on the blackmarket. It's how I pay my bills," he replied dryly. Kent's derisive snort made him smile. "It doesn't matter where it came from, Aisley. It's not from a rogue that walks for the Dark, I can promise you. How do you feel?"

"A little drunk, to tell the truth. I haven't felt like that since…" He trailed off, then deliberately cleared his throat. "It's been a long time."

Michael wasn't educated on vampire physiology, beyond the means to kill them. Still, he knew that it took an awful lot of alcohol to get one drunk. He would never had thought Aisley would be the sort to go out of his way to consume that much. Given the bleak expression that flickered on his face before vanishing, the occasion had not been a pleasant one. He let it pass without comment as Alex returned with the water.

"Thank you." Kent took it, sipping steadily for a few moments. By the time he put the water glass down beside the bloody one, he had regained all of his color and his eyes had lost the red tint. "Alright. Here."

He took two objects from the desk to hold them up. They looked like compasses.

"These are your trackers. I've done some testing with the necklace you gave me. The range is around a mile radius. The needle will point towards the amulet." He handed them over.

"It works like a compass?" Alex studied hers thoughtfully.

"Yes. However, you'll need power to make it work. It's a simple spell and doesn't use much magic to sustain." He passed them each a sheet of paper. Michael read the spell's instructions.

"Most of the parameters for this are embedded in the tracker." It was an intriguing technique. "You'll have to show me how you did this."

"It's the same principle as purposing an object."

"Like your dishes," his partner interjected. "I guess. It's not really something I'm schooled in."

"You have purposed dishes?" Kent gave him puzzled look. "Why?"

"So I don't have to cook." He folded the paper to tuck away in his coat pocket. The vampire opened his mouth to follow up on that, then changed his mind.

"I've made a few more of these. I'll send others out with them when I can. There aren't many of us that go out in the daylight."

"That's okay." Alex gave him a smile. "We can get started on this. You get some rest."

"Be careful." He shifted his amber eyes to Michael. "Both of you."

"We will be."

With that, they left.

The first thing it noticed was the stuffiness of the air. Its eyes blinked open to stare, uncomprehending, at the crumbling ceiling tiles above it. Confusion swamped its mind. Where was it?

It remembered pain. Suffocating pain. It hadn't been able to breathe, to move. All it could think of was not giving up. Warriors never gave up...

There had been a brown box on wheels. Packages in the back, the sound of water striking the metal roof. The delivery truck. The driver – the rite. The back had filled with smoke and heat. It recalled most of it now. Had it stumbled out while it was dazed?

The fingers of one hand twitched. It turned its head to see them curled around – the amulet. It bolted into sitting position, cupping the thing in its hands. The one that had clenched around it was scarred now. The tissue was smooth where the metal had burned it. As for the silver pendant, the hammered details of the decoration had softened or partially melted. It had been that hot.

It hadn't destroyed it, yet it was weaker than it had been before. It could sense the restraints stemming from it as being fewer in number, more lax, flimsier. Its lips peeled back in a fanged grin.

Yes....

Its stomach rumbled.

Hunger pangs stabbed through the elation. Casting around its new surroundings, it saw boarded windows, trash left by squatters, a heap of clothing and newspaper in the far corner. Raising its stubby snout, it scented the air. It was musty. Under the staleness of it, it could smell old sweat. It could smell human male.

It lurched to its feet. Swaying, it fumbled with the leather thong of its amulet. It slipped it over its head, patted the pendant against its chest. Satisfied that it wouldn't be lost, it ambled in an unsteady line towards the man hidden in the pile.

First it would feed. Then it would see what it could do.

8o

"So, shall we take a tour around the city and see how the magic sniffers work?" Alex gestured with her tracker at the one Michael held. "I have to say that I'm rather antsy to try them out."

They stood on the corner of Parker and East Church Street beside his Firebird. Behind them was Aisley Printing. Overhead, the overcast sky was darkening. They both looked up to study it.

"That's the *hamrammur*," he murmured as the wind began to pick up. "It's either killed again or is getting ready to."

Alex lifted her device, watching as the needle on it wobbled slightly.

"I think it's just out of range."

"We'll have to split up." He gave her a warning look. "Do not engage it alone."

"I don't plan to." She sighed. "As much as I hate the things, now would be a good time to have cell phones or walkie-talkies." Seeing his frown over the term, she elaborated. "Hand-held two-way radios."

"Ah."

"Since we don't have anything like that to work with, how do you want to handle this?"

Again, he lifted his face to the sky, considering.

"I have enough energy invested in the chassis to track your location." He lowered his gaze to hers. "I can also use it as a conduit for telepathic relay. You just have to be in physical contact with it."

She raised an eyebrow.

"So you could read my mind from anywhere in the city so long I'm in contact with your car?" Running her tongue over her teeth, she looked back at the sleek ebony machine. "How often have you done it?"

"I don't, generally." He inclined his head towards her as she contemplated all of the things he could have eavesdropped on. "As fascinating as your thoughts are, I've resisted. Will you consent to it in this instance?"

"Yeah, I will." There wasn't another handy alternative that she could see. "So I'll take the Firebird and you'll be…?"

"Don't worry about me. Shape-shifter, remember?"

"Right." She glanced down at the tracker, frowning. The needle was slowly edging to the left, pointing south of their position. Looking up in that direction, she realized that the best part of downtown was that way. "It's fairly close to the river."

"The clouds are darker that way." He handed her the keys. The temperature began to drop as the wind whipped around. Alex dug into her pocket for an elastic band to pull her hair back as he raised his voice. "You scout from this side. I'll scout from the other side."

"So we'll meet with it in the middle?"

"Exactly."

She grabbed his jacket, yanked him forward for a kiss. The heat of it warded off the chill that cut through her clothes.

"Don't take it on without me, Keegan. I mean it."

She let him go with a grin, then got in the car. After buckling in, she looked back at Michael. He was gone. Her stomach jittered with nerves and anticipatory adrenaline as she placed the compass-like tracker on the dashboard. If all went well, the hunt would end soon.

Cranking up the engine, she pulled away from the curb to head down Parker Street.

81

Michael materialized next to the Friendship Fountain, by the railing that lined the walk along the bank. Across the river, the Modis Building's letters glowed against the dark grayness of the clouds. A small droplet of water landed on his cheek, a precursor to the waiting deluge above.

The wind was blowing in the opposite direction here. He scanned the choppy surface of the river, the churning sky. He was beginning to feel uneasy about the plan they'd made.

"You had better be careful, Alex," he muttered. He held up the tracker, waited as the needle moved back and forth before pointing south-west. Given the way the river curved around, it was difficult to determine which bank it was on.

The cloud cover was so uniformly dark now that he couldn't make out an epicenter. That was probably because it was moving. If the wind direction was an indication... He visualized a map of the area, tried to judge the convergence of the winds on either side of the river. It didn't get him anywhere.

For all he knew it could be on a bridge, or near one. There were two close by – three if you counted the railway that ran alongside the Acosta. All of them were in the general direction indicated by the tracker. He would start there.

Device in hand, he trotted towards Prudential Drive and the nearest bridge.

The *hamrammur* had walked out of the empty store front to see the streets of downtown virtually empty in comparison to the last time it had ventured out this way. There were some people still out, mostly business or police types. Shops were boarding up their glass fronts. Restaurants were closed.

A pair of female employees came out of a café to close the shutters on the 'to-go' window and drag the metal table and chairs inside. They chattered about the coming storm in worried voices. It shambled past them, now a dirty, smelly man. Their gazes skittered past him as they hauled chairs. It snarled at their backs, hunched its shoulders, and fingered the amulet around its neck.

It felt the prickle of magic against its palm.

What would happen, it wondered, if it tried something now? In the middle of all these people?

"They would run – run away. Run, screaming." Its muttering earned a few disquieted looks from passersby. It ignored them. "No fun in that – no power. Need power. Need to fix this – " It tugged on the pendant. "Need havoc, fear, blood…"

It stopped to stare at the overpass a block away. Lots of

vehicles were on it, moving to and fro. There were only two directions to flee in. What if it blocked one?

Grinning, it marched purposely towards it. There would be a way up there. It would find it.

For the first time since waking, it tried to gather it's magic. The clouds rumbled, light flashed in the heavens, a gust sped down the street. Its filthy coat flapped in the gusts as they whirled around it. Elation filled it as its call was answered.

People began to leave the streets, seeking shelter from the elements. So focused were they on getting inside before the rain fell that only handful of pedestrians witnessed the homeless man being lifted up by the gale. No one heard the manic, grating laughter above the rushing wind as he rose.

Kent's gadget had pointed that way, and that way was where Alex had tried to go. The dead-ends and one-way streets of downtown soon had her completely lost. Within the first five minutes of leaving Michael, she had cursed the founding fathers of Jacksonville, Florida. Then she expanded that to include everyone who had agreed that this type of road plan was the best way to get around.

They – every last one of them – had been stark raving mad or as intelligent as a newly hatched tadpole.

She snickered at the image that popped into her mind. Stark raving mad tadpoles running for mayoral election was just funny. Shaking her head at herself, she glanced at the 'sniffer.' She assumed that it still pointed at the St. Johns River. Two SUVs passed her, and someone in a convertible honked his horn at her. They'd all have to get over her slow progression. There was a reason she was going only 20 miles per hour.

Finally seeing a familiar street name, she guided the Firebird onto it. Two blocks down, she could see part of the Landing. As she neared it, the needle slid slightly to the right. She came to a stop in the drop-off area in front of the Landing to peer in that direction. It was pointing at the Fuller Warren Bridge. That meant she had to find an I-95 south on-ramp somewhere.

She re-entered the flow of traffic, made two left turns to head towards the bridge. She'd just spotted the sign pointing to the interstate when the compass arrow began to spin. Pausing at a red light, she stared as it jerked to stop, indicating the heart of downtown.

Weird.

A blaring of horns caught her attention. Up ahead, several vehicles plowed through an intersection, with more following them from an exit ramp. Even though her light had changed to green, she stayed where she was as a truck narrowly escaped getting T-barred by a car. Several cops jogged past her on the sidewalk, heading toward the commotion, shouting. She rolled down her window and caught some of it.

" – nado on the bridge! Everyone stay where you are! We'll tell you where to go!"

She picked up the tracker. It was pointing to the bridge again.

Checking to make sure the way was clear, she turned left again, going back to the Landing. If she went down two blocks further before the turn that would have her going in the right direction, she should be able to bypass most of the confusion and get on the bridge.

Buoyed by the wind in the middle of its vortex, it hovered half over the concrete, half over the river. Air and water rushed around it, funneling up towards the sky. In the compact eye of the tornado, it barely felt the fine spray of moisture that whipped around it. It listened to the roar of its creation, grinning.

Flinging out an arm, a smaller vortex spun out of the main one, careening down the lanes of the bridge to tear into oncoming traffic. It squinted through the mix of cloud, wind, debris, and water to see the automobiles crash into the cement walls or each other. Some flipped over the side. As they raced towards the river, it could sense their fear, almost hear their screams. It drank it in as it unleashed another attack.

85

"What the hell is this?" Alex pressed down on the brake as the sky opened up. The deluge was so thick she could barely see. "Not good, not good, not good at all."

She had managed to get onto the bridge before the police blocked off the on-ramps. She'd turned the radio on, channel surfing until she had found one featuring local news. According to the guy covering the traffic reports, the Fuller Warren Bridge – the one she was currently on – had a tornado sitting right in the middle of it. According to the tracker, that tornado was probably the creature she was after.

Slowing to a halt in the emergency lane, she put the Firebird in park. Hands gripping hard on the wheel, she peered into the downpour, catching a glimpse of something dark flying across the bridge. Had that been another car?

"Michael, where are you?" Could the telepathic communication thing work both ways? "You never know until you try." Concentrating on the Pontiac, she tried to mentally reach for Michael. A dull ache began to form at her temples. "Please let this work…"

A strange feeling welled up inside her head. It was as if someone was peering over her shoulder, only in her mind –

Alex?

"Michael." She allowed herself a moment of relief, then got down to business. "I'm on the Fuller Warren Bridge. I don't see it yet, but it's here."

Something big streaked through her field of vision, sailing over her hood to fall beyond the outer cement barrier. Catching a glimpse of wheels, she watched it disappear in horror.

I saw that. I'm coming.

"Hurry."

The rain stopped.

With her view unobscured, she gaped at the carnage. A van rested on top of a toppled partition. It was the only vehicle in sight. Automotive scrap was strewn across the lanes. A body lay amid wreckage, unmoving. Deep pits pocked the cement. Lightning flashed down in front of her, creating one more gouge. Above it all, a figure floated, bouncing, on buffets of wind.

"Michael, you had better get here fast."

The *hamrammur* gestured. Electric bolts lanced down around her. Chunks of concrete flew with each strike. The simultaneous thunder was deafening. Ears ringing, she threw the shifter into reverse, flooring the gas. The car shot backwards as the creature flung out a hand, fingers hooked like claws.

The storm responded like a dog eager to please.

The wind tackled the Firebird as it retreated. She felt the tires lose traction, panic rising even as she did. The vehicle jerked to the side. Alex's head hit the door window. Dazed, she kept her death grip on the wheel.

The world began to spin.

Fighting fear, nausea, and shock, she caught flashes of water, of the bridge, of the enemy. It drifted closer as she twirled in mid-air. Then it turned away from her.

The car crashed into the side of the bridge, before tumbling on. Alex could only watch as the view in the cracked windshield flipped from the churning sky to the turbulent river and back again.

Michael couldn't home in on the Pontiac.

There was too much arcane interference in its location to get a firm fix on it. Instead of teleporting there, he'd had to go on foot.

Paws were faster. Abandoning his human form for that of a wolf, he raced across the pavement, dodging officers dragging a blockade in front of the on ramp. Leaping over damaged and abandoned vehicles, he ran towards the middle of the bridge. A wall of rain loomed up ahead. He dived into it as thunder boomed.

His paws stumbled over wreckage. Slowing, he shifted back to his human shape. He almost tripped over an arm as he fumbled through the downpour. Kneeling, he felt along the limb to find the rest of the body. He sought for a pulse in the throat and found none. He pressed onward.

He broke through the deluge into a space devoid of rain. The first thing he saw was the *hamrammur*. The second thing was his car being tossed about in the air like a child's toy.

"Alex!" Running forward, he tried to think of a way to reach her. Then the creature turned to face him. The battered Firebird hit the bridge. It dropped out of sight.

His heart stopped. His mind blanked.

A torrential gust of wind hit like a huge fist. He went flying, hitting the pavement hard. Rising, he let the pain feed his anger. It was anger, not fear, that he needed now.

He let loose a levin bolt. Then another. Gaining ground with each one, he continued the assault. He dodged lightning, pushed through the gales, until he finally reached the edge. Firing one last bolt, he dove into the river after Alex.

Alex came to, smelling water fouled from the city and chilled to the bone. Water leaked through the cracked windshield. It was also seeping up through the floorboards. On the other side of the glass she saw a black void. She stared, uncomprehending, before she remembered. Fear was close on the heels of memory.

I am not drowning, I'm not going to die here. Please. Oh, God, please...

She had to keep calm. That was the key to survival. She steadied her breathing before fumbling with the buckle of her seatbelt. The water was up to her knees by the time she'd gotten loose. Her body was beginning to ache now. She caught a glimpse of herself in the rear view mirror. Blood trickled from her hairline, the skin was abraded on her neck from the shoulder strap, and her chest felt as if a ton of concrete had slammed into it. Underneath the clothes, would be a lot of bruising.

The water level had come up to her waist. She couldn't tell how far she'd sunk, but she didn't think she'd hit bottom yet. She tried to open the door. It wouldn't budge. She closed her eyes, fighting against a sob.

She wasn't dying in this trap. She'd be damned if she would.
Calm. Remain calm.

Tears leaked from her eyes anyway. The water was up her chest. Her time – her air – was running out.

Wait, wait. If the water filled up the inside, the pressure would be equal inside and out, right? She would be able to open the door. After that, all she would have to do was swim to the top.

The car jolted a little as it settled on the river bottom. She quelled panic as best she could as she waited. The water reached her nose. She angled her face upward to take one last gulp of air before she was submerged completely. She felt for the exit, opened it. She pulled herself out, braced her feet on the body of the car, then kicked off towards the surface.

She swam blindly through the murk. Her lungs began to burn. Her limbs grew heavy with cold and fatigue. Soon she was flailing in the water more than swimming.

Keep moving – got to keep – going –

Seconds ticked by like an eternity. She couldn't feel the cold anymore, only the burning in her lungs. It was painful, in a distant way. Could she feel her limbs? No. There was only the burning. Then not even that.

Grayness was creeping into her awareness.

No...

She began to sink.

...can't...die...

As consciousness slipped away, flame flared in the watery dark.

Michael had changed his form the moment he'd hit the water. As a dolphin, he surged into the darkness, blocking out panic as he searched. Following cetacean instinct, he made continual clicking noises. The echoes came back to him, painting the river-scape he swam in. There were fish, some rocks, floating trash. There was no Alex. Surfacing briefly for air, he angled downwards.

He had to find her.

The temperature began to change. The murky chill was warming. Seeking the source of the warmth, he dove deeper still.

In the darkness, something glowed. The heat of it was fierce enough to boil the surrounding water. He came as close to it as his dolphin's body could stand, swimming around it as he probed it with his mind.

It was...Alex?

Leaving his confusion and questions for another time, he gathered his power around both of them. In a wavering shimmer, they vanished from the river.

The Wood

Gwynn sensed the incoming teleportation. He sensed, too, His adoptive son's mental state. Fear, worry, and bafflement warred for prominence. It was partly because of this that the teleportation faltered before it could be completed.

The deity stood in His camp, casting His will out to catch them. They appeared in a flash of blinding light at his feet. Michael lay cold, drenched, once again in a man's guise, breathing heavily. His mind reeled from the backlash of failed magic and fatigue.

Alex was naked, curled in a fetal position. She was as dry as her partner was wet. Gwynn pulled several furs off a nearby rack to bundle her in. Lifting her up, He carried her inside the tent. By the time Michael had recovered enough to regain his feet, He had Alex tucked in amid blankets.

He heard Michael lift the flap, was aware of the hounds as they crowded past him to lay next to the sleeping woman. When He looked up at His son, He saw everything he was feeling cross his pale face.

"Is – How is she?"

"She will be fine." He touched her cheek in a small gesture of affection. "She just needs rest."

"What happened to her?" Michael continued to stare at her as he spoke. "It looked as if she was on fire underwater."

"There are things that you do, and do not, know about yourself," He replied, choosing His words with care. "Things that you learn as you live your life. It is the same for her."

"Does she know what happened?"

"No." Gwynn rose to stand in front of him. The dragon looked vulnerable now. It pained Him to see it. "Whether or not she remembers will be up to her. She may not yet be ready. Will she understand what it means when she does? No, she won't." He held up a gauntleted hand to forestall the next question, then laid it comfortingly on Michael's shoulder. "Answer me this, My son: do you love her?"

"I thought I'd lost her." His voice was raw. Swallowing, Michael rubbed his face with his hands. "I was so afraid I'd lost her."

Gwynn waited as he pulled himself together again.

"Yes."

"Be with her." He placed a hand on the side of his head. "Don't think about tomorrow. All that matters now is today and that she lives."

He hesitated.

"The *hamrammur* –"

"Has moved elsewhere. You cannot face it as you are now."

The deity stepped aside so Michael could join Alex. He watched him strip the sodden clothing off then lay down next to her, before leaving them alone in the tent. Outside, He studied the darkness on the horizon – a reflection of things in the world. Under the faint rumbling in the distance, He could hear a crazed cackle of laughter.

Let the Bound One laugh, He thought. The battle was far from over.

Jacksonville, FL

"This one's from Washington, D.C.," Nate announced as he skimmed through a report. He'd done away with his country accent some time before. He sounded faintly aristocratic – like his father, Teri mused.

They sat at the dining room table, which was now covered with papers, envelopes, notepads, and folders. Richard wasn't there. With Janice looming off the coast, the Hidden Reaches had decided to throw a hurricane party in the gym. Those who weren't heading out of town would wait it out there. Since it looked like they would be joining them, the chef of *Candlelight and Magic Café* had offered his services.

So while he set up a makeshift kitchen at their hurricane shelter, the rest of their troupe rummaged through the packages that were coming in for Michael.

Teri made a humming sound in her throat absently as she read through another news clipping, one of several that had come in during the day. Across from her, Lys neatly organized notes of dates, places, people, and things. The chart she was drawing up already spread across several pages.

"Mine's three in New York," Teri murmured. "One was at the airport." Intrigued, she read a little more of the report. "The first victim had been a Peter Browning. He'd been a passenger on an incoming flight. From Iceland."

That got everyone's attention.

"Say again?" Nate asked, setting his portion of the papers aside. "Who or what is from Iceland?"

"The vic in New York," Teri answered absently as she continued to skim through the details. "He was killed at the airport, after flying in from Iceland. He'd been with his wife. They never found her, though, just him. Browning was found in a janitorial closet. According to this article, the coroner stated he had died shortly after his arrival at twelve-fifteen. However, he was seen leaving the airport at one-forty-five." She showed them a grainy picture beside the text. "This is from the surveillance camera."

It wasn't the greatest picture, she had to admit. The quality was pretty poor. She could only wonder where they'd gotten it from, as she doubted that the FAA would have allowed its release to the press – if it was legitimate.

"The creature," Nate said, golden eyes narrowing thoughtfully. "Came in as the wife, maybe? Then got the husband."

"Kind of looks like it, doesn't it?" Lys murmured, snatching another piece of paper from somewhere on the table. "Why go about it that way, though? I mean, it seems to be an awful lot of trouble to kill someone, fly over with the spouse, then kill the spouse. Wouldn't that attract more attention?"

"It's not the way I would have done it," Nate muttered, frowning at the picture. "If I had to kill someone and take their identity – which is the monster's MO – I would have chosen a loner. Someone non-descript, with few or no attachments."

"What's the date?" Lys began making notations.

"July 8, 2000." Setting the clipping aside, Teri rubbed her tired eyes. There was a dull ache beginning to throb in her left temple. "I need a break."

"I think we all do." Nate sighed as he pushed back from the table. "We've been at it for most of the afternoon. Is there anything in the fridge ready to heat up or do we have to suffer through cooking?"

"There are ready-to-heat meals in the freezer." Lys gave him a quick smile. "Richard makes them up for Alex and Teri."

"Did he say when he'd be back?" Teri got up to stretch as her friend shook her head. "Oh, well. I think I could use a nap."

Lys continued to shuffle through her notes as Teri went to lay on the couch. Closing her eyes, she let herself drift. She could hear the others murmuring softly. The microwave hummed, then beeped. Nate's meal. For a half-vamp, he certainly ate a lot of solid food. She wasn't hungry, though. In truth, she hadn't had much of an appetite since – the incident at her house. Maybe she'd eat after she woke.

Her thoughts soften, fuzzed, and faded. She was just on the edge of sleep when fingers brushed over her cheek. Irritated, she swatted at them, opening her violet eyes to glare at Nate.

"What?"

"You need to eat, sugar." It was so odd to hear him use that casual endearment without the affected redneck twang. "It'll help with the headache and put some color back in your cheeks."

"What are you? A doctor or something?" She scowled as she sat up.

He smiled. "No, sugar. You just look like the wrong side of hell."

He held out a bowl of something steaming. She took it reflexively, a bit surprised to find the aroma stirred her listless appetite.

"I'm not hungry," she said, resentment trickling into her voice as she glowered at the bowl of soup. The scent of chicken, spices, and vegetables hit her like a sucker punch. When her stomach gurgled in anticipation, she gave in. "I need a spoon."

"Right here, sugar." Nate held it out. Taking it, she dug in.

The phone rang.

They let the answering machine get it. It wasn't their phone, after all. Teri absently shoveled in soup while Alex's recorded message played through the speaker. It beeped.

"Nate, Teri, pick up the phone."

Kent's terse command had Nate across the room in a flash. He picked up the receiver from its cradle on the bar.

"Sire." He paused, his amber eyes deepening in color as he listened. His mouth firmed in a grim line. "No, neither have returned here. We haven't heard from them since they left to see you. What's wrong?"

Teri's heart leapt to her throat. She tried to swallow it back down again. At the table, Lys glanced at Teri anxiously, gripping her pen hard in front of her.

"No, we hadn't heard. We've had the TV off, going through the homicide reports that Michael has coming in. What –" He broke off, listening, as worry creased his brow. "They took Michael's car. It's a black Firebird." He paused again. Teri set the bowl aside. "You're positive?"

"What?" Teri rose from the couch, hurrying over. "What is it?"

Nate signaled for silence.

"Which bridge? They found only scraps – parts on the road?"

She felt her gorge begin to rise as Lys went as white as a sheet.

"Are they okay?" she asked.

"A moment, sire," he murmured, then shifted the phone away from his face. "There was a tornado on the Fuller Warren Bridge. One of the news cams – the ones they have sitting somewhere on buildings that overlook the city – caught it all on tape. Several cars went into the river. One of them looked like Michael's; it hasn't been confirmed that it was his. Kent's trying to find Alex and Michael to make sure that they're okay."

"Alex. God, Teri." Lys turned to Teri. She reached out to take her hand and gave it a comforting squeeze. The petite blonde had gone stark white, her brown eyes dark with fear. Tears were starting to pool in those eyes. If Lys broke down, Teri would as well.

"Alex."

"She's –" Teri fumbled for the words, striving to keep her own growing dismay in check. "She's gotten in and out of scrapes before this."

Yet Alex had never been thrown off a bridge. Could anyone survive that? She screwed her eyes shut, taking deep breaths. She didn't hear Nate as he continued to talk with his father. Her friend couldn't be dead. She couldn't be.

God, please, let her be okay. Please, let her be okay...

Warmth seeped in, burning away the chill of fear. Then she knew. The knowledge swept into her heart on a wave of faith-based reassurance. Quelling her tears, she reached for Lys' hand. She gave her a shaky smile.

"She's alive."

91

Alex awoke to find herself bundled in furs, snuggling into Michael's bare chest. Her first thought was that this was exactly where she wanted to be. Her second thought was that it would be nice to wake up this way every day. It wasn't until thought number three that she realized that she couldn't remember how she'd gotten there.

Lips pursed, she pummeled her brain, and came up with her most recent memory: swimming for her life in the St. Johns River. He'd rescued her, obviously, then brought her...where? Shifting slightly, she looked around the tent. They'd gone camping? That didn't make any sense.

His arms tightened around her as she tried to sit up.

"Take another minute."

She would have to, she realized. Underneath the furs, she was naked. She settled back down against him. He buried his face in her hair.

"Michael? Are you okay?"

"No."

Concerned, she attempted to turn into him, stopping when his hold on her tightened again.

"You may not need another damn minute, Alex," he muttered, temper creeping into his voice, "I do."

"I wasn't going to get up." She sighed into his shoulder. A moment of silence passed between them. He relaxed. "Um... where are we?"

"The Wood. Gwynn's tent." He lifted his head to look at her. "Do you recall anything?"

"I was swimming." She frowned, examining the memory. There was something there that she was missing. "We'd split up. I used the magic sniffer thingy Kent gave us and ended up on the bridge. It was there. Flying." No, that wasn't quite right, was it? "Hovering? It was in the air. It seemed to be controlling the wind and rain around it. It tossed me into the river."

"That much I saw."

There was anger in the flat tone. His eyes, dark with emotion, had little flecks of purple and gold in them. Sexy eyes, she thought. Too bad he was pissed. Then she realized part of what he was pissed about.

"I'm sorry about the Firebird."

He growled. She blinked.

"I don't care about the car." He bit off each word with angry precision. "You almost died."

Oh. She considered that a moment. Yes, she could see how that would get to him. It would get to anyone. If her mind hadn't felt as if it had been stuffed with cotton, she might have come around to that conclusion sooner.

"I scared you. I'm sor –"

He shifted, his mouth claiming hers. Heat began to pool inside her as he took her deep into the kiss. Then he broke it off as abruptly as he'd started it.

"Don't *ever* do that again."

"I'll never get tossed off a bridge again." Her lips twitched. "If I can help it."

"Alex –"

"Michael. If our roles had been reversed, could you make that promise and keep it?"

"Fine." He rested his forehead against hers. "You have a point. I do not, however, have to like it." He kissed her again, softer this time. "I didn't take it well, seeing you like that. By Gwynn, Alex, I didn't know if you were dead or alive when I found you in the water."

His face darkened. She reached up to caress his cheek.

"Thanks for getting me out of there."

"You don't recall anything that happened after you were in the water?"

She shook her head.

"There's something else. I can't put my finger on it." She studied his expression. "What did you see?"

"I'm not sure." He brushed her hair back from her face. "You were suspended in the water; there was a great deal of light and heat around you. I haven't seen anything like it before."

"Weird." Her mind searched for answers or comparisons. It came up blank. "Very weird."

"You're safe. That's what matters." He shrugged it off, though she could tell he hadn't quite dismissed it. It was nagging at him as it would nag at her for the next little while. "Let's get you dressed."

Twenty minutes later, Alex left the tent wearing an outfit that could have come from her bedroom at home. Michael hadn't said where the jeans and pull-over blouse had come from. She supposed it didn't matter.

Her partner stood by the campfire, his hands in the pockets of his own black jeans as he stared at the flames. He had the brooding look again. Gwynn sat across from him, absently scratching the ears of the white hound.

"Welcome, Alexandria Rosselle," Gwynn intoned formally. "Daughter."

"Ah, thanks." She gave Him a puzzled look, then turned her gaze to Michael. He just looked at Gwynn with a thoughtful, almost suspicious, expression.

"You are coming into your own, much as Michael had some

time ago." Gwynn inclined His head as He spoke to her.

"What does that mean, exactly?" she asked, looking from one to the other.

"Only that." He put more effort into the scratch. White's foot began to snap to and fro with enthusiasm. "Things are moving quickly. You will find that few things are as they seem."

"Okay," Alex said, a little baffled. "I'm going to pretend I know what that means."

"If you don't now, you will in the future," was the deity's only reply.

She rolled her eyes. Michael held out a hand for hers. She took it, allowing him to pull her close.

"So what's next?"

"I think the two of you can figure that out on your own." Gwynn rose to His feet. "Your hunt continues."

"It's time we returned to it." Michael gave the helmeted figure a slight bow. "Thank you."

"Any time, My son." He inclined His head toward Alex. "That goes for you as well, Daughter."

Before she could say anything in return, Michael was teleporting them away.

It was almost completely free.

Technically, it was free. It had the amulet, the key to its chains. It had control. Hadn't the weather answered its call? Hadn't it tossed the wheeled contraptions of this era into the river like rocks into a pond? Still, it wasn't enough. It wouldn't be enough, not until the last vestiges of its enslavement were gone. Only then would it be as it once was: unfettered, unhampered, unchecked.

For that, it would need more magic.

The blood rite hadn't generated enough arcane energy to destroy it. It could acquire more victims for another rite. Ten or so might meet its needs. However, there were other issues to consider. It needed a secluded place and ropes to secure the sacrifices until it was ready for them. With the police scattered around the city, managing transportation venues, that method might be difficult to use.

It drifted on its vortex of wind until it settled onto the middle of a downtown street. Where there had been people before, there were now none. Puzzled, it scanned the sidewalks, the buildings. There were only vehicles on the asphalt, and not many of them. Without prey, it was left with its new knack with the weather. For that, it would need a tall structure, a tower, something- that would be fairly easy for lightning to strike. It would also need to be able to access it.

It took hours of inspecting buildings before it found one it was satisfied with. Remembering what the master had taught it about breaking and entering, it sought out the loading bay. It marshaled its new power as it progressed to the main door leading into the basement level.

Lightning fried the electronic locks on the fourth try.

93

"Alex!"

"What happened?"

"Are you hurt?"

"My sire's been looking for you."

Teri, Lys, and Nate had rushed to the foyer the moment Alex and Michael had walked into her apartment. Alex clasped her friends' hands with a reassuring smile as her partner gestured for silence.

"Okay, one at a time. We just walked in." In fact, she reflected, they hadn't even had a chance to shut the door behind them before the bombardment of concern began. Michael did so now while she addressed everyone's questions. "Hi! I took a swim. I'm fine. What did Kent want?"

"He wanted to verify that it wasn't either of you in the black car that got tossed off the bridge earlier today." Nate gave them a stern look. "Was it?"

"It was. Let's sit down."

She ushered everyone to the dining area. Michael pulled out a chair for her, murmured that he'd get something hot to drink, then delved into the kitchen. As he busied himself with her coffee maker, she told them about what had happened on the river.

"Several people died," Lys said once she'd finished. "We were afraid that you were one of them."

"I'm sorry." She touched her arm. "I didn't mean to worry you."

"At least Michael was there." Teri took a deep breath, releasing some of the residual tension. "You had better call Kent."

"Be prepared for a lecture on carrying cell phones." Nate gave her a humorless smile. "It would have saved a great deal of heartache if we'd been able to reach you."

"Okay, I'll do it in a minute. Where's Richard?"

"At the gym, helping with preparations there." Lys shrugged. "It keeps him out from underfoot here. He's happiest when he's busy anyway."

"Right." Alex remembered Richard's thinly veiled disapproval of both Nate and Michael. Keeping him apart from them was probably for the best. "Does anyone know the latest news on Janice?"

"She'll hit in less than twenty-four hours at her current speed." As Lys spoke in her soft, serious tone, Alex saw Michael reach for the phone on the bar. Calling Kent, she thought. "There's still some time for her to turn away from Jacksonville, but they don't think she will. They don't anticipate a direct hit. That's the only good news they had to say about it."

"The highways have been converted to go north or west only," her neighbor put in. "They're packed with people trying to flee the city. Hidden Reaches is holding a hurricane party in the gym, as that's the strongest structure in the complex. Most of us will ride it out there."

Us. The residents. How many will remain?

"Orlando only got the outer bands." Teri picked up a pen lying on the table, fiddled with it. "They took a lot of damage – are still taking a lot of damage. It's a huge system. There's a ton of flooding, some fires from lightning. The winds have been terrible. They had thirty-eight confirmed deaths from hurricane related incidents in the last newscast."

"The Reaches has survived hurricanes before." This came from Michael as he set a mug of fresh coffee in front of Alex. He'd muffled the mouth piece of the phone against his shoulder. "When Dora struck, the damage here was minimal. There were no injuries incurred by anyone who stayed. They'll be safe here." With that, he stepped back into the kitchen to resume his conversation with Kent.

She nodded as she cupped the mug in her hands. The warmth was comforting.

"It doesn't leave us much time to finish this thing." She sipped, considering. "We don't know where the *hamrammur* went after our last encounter. The trackers Kent made do work, though. That's something."

"The news forecaster said that there was an awful lot of storm activity downtown. That hasn't let up since the tornado on the bridge," Teri put in. "That helps, right? It's a sign that the monster thing's in the area."

"We'll have to get over there soon. It's most likely looking for a way to destroy or nullify that amulet – which it now has, by the way." She frowned as her partner rejoined them at the table. "What's up?"

"Kent will have cell phones ready for us when we meet him next." He ignored her pained expression. "Deal with it, Alex."

Nate chuckled at the two of them. Alex kicked him from under the table.

"Kent has a few people with trackers scouting the city. When we find it, there are a few ideas we can try to resolve this. Meanwhile, we're to meet him at his office to coordinate the rest."

"The rest of what?" Lys asked. Alex gave her a fierce smile.

"Oh, just a little game we call killing the monster."

94

Buoyed by the whirlwind conjured to keep it aloft above the plants in the lobby, the *hamrammur* considered its current lair. It was nice, roomy, tall. Suitable.

It wore a different shape. A member of the building staff had remained to monitor the generators – which it then turned off. It had no need for them. His memories, so crystal clear in its mind unlike those of the people it had killed prior to claiming its amulet, had been most useful. Drawing on those memories, it had managed to rig an antenna to attract the lightning, and disabled the grounding rod. All it had needed to do then was connect the antenna to the main wiring for the building. Things would be trickier from there.

Lightning was only a untamed form of power. It was all related, the master had said, electricity and magic. Handling either was only a matter of will. Yet if it didn't have enough will or strength to control it, it would come to harm. That was a risk that it was not willing to take.

Turning in mid air, it studied the rest of its work. A restaurant provided the closest electrical outlet, along with a few other helpful items. It had found an extension cable, running it from the outlet to the floor in front of it. At the end the insulating plastic had been stripped away to interweave with the bare wires of a hot plate's power cord.

It would work. Shouldn't it?

It dropped lightly to the ground to study the hot plate. Groping at its neck, its fingers closed around the amulet. Once placed on the metal surface, all that needed to be done was to wait. The wild energy – lots of it – would come. The huge electrical surge it hoped for would hit the metal, frying the pendant. It would be free.

Of course, that wasn't all that it had to wait for. Where at least one of its pursuers had fallen, several others had sprung up. If they came, it would have to be ready.

Idly fiddling with its prized possession, it mulled over its options. It smiled. It would destroy the amulet and its hunters in the same blow. It gestured.

Outside, under a sky so thick with thunder clouds it looked like night, thousands of jagged bolts struck the area. Inside, more shot out from the creature's fingers. Glass shattered, lights went out. It grinned in the blackness.

Its best hunts had been in the dark.

95

"They've just closed the bridges. Are Teri and the others safe?"

"Yep." Alex gave Kent a grin. "They're having a party back at the Reaches."

"They'll be fine," Michael assured him. "Your people?"

"Those who needed to leave, have."

The three stood in Kent's office, Michael and Alex having teleported in moments before. Kent leaned against the front of his desk, regarding them with sober amber eyes. Michael was a statue in comparison to Alex, who kept shifting her weight from one leg to the other. It was evident that she was a bundle of energy at this point, anxious, perky, and excited all at once. If it went on for much longer, it would start to get on his nerves.

"If I agree that you're right, I'll carry a cell phone, etc, can we skip the lecture?" She pursed her lips as she looked through the pane behind the vampire lord. "We need to get started."

The two men followed her gaze. Outside the conditions had deteriorated fast. Winds had become gales. Most cement and asphalt surfaces bore pits from lightning. Moving out in the open would have to be done as cautiously as possible.

"Fine." Kent went around his desk to open a drawer. Taking out two cell phones, he handed them one each. "The numbers are preprogrammed. Keep them on and with you." He gave Alex a meaningful stare. After receiving a meek nod in return, he continued. "I got news just before the bridges closed that the thing is at the Modis Building."

Michael considered it, factoring the information into the various scenarios he and Alex had discussed prior to arriving.

"Hmm." Alex tapped the new phone against her palm lightly. "Do we know what it's doing there?"

"No. I've gotten a few reports. It seems to have some mastery over lightning. It blew the glass fronts out, on the first floor. It had also done something on the roof. No one is sure what. Aside from that, it has remained at ground level."

"We'll need to find out what it did on the roof." Michael's brow furrowed. From the look in Alex's eyes, he could see that she was one step ahead of him.

"I think we can accommodate that. It shouldn't change the overall plan too much."

Kent's eyebrows rose.

"You have a plan?"

"Why, yes, actually." Alex's eyes were a vivid emerald as they twinkled at him. Michael nodded, somewhat amused. "We do, and you're part of it…"

Alex trudged down Ocean Street, having left Kent to continue his journey alone on East Bay Street. She kept close to the buildings, moving slow against the wind as she headed towards the river. Glancing up at the sky, she winced as light flashed ominously in the clouds.

Michael had better know what he's doing up there.

He had to, right? He had volunteered for it. Still, dragon or not, he could still be fried or crash to the ground. If anything happened to him, their plan – her plan – would fail.

Trust that he'll do his part. Think about something else.

Like Gwynn. He was, according to myth, a Welsh deity of the hunt, war, death, and vengeance. Well, He seemed to have an interest in the conflicts with the Dark. They often included elements of death and vengeance. Hunters, too, were frequently involved. She wondered if anyone else in the Hunters' Guild had encountered Him.

Would the wind ever let up? The wall next to her provided some protection. Still, the press of the gale was hard. At this rate, she'd be exhausted from fighting it before she arrived for the real battle.

Hey – Water Street!

Straight ahead was the Main Street Bridge, marking where Ocean met Water. She turned south at the corner, freezing in place when a stray lightning bolt struck the pavement a few feet in front of her. The pockmark it left behind was the size of her hand.

"Well." She took a deep breath as adrenaline pumped. "If I wasn't awake before, I sure as hell am now."

A tiny pebble landed on her head. Another fell at her feet. She bent to pick it up for a better look as more began to rain down all around her. *Hail.* At least they were small. No problem. She braced herself against a store front and continued down the street.

One block later, her goal in sight, something big hit her shoulder. Throwing herself against the wall beside her, she rubbed it, looking around to see what it had been. A chunk of rounded ice the size of a golf ball lay on the sidewalk. In the middle of the road, she could see a few larger hailstones scattered about.

Great.

Better to move fast. She began to run, her progress going easier as the wind had dropped down a bit. Skidding a bit on the ice pellets, she closed the distance between her and the Modis Building with a handful of hail related bruises to show for it. Once at the entrance, it began to rain.

Shivering a little from the wet, she crouched outside the doors, mindful of the glass that lay in shards all along the building front. The air here felt weird. Thick. Was it…pulsating?

Power's building up…

She peered inside. The interior was dark. Still, she thought she saw something move inside. If that was the *hamrammur*, then it probably could see her. She looked around. There was no cover, not even an awning – no place to hide, no place to take shelter.

She fumbled with the cell phone, dialed Kent's number, let it ring three times, then hung up. He called back. Set on vibrate, the phone buzzed twice before disconnecting. He wasn't in place yet. She'd have to hold.

Shit, shit, shit.

At times like this, with her nerves strung tight, adrenaline rushing through her bloodstream, she wondered what it might have been like to be just an artist. Nothing else. Not a hunter. Just an everyday person, totally ignorant of the Dark. No getting thrown off bridges, no near drowning in the river, no having Egyptian coffins thrown at her from across the room...No Kent. No Michael. Would it be worth having?

I would be so bored. She laughed a little at herself, watching for whatever was inside the building. *Okay. That's done. Focus.*

There were a few bright spots to this. She had a lot of weapons strapped to her person this time. There were no sarcophagi for the thing to throw at her.

Kent's research on the building had revealed that it was being renovated. She remembered that there was an open atrium of sorts in the lobby area. There would be plants, maybe some tables and chairs from the bistro inside. That would be...to the right of her position. She couldn't remember what was on the left. In the middle would be the stairs zigzagging up to the second floor. Behind the stairs, were the elevators...

Trying to anticipate what else she might encounter inside, she did the only other thing she could do.

She waited.

97

Lightning flashed, a blazing burst of white-violet light in the darkness that lasted only three seconds. It was enough for Kent to see the silhouette of a huge winged creature passing high overhead as he trotted down East Bay Street. A little voice in the back of his mind observed quite calmly that it was quite likely the largest – never mind the only – dragon he had ever seen. Another voice, shaky with nerves, stated that it couldn't have been a dragon. They didn't exist outside of legends, fantasy novels, and movies. A third voice, full of speculation, interjected that Michael –

"I don't want to think about it," muttered the vampire lord. "I really don't want to think about it."

Hand on the sword scabbard belted at his hip, he ran down the deserted street, ignoring the hail, then the downpour, as he made his way to the loading dock. He found the doors easily enough. They were hard to miss. Dented and scorched, one lay discarded on the ground. The other hung drunkenly from its hinges.

"That makes things a bit more convenient."

Drawing the sword free, he stepped into the basement level and smelled it. Blood, death. The air here was full of it. Underneath the scent, he could sense a faint throbbing. Gearing up for the fight, he thought. It knew they were there or were coming. Still, he had to check. If there were others down here, someone who might have survived or hidden from it…

He followed the stench to its source in an alcove off the main area. Taking a pen light from his pocket, he used it to find the body. It lay sprawled off to one side. There wasn't much left recognizable as human.

Did you enjoy that or were you just pissed off? He shook his head. It didn't matter. It would end, one way or another, very soon.

Angling the light over, he saw machinery. Generators. Still operable, he observed. They'd been shut off. The smear of blood on the switch told him by whom. It hadn't wanted the auxiliary power.

He checked the fuel levels, then considered ruining someone's night.

98

Above the city in the form of his birth, Michael twisted in midair to dodge a streak of lightning.

Teleportation had not been an option. While he could travel anywhere with that method, there was still one limitation that had proven to be a stumbling block here. He had to have seen or been to the place he was teleporting to before. The roof of a downtown office building had been outside his repertoire of locations. That had meant arrival by foot or wing. He'd chosen flight.

Flight was extremely difficult. The cross winds, the tail winds, the hail, the rain – it made him question what he had been thinking when he'd decided to make his approach from the air. Aside from securing the roof of the building.

If the creature had an interest there, so must we.

A gale came from below, tossing him up. Partially furling his wings, he dove through it. He fanned them out, angled them, sensed the air currents around him. He glided closer to the Modis Building, spiraling down towards the roof. The closer he got, the thicker the air become. It wasn't humidity or heat. It was magic, of the same signature that permeated the clouds, and it was alive.

There was a slow, rhythmic beat. Like a heart. It was eerie.

As a dragon, Michael had never experienced goose bumps before.

The wind, too, reacted to it. It swirled around the structure, gaining speed as it went. Yet the focus of the power, the focus of the storm, was not the top of the tower as Michael had half expected. It was at the bottom of it.

Though there was now a vortex around the building, he still had to land. Another challenge. At least the hail was subsiding.

He slipped into the whirlwind, letting it take him around. As he had done with the gale, he folded his wings, let himself drop in altitude. Little by little, he drew closer to the roof. Finally he caught the edge, using the momentum of the wind to swing his body up and over the edge. His form shimmered, shifted, shrunk. He hit the rooftop as a man, in the relative calm of the vortex's center. Straightening, he spied a rigger antenna.

It was time to get to work.

The Master watched from across the street. He stood in the Landing parking lot, sheltered by an overpass leading onto the bridge, with his hands in the pockets of his slacks. He smiled coolly as Alex continued to wait, her attention centered on his former servant.

Soon, he would lose either a tool or an enemy. Which would it be? The outcome hardly mattered, so long as someone died.

It was a kill or be killed world, after all.

Alex's phone began to vibrate in her pocket. She fished it out, checked the display. Michael. It buzzed three times, then cut off. Inside the building, the auxiliary lights flashed on. Head jerking up, she saw the *hamrammur* as it twisted in the air, snarling at the lights. The phone in her hand began to vibrate again. Once, twice, three times. They were ready.

"Alright, Alex," she murmured to herself. "Showtime."

She rose to enter the lobby.

101

How dare they? How dare they ruin its advantage?

Rage surged through it. Wind tore through the openings of the ground floor, whipping around it to raise it higher. There was a roaring in its ears, a tingling in its skin. Static sparked along the metallic surfaces nearby.

Something moved at the end of the lobby. It flung out its arms, throwing its head back in a challenging cry. The air around it exploded.

Tables, seats, foliage, drop-cloths – all of it went flying out from the *hamrammur* towards the farthest reaches of the lobby. It watched its missiles shoot away, saw a figure duck beneath them, auburn hair streaming behind her. Then she was up, green eyes bright and glowing, one hand delving into her jacket to pull out a gun as she ran towards it.

Her.

She had drowned – died. It had seen it, flung her to her death personally. The shock became fury. If the river wouldn't take her, it would.

It would kill her again. There would be no errors this time.

102

The whole tower trembled as the scream sounded from the lobby.

Kent flung the stairwell door open, dashing onto the ground floor. He saw the elevators, heard the impact of many objects colliding with the marble-sheathed walls. Stopping to orient himself, he saw a chair rocket past him. It hit the wall, cracking the stone.

He adjusted the grip on his sword, wishing briefly for a shield. He'd been a knight once, trained to fight in the crusades before vampirism had taken him. Shields had been standard equipment back then...

They aren't now, Aisley. He moved to the far end of the row of elevators, side-stepped around the corner. Gunshots fired. Electricity began to crackle in the air.

He abandoned stealth for speed, darting into the open.

Alex fired several rounds at the thing floating in the air. The bullets bypassed it, hitting the central marble staircase behind her target. Curses ran through her mind.

"Damn it!"

Alex swore. Her aim had been off. Worse, her glock had jammed. She got behind a supported column to eject the magazine and pull back on the slide. The jammed bullet fell from the chamber. Reloading, she stepped back into the fight. She saw Kent come out to run up the stairs to gain higher ground. She fired again, lunged to avoid a potted plant thrown her way. She'd missed.

I'm not a crap-shooter, What gives?

It had to be the wind. Holstering her gun, she pulled out throwing knives. Seeing her enemy beginning to turn towards her ally, she tossed a blade.

"Hey! I'm not through with you, buddy!"

A blast of air deflected the dagger to the side. Whirling back to her, it snarled, the features contorting grotesquely. It was losing its assumed form, she realized. Was that because of the amulet?

It fisted one hand, swiping it at her. A gale answered the command. She felt herself rise into the air and sail towards it. As it caught her by her shirt front, it grinned at her. The eyes glinted with a sulphurous light. She grabbed its wrist, pulled hard, braced a foot on its thigh. With her free hand, she reached for the glint of silver at its neck. Behind them, Kent leapt over the railing, sword raised in both hands to plunge the blade into the creature's back.

Power jolted her.

The *hamrammur* howled.

She found herself speeding towards the wall above the entrance doors. Rolling as she fell, she landed on her back. Stunned, ears ringing, she lay gasping. She snapped out of it as she heard Kent scream.

Fumbling onto her hands and knees, she saw him crumple to the floor, wisps of smoke coming off his clothes. The sword dropped onto the tiles beside him, blackened.

Cackling, the *hamrammur* set itself down on the ground. It no longer looked remotely human. The nightmarish visage rid itself of the last remnants of the uniform it wore. It raised its clawed hands, shouted something in a language she didn't understand. The building began to tremble.

Michael, where are you?

104

I t hadn't worked.

The thing had rigged a contraption to harness the lightning of the storm. Michael had taken it down, severed the wiring. It hadn't mattered. Now deep within the stairwell, two flights away from the second level, he felt the structure quake. The lightning had struck, en masse, anyway.

What was conducting it? He laid a hand on the cement wall. It was hot. Something within it was carrying that raw electricity down to its main focus below.

He hurried down the remaining steps, opting to come out on the second floor. It overlooked the lobby, he recalled. He'd be able to see what was going on from there.

105

Outside, the rain was coming down in torrents. It drowned the street outside, blew through the broken panes lining the building's front.

Alex crawled through the water and shards of plexi-glass until she was behind a pillar. Her body wouldn't cease shaking. Shock, she thought. She was in shock. Couldn't have that. She had to pull out of it. Kent would survive – he was a vampire – but he was out of the fight. She had to believe that Michael would make it in time.

Okay. Options. What are my options now?

"God, please help me think. What do I do?" Their plan had hinged on the thing's power wearing down as they fought it. Instead, it seemed to be increasing. *Abandon the plan.* Play it by ear.

Something popped. The sound was sharp, quick, almost electrical. Then there was another. Another. The air filled with a cacophony of noise.

She peered around the column, saw it just standing there, head back, as white and yellow tendrils of energy crawled over the marble. They came from pockmarks in the walls, the ceiling, slithering towards the one that called them.

Alex had never been a fantastic student of magery. She could do simple things, invest positive energy in a weapon, bolster it with faith, and use it to dispel negative energy. Her practices, her experiences, had been nothing like this.

Something zapped her foot. Jerking back, she saw more of the arcing lines surrounding her. Most crept past her. Others were converging on her position. Without thinking, she put a hand up, spreading her fingers out in front of the advancing streaks of magic.

"I'm not done yet," she muttered, her mind clearing a little more. Her hand still shook. She willed it to be steady. "With God as my witness, I won't be done. I'm a hunter. I'm a fighter. I have faith, damn it. If that monster wants power, I'll give it to him."

She closed her fingers tightly as the tendrils reached them. Light flared around her hand, first a brilliant white, then with a fiery corona. Deep inside her, magic began to gather. The serpentine streams of yellow began to turn a blazing orange.

All of the aches faded from her body. She'd pay for this later, she thought as she rose to her feet. Palming another knife, she suffused it with energy. It wouldn't be enough. It was too small. She needed more reach. Then she saw it on the floor not far from her.

Kent's sword...

It fell into place in her mind. She knew exactly what she had to do. With a surreal calm, she readied the arcane blade and walked away from her shelter towards the creature.

106

This was interesting.

The Master hadn't expected this kind of reaction from the girl. Who would have? She had never evidenced anything like this before.

Frowning thoughtfully, he watched from the shadows of the bistro as a human woman advanced on an inhuman monster. He wondered if she was aware of the glowing aura around her. The color of flame, the shape not fitting her own, it reminded him of something.

As he mulled it over, she flung the knife, diving for the discarded sword nearby. The small blade burned like the sun as it buried itself in his tool's torso. It shrieked. The pattern of magic it had been forming unraveled. The lines snapped backwards, writhing. With arcane force surging in flux, the wooden floor of the little restaurant began to scorch.

Seemingly oblivious, he watched his former servant wrench the dagger free, give a wrathful bellow. A movement above them on the second floor caught his eye. Her partner had finally arrived.

107

Michael made it to the sidewall overlooking the lobby in time to see the *hamrammur* rush at Alex. She was glowing. Kent lay still nearby, his sword now in her hand. Physically, she wouldn't be a match for it.

He let a levin bolt fly as she raised her weapon, fire erupting along the blade's edge. The bolt raced towards the creature, then curved up to hit the ceiling as she side-stepped then charged and swung. The sword tip sliced into shoulder muscle. The monster broke its forward momentum, lashing out with its injured arm. The fist slammed into Alex's chest. Air was forced from her lungs. She stumbled away, lost her grip on the sword, struggled for breath. It skittered across the floor as the creature tackled her.

Michael jumped over the wall, changing form as he fell. He opened his maw as he landed, shot dragon fire at the enemy. The blast of flame missed its mark by inches. Alex bucked beneath her attacker, shot her knee into its groin. It grunted, closing one clawed hand around her throat as she twisted. It began to squeeze.

Wind rose, whipping around them. Leaping at the creature, Michael was shoved back. The gusts circled their master, a protective barrier. He couldn't give up. He could see Alex, saw the blood seeping out from under her. If he didn't get to her, didn't kill the creature, she would die.

Inhaling deep, unwilling to hurt his partner, his woman, he aimed high and opened his maw to let fire loose. The torrent hit the whirlwind. It deflected a few degrees to the side. He adjusted his aim, breathed flame again. It hit the *hamrammur's* back.

Alex felt its grip loosened, its body jerk. Still gasping for air, she knocked its hand away from her throat. Her body bucked violently. It raked its claws across her front.

Pain exploded. Flesh tore. Weight crashed down on her. She could smell the metallic tang of blood. Pictured droplets on the tile. Remembered the girl. Brandy. Torn apart in a stall. Without a chance. Helpless. Hopeless.

She heard Michael's anguished roar. Felt his fury, his fear. The job wasn't done. She couldn't leave with THE hunt incomplete. Fighting the pain, her mind reached out for his.

Do it. Now.

There would be no other chance.

Michael's grief and anger poured over Alex as her awareness drifted back, as the creature dug in to tear her apart. Teeth fastened to her neck. Breath clogged. Pain began to recede.

She had faith. Closed her eyes. She had Michael.

I love you.

With a mournful cry, the dragon seared the darkness with a

mage-born firestorm of white and blue.

Alex smiled, fading, as the world was incinerated.

109

The Master grinned as the flame engulfed the servant and the woman it grappled with. Its short shriek of shock and pain was sweet music. From behind a pillar near the entrance, he watched as flesh turned to ash and marveled at the strength of dragon fire. It really was hot enough to melt steel.

As the blast abated, he turned to leave. There was no further need for him to stay. The creature was dead. So was Alex. He knew what Michael Keegan actually was. While the 'man' would still be a knot in the skein he could be dealt with. No dragon lived in this world without making enemies somewhere. All the Master had to do was find one.

Then the next phase of his plans could commence.

Satisfied, he walked out of the building. The streets had filled with water, the wind driving to lap at the steps leading down from the entrance of the Modis Building. Heedless of it, he waded in. He would be gone long before the storm had subsided completely.

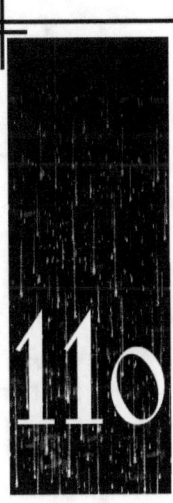

110

Atlantic Beach, FL

Gwynn had watched the events unfold, standing witness to both the fight and the storm from atop the Main Street Bridge downtown. He had seen the river overflow, had felt the sacrifice made, had experienced His son's anguish. The *hamrammur* was dead, yet there was still one thing left to do.

Now He stood at the beach, knee deep in the violent surf. In front of Him was an oncoming wall of cloud, rain, and moving air. Janice still obeyed its master's command. Unmoved by wave, wind, or riptide, He listened. Weather had its own melody. The harmonics, once disjointed and harsh, were falling back into place. Given time, the system would normalize on its own.

The city didn't have time.

He raised one gauntleted hand high above His helm. Behind Him, the storm over the city stopped its aimless churning. He clench His hand into a fist, gathering all the threads of magic that linked the hurricane to the other system. He then hurled those tethers back at Janice.

The hurricane they chained raced over the sea. The bands churned. The eye shifted.

Janice was turning out into the empty Atlantic.

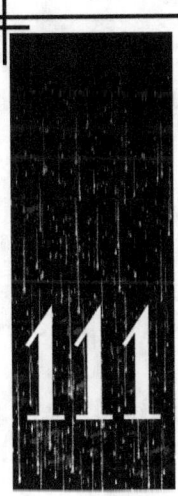

111

Jacksonville, FL

In the lobby of a downtown office building, a dragon was grieving. Michael swayed his head over the spot where she had died. All that remained of Alex and the enemy she had fought, were embers, ash, and cooling molten silver.

It was written somewhere that dragons did not cry. They couldn't cry, because they couldn't grieve. Tears were as foreign to them as flying was to a worm. Whoever had written it was wrong. Dragons wept, their tears ranked among the rarest things on earth.

MICHAEL.

Tears splashed in the ashes, sending up puffs of steam into the eerily still air. He'd lost her. He'd just found her, and now he'd lost her. He was alone. Lost, and alone.

The waves of his grief crashed over him repeatedly. His chest constricted. His throat closed almost completely, cutting off his keen. In his mind, he kept seeing her as she had been before the before battle. Before he'd killed her.

He'd killed her.

Blindly, he threw himself away from the ashes, striking one of the columns. The building shook under the impact. The marble fractured. The death song took on a self-accusatory note as he smashed himself into the pillar again. This time it crumpled beneath him. Sprawling on top of it, he made no effort to get up.

You did not kill her, Michael.

Silence descended. From somewhere to the right of him, Michael could hear footsteps echoing. He didn't open his eyes, even when he heard the figure kneel beside him, even when he felt the armored hands stroke his muzzle.

You did not kill her, My son, Gwynn repeated, more gently. If there is blame, it lies with the HAMRAMMUR AND ITS MASTER.

But she was gone…
Gone…

She never left you.
Gone…

She isn't gone.

112

Flame.
  Heat.
 Ash.
 White.
 Was this death?

Alex wasn't sure. She couldn't tell. In a world that was all color, all light and shadow, she had no way of knowing. Her conscious drifted, lacking form, direction, purpose. Yet a sense of something left unfinished persisted.

What was it?

She tried to focus her thoughts, felt them scatter as if on a breeze. Gathering them, she made another attempt, heard a faint song. A snatch of sound, of emotion. There was pain in it. No, not it. Him.

Michael, don't cry. The words formed, then vanished. *I'm right here.*

Could he hear her? As the keening continued, she didn't think so. She had to get to him. Had to reach him, assure him that it was alright.

DO YOU HAVE FAITH?

The question was whispered in the light. She answered it without thinking of who it was or where it came from.

Yes.

DO YOU BELIEVE?

Of course she believed. Wasn't that part of faith?

SO LONG AS YOU HAVE FAITH, AND BELIEVE, ANYTHING IS POSSIBLE.

Heat flared. The spirit of Alexandria Rosselle was sucked down, down to where the glowing embers had died, and the ash was soaked with tears.

113

Michael opened blue eyes dark with pain. Reluctantly, he lifted his head. Gwynn stood up, stepping back, turning his antlered helm towards the place she had perished. Dazed, he followed the deity's gaze.

The embers were red.

He stared, not comprehending what he was seeing. He found himself moving slowly, stiffly, making his way to the spot. By the time he was within ten feet, the embers were bright orange. He felt the heat. The air stirred as he hunkered down beside it, lowering his chin to the floor. He saw the ashes give birth to the merest flicker of flame. Within moments, the tiny spurt of fire had grown waist high and was spreading out.

Mesmerized, Michael found himself shifting from his draconic form to his human one. Gwynn came up behind him to lay a hand on his shoulder. Together, they watched the flames flare incandescent, piercing the gloom around them. Then they died away.

There, in the bed of ash, lying naked in a fetal position, was Alex.

With a hoarse cry, Michael gathered her to him, cradling her in his arms as he nuzzled her face. Tears streamed down his cheeks. One fell on her lips as she opened her brilliant green eyes.

"Michael?" she murmured.

"I love you." He buried his face in her hair, rocking. "I love you."

She smiled.

114

Alex set down her brush. Reaching for her coffee, she sipped as she contemplated the painting. The form was fluid, the colors vibrant. In the center, the regal figure of her black dragon looked out from the page. She liked to think that it was one of her best pieces.

Pleased with it, she signed and dated the picture within the Celtic circle she'd placed in the corner for that purpose. She rose, setting the coffee aside as she checked her watch, then swore. She was running late.

Dashing out of her studio, she ran into the bedroom to dig through her closet. Her date would arrive within the hour; why hadn't she kept a closer eye on the time?

Kent, having recuperated from the ordeal at the Modis, was holding a party to commemorate their victory over the *hamrammur*. It would be her first public appearance since the fight, her last carefree event before she had to settle back into the more regular rhythm of her life. She was determine to have fun.

"Come on, Alex, find something…here."

She pulled out a blue sundress. Changing into it quickly, she hurried to the bathroom to fuss with her hair. She paused, smiling, as she caught sight of the silver around her neck. Fingering the dragon pendant, she turned it over to read the inscription on the back again. *To My Lady Faire*. Michael had given it to her two days ago. He'd bought it at the jewelry store they'd visited.

"Alex, are you ready yet?"

Teri's voice jolted her back to the present.

"Coming," she called out. A glance in the mirror told her that she looked fine. Abandoning the bathroom, she groped under the bed for her shoes, then slipped them on. Her bedroom door opened to reveal her friend in a little black dress, her chestnut curls bouncing as she shook her head in exasperation.

"Michael's here, and the others are already on their way to Kent's." She looked Alex over critically. "Are you sure you're up for this?"

"Yep." She grinned at her. "I'm fully recovered, full of energy, and raring to go."

They walked into the living room together. Her partner was there, talking with Nate. Both were wearing black. Alex rolled her eyes.

"Did I miss the memo? Is this a black-attire-only party?"

Nate chuckled. Michael crossed to her, caught her hands, and kissed her.

"Okay, okay, let's go. We're going to be late."

"Aw, let them be, Sugar. It's sweet."

Alex stepped away from her man.

"Why don't you two step out for a minute? I've got to show Michael something before we leave. A few more minutes isn't going to hurt anything," she said, anticipating Teri. She gave her partner's hand a tug, leading the way back to her studio.

"What is it?"

"You'll see."

She opened the door, letting him inside first. He stopped two steps in. She'd left the painting on the table-top easel. The black dragon looked out from the paper, the vivid blue eyes so much like Michael's own. Seeing the two together in the same room, the dragon man and the picture, she knew she'd gotten it right.

"This is the picture you were sketching at the café. You finished it."

"I did." She came alongside him to see his face. "It's you."

He came closer, raising a finger to touch the signature in the corner. His lips curved.

"I don't wear a collar or horn caps."

"No, but it's still you." She picked up the illustrator board the painting was mounted on, handed it to him. "I want you to have it."

He took it, reaching out caress to her cheek.

"I love you."

Hearing the words brought joy to her heart. They always did.

"I love you, too." She kissed him lightly, the picture held between them. "Come on. We've got a party to go to."

They would let tomorrow take care of itself, she thought as they hurried to rejoin the others. Together, they would enjoy today.

About the Author

D oris Ross lives in Jacksonville, FL, where she drinks coffee by the gallon, writes, works, and occasionally plays video games. Her current favorites are *Halo, Minecraft, Diablo III,* and the *Fable* series. Sometimes, when she's met enough of her writing goals, she gets to have LAN parties with friends.

A resident of the city since 1987, she began writing *Blood & Rain* in early 2004 and finished the first (very rough) draft in 2005. The next nine years were spent learning more about the writing craft, confronting the monstrous job of revision and editing the book, and educating herself on the ins and outs of publishing industry.

In June 2012, she co-founded the publishing house Trinity Gateways LLC with fellow authors and long-time friends LJ Gastineau and Tricia Sparks. Not long after, her father pushed to have *Blood & Rain* readied for publication. So after a final edit and revision, she did — much to her father's gratification.

Today, Doris is working to finish the *Descent Into Darkness* dark fantasy series and revise the completed draft of *Blood & Rain*'s sequel. You can follow her progress at DorisRoss.com, and find out what other publications she's been involved in at TrinityGateways.net.

DESCENT INTO DARKNESS

VOLUME 1

HE BEGINS

BY

DORIS ROSS

From obscurity into infamy, Ba'tvian Delthanurk blazes his wicked trail. He is both hunted and hunter, a blood mage seeking to carve his deep into the history of Einlienn. Some will follow him, others will seek his death.

Meet the loyal Nerisse se li Astorae, an elven woman intended for the priesthood and the determined Absol Omine, the Mancer whose name fills Ba'tvian with hate. More will cross paths with the blood mage Delthanurk. Only a chosen few will survive, and none—living or dead—will forget him.

This is his journey into villainy – Ba'tvian Delthanurk's *Descent Into Darkness*.

He Begins is the first printed omnibus containing the initial three novellas, *Part 1: His Own, Part 2: Her Lord,* and *Part 3: His Beast,* previously released as e-books.

ISBN-10: 194142600X
ISBN-13: 978-1941426005

MANTLE OF THE GODS
BOOK 1

QUEST FOR TRUTH

BY
TRICIA SPARKS

A mysterious discovery leads one woman to stumble upon a startling secret of the ancient world...

Annalynn Gallagher is an archeologist working the find of the century with the last person she ever wanted to see again: Dr. Ian Broody, the man who'd ruined her life. Now trouble is brewing at the dig and Anna is determined to prevent the past from repeating itself.

Some secrets should stay in the dark...

As she delves for the answers about the rising turmoil she finds only more danger. From her dig site to her home back in the States, she encounters sabotage, ominous tails, and threats to her safety and sanity. Seeking help, she turns to a man with a history darker than her own.

...or they will drive you over the edge.

Sam Abrams left the blackness of his past behind a long time ago. With his career as a professional fighter on the rise, he has little

interest in aiding a prim and proper archeologist with her issues –
especially when he has enough of his own. Then he catches sight
of what's followed Anna and can't turn away.

Some things have to be fought...

At Anna's dig site, an ancient evil stirs awake. As it reaches back
into the world, Ann and Sam land in the heart of a dark storm that
could mean the end of them.

...others have to be survived.

The clock has started ticking and the world may never be the same.

ISBN-10: 0988195151
ISBN-13: 978-0988195158